LIVING
DANGEROUSLY

Donald Tate

LIVING DANGEROUSLY

IN SWEET DELUSIONS AND DATELINES FROM SHRIEKING HELL

Addison & Highsmith

Addison & Highsmith Publishers

Las Vegas ◊ Chicago ◊ Palm Beach

Published in the United States of America by
Histria Books
7181 N. Hualapai Way, Ste. 130-86
Las Vegas, NV 89166 USA
HistriaBooks.com

Addison & Highsmith is an imprint of Histria Books. Titles published under the imprints of Histria Books are distributed worldwide.

Library of Congress Control Number: 2021942637

ISBN 978-1-59211-103-9 (hardcover)
ISBN 978-1-59211-196-1 (softbound)
ISBN 978-1-59211-257-9 (eBook)

CONTENTS

For Fran,
who saw some of it in the flesh,
and heard echoes of it from chilling dreams in the dark.

BOOK I
EXPERIENCE BEYOND THE PALE

As one hopelessly obsessed viewer slightly overstated:

You are the most charmingly delectable of earth's destructive creatures, sweet, I can't take my eyes off you, sweet. It must be, well, a personality thing or something, the fetching swing of your personality or something, or the warm, contemplative signals emanating from your great beautiful sweet brain when you walk in a certain way, and so I beg you, don't walk that way or bend over that way or, dear god, breathe deeply in my field of vision, and kindly withdraw your flaming pitchfork from my groin and let me think. Could it be a force of ancient mammalian attraction, of beauty beyond heaving shimmering bosoms and stimulating chemical pitchforks? What else could it be? Perhaps a call from romantic mists of olden days, of simply brave togetherness, of undefeatable love.

As One Grand Master Of Strategy Grandly Understated:

"Vietnam is not an excessively difficult or unpleasant place to operate..."

Said a grand master advising the highest of authorities, of how war in the steamy low jungles, stormy hilly jungles, and fierce heat of the rainy rice paddies of the cause called Vietnam would likely unfold, which was a heady thumbs-up for those who'd heard they were on their way to war's infernal region. But from the highest perches of strategy, in possession of a veritable Matterhorn of military expertise and geo-political data, a more cheerful view was spread down the ranks, "about a glorious end to it all.

This from serious experts who were very brave in theory and never lost a battle in theory.

It rained experts, but the boots-on-the-ground lads would soon see for themselves (What's it like up ahead, sergeant? Like you don't want to know, soldier) because there in the distance fumed smoke, sudden leaps of fire, and whiffs, ever stronger, of burning flesh. If you're not truly brave, they were urged onward, at least act brave. As the Army's creed says, "I will never accept defeat… never lose… I am an American soldier."

In Other News

With loathsome thoughts to sell

Secrets of death to tell…

But a curse is on my head,

That shall not be unsaid,

And the wounds in my heart are red,

For I have watched them die.

— Siegfried Sassoon
A serious poet

1
APPROACHING DEADLINE:
JUST GET THE DAMN STORY, BEFORE IT GETS YOU

It was Sunday when it finally stopped. It had rained from that wrath-of-god sky with the wind bending and cracking trees as if about to blow the war away. Unseasonable, complained experts on rain. It rained anyway, and it rained. In that howling mad year of what observers called a cascade of deteriorating events, he lay among the dead in a forest blacked and twisted and clawing at the sky. A red sea of words sloshed in his head. He couldn't stop the rain and he couldn't stop the dying. His interesting work was to chase datelines of shrieking hell, pluck war's eye from its flaming socket, and bring it back cool and cleaned-up in news-friendly sentences of 10 to 22 words, from what headline writers were moved to call the eerie trail of death. *The Story*, nothing got between Jim Jordan and the story, outside of speeding objects of flesh-seeking steel, and this libido-scorching, attention-whoring dream walker, who other than people in the story who might kill him, set his piece of war on fire, who looked so good he couldn't stand looking at her or, worse, not looking.

By the norms of risk-ratio, his stories needed intense, very intense focus, or express delivery to bad-news Valhalla in bright red bits and odd jigsaw pieces loomed. Even venturing forth to such work was like scary-stupid and so unhip, man, opined groovy folks of the day, Likely, he'd over-dosed on low-quality loco weed. Patriots blowing in winds of less than 4th-of-July fervor, fought the unfeeling draft by song and shouts of peace and love while digging up buried principles most high and noble, while agonizing over falling arches, angry bone spurs, and protesting backbones, even as Jim's curious breed tripped out chasing that unpopular, uncool bitch of a war. Yes, those were the days.

This day, wounded, bleeding, he's seized in spasms of clarity and flashbacks, some as visible and sharp as shell bursts, others dreamy dark and close to crazy. Like Susanna, dancing as if breathed on by the *wicked one*, and guys milling and mooing around her like testosterone-besotted loons, drunk on anatomical numbers. Her once red-hot-numbered Mama, matured into a booze-lunching pork belly, taught her the moves. Enjoy blowing the doors off their egos, the brutes, Mama advised with feeling to her shaped-dynamite-with-her-fuses-on-fire daughter. One gentleman body-language expert, doors blown off, swore he saw her dancing naked in the moonlight waving a flaming pitch-fork. Jim hoped such mesmerizing facts-of-nature were ultimately harmless, and usually, they were, until the Saigon sun went down, and nature might slip off its brain, make a few of those moves, and the pack prowling under the wolf-red moon howled for more.

***

Quiet now, no dancing dreams, just that murderous quiet. Dawn creeps across the graves. A huge ugly cloud sits overhead like some voracious maw looking for a body to swallow. The sky shakes, once, like the beast clamping something in its jaws. Jim's half-buried in a scene that would have unsteadied the hand of Goya, or to a midnight writer muttering *No words can describe it.* More describable is the smell of cordite and smoked human stuff floating all around. Scorched leaves still tumble silently down over this battered old bone-orchard of communist soldiers buried back in deep jungle that, in the last hours, has been restocked with curious Americans who couldn't stay away.

Something moves, his bloody tongue, the only thing warm, the rest of him shivers. His is the only corpse stirring. He's trying to move his legs, to spit dirt, to suck in a breath, and avoid ending up in a buzzard's belly. In that early light, he sees many bones in the waving earth, moldered old bones and fresh-cracked new bones. Perhaps someone somewhere thanked them for their service, even if they are all mixed up in slivers of flesh, shards of shrapnel, the scattered remains of hands, feet, legs, cracked skulls, gun barrels, tree limbs, and big dud shells sticking up at odd angles among the graves. A maddened rat gnaws at a skull. Columns of big red ants and smaller black ones swarm over a soldier blown so perfectly flat he seems painted screaming on the ground.

The fires are mostly out now. A riddled canteen with last drops of cognac slides down into a watery crater near Jim. Water still drips from blown-sideways bamboo and the wild-reaching roots of great trees up-churned and sawed off by thudding storms of shells and bombs, leaving all sorts of twisted steel, live and dead thunder, sticking up through the gloom.

Jim hears, thinks he hears, a howl, turning into a muffled wail, as if out of the earth itself. Perhaps it's just the wind muttering, only there's no wind. Or last sounds from some hurt animal, but there's no animal. Or a final protest from that NVA who lay screaming and cursing all night before something shut his mouth. Or maybe just more noises in his head. That's probably it. Still, he must drag himself out of here or be lost forever.

"It is a rare privilege to die well," a living poet wrote, but through that smoky first light, Jim Jordan cannot tell which piles of shrapnel-gashed skulls feel the poet got it right, and which might request a rewrite. The last man breathing affirms he's alive when he hears a flapping noise from a shell-blacked tree, sees small red ponds pooling beneath him, which is the color of luck in Vietnam. He feels dim verbal rhythms trying to form some coherent order, sees word shapes trying to write themselves in longhand, but can't spell them out.

Perhaps the timely news nugget, the instant analysis, "and that's the way it is" even when it isn't, haven't been invented to convey what's gone on here. Or they could just bomb it again, pound the ghosts of nameless soldiers, pulverize the bones of glorious causes to be dug up someday as fossils from that misunderstanding so full of battle fury, media bombast, and ten kinds of confusion.

If there's enough left to box up they could ship him home and lay him down on the hill beside his father who, with the battle in his lungs lost, took him one evening to the cemetery dating back to Confederate days, as the sun sank into the big river like floating fire in the distance. "See, not so bad here, son," his old man said, aiming his eyes downhill over rows and rows of stones and crosses, "we've got the high ground."

"*Happy are those who die in great battles, lying on the ground before the face of God...* an enthusiast close to the spirit world once wrote. Jim knew carolers, usually far from battle, singing that battle hymn, but only one who seemed eager to take the trip. Now he's half-out of the grave of his own trip, pushing off dirt when he glimpses objects moving over wet leaves. Hears whishing shadows riding down the wind, settling in a squawking flutter, hopping all around in fat feathery coats and long necks dripping pearls, icepick eyes staring, red-smeared beaks jerking.

***

He had wanted work that meant something, like life beating back death. He found it along war's murderer's row, in a land where the sky thudded with clattering mechanical birds under whirling swords, and all the truth-seekers rushing from the Delta to the DMZ, getting the dirt on war, sorting through the over-speak and the gun-smoke during hot and steamy days and dark and bloody nights, which noises rolling out their bones made sense and which just more clueless rattle.

There were raging doves, "*Why are we in Vietnam?*" And others drank the adrenaline, chasing battles like they were destiny's last hot breaths. See more, risk more, top this with that, and bring it back screaming, sobbing, or growling, just bring it. Some dared the story too far, went searching, got destroyed. Others, who should have called in sick, crept down roads winding into dark trees and never came out.

On such a road one day Jim saw an enemy soldier crawling from under trees, a trigger-pull away, who pulled the trigger. Jim was dead. *Click...* Nothing. The trusty AK didn't fire. And trigger-puller rolled over a moment later a red smear across his neck. *Not meant to die today, Jim thought. He remembered the time his belly was traversed by the big tire of a car rolling backward out of a driveway, that took pity and didn't split him open, indeed big tire scarcely bruised him. It was the first time he played dodge-ball with the Demon of Sorrows. He was five-years-old and his luck was still holding.*

***

Passing out... He's on the train, hearing its mournful whistle in his head. Sick-bellied on the train, through tunnels of twilight, color vision going fuzzy, sweating cold, then hot, and the pressure on his chest so heavy he's pulling in air like it's a rope on fire for one more living breath.

Life brushed by death. Some said it flashed before your eyes, but his came slogging through miles of fever swamp. There had been a romantic, even sportive air to the early jousting, mainly in his head. He had read much on white-gloved stout-hearts trotting about on horseback, of plume-helmeted charges and flashing lances, glorying in the clangs of sabers and blasts of bugles in exhibitions of brilliant valor. These days there were exhibitions of great dark angels spreading their wings and sending down greetings from 30,000 feet up, shattering carpet bombings of the senses, that tilted one's poetic plume, and scattered one's brightest metaphors into far dark places.

And they will define him as one of the more curious ghosts prowling the boneyard. Got smoked in the jungle along the Nam-Cambodian border. Didn't have to be there. Kept saying he wanted experiences beyond the usual ho-hum, before almost getting blown into irregular pieces beyond anything. On the brash side at times, an unguided news missile. Did a little evil, witnessed an awful lot of it. In the storied tradition of journalistic cannon fodder, perhaps rates a posthumous award as a gatherer of chancy-to-come-by quotes and brutally-specific details, like that one over there, that blood-streaked eyeball staring at him below the slowly-swinging threads of a burnt eyebrow hanging to it, stuck to that tree stump there.

Now in the gloom through pockets of mist, as if out of the eyeball itself, something comes slow-dancing over the graves, an old wrinkly-faced apparition in high-topped, blood-soaked shoes, carrying a thick black walking stick and wearing a black derby cocked over a malevolent grinning sneer. It seems to change shapes. It prods the dead with the stick, until it is right there, prodding Jim once, then hard again. Now it's humping over him, who had always wondered what it was like at the end.

Did you find it, seeker of experience beyond the pale? Describe your pitiful plight, your last gasps. And now that you are no longer viable, is there any sentimental slop you wish to pass on to your hot silk honey with the fine cruel legs? What? No last sliver of unhinged wit? Then slouch off quietly. The Perdition editor awaits. Jim spits dirt and makes noises, unhinged, that Perdition might not enjoy editing.

All right, cease muttering! Enough word games! Your hallowed platitudes are forgotten even by those who will believe anything. Now cease struggling! Shut up! Cease! Don't you know who we are?

***

For a time, he had carried a camera, but found his sharpest focus on the heart of the story was with words and a strong sense of that rare quality called journalistic purity, of trying to track down and capture the slippery escape-artist called truth.

"It's as easy," Ernie once advised, "as having a pleasant interview with the shadow of death. You might even have as much as a half-second to decide which is shadow and which is truth."

Jim found the impurities of actual battles lacked the romance of covering them in the cozy haze of the hotel bar after a poetic drink or two. Nor were those fleeting jungle phantoms and blinding killing flashes, that usually hit before the coffee got warm, readily visible to the high priests of authority and deep bunkers of delusion back on that lost-again planet, Washington D.C.

Back from action, he would erupt with words that sweat-dripped, smashed into, and leaped upon each other with gut passion, to action that kept pulling him back and back like some spellbinding temptress, insatiable, *"I'm waiting..."* as she extends her arms so like Susanna's and invites him lovingly down, down where, sneering and bloody, it's the old Demon of Sorrows under the black derby pulling him deeper, deeper, and each time he rises jamming him back with the big stick. And suddenly all over him smothering, stinking and snarling that this is the way his interesting work ends.

Surviving such a story might even serve as a career enhancer, if there's enough left over to enhance. As the hanging brow swings, still just holding to the blood eye, he hears whispers that he's still alive, with time to act brave and even be brave. He blinks, stretches, there's something wet on his face, it's raining again. And it's still Sunday.

2
REPLACING ERNIE

"Let every nation know whether it wishes us good or ill, that we shall pay any price, bear any burden, meet any hardship, support any friend, oppose any foe, to assure the survival and success of liberty."

Such words were not only uttered but ardently cheered on that dazzling day. Another mission for America the mighty, America the good. And a young newsman broke out in a patriotic sweat, and the president who spoke the words got killed. And across the sea raged the war many lamented was immoral and insane, and the blood ran, the cheering faded, and back home returning warriors got spat on, things grew ever more spooked. Strange spells seized the American land. Headless history seemed in the saddle, thundering right, lurching left, shouting unspeakables, and galloping to where nobody knew.

You may know how it goes, being there at the grinding point of history's sausage being made, and how it might benefit the sensitive reader to white-out the blood and go easy on the grinding. But that would not communicate reality. So report it again, carefully, bloody but with style. In a few weeks in this work, you could see a lifetime of experiences beyond the pale, what news folks called war reporting. And with a touch of swagger, a dash of young Winston, a jigger of vintage Hemingway, and a stout snort or three of straight Ernie J. you might feel elevated to a more intrepid calling, as *correspondent of war*.

Military people, especially under stress, have expressed less laudatory notions about those "expletive-deleted conniving jackasses… those bleeping piggish creatures with long bleeping snouts." And consider General William Tecumseh Sherman's untidy outburst: "I hate newspapermen. I regard them as spies. If I killed them all, there would be news from Hell before breakfast."

Having read much on war, Jesse James Jordan, usually called Jim, thought himself as knowledgeable as any fellow who hadn't been in one. He knew the generals and the strategies. Like those British longbows, 80,000 arrows flying in minutes at Agincourt. He moved armies, from fierce Johnny Turks to goose-stepping purveyors of pure Aryan blood, around in his imagination. He kept the right flank strong. He studied the mad valor of Verdun, the bully brilliance of Austerlitz. When advancing his valiant razor, he maneuvered stubborn enemy shaving cream into futile pockets of resistance, dispatching them with deft pincer strokes, sustaining scarcely a nick. He had read much of heroic sacrifice in battle. His father knew it in the shrapnel-stitched flesh. He had read of brave Josh Chamberlain standing with the flag on Little Round Top as Rebel fire fusilladed around him. Query him on gallant charges that never made it and he would describe the British cavalry near Mons, legions of the hard-galloping blind, moving forward with shining lances as shell after shell crashed into them and they were blown up and mowed down and blown up again by an enemy they never saw.

He poured over pictures of the brave bayonets of the old Western Front going over the top at dawn, those clanging sweeps *(they went with songs to the battle, they fell with faces to the foe)* across the thunder fields of the Great War. And how the Boche bruised the terrain industriously with sheets of machine-gun fire as the helmetless *(wearing one stained one's manliness)* silly French came on in their attractive red pantaloons and were chopped down row upon row like fields of screaming roses. So, he knew the words about lightning thrusts and mortal blows, and was enthralled but not frightened.

Consider the combat aeroplane. He could wind up and spin off on one who truly enjoyed the jousting, Rittmeister Baron Manfred von Richthofen, the Red Baron *("I am a hunter. When I have shot down an Englishman my hunting passion is satisfied for a quarter of an hour...")* until the ace of aces saw the sparks from his red Fokker fighter taking hits that last time near the Somme, heard the engine sputter and stall, his eyes glazing through his goggles, then spinning, spinning, round and round all the way down *(he had dispatched 87 souls to flames himself)* all that time. He was not quite 26.

Turned desperately 26 himself, Jordan had been captivated from an early age by the rattle of guns between the pages, in the headlines, and by word of mouth. Growing up, it seemed that's all there was. Here came the treacherous Japs screaming "Banzai!" And the rotten Nazis shouting "Heil!" Somebody evil is always on the march. And in his imagination, he faced them down, maneuvering toy soldiers through his bed covers, playing out the dramas in the wrinkles and the furrows. He rode a tank with Patton over lumps in his pillows, charged up the hill of his headboard with TR in his rough rider duds. He buckled his chin strap and tromped muddy-booted into the misery of the Western Front. Across a red-checkered blanket, he witnessed monstrous artillery duels across trench lines and bloodied thousands charging against Fate in spiked helmets. It was play war, and he was undaunted.

As a young man, he would sit by a window with a doomed poet look and listen to the *Warsaw Concerto* and write wine-inspired stuff but he didn't know enough to be doomed. The more he didn't know the more he longed for experiences beyond the pale, for the story to deliver him from the Devil's Island of an adventurous young man's existence, that cruelest of sentences, the prison of boredom. Day-to-day dramas left him yawning. Worshipping in the cathedral of money was not his religion.

The backyard barbecue or how to make the perfect burger or even clearing the yard with a chainsaw were not heroic events. Mundane news *(the invisible man was not seen again today) and tiny ideas* cloaked in fatuous overspeak caused him to go numb in places like his mind. Sadly, the grand old growl of the city room, of his editor jerking out his cigar and shouting "Jesse James, spur up, go, go!" That sent him galloping across town to lasso the latest pillage or plunder, had lost its early thrill, as had mysteries of the local health universe like why old men got bowlegged, or took off their glasses before peeing. Not all did, he found, how interesting.

In search of insights, he playfully arm-wrestled a paranoid schiz with bad feelings in his face and let him win. Good feelings all around. The chief psychiatrist, weaving a bit in his chair, with a sly look ferreted a bottle of Scotch from his desk, offered Jim an insightful swig, and allowed him to try his art of the interview on a blank-faced fellow diagnosed as an inarticulate idiot in a state of catatonia. Blank-face didn't twitch to Jim's art, and the friendly shrink concluded that if you were an idiot or a psychiatrist these days, it was best to be a silent one and get brain-drip drunk. Have a drink, but don't write that.

Weekends, musing over what it all *meant* — it couldn't just maunder on and on — led him to seek off-beat adventures, and waking up under a cement mixer somewhere, grew ho hum. Nor was his passion for experience satisfied by civil rights riots that got him tear-gassed, but still unfulfilled beyond the pale.

And then one day he listened to JFK, stoking the flame: *Let the word go forth…"* He heard a stirring ballad of men with *silver wings upon their chests… America's best…"* engaged in a serious battle in Vietnam over there somewhere by the South China Sea. The very sound of it, the *South China Sea.* Who wouldn't want to go to the South China Sea? Apparently, most everyone he knew and more, heard *"Hell, no, we won't go!"* he turned off the music, while he got high choruses of just musing on the mystery and challenge of *over there,* and beseeched the *Spirit of Great World Happenings* to make it happen before he and his malady grew too ancient to care.

His city editor, an old news salt who often shouted, "This doesn't read right! Get the story, get it right, or don't come back alive!" leaned back in his swivel chair, prepared to spit where the spittoon once was and sprinkled the young tiger with salty advice. "Some people are hot for action until they find it, then even hotter to get the hell out… Why don't you find some hip little smarty-pants to go to a cool hootenanny with, or some tidy home-maker to make a home with? Settle down. Buy her a crock pot."

But the smarty-pants Jim knew were already blowing in winds way off his course, and the crock-potters seemed more interested in terminal nesting and great shopping expeditions than deadly doings in faraway lands. Better, he thought, to be lost in a pitiless jungle than in an oasis of dreary domesticity, no matter how challenging the shopping.

That was just him. Perhaps as a boy, he had watched too many movies about daring young men, cowboys battering and shooting each other in wild west streets and saloons and neatly picking up their hats afterward, and read cave-man books in which the good club-swingers always got in the last swing.

Or perhaps his predilections were blood-linked to forebears that included volunteers with muzzle-loaders battling Bluebellies to the last shot and shell. There was an ancestral specter who, the story went, escaped Grant at Vicksburg, then, with one leg amputated, got shot-up waving his saber while riding beside one J.E.B Stuart looking for a last chance called Gettysburg. At his funeral, Aunt Tettie

Pickle, a desperately sociable lady who went to funerals to exchange pleasantries, sat in a long black dress by his casket with her violin. Hands shaking, she began scratching at it with such inchoate passion that cringing mourners swore the casket dumped over, but saber-rider's remains were not there. Some delirious attendees amazingly saw him one-legged astride his steed galloping in the distance snorting fire and belching under. Ah, the stories. Then there were WWII tales of his father going over on the Queen Elizabeth turned troopship to fight the Nazis, and sailing home wounded on the Queen Mary, listening to "Sentimental Journey" all the way — no ghost stories needed — at ease now on the hill by the river.

As it happened, Jim was summoned to Washington. An urgent replacement was needed in Vietnam. Checking out the would-be daring young man's reflexes over lunch, the head editors of the chain to which his paper belonged, asked if he understood that beyond the gathering and writing of information, the risk-ratio he'd face. Yes, he replies that he wanted work that meant something with life and brushes of near death to bring out the essence of the story. "No risk-ratio, no gain," Jim made a sort of joke. "Just send me to the action."

The chiefs looked him over. Perhaps, he was sane. Had he considered stress tolerance, that war might render unto him what it had to others? Was he ready to trade the satisfaction and security of interesting office work for chancy action in a brute Asian landscape of steamy jungle and rice paddy?

He replied with vigor that he was ready for the paddy and stomping, eager to try on his jungle boots.

They warned him how eager others had regretted such words after experiencing the extreme adrenaline jumps and dumps, crazy working hours, crunching noises that deafened hearing and disharmonized the universe, along with sharing battlefield amenities with endless rats, snakes, spiders, scorpions, leeches, creeping fungi, crippling immersion foot, and other creepy-crawlers along with thousands of stealthy human killers. They did not want a Nervous Nelson or Fainting Freddie safely in the rear echoing mere handouts and briefings, but they also warned about becoming "too emotionally invested in the story."

He longed for strong emotion, Jim replied, but not to overly invest in it. It was suggested he cover the Washington scene first, to get the feel of things. He replied he felt more motivated to get the feel of war than the creepy-crawlers slithering around Washington. It was another sort of joke. After a pause of hours, it seemed, he heard a chuckle, then more chuckles. The chiefs looked him over carefully again. They had a live one if he had all his marbles and lived. Soon enough he was packing his action marbles and slashing verbs to capture the reality of the clash-of-arms called Vietnam, just cramming for war.

"Wish I could go with you," said a chief, clapping his shoulder. "At my age, too slow to duck."

"Sorry, sir, some of us were just born under that lucky star," sympathized Jim, although his experience with luck in the stars was as limited as his experience of reality on the ground in Vietnam.

"*Jim Jordan has a new by-line,*" read the announcement. "*Jordan has been chosen to relieve famed war correspondent Ernie Johnson in Vietnam. Jim's dispatches on the fight America's young men are making for freedom in that far land will come to you exclusively in United Newspapers.*"

Looking tired, famed Ernie, great in WWII and Korea, winner of every award that didn't get him killed, but now back in Washington, narrowed his puffy eyes and stated that he expected to rest up and head back to the action before long. "I may be down, young Jordan, but I'll *pop right back up,*" drumming the last phrase two beats longer than the first.

It was not easy getting old Ernie and young Jordan to discuss the reality of war or of each other. Ernie had dodged death many times and had started drinking a goodly lot. Among the creatures of Washington, he was not a good ol' Washington boy, but he epitomized the United tradition of war coverage, mostly at the front. With the troops. Butt on the line. Clean razor's-edge sentences. And large enough testes to go out and get the high-risk stories and bring them back kicking and readable alive. It was for greater scholars, observed Ernie, to pontificate the complexities and bang their pundit spoons from the dizzying heights of the all-seeing highchairs of the clear-eyed.

Once a Marine, Ernie kept coming down with what he dismissed as small power outages, and something with bitter little teeth gnawing at his liver. There was also an unpleasant situation in his left eye, got crashing into a sandbag while diving from a mortar burst. Hadn't even noticed it until he looked in a mirror and saw shimmering halves of himself.

"Nothing to that," he shrugged, because Marines, even halves of ex-Marines, don't boo-hoo. On Ernie's scale of horrors, it was nothing a drink or two couldn't put a shine on. He was always ready to go out one more time and give it the old shot, and said the only combat he felt trepidation over was when the major action of the day became the stubborn battle of the bowel. "There's no hero in bowels."

When Jim asked what it was like being back from the hot war to thrilling, freaking-out old Washington with its political bang-banging and gas-bagging, Ernie gave him a second once-over. "Thirsty, kid?" So they stopped for one in a smoky place Ernie knew. Kid 1, Ernie 3.

It was dialogue for the ages that Washington evening as Jim listened respectfully to Ernie's litany of disgust about the stunning cluelessness of some of the political cluster-fucks running the war, and his admiration for patriots marching the streets shouting the trendy "Ho, ho, Ho Chi Minh, the NLF is gonna win," and spat on returning Medal of Honor winners. "If they had the brains and guts it takes to spit-shine a boot they might recycle that."

Ernie's eyes darkened, staring into somewhere else.

"Of course, that is just old-school thinking. I come from a quaint school of war correspondence. I mean the Second World War. In those days we were all joining up. Everybody doing something. Not just parading around shouting shit. I was lurking in the vicinity of men who climbed that cliff straight up under fire at Pointe du Hoc. That was Normandy. In the country of France. With a spirit, the new mob expectorates on. But I proceed from the premise that ours is still the best country in which to get a drink. Therefore, I am fiercely anti-communist. There's also a badass Soviet Russia to consider. There's a Berlin Wall for the mob to climb on and smoke clouds of pot. There's that pork-chop Mao making great leaps forward over millions of corpses. There's Uncle Ho working for the greater good of his people, and like any good Communist if you're not for his greater good he whacks you out. But why worry about the new mob? There are always relics of the old guard around to save their silly asses. And that's what I am. Old."

Ernie drank on with that dark stare, gazing into spaces the kid might soon be visiting. When the aspiring reporter of carnage said he had read and heard so much, it was as if he had been there, Ernie scratched at traces of scars on his neck and his reply came scraping out full of whiskey and smoke. "So, you're all set then. I saw an Arm-and-Hammer commercial on baking soda once, and now I'm an expert baker."

"Still hell of a story," Jim said. "Any scraps you left over, I'll get a nibble of, hopefully."

"And hopefully you'll let me know what it's all about," said the old guard, who went quiet for a moment.

"Well, kid," Ernie said softly, for Ernie, "I wish I could just lay it out for you. All you have to do is strike like a cobra and squeeze like a boa until the story spills its guts on you. Be aware that boxcar loads of BS will unload on you, all the news that's fit to dump. In this era of intellectual honesty, all sorts of heads that talk will tell you what to think with the garbage that should immediately be bagged. You'll hear the usual cuckoos singing their usual cuckoo songs. The less they know the louder. they cuckoo. Remember that out where it counts, you'll need keen ears and the eye of the eagle. You'll learn how to get close to the hard stuff, and when and how to get out, hopefully. There's a dark art to it, edgy, instinctive, staying-alive art. You are not a warrior, theoretically, but mistakes are made. It might all seem very glorious. In the beginning."

When Jim asked what the maximum dangerous time was for a new guy learning war art, Ernie sipped his whiskey a little faster.

"Know that the cunning enemy grows fat on beginners — noisy trigger-pullers and naive seekers-of-truth-and-light, easily edited out by too close proximity to speeding steel. Keep your head down. Save your best ammo for the hard stuff. You're doing the story on war and the war 's doing its obituary on you. But if you intend to seriously cover it, and make it past the first six months, you'll probably make it home, alive more or less So lock and load, young man. Are you really ready to give it the old shot?" Yes, said the young man, he felt ready to give it the old shot, and Ernie lifted his glass. "To the hard stuff," he said, very softly, for Ernie. "But you'll never be the same. War doesn't wash off."

**

And so it was in that summer of riots, protests, draft-card burnings, marches on
the Pentagon, the summer of love, free spirits called it, the stinking 60s, others
sniffed, with that country over by the South China Sea firing up into a more ferocious dragon than anyone had dreamed, that the young man set forth to seek his
fortune of experience beyond the pale.

There was of course Ernie's eye of the eagle to remember. Not to be forgotten
was the once-French spirit of the attack and the all-conquering will, which trans-
lated into *audacity, audacity, audacity.* He would have to balance audacity with the
enemy growing fat on beginners. He had read of the unique discipline of the Red
Baron, purging himself of all inner *Schweinehund* to find stainless-steel purity of
focus in battle, a quality of value, Jim thought, in pursuing heroic journalism or
heroic anything.

Imagining what was ahead, he further told himself he must be afraid of nothing
he might find out about war or himself, even as people around him died like flies
being switched off a horse's behind. Looking into the darkness, that was how Ernie
had described it. Jim reflected on such things along with the story of how his father
had handled *Schweinehund* in an unscheduled swim and rough-landing on a beach
called Omaha far from Nebraska.

Another lesson for a news knight in the war-covering biz, armed with fierce
pens and notebooks, was Ernie's dictum on how a mission looking so gloriously
purposeful and passionately doable in the beginning, could end up so miserably
fu'qued up as people kept getting wasted with no more seeming meaning than flies
being switched off a horse's behind. Ernie said that about horses' behinds more
than once, and Jim pondered the symbolism of the flies, and beyond the flies what
the greater meaning of this war meant in the grand sweep of history. Ernie had
cautioned him to spare the reader the righteous agony of his heartfelt political
hang-ups, and how at times he might be driven to feeling absolutely crazy while
hopefully remaining relatively sane. That, while finding the right words to capture
the slam-banging music of battle with its badly-singing bullets and decapitating,
heavy-metal drumming. That, and making it past the first six months.

3
THE CALLOW CORRESPONDENT MEETS THE LORD

It was another very hot sunny day and he was right there, in God's big bloody East, enjoying his first sniff of Saigon, smoke-gritty, breathing it, and chewing on it at the same time.

Though a bit numb from the long trip over, Jim Jordan felt rushes of sweaty joy as they rattled in from the hurl-burly of Tan Son Nhut Airport in a blue and yellow little trick of a taxi, a tinny Renault so bent and rusty his left foot stuck partially through the floor-board. It did not matter, nothing mattered until the war showed itself. Where *was* the war? He saw military stuff all around. He had half-expected instant hot war. No war, just plenty of smoke and heat and honking mad traffic jams.

"The Continental, right?" directed the British correspondent, one Eric, or E. Drudgington Blow as his by-line declared, jammed in the back with Jim.

"Sure, sure, my know," replied the driver, thrusting up a thumb while happily sharing with them that he was the greatest driver in all of Vietnam.

"How *much?*" pressed the Brit, who had been over-tripped to Saigon before.

"*Ti ti,* no sweata," assured the greatest driver, turning and smiling as the sun tiptoed across golden teeth, the ones not missing. In the center of his forehead, as if stamped by a branding iron, were several round red and blue spots. Jim and the sweat-dappled Brit, a loquacious fellow whom he had met on the plane from Hong Kong, were half-buried under their luggage. Elbowing against each other, they tried not to breathe the fumes floating up from the floorboard as the greatest driver, a babbling yellow brook of news and views, puffed a Camel and whipped his smoking sardine can along the edge of the road.

"Hey, *watch the bloody road!*" yelled the Brit, veins bulging in his neck. E. Drudgington Blow wiped at his face with a handkerchief and informed Jim that he could feel his ulcer, his suspected dreadful ulcer, rapidly enlarging at that very moment.

"My know, my know," cackled the greatest driver, driving faster, pausing once to scold a traffic cop before cranking forward and nearly plunging into a roadside market full of squatting women in black pajamas, who scattered like a flock of squawking crows who couldn't take a joke. Looking back at his passengers with what Eric called his golden grin of sheer idiocy, the greatest diver courteously informed them that his name was Mr. Ngo, but that his many dear friends among the number-one Americans called him Mr. Go, who would take them anywhere for "rary sheep" price.

Careening onward, he explained that he was now a part-time soldier who had once been rary brave until he caught a terrible pain in the rain that had dampened his bones for battle.

"Now my carry the talkie-talkie. No more fight. *Beau coup* talk."

"Through those holes in your head," said Eric.

"No holes. Before, every morning my head have the heading-ache and car go poot. Then my press the hot coin on it…" he turned, wagging his head, "and now no more heading-ache, no more poot."

The story of the medical-mechanical miracle was worth a paragraph, Jim thought, but he had expected to hear the sound of guns by now. Here and there he saw sandbagged positions manned by South Vietnamese soldiers (ARVN) looking rather nonchalant in the sun, but the closest thing to battle were narrow escapes in the increasingly manic traffic full of quaint foot-and-motor powered contraptions that the greatest driver swore at. "No damn good!"

"So, who's winning the war?" queried Jim.

"Not this sluggard," groaned Eric. "Not this thief."

"No! The soldier must never become the thief!" protested Mr. Go. "If the soldier steals the pig from the people, then the people follow the VC. My never steal the pig."

Agog at Saigon Street life, Jim gazed at a Vietnamese woman in a creeping pedicab, her skirt hiked high. She was heavily painted and looked a bit tough, though her legs seemed a winning pair.

"Numba wan nice girl," observed Mr. Go. "You want? My take you. My know *beaucoup* nice, not 'spensive girl."

"How *beaucoup* not expensive?" asked Eric

"As you like. Me know what you like."

"You *don't* know what me like," snorted Eric, flicking beads of sweat off the end of his nose with two fingers. "So how much for not expensive *beaucoup* bad girl?"

"Vietnam bad girl rary 'spensive. Every day the perfume. Every day the this, the that."

"My have too much wife. Always make hard time for me. Always make…"

"Watch out *YOU IDIOT!*" bellowed the Brit as Mr. Go just failed to splatter several Buddhist monks in ethereal float beside the road. One of the monks turned and flapped his robe in monkish disapproval.

The greatest driver gave the monk his golden grin and rattled onward. From a side street

Jim heard a clatter of gongs, drums, cymbals, and bamboo flutes, then a lot of horns starting up. It was a funeral procession led by a man beating a big orange drum following a hearse and floats and all of it disappearing around a corner, drums banging, horns bleating, banners waving.

Now traffic squirted this way and that like drunken water bugs; the ancient midget taxies darting about; the clack-clacking motorized pedicabs belching out black kerosene and sounding ready to go up in smoke; the open-backed, people-packed Lambretta minibusses called *pouse-pousses* sput-sputting along; and there, weaving past, a family of four squeezed precariously together on a motorbike next to a stopping, going young Vietnamese cowboy type scooting and bucking in and out of traffic through a pall of smoke.

More stoically came two pale yellow princesses. The steering one rode with legs snugly astride their Honda, the silken tail of her *ao dai* flapping back at the second princess riding side-saddle, white-gloved, wearing white silk pantaloons, her black shiny hair in full flow as she thwarted the evil sun with a pink parasol, her cool apple-seed eyes going blink, blink at Jim. When she stared his way, twirling the parasol, instant warmth swept over him. He leaned forward, but she was gone, swallowed in smoke. Terence, this is stupid stuff, Jim reminded himself, not what he had come for.

The greatest driver turned around again, waving a crooked finger. "No messy round wid sixteen-year-old Vietnam cherry girl!"

"Sorry," Jim said. "Hard to tell."

"Nice figger," Eric noted. "Fetching, fetching. There's nothing like pursuing or being pursued by a beautiful she-wolf on a motor scooter. Maybe we can catch her."

The taxi swerved badly again. Mr. Go was agitated. "No catchy!"

"Quit your clucking!" commanded Eric, "and watch where you're driving, you demented blooter. Now *slooow* down, I say! Stay on the stinking road! I bloody *beg* you!"

They were into the heart of Saigon now, jammed between a honking, grunting convoy of army trucks, a rolling lunch stand caught in the crush, a whoop-whooping ambulance, a wow-wowing military police jeep, a 1930s Citroen squeaking forward like an old black shoe on wheels, and many muttering, sputtering motor bikes.

Jim had been warned how ungracious the living was in the mushy damp heat, how things broke down, got fixed, broke down again, the plumbing, phones, lights, bathroom fixtures falling out of walls, toilets collapsing, how you didn't drink the tap water, it wasn't potable, how noisy and dirty and corrupt and sweaty and all-around wretched it was for the cool and comfortably inclined, just no place to enjoy life. He had not come to enjoy life.

"Oriental clutter," remarked Eric, flicking sweat off his nose onto the back of Mr. Go's head.

Now, in the afternoon heat of Saigon's siesta time, the taxi rattled past sleepy-looking Vietnamese police known as White Mice in their little white guard posts, and then up beside the potted palms outside the Hotel Continental Palace. After a brief haggle over what this day's fare had evolved into for foreign devils, the greatest driver said he must hurry home to lay his bones down to nap.

The Continental — E. Drudgington Blow had declared he would stay nowhere else — was a quaint, white, green-shuttered, four-story leftover from French colonial days with a noisy metal cage of an elevator, faded, red-carpeted stairs, room boys asleep on grass mats in open-air corridors, dark thick oaken doors, and big, high-ceilinged rooms with squeaky over-head fans and cranky pull-chain toilets.

Indeed, enthused Eric, this was once the Paris of the East, Pearl of the Orient, all the exotic old rot where Somerset Maugham and Graham Greene had once happily dallied and written serious drama in olden Vietnam before Uncle Sam's mad wooly mammoth, emitting deafening bleats and bloody burps had blundered in and wallowed all over it.

"Good to know about the mammoths," Jim said.

After a shower and a fast victorious skirmish with red ants surrounding his toothpaste, the new Asia hand walked down and met E. Drudgington Blow. They sat in rattan chairs on the terrace of the Continental at small round tables with white cloths, looking rather worn but quaint, and were served by an elderly waiter in a white-duck jacket looking quaintly worn.

Sporting his rich voice and nice teeth, though yellowing, Eric smoked and held court. "As sporting gentlemen in the game of war, let us talk about a subject of supreme interest in my life." Wiping at his he revealed he was a three-shower-a-day man. As soon as he walked into the Saigon sun in the morning, he broke into a sweat and required another shower. "Wasn't that interesting? But perhaps you would prefer to discuss the illumined well-springs of my artistic unconscious? Well, enough of that." He wiped at his brow and drank gin and something in a lordly manner as Jim brushed away ants trying to colonize the sugar.

"Now, the ant problem. I do not object to the individual ant. It's the bloody heaps I object to," said Eric, looking toward the street. "Gawd, these antlike masses. Never mind. I am passing into a great new phase, with a veritable cornucopia of ideas. The moving finger having writ rages on. I've a rage to write beyond mere pap journalese, to be an eagle among yawping boo-birds, to be a litterateur. Having used up the 400,000 words in the language, I'm raging to invent more. I can do it in Swahili. All I need to get the old girl going in this frightful heat is a cool quaff or two of something cool. You too, what?"

Between quaffs of getting going Eric displayed, as if button-pushed, rows of those splendid though tobacco-yellowing teeth. Jim noticed his talent for talking non-interruptus with a slight hissing sound through the smiling teeth while hardly moving his lips, the smile lingering after the moment of mirth had passed, as his eyes made little moves past you. "Did you say something, sport? No? Well, think of something to say, profoundly witty. Are you witty? Are you profound? My reliable sources say you are. What sources? Sources said to be close to the planet earth. *Haw.* So prove it to me, what?"

A tall, good-looking fellow with sandy locks spilling over his brow, a lordly voice when he wasn't hissing, an almost-Roman nose, the Eighth Earl of Something Once Big, as it were, entered a room in the manner of a brisk English breeze, a fount of jocularity and such jolly charisma as to give targeted femmes (whispered Dame Rumor) a rocket rush to the moon of amatory delight, and leave them just all-dither and a-sighing "so utterly brilliantly charming," sentiments to which the Eighth Earl had to humbly admit were, yes, fortunately for the ladies, just utterly true. In his early 30's, Blow, despite his disclaimer "I am neither proud nor unproud" was proud to the bone marrow of his tattered nobility, with a core bitterness about his family's financial demise brought on by hard times, devastating (passionately denied) Blow debauchery, and disastrous for Blow world societal changes after Big War I. As fortune vanished, and following a not-so-jolly slough-of-despond, he came to fancy himself as a breed of revolutionary knight, jousting his way through the ignoble workaday world, temporarily rubbing elbows and intelligence quotients with graceless dolts and bad-breath peon swine who, in days of empire, would have been grateful to kneel to clean the unspeakable off his boots. As far as bloodlines went, he made it unequivocally clear that he was still, yes, indeed, jolly well entrenched close to the Puddingham tribe. Quite. No doubt about it.

Based in Hong Kong, the Eighth Earl had earlier reported from Moscow and Beijing and despite logical lapses, been smitten by the rising of the Reds. He felt certain his gut instincts were more than gas pains. Brilliant bursts of dopamine in the brain confirmed his genius, he felt. At least the relentless bastards. Reds, not gas pains, knew how to put the swift boot to the feckless slugs of the bourgeoisie.

Of late it had been on and off to Saigon to get the goods on war, mainly the political goods, for his London journal before he and his suspected dreadful ulcer would fade back to Hong Kong to China watch. He said that even as he soared in the metaphorical trenches, war's unseemliness was not his game. Only now, *now,* his new detestable militaristic editors, the blood-lusting swine temporarily in charge of his emotional serenity, urged him to bless them with more of his analytical and eye-witness wordsmithing on the beasty side of the war, beyond the bars, eateries, and wild rumor mills of Saigon.

That was the beasty, the drama, the challenge, Jim was looking for. He said he wanted to hike on over to JUSPAO, the Joint United States Public Affairs office, to secure his press credentials so that he could get cracking out to the action. But Eric insisted, no hurry, time was slow and plenteous here.

"Think of this as another long march," he advised, ordering another gin and something, and drinking on like any Eighth Earl would on a muggy afternoon. "So be a good egg and hear how to be a demon correspondent without the usual dirt, sweat, toil, and gore of war without going to war. At the risk of sounding too warlike, I will explain to you about war, friend student. Why in Big Show One we Englanders lost -60,000 first day at the Somme. Pressing on brilliantly we lost a million in a single battle. Now that's the old boffo spirit, young pickle. However. The truth is there's a mirror of this war so hallucinatory it turns the brains of poor ordinary maximization-of-minimum-content news blokes churning out their schlock into blocks of stale cheese-- rancid, cliché-ridden, rat-nibbled, *haw.*

As Jim listened to his new mentor's theories on cheese and war, he could almost hear Ernie growling, *"In country three hours and still sitting around jaw-jawing. Get to the action, kid, the action!"*

"*Oh, posh.* Such an anachronism," remarked Eric on Ernie. "Yes, I know, the USA never lost a war. The armies of Snow White, Santa Claus, and General Patton always rout the Awful Red Baddies. *Rah, rah.* Here come the whites of their eyes, expounds gung-ho Joe!. Charge by golly, by gum. And don't dangle your participles. As you know, Yunkies, *haw,* in their passionate pursuit of ignorance, absorb history by going to idiot-delight movies. Now, on war, the terrain and style of fighting, the other side's use of sanctuaries, not promising for the Yunkie military machine everyone keeps expectorating about. Your lads have gismos of firepower, their chaps endless well-springs of cheese power. They *believe*... in Ho Chi Minh cheese. I lay my quid on them. Why just listen to the squeakings from Mickey-Mouse land already, like its tail caught in a trap? Best to flee back to their safe holes and be good little rodents."

Although the declarations tripping off Eric's tongue seemed so absolutely certain, so arrogantly entertaining in words delivered in bursts of gamma-ray brilliance, as Eric put it, Jim still thought it possible to learn something useful from the lord, who warned him there were too many arrogant motor-mouths and pundit-pretenders over here telling the world the way they think it is. No doubt about it."

"Have you ever been doubtful of anything, by accident?" Jim asked the lord politely.

"No, Well, yes. A once. In April. A day of my birth. A Tuesday, no doubt about it. Moving on, so unless your mice invade North and overrun their cheese, can't win. Clearly, Mickey's mob lacks the sand for such serious cricket anymore. So there, friend student, I pronounce you a demon correspondent of war without the untidy show of going out to prove it, what? In any event, battlefield bravado is but a flighty floozy bouncing bed to bed, any insensitive boob can have her on occasion. I choose to ignore the dear dumb duckie-poo no matter how much she wants me. Of these are my thoughts."

"Why are people so eager to pervert General Mickey's purpose here?" Jim asked his mentor.

"Firstly, lastly, as an expert journalist, I stand by my perversions. As a trained interlocutor, I pose questions, pay little attention to vapid answers, because. I am fact-driven. Facts are fortunately what I say they are. I write the lightning, I blitz mercilessly with poesy. My cutting-edge iambic pentameter, when not making the birdies sing and the flowers grow, is lethal."

"Mickey says poesy does not win wars."

"Ah, the arrogance of ignorance, the passion of stupidity." Eric showed the handsome though yellowing teeth. "Just assure me, friend student, you don't believe all that hyper-patriotic word puke."

"Not quite all."

"So, then, bombs away. A little more mass murder never hurts, what? If that doesn't work out, try enhanced radiation devices. Any unsizzled leftovers, sell 'em ice cold cokes, *hoot, hoot.*"

Lighting up again, Eric jabbed a finger through his smoke rings. "If any survive, what's more patriotic than standing over a hot machine gun all day shooting innocent peasants? There's also the matter of the trees. These subversive, uncooperative coniferous forests with unruly branches blotting out the sunlight, blinding your lads from seeing the creepy-crawly Reds. Thus your lads, in good conscience, must bomb all un-American trees into the Golden Age of the Parking Lot. If that doesn't work out, empty your opium dens, death rows, copious insane asylums, and cemeteries of the undead and send them over to spread democracy and defoliation. If that doesn't work out, go bomb the fierce Liechtensteiners, always spoiling for a fight. And there's always that misty mountain top in Nepal where you can rent a vacant rock, indulge in moments of meditation, spots of pot, and decide whom to defoliate next, what?"

The tables all around were crowding up now, as was the long bamboo bar overlooked by a wooden World War I fighter-plane propeller. It was mostly a round-eye crowd, several tables populated by a few deep-sunned soldiers in from the boonies, several correspondents in wash-and-wear, and a gaggle of ruddy-faced civilian engineers, one of them escorting a tight-skirted, plumpish white woman under a swirling stack of lacquered red hair. Then, tail twitching, a native dragon lady in white boots and purple hot pants cruised past with a smiling look-over of Eric and an eager brush stroke at Jim.

"See the harlots come and go, whispering of Michelangelo, and me," chuckled Eric. I prefer quality breasts 'o white, or pleasantly pink, myself. *Hoot, hoot!*" Eric was in the midst of his pause for applause when a television correspondent walked by. "Back again? How're things, old Blow?"

"Bloody."

TV-man sat down nearby with several others who waved at Eric, who gave back the classic smile while offering analysis. "Now there are motor-mouth news-nits assaulting the king's language with delusions of adequacy, who poke a mike at some bleeding mouth and say, 'Bite me off a second of sound, Marine dude. Tell me how devastating is the devastation, and how, after a brief commercial break, your world ended today. And is it ever going to stop raining?' Now some of these talking fire hoses articulate their idiocy well enough but leave me drenched in boredom. One feels surrounded by such dreary puddles of clueless news dung, doesn't one, friend student?"

Eric then revealed in so many words that his own words were drawn from a treasure trove of near epistemological light, that mere facts were very thin noodles of information and how he added layers of irony and mordancy to give them meaning and how lucky friend student was here to hear this. He was in his flow again, the moving mouth droned on and on, putting a fine point on a fine point until there was not point. Friend student's eyes and ears had glazed over until he roused himself to say that he must nit on over to JUSPAO to get properly credentialed so he could then head out to the troops and get his boots properly muddy, where he could experience epistemological adequacy and not feel like a puddle of clueless news dung.

Eric showed the teeth. "That's so American. Muddy your boots to the last drop of somebody else's blood. *Haw.*" Smiling, he raised a hand "Well, chin-chin. One more and we'll be off. *Garcon, garcon,*" he called, waving at the elderly waiter. "One fresh-baked baguette and a screw driver. Light my lamp, old thing."

At that moment Jim felt a fresh-baked pang of urgency. Hand to belly, he stood up. "Excuse me." He hurried, then fairly charged back past tables to the dark wooden stall marked *Toilet Messieurs.*

Though forewarned of Ho Chi Minh's revenge, he had assumed you had to eat a bite first, his first Vietnam mistake. Fortunately, revenge passed quickly. Upon returning to the table, he saw an aroused Eric, his face fueled up tomato-juice reddish about to spill over. He was losing his jollies.

"No, it's *your* mistake, old thing!" Eric lectured. "I asked in *small* words requiring minimum intellect for a fresh-baked baguette, and a screw driver. A *ski-ruww* driver! Bloody *ski-ruuuwww* driver! And why not oysters or eggs on the half-shell? The eggs should be fried and turned over. And a bit of ice cream garnished with green peas would be nice. Have you got that? Do I need to spell it out?"

Slowly, the waiter shuffled off to fulfill his mission. "Beastly heat," Eric wiped at his face. "No wonder these people have problems. Why do such people exist? Why do I have to *know* they exist?"

Now a black-patched Viet with medals dangling from his chest and a portion of his face shot off, limped over. Leaning on his cane, he extended a hand half-covered with a dirty bandage. The hand held a magazine, tattered at the edges. "Sunny Vietnam picture book. You like buy?" Beside the man, a tiny girl in scruffy flowery pajamas offered Eric necklaces of fresh jasmine. "Me no VC. You buy for your girly friend, papa-san? Make so happy?"

"I am not your papa-san, and I have no girly friend I'll admit to in this pestif-erous place." He waved a hand. "Now away! Shoo! Begone! *Hoot!* Do I have to call a gendarme? Why do these scrofulous sneckdraws always pick me? Blasted people! Blasted country! Blasted heat? 'tis ever so disturbing."

The girl scooted behind the man with the part-cheek, half-lip, and sunny pic-ture book leaning on his cane for a long moment while staring one-eyed at Eric before tightening his half-jaw and tapping away with the girl hanging to him. Eric wagged a finger at Jim. "Hark, friend student. So, sit there in your insouciance while I fight off the Philistines. Of course, a little red spanky-spank might have a bracing effect on such irredeemables. Might give the lumpens a bit of the bottle, what?" Midway between a mock and a sneer, he jerked around. "Look there… that 70-year-old, baldheaded hooker leering at me. And there, what comes… that lice-crawling, raggedy-tail bugger straight at me. Do I look like the great white rice bowl? How much can a man take? Did I tell you of my book to come, *The Secret Joys of Cancer and Vietnam*? Quickly, before they charge, let's bang off."

Banging off through the buzzing, smoking traffic, Eric began explaining why he was so verbally infelicitous toward the native poor, lame, and worthless simple-minded. "My attitudes are not, as some insinuate, based on the begetting of little bastards all over Asia, what? I say rot. Not *all* over, friend student. Deep down my essential humanity shines as a beacon for all the little lice-crawlers, though some drive me a bit wa-wa."

As Eric dissertated on his relationships with lice and the natural order of under-creatures, Jim felt a lightness in his back pocket and reached for his passport.

Missing. Asking Eric to wait, he rushed back through the sidewalk jam of parked bicycles and found the precious document in the *Toilet Messieurs*

What an immaculate beginning, he thought, flapping it back and forth. What would Ernie say?

Back on the crowded walk, E. Drudgington Blow oozed sympathy. "You look a bit pale, friend student. Now man up. March with me to the glory of the Five o'clock Follies and be serenaded with the usual rot. Go steady now. I am with you."

As Jim marched with Eric and worried about finding his first war story, the battle in the *Messieurs,* perhaps, he saw newsmen streaming from the press briefing.

"You have tragically missed that gaggle of misinformation called the Five-o'clock Follies," congratulated Eric. "Their every evening deflowering of the language on how the military is bonging the godless Cong, to which I say *poo,* and a big fat *faw,* that requires a willing suspension of disbelief that makes my ulcer cry out. I've a dreadful ulcer, you know."

A moment later, as Eric introduced Jim to a pair of veterans of the Follies, there sounded sudden rattlings from above, then slam-banging shatterings below. *The war.* Jim went into fast-twitch defense mode, ducking, eyes darting, body crouching low as he had seen -in the war books, steeling himself for the worst. The seasoned vets of the Follies looked down at him steeling himself, and laughed.

The *attack* was but a Filipino rock band racketing forth from the roof garden of the Rex BOQ an American billet beside JUSPAO. The shatterings and splatterings were but errant splashes of Saigon evening frolic, friendly fire from five stories up, and a tray of tipped-over, tumbling beer bottles, rarely fatal. Eric said that this was no way for a laddie buck to begin his tropic adventure and urged that they all repair to the Continental where one could regroup one's wobbly nerves.

"Pray, pull yourself together, friend student. As one of the easily excitable, try breathing with your mouth open, allowing more O-two to reach your cranial cavities. I say, war nerves before you reach the war, not promising."

Instead of his mouth, Jim's eyes popped open. Curved lightning in a skirt went flashing by.

"Whose army is that in?"

"I do think…" said Eric, "what we have here is… I do think… To my mind… What we have here is… As I stand here… Indeed… Bloody army of the night, I'd say… *Hoot!* Gentlemen, control your knickers! All these ugly people, and suddenly that *figger*. Why don't I know that *figger*? And that *caboose*? Why it's singing to us? It's bloody smoking. Why it's about to fly off the rails. By order of the Royal and Ancient Garter of Wicked Cabooses, I must investigate it. I'll tempt it with strawberries and cream."

Jim's eyes remained riveted on the wicked caboose flying off the rails as did the eyes of the others.

"Gentleman, I must say…" said Eric, "with that concatenation of moving parts, that flow of kinetic energy, I say again… What we have here is… um, I am filled with a burning desire to… hoot! hoot!"

He burbled on, licking his lips like a dog mad to take a bite out of a fleeing pork chop.

"Gentlemen, turn on your engines," said the taller vet. "How she cranks it along."

"Uh…" replied the shorter vet. "Uuh…"

"Original sin," said Eric." That curvilinear design leaves me speechless, and virtually, makes my viscera rage! *There*, gentlemen. How did random evolution produce such an objet d'art? This may never pass our way again. Our viewing time lasts eight seconds. She obviously is the daughter of the devil. Can any manly flugelhorn remain unhonked? Did not Aristotle in his treatise on flaming cabooses from hell have a word on that?"

Jim's gift was that he could make a story out of almost anything, even Aristotle on cabooses. Eric tried restraining him, but the new correspondent of war thanked them for their keen insights on beer bombing and cabooses, bid them adieu, and promised to see them again down the road of war once his viscera stopped raging.

"Well, toodleoo. But beware," warned Eric, "it behooves one to know only heap trouble come from chasing squaw with tail on fire without press cards. Well, bung-o, look at the callow fellow go. Quite the aggressive lad. Doesn't he know cowboys get rather shot up over here?"

There were risk tendencies in Jessie James' nature, like acting out sudden dares into dangerous unknowns, which he was prone to do and did now as he wondered where the Charles Dickens that undulating bolt of female lightning crackling *follow me* was leading him.

4
MYSTERY OF THE SUN GODDESS

She wasn't in the plan. But after standing on a street corner with a vacant look more common with munching bovines than a man in search of dynamic action, Jesse James Jordan had emitted a libidinous little snort, lost his balance for a moment coming off the curb, and lurched forward.

Her magnetic field preceded her, just following the sun sparks, the turning of heads as the little people of the East stared at America the Beautiful, blond-gold hair on fire with sunshine, lovely-limbed and rippling along in a high skirt made for sculpted legs, and a clinging pink top over breasts like shivering moons rising.

He was tracking her on a street with wide cluttered sidewalks called Nguyen Hue, which came out in his head as Newgooyan Hooey. When she paused, half-turning, glancing in a shop window, the visual effect of everything he could see jolted his loins so sharply that he tripped into a sea of black marketers squatting on the sidewalk. The hawkers of PX watches, cameras, stereos and other pilfered riches stuffed into pilfered U.S. mailbags glanced up hopefully at the stumbling round-eye. How could they serve him? Nothing right now, thanks, he had to see the full front of that caboose.

Apologizing to the free black market, Jim righted himself and dodged on through a sidewalk zoo featuring fortune tellers, a half dead-python, and a swarm of babbling little kids in unclean pajamas selling peanuts "for lucky" while clawing at his watch and wallet. "No, no, not for you!" He wrested free.

Now a barefoot boy in raggedy shorts confronted him, planting dirty little feet defiantly apart, and two filthy fingers to his lips while screwing his face into a mask of fierce misery.

"You, man, gimme smoke. Hokay?"

Jim shook his head. "Smoky no good for you."

"You, papa-san, gimme money for chop-chop. Hokay?" The boy rubbed his belly, rolled his eyes, and stuck out his tongue like a starving dog. "*Beaucoup* hungry."

Jim hesitated too long. The boy kicked him in his left shin, shouted "Numba ten!" and scuffled off down a narrow street before dropping to his knees laughing and wrapping his arms around a gaunt old dog the color of the gutter. Behind them twisted a smoke-drifting maze jammed with refugee shanties built of canvas, scrap wood, flattened beer cans, and tin roofs with sandbags on top. Crap floated in the gutter.

From a bamboo pole outside one shanty dangled a hunk of raw meat humming solid black with flies. Flapping through the canvas doorway appeared a scrawny woman with dark baggy slits for eyes. With a sweep of an arm, she tossed a plate full of fish bones into the gutter near the crap, then squatted beside a sidewalk water pump. Slipping out of her blouse, washing it under the pump, wringing it out quickly, she stuck it back on and stood up wet and bowlegged with reddish betel-nut juice leaking from a grim mouth full of blackened teeth. Her cheekbones and her ribs looked as if they could cut you up.

Spotting Jim, she thrust out her bony chest, pointed a crooked finger, squawked like a wild bird, and raised her arms as if to swoop at him. Noting the amazing range of reaction the female configuration could arouse in the curious male, the intruder hurried away, searching for the curvilinear design on which the sun dazzled and called him from wild places.

He hurried past a gray-bearded fellow sitting beside a lizard-crawling wall making music with a one-stringed instrument sounding *ayeeeee* with his hands while going *tap, tap, clop, clop* with bamboo clackers tied to his gnarly feet. Then on past, an even gnarlier fellow hunkered down in a narrow passageway, his wispy-bearded face contorted into a wrinkled map of old Asia, as he relieved his venerable self.

Jim halted his own self. So absorbed was he in the chase, he had forgotten to ask what he was chasing exactly. *Terence, this is getting stupid.* And then he caught a view of golden wheels flashing past a boy peeing on a wall from which election posters peeled. He jerked onward, kite without a tail, toward the bright red door through which golden wheels had passed.

Due to the Emergency this Club will be Closed until further Notice advised the notice on the red door. Which emergency was that? The club, named the International Club, was running wide open awash in happy-hour drinking. and non-thinking. Was this the terrible Vietnam war? What would Ernie say? All drinks two for the price of one until 7 p.m. A double for 25 cents. Beer 15 cents. The place was packed, with raucous talking, rolling slot machines, and free popcorn. There were chattering women, round-eyed and oriental. There were U.S. rear echelon types, variously known as Saigon warriors, REMFs, mother-fugs of the Saigon rear, plus assorted civilian beer bellies and all the South China Sea shrimp you could eat, $1. Morale seemed high. It was a club run by foreign devils mainly for the morale of foreign devils. Jim wandered on through, past a flabby-armed white woman with pizza-bulging hips ferociously jerking at levers in a row of slots. Which blubber-butt army was she in? *It's getting ever stupider, he heard Terence advising. Chasing a caboose like this is truly stupid stuff.* I truly believe you, Jim thought but continued on up the stairs to a bar that tinkled with a piano, but he wasn't looking for a tinkle. He felt by that figure possessed. Where was *the figure?* Then back downstairs through swinging saloon doors into a dim crowded room full of smoke and laughter, drinking and war stories, the stories coming out funnier than they ever were, brave birdies tweeting after a storm.

A song trembled from the jukebox… *"Those were the days my friend…"* And there, across the room, at the small brown bar she sat, enthroned like Apollo's bride on a high stool, hair shining, golden legs crossing and uncrossing adventurously as she rolled dice out of a cup with a big jovial naval officer. Jim walked over and sat at the end of the bar just behind them. It was happy hour.

He ordered a beer from the Filipino bartender who kept glancing at *the figure* even as he slid a bowl of popcorn nearly into Jim's lap. As a journalist, Jim was on occasion given the power of truly close observation, and closely he looked for flaws in that racetrack of curves forming her backstretch. He heard her laugh, watched her repositioning her — the word *bodaciousness* popped into his head — rear on the stool. He heard her giggle, saw her wriggle deeply-tanned shoulders as the naval officer tippy-fingered across one of her happy-hour knees.

"Hey, is there a Tommy Sullivan here?" called a woman's voice through the swinging doors.

"No, he's not here," called back the officer. "Him go Vietnam. Stay long time."

"Calling Tommy Sullivan. Commander Tommy L. Sullivan."

"Hey, I'm not here. I never come here."

"It's your mama-san and she want you home right now. Or she's coming right down here and spank you, Tommy-san."

Commander Tommy-san, a bear of a fellow, reluctantly got up to leave, giving the lady a last chummy knee-tickle with one of his paws. She gave him a pat on the shoulder and a quarter to drop in the jukebox on the way out. *Those were the days, my friend, We thought they'd never end…*" trembled the voice from the jukebox.

The object of Jim's story was alone now, still aglow, her racetrack quiet, fiddling with her drink, tapping her nails on the bar, and Jim sat there yearning for the story of her front. He felt the steamy bubble would soon fizzle and pop. In his experience, beneath the curvy clothes, the magic make-up, the usual push-ups and squeeze-ins and smooth-overs, just another booby trap full of fetching emptiness.

Although he longed for substance, in truth in those days his yearnings had less to do with learned sweethearts with whom to discuss life and literature, war and economics, than for some flawlessly formed creature posing for him in the mythology of his imagination, undisturbed by imperfections like being alive and noisy. He decided to say goodbye before saying hello and started to stand up.

He was halfway up as she turned a bit. And a bit more, her eyes burned across him. The dream figure was coming about, three-quarters now. Here she came, slowly, and then the full-frontal assault, her boomers aimed at him, no mythology needed, maybe a heat shield. He decided not to say goodbye just yet. (*Terence, you poor fellow, turning stupid again.*). Then, dimples winking, the Sun Goddess moved her lips.

"Hi, bum a quarter?"

Bum anything you want, he thought as she smiled so hot and bright and sweet he saw sunflowers, and smelled honey-suckle. He dug into his pocket for quarters and placed a couple in her hand while not knocking over his beer. He watched her swinging over to the jukebox in a rhythm that his animal appetite imagined went back to the first man glimpsing the original woman in the garden, watched her there in the pulsing glow, making original hip magic.

Swinging back, she sat on the stool next to him and crossed her legs, a show of leg art, the rousing effects of which had the happy-hour mob grinning like loons, especially when she recrossed them, *(Mama couldn't have performed it better)*. Now the bartender grinned like a loon, and Jim wondered if the lady calculated it or if it was just the nature of her beast. He wondered what she was thinking. Or if one put together like that bothered to? Looking at her affected his reflexes. He felt her magic touching and she hadn't even touched him yet. Well, he wasn't thinking too straight or breathing right. He had fancied that after escaping Glamorous Gloria the idiot model's moon-beam asylum he was well past all the silly surface glitter. He had fancied wrong.

They began talking about something. She seemed to need to talk-talk like he needed not to. There might even be words of substance emanating from those lips that seemed designed to send the receiver of the moment into the hot-shock kiss of his life. He must cease these manic imaginings, he thought, and focus on the innocence of the freckles on her forehead.

The bartender was looking at him knowingly. What did the bartender know? Jim shifted his attention to the seductive popcorn. What did the popcorn know? Summoning up journalistic steel, he decided to view her as merely today's leggy headline, perhaps a few minutes of bliss followed by endless hours of non-bliss and a heavy load of womanly woes irrelevant to his mission and would make his head hurt.

That would be tomorrow. Today her body rose and fell in stunning swells and ripples. Today he learned that Susanna the sun-dazzler had been a Louisiana army brat who got moved around a lot before fully blossoming on the beaches of Florida. In Saigon, she worked hard for the Red Cross, hair swept up, dress longer and looser (skirts should be not more than one inch above the knee) consciously drabbing herself down to help keep the grab-and-growlers at bay, unless she felt in a certain rush of a mood, although she did not tell Jim of the moody part.

Day work was straight and pure Red Cross. After work, she sometimes felt moved to put on a different uniform and show herself out a bit, well, quite a bit. There was no need to tell him of that either. Anyway, it was just to have some fun, maybe trigger an innocent eyeball riot like she was doing now, until some other highly physical event might occur, which she did not speak of either. In any event, she was through with all that, she felt fairly certain, and when he asked for her full name, she smiled again so hot and bright and sweet.

"Susanna... Diane... Robinson..." she said slowly. Jim repeated it slowly as if tasting her.

"So, Jesse... James? Where's your horsey?"

"Resting. Got tired out chasing you."

Jim glanced down to where she doing little tricks with her legs again. He wished she wouldn't do that. It turned him sappy. One sappy stretch with Gloria the idiot model had been enough. He was now a free man. And yet this one was even more formidable, who had a way of tossing her head just so, golden ear-rings glinting, hair caressing her shoulders just so, who kept sending such hot smoky signals from the shadows of her eyes that he could not tell their color exactly, speckled blue or green touched with traces of she-devil?

"Don't you like a little mystery?" she asked, half closing them, leaning forward playfully, bosom blooming. "It makes you want to know more, huh?"

It made his mind jitterbug around and breathing stop.

"Mystery ladies are a little scary," he breathed out.

Susanna liked that. It was exciting to scare aggressive gentlemen. When he confessed that he had actually gasped, and broke into an unseemly sweat the first time he saw her, she liked it even more.

"That's nice. A small gasp is nice A little unseemly sweat is nice. Being a mystery lady is nice.

Don't be too scared," she reassured him, with a little hip twist, "I won't hurt you."

He started to say something witty, like where was she on the pleasure-pain principle that might drive a fellow to lose his boyish innocence and just pounce on her, but restrained his wit.

"What are you looking at?" she asked. It seemed she had hooked another live one, eyes dancing to her every move. Should she jerk the line, dangle the poor fish, turn him dizzy, or flip him a little for fun?

"Just wondering, you know," he wondered, "what got you over here?"

She tapped her nails for a moment, fiddled with her wallet, then pulled forth a picture of a Hawaiian coconut tree under which she, wearing very little, was all squeezed up in the arms of a big fellow with an upswooping blond mustache, wearing a green beret.

"Robby. Captain Robinson... KIA. Two years, going on...."

When Jim started to commiserate, she shook her head, gazed at the picture, slid it to one side, and made a decision. The one-more-drink decision.

"Jess... Jim," she asked, drinking, "what do you do in the war business? Some kind of secret spook? USAID? Embassy? Barfly commando on a mission? Can you reveal it to me? Can you?"

One moment Susanna Diane Robinson, in her twenty-fourth year, seemed to be appraising him with sunny warmth, but then her lovely sky changed expression, darkened, gloomed over.

When he told her, he was a newshound, she flared her nostrils, slowly uncrossed her legs, pulled back, and straightened up as if looking down upon one of the low ones.

It seemed her late captain had drilled it into her — he was a heavy driller — to accept nothing the media boo-hoos whined about the war or anything. Susanna herself supported the war, or at least the wounded warriors, and noted that thus far her encounters with a few of the know-it-all-before-they-get-here media hot-shots had lived down to her captain's descriptions.

"There's also the media meek and humble," Jim said. "Poor peons of the written word, just trying to get the story straight. You're looking at one. Be kind to the poor."

She still looked down upon him.

"The fact is, Red Cross lady, I just got here. I'll surely know it all tomorrow after I get my press cards. Right now, I'm still wondering what got you here?"

"In this beautiful bar? Talking to you?"

"In this beautiful Vietnam, talking to anybody?"

She touched the picture, sipped at the drink, unstiffed a little, and repositioned her legs. "I got tired of feeling sorry for myself. I wanted to come over and do some good, you know. I hope I am, a little. I needed something; you know. More. I needed it. Maybe I've found it."

As probably the most eye-pleasing contribution to the American expeditionary force in Southeast Asia, Susanna had served as everything from a Donut Dolly, going out with big smiles and coffee and doughnuts to a few of the safer bases, cheering up soldiers, helping out however she could. She said it beat throwing beer cans on the beach and getting stoned and grooving on the BS Express back in the great discombobulated rear. She said she owed this much to Robby. And it was quite an adventure. And now in Saigon, she was doing this counseling work, emergency leaves, family problems, other problems, like tending to their mental health and general welfare, helping the guys work it out.

Ordering another drink, discussing helping the guys work it out, she began throwing serious psych verbiage at him. She had been working toward her degree in psychiatric social work but said this was an experience beyond any psych degree.

She had shifted into another mode, lashes fluttering, mental gears clanking, Susanna Robinson asked Jess… Jim… if he felt comfortable in his own skin, deep down, about what he, Jess, or Jim… would in fact be doing over here? Did he actually, truly, in his own skin truly know?

"Well, I truly can't wait to find out."

"You might be sorry."

It struck him that he had honed in on a sex bomb and exploded a social worker. But he truly liked the way the blood rushed to her cheeks when she grew contemplative. He truly liked the soft rhythms emanating from those lush social worker lips that caused him to lose the meaning of the words in the sweet music of the voice that went suddenly flat.

"Sorry?" he said. "Say again?"

"I asked why do press people's eyes light up so when reporting the horrible stuff?"

"Give me a break, Red Cross. Be nice."

"I am being nice. I can be a lot nicer, too."

Nicer Susanna began expressing concern, more than concern, for the heroic, psychologically damaged. "I find them very sensitive people under their scars. Counseling can get incredibly intense, with incredible depths of feeling explored."

Moreover, she went on, drinking, it could get incredibly complex, even frightening, but the saving grace was that the men with whom she counseled did not usually regard her as did some of the hungrier carnivores in this bar.

So why, Jim thought, but did not ask, was she swinging her chariot of fire around in this fine bar?

"The female experience, being a woman here, can be a dilemma," she went on, biting into an olive, empathizing with herself, and with the war wounded, people whose lives she said were forever changed.

"Commander Tommy-san seemed to be feeling no pain."

"That naval officer," she said, nostrils flaring, "won medals for deeds very self-sacrificing and brave. He was badly wounded and now he is healing. And I am helping him heal. It is a form of counseling, even here. But how would you know? You don't have your press cards."

She spoke of other wounded heroes she had known and wondered what wounds nosy newshounds got.

He rubbed his nose. "I'll let you know."

"I'm sorry," she said, fiddling with her glass, "I'm sorry. I guess I love those guys..."She finished the drink. "I mean in a generic, psychological way, you know, is what I mean."

"I'm sure they appreciate the generics," Jim replied, imagining what every horny toad in the country would give to lay down a night's fire on those wondrous peaks and valleys. What were they supposed to do, go blind and walk around them?

"I really do," she went on, voice softening again. She called for just one more drink and her voice grew ever softer. She leaned toward him again. "But I can't go around loving them all at once or something, can I?"

He had never seen anybody better equipped for it, he started to say but held on to his wit.

"No, that doesn't sound right," she gave him a little shove to the shoulder. "See, you're getting me confused."

The widow of the late captain now confided in near secret-society tones that she had drunk perhaps a tiddly too much and was about to bubble over. Once reaching that point, she confided, she might giggle and gabble on a bit, saying stupid things and sometimes doing even stupider things that she couldn't even remember but didn't desire to talk about.

See, you've got me talking. You're interviewing me, aren't you? Do I talk too much?"

"A good reporter remembers the good stuff."

Yes, she had now reached that tiddly point or had proceeded beyond that tiddly point, she confided. Thus, she must say goodbye. She was having a really, truly pleasant, informative time conversing with the nice, knowledgeable, non-know-it-all newsman, but it was time to say goodbye. Because she had made this pact of discipline with herself. No more ones-too-many with silver-tongued strangers, especially ones who kept looking at her like that.

"But it feels good talking to you. You *do* listen. Anyway, it's been nice, and you're nice, and I'm sorry if I said unkind things about the media. There must be kind ones too. And you must be one of them, to even listen to me and remember the good stuff."

Easing off the stool, Susanna stood, a bit unsteady, pressing toward him, blood up in her cheeks, the tips of her breasts briefly scorching his forearm. She thanked him again for sharing this talk, because she truly needed a talking bud, truly, a straight-shooting talking bud.

"Jesse James, an incredibly nice cowboy without a horse," she said, smiling, edging away. "Hey, I'm only kidding. But you *are* nice. You really *are*. An incredibly nice cowboy without a horse. What are you looking at?"

"Nothing.

Jim noticed the bartender, stuffing his mouth with popcorn, also looking at nothing. The happy-hour gang also looked at nothing eagerly As she moved off, Jim looked down. Her late Green Beret lay in a wet spot on the bar.

"Susanna."

She turned back, shaking her head. "See, who's dumber than me." She wiped her late captain carefully dry with a napkin, then reached over and patted Jim's shoulder, and they smiled at each other through the happy hour noise and smoke and singing of the days that would never end. So he asked her if she might spare a little counseling time for him?"

"Sure. Some day. Bring your horsey." She gave him the smile, and went moving off in that way that so delighted the carnivores and made their flugelhorns honk.

Only once before had he gone balmy over beauty, and vowed nevermore. That one was glamorous Gloria, the exceedingly ambitious model whose idiocy had finally exceeded her glamour, who put in full days preening in a house of mirrors while obsessing on getting her picture emblazoned on the front page of his newspaper with the caption *Leisurely Lovely of the Lake,* adored center of the miserable male can't-keep-their-eyes-off-her universe, while in her scanties and smoking a joint, who kept pestering him why the selfish pig hadn't plastered her in the paper yet?

In the highest heat of that very hot summer, the selfish pig tried to escape from the leisurely lovely to an animal-infested forest outside town. He told her he felt moved to go live basic tent life. "I am a natural man," he asserted, "and that's where I choose to make my natural habitat." Raging that no man naturally dared dump Gloria before Gloria dumped him, she had stubbornly chosen to accompany him out to prettify pristine nature.

They slept on sagging cots on opposite sides of a sagging brown tent with no mirrors, separated by smoke pots to discourage stinging. biting, yucky-sucky things.

"You never take me anywhere!" she had screamed that first night. By the third day, after a night of rain dripping on them through the leaking canvas, she rebelled. In a frizzy-haired fit, Glamorous Glo roared wildly away in his car in the early morning, dragging a tent post down a forest road before leaving the car in a ditch, and her feelings toward natural man smeared in lipstick slashes across the windshield.

Now comes this high-skirt dancer making moves naturally that Glo never achieved in her highest cloud-of-pot dreams. And there she went. Jim fancied he had the free choice not to look. What was free about it? In the great scheme of things, for one covering the deadly-serious subject of war, she should have been but a vanishing blip on his big-story screen, one would think. One would think wrong because this blip sucked the oxygen out of his not-so-all-conquering will. Rapping his knuckles on the bar, Jim swore a silent oath to Ernie that nothing in a 38-caliber bra was messing up his critical thinking unless it was packing an AK-47 on full automatic.

"Another?" asked the knowing bartender, a kernel of corn stuck to his chin.

"Not without a helmet," muttered the critical thinker, wondering what nonsense wouldn't a man utter to get that gorgeous thing snuggling into his arms. *Well, this sucker's not uttering it, Terence.* Still, he had to wonder what might be a sun goddess' view of leaky tent life amid the bug-infested wonders of nature.

5
HARD HANDS

I am getting so soft,
Like a flower, I like
Being a flower

— Susanna, age 14

A beautiful flower in full bloom is not for trouble formed but pray for its blossoms in the wrong hands. At two 'clock in the morning, Susanna tries to roll away. The half-asleep soldier's big hard hand lay like a cold hammer on her bare breast. She pushes it, and feels it slide away, one ringed finger scraping her. She lies there wiping at a trace of blood, trying to think. What in the conscious world did she do to get here? She had flaunted herself, hadn't she? Well, a little, maybe, you know.

The ceiling fan revolves over them in the bed like a circling hawk. It is very hot. She feels sweat trickling down her neck and like little spiders crawling on her belly and the sheet wrinkling wetly under her back. She thinks of Jim Jordan but he is not here, and she thinks of Captain Robinson, poor Robby, who is not here and will never be. She lies there under the snicking fan in the nearly dark room with a twist of the damp sheet between the heat of her legs.

What is she doing here? She remembers the counseling session, some of it. Her counseling him was the start of it. She remembers him being about fifty percent unattractive in his manner, but so very needing. At one point he told her to take her empathy and shove it. She refused to accept that. He was hardly her plan for the evening, but he was a challenge. Somehow, she had started drinking with him, drinking with empathy. She could drink a lot of empathy.

She had been helping him heal a little, just talking with him, trying to open him up. Someone said her counseling could get a little too sweet. That she tried to step around the body of the war and offer them the sweet healing cookies of her smile buttered with sighs of empathy. She told herself that she was just always trying to see the good in them and not the bad in herself. But after a few drinks, this one didn't seem to give a hoot about healing, and she could take her lovely empathy and… It had gotten a little out of hand. Earlier, a part of her had wanted to please him not in an animal way but in a counseling way, she told herself. He had been through a lot like Robby had been through a lot.

Big like Robby. Big hard calloused hands like Robby's had gone bumping over her and he had climbed on top and boozily held her down like Robby once held her down, but this one going nowhere before he toppled over as graceful as a sandbag tumbling off a roof.

I must stop this, she thinks now. What's *wrong* with me? How do I get into these things? There were just so many of them coming through Saigon, lost, needing souls, so damn needing. They usually said pretty things once or twice about what a gorgeous sweetheart she was with a body too hot not to touch and burn in hell with, but not this one, she's growing a little frightened of this one. She starts to slide away from him, slowly rolling and slipping away.

Hard-hand moans, rolling toward her, putting out his arms, fumbling to pull her back, and then rising again and that sandbag falling *whump* back on her again. She feels his whiskey breath and big mustache almost like Robby's flying over her. She feels that hand scraping up the inside of her thigh like it's a rifle and he's searching for the trigger, and then clamping there as if to keep it from running away.

He's trying again, hugely pressing downward. Then reaching under her, making her back arch, pulling her up toward him until she thinks her spine will crack, is he a lover or a wrestler? Robby always said she was nothing but a mechanical doll. But the ways she makes them carry on are hardly mechanical anymore, and she briefly closes her eyes, letting him. You can't stop the big ones, she feels. What could she possibly do? She could never stop Robby, but, please, get it done, soldier, *why can't you get it done?*

A part of her wants him to hurry to wherever he's trying to go. Another part wants just to get herself out of there now. But he's stoking up again, blowing like a downhill train. Now, Robby, she thinks, the crushed doll beneath the train, am I maxing my efficiency report?

You're maxing it, all right, you show-off tramp. You'd be Dr. Freud's worst patient. It's that mean old fool noise from far down in some bat cave of her head, unforgiving old scold that refuses to ever give her the benefit of any doubt, never letting her explain, but please, soldier, *just get it done.*

With no invocations to carnal bliss, he suddenly slides one big hand under her. She's his beautiful flapjack and he flips her over.

"Don't, Robby, please!"

This soldier couldn't care less about *Robby please* whoever the C-rats he is, or whoever the C-rats she is. She started it, he's pretty sure. She was sure as hell advertising it, he's pretty sure, showing her counseling hot stuff. She's here, isn't she? Making stupid noises.

She can't stand what he's doing. She squirms and rolls… "Please, Jesus, somebody, *please!* but he keeps jerking her back into position doing whatever he's trying to do and not doing it well. Her eyes are tightly closed. Her little fists are tightly clenched. She can hardly think. It is very, very hot. She had felt in control, even making his eyes cross looking at her, beauty blinding the beast, but now the beast has the power. She had the power but the spell is gone and her back seems about to crack. I will not cry, she thinks, I will *not…* She hears the fan snicking through the heat. It is very, very hot.

Without War

It was the summer the civilized world, grown plump with peace, patted its belly, looked in the mirror, and went mad. A perverse spirit was at work, analysts noted. The tension seemed unbearable; it was reported. Something strange was going on beneath the stolid prosperity, "a surfeit with peace, a lust for violence, a belief in death, a passionate mystique with war," a historian would record.

"Without war," declared the German chief of staff, "the world would
quickly sink into Materialism

Of Thee, I Sing

"I have heard the bullets singing, and there's something charming in the sound."

— early George Washington

Did You Miss It?

"Oh, if you could have but seen, some of the charges that were made... I could not but exclaim—oh, glorious war!"

— early George Custer

You Heard What?

"We heard we're over just murdering innocent peasants. So where did all these tough bastards trying to kill us come from?"

— early Vietnam participant

6
THAT FIRST TIME:
IN THE CAFÉ OF LAST RESORT

Con Thien, South Vietnam: "We don't kill. We service the target." Big old burly, warty-faced gunnery sergeant who from his basso profundo neck-swallowing-his-chin voice box confided how he had field-stripped about every nut and bolt of every piece of equipment and knew every maneuver and gunnery technique and serviced every target of Marines since the age of throwing stones.

Said he didn't want to repeat stories he had already repeated but was happy he could still remember to repeat them. So, yeah, I've been there done that and been done that too. So yeah." Said he was born a bad boy back during the Great Crash and has been skidding downhill ever since. Holding forth now on the way it was and the way it oughta be in his sacred Corps. He also started to share his views on

"Some of these highly paid correspondents who, well.... Now don't get me going. See, you got me going."

Sergeant Billy "Bad Boy" Redd rarely paused as he recounted tales of the only Marine he ever knew, which was himself, who had the balls to never duck and still get shot in the foot, who passed his driver's test when stone drunk, who was deaf in one ear but felt lucky to still have an ear to be deaf in.

Jim Jordan longed for even a little of what old three-wars was rambling about as he reeled off the names of generals, battles, what kind of booze he drank, and what the horrors and finer whores were like in this hellhole or that.

"So found myself in this house of heavenly bliss in Honolulu when the Japs hit Pearl. Bombs started bursting, and one come nearly down my smokestack, bounced me so high off the bed thought I was bound for luv's pearly gates. Okay, you got me going."

This was the night before Jim's first action, perhaps, because outside it kept raining hard. Inside, he sat antsy in his stiff new black-market boots and too-clean jungle fatigues at a table of jolly, mouthy, old-timey Marines now serving in the relative rear and populating the dining and drinking rooms of the noisy little compound by the DaNang River known as the press camp.

"Nice thing about the Chinks," gunny got to going about Korea, "was that they let you know where they were, all eighty-eight billion of them. Loved to blow those bugles. Then romp all over you like Friday night in a one-star Shanghai house of blissful clap. The bad thing about Charlie, 'he careened on to Vietnam,' is you can go weeks and never see one of the little slobber knockers. I raised up to say come on out and fight like a man and get in one clean shot up and the little slobber knocker got me. The week I got this we took forty casualties and didn't see one live dink."

Pulling open his fatigue blouse, he showed a twisting scar on the grizzly-bear mound of his belly that looked as if it had been stuck by a twirling pitchfork.

"Naw, not that one," he turned sideways, jerking the blouse higher, pointing to a small scar under his ribs. "Little baby right here nearly ate my lunch. Charlie snuck up and drilled me with his pig sticker, five inches to hit bone. Well, the crazy thing was the draft board kept sending me letters warning I better come sign up. Said I had run off to Canada and they were looking to arrest me.

Said I was 4 feet 11 and weighed 112 pounds. I wrote kindly back that I was a little bigger and was in the jungles of Vietnam so please come on and arrest me. Never showed up. Well, boys, this is my last tour. Just don't want to croak in bed, a fate worse than pig stickers. I am a Marine. That's what I am. Hell, last night here in '65, throwed a good one. Drank too much lemonade. Fell into a ditch and thought I'd been shot again. Well, boys, started out a slick-sleeve recruit and had more stripes than the star-spangled banner, but kept on fallin' in damn ditches. Enjoyed the lil' gals. Had a drink or two.

Played a few hands of poker. Played everything. Semper fi. Just a tub of guts and a half-jug of brains and figured might's well do my jollies cause I was bound to catch the grease any day. A little low-grade insanity never hurts in a place like this. I can make fun of it now cause the jug didn't finish me and no piss ant war. Hell, I've eaten monkey feet, snakes, and mule meat, which is better than horse. Had beriberi, pellagra, scurvy, dengue fever, got so weak couldn't hold my head up, called it limberneck, got a sort of jungle rot of the face which the gals say marred my youthful beauty. See my old gal here."

The gunny rolled his right forearm over and pointed to a purplish patch of skin that looked like the ravaged tattoo of an aged, hairy sea nymph. "Don't know what it is. Never goes away. Itches all the time. There's always a fungus among us. It's alive."

"I remember," piped another old Marine, "a Marine captain in Korea who had a tattoo just like that."

"Marine," guffawed gunny. "Naw, he weren't no Marine. He was in the band. Captain of the band played the trombone. The combat trombone. They found it frozen to his lips at the Chosin Reservoir. Got hit in the ass first day of combat. Old Frozen Chosin. Now don't get me started."

Getting started, his face disappeared into his beer mug like a man drowning his nose. Jim laughed on cue but was scratching an itch worse than gunny's. Just balls-to-the-wall to get on up to Con Thien, which meant "small mountain with heavenly beings," an American strong-point hard against the DMZ, under artillery attack for weeks from big guns firing from North Vietnam, and NVA (North Vietnamese) infantry probing its wire by night. Jim had urged Eric to come on up with him, he wanted some company, but Eric had demurred, saying it wasn't his kind of show. What better show than this Damn. It's what he had come for. *Frontier Bastion Hit Again.* His adrenaline's fast-dancing again. What it was all for. Front page all the way.

He got up now and paced like a hound panting to get to the rabbity woods, just hungry for action. He paced into the crowded little bar by the dining room and checked with some Marine PIOs, public information types, and yelled at them over the throbbing jukebox. Was the morning mission to Con Thien on or off? Yes, it was, on and off. Con Thien taking *beaucoup* incoming. And the weather was number ten. Raining *beaucoup* out there. All socked in, nothing flying. Everything off. Could change, of course. Probably won't. Number ten. What paper you with? Jesse James Jordan? Ho, ho.

That was gunny Redd addressing Jim. "Along with life's other great question, like why do flies love a horse's ass, why the hell with a name like that are you in

Vietnam? The wild west is in the other direction. Have a drink, JJ. With a name like that have two or three."

There was a radio squawking between serenades from the jukebox. "So all you guys who want your big blue yearbook, send four dollars," said the radio voice. "However, the folks who publish the yearbook way back in Georgia say they're getting piasters and MPC for payment, and to please stop sending that kind of money as they are not negotiable in Georgia. Now, corporal" said the radio voice seriously, "tell us all about, I mean *all* about, those big beautiful Australian girls you saw on R&R"

"Well, yeah," answered the corporal. "Big. They sure was. Like, yeah, they was. Beautiful. Yeah."

"Man," gunny Redd was telling Jim, "you look like a grenade with the pin comin' loose. Don't make such a big deal over a big deal. Never seen a cherry, a press cherry at that, so eager to get his ovaries blown off. Two bits of common sense'll tell you that won't get you to social security days."

"You're just trying to make me feel good, sergeant."

"Now don't foam at the mouth there, JJJ. We'll get you out there. Cool it. Isn't that what all the dope-fiend foreign policy studs say back there... *coool* it? Why we had one hot-shit, cool it *correspondent* come in here so *coool* in three days he said he was too *war-weary* to go on. I said go home, young stud, or sit over there in the corner and get intoxicated. Well, have a drink, JJJ, like Ernie would. So you're taking over for Ernie, ay? Well, *cool.*"

Jim drank beer and listened to the Marines tell tales of Ernie, who had spent a lot of drinking time with them and was their kind of *co-respondent*, and happened to be an ex-Marine.

"But too many monkey-see, monkey-do candy-asses come up here to get their tickets punched. Don't know combat from a kumquat." The gunny shook his head. "You're not of that wild bunch, are you, JJJ? You won't be callin' in cryin', will you?"

"Guess I'll soon find out."

"A few rounds come in and you can see they don't know jack shit about war than they know how to culture bacteria from shit. Why I've seen some of these highly-paid weeping weenies writing their eye-witness reports while peeing on the floor under that table over there. Now don't get me going. Some of these tinker-bells piss and moan all we do is kill babies and count bodies while blasting the *always* innocent peasants, like there's not a mean-assed killer in the bunch who'd slit their throat and stuff their balls in it with a cherry on top. In WW Two days we blasted the boola-boola out of anybody blasting us or thinking about blasting us. They kill us, we kill them, that's it, count 'em or don't count 'em. So where do they enlist you, cry-me-a-river boys? Not that you're not fine, sensitive folks back in the world, but out here highly sensitive folks can be sorrowful-ass Marines. As I told one highly sensitive *correspondent,* the Germans called us Devil Dogs. Because Marines accept the heat and rain cheerfully. Catch a bullet cheerfully. Marines laugh in the face of death cheerfully. There's nothing crazier than a crazy-thirsty Marine. Where's my beer?"

"I'll write that down, sergeant," Jim said, "and tell you there's nothing crazier than a crazy reporter hot to trot to the fire, not from it."

"As the days trot along, we'll see which way you run, cherry boy," laughed Bad Boy Redd.

***

Dreaming of the Sun Goddess, and waking up at 0400, he stared at the shadow of Bad Boy hulking over his cot, flashing a light in his face.

"Come on, cherry, go, go."

"Go?"

"Con Thien. You wanted it, J.J. you got it. Lock and load."

Jim struggled upward, cold, queasy, leaning 30 degrees to starboard, head full of beery weights tilting at odd nauseous angles feeling about to drag him off his cot. Asking the dark-how could they be going? Weaving through the beer and rain to his hootch following the ninety-ninth war story past midnight, they had assured him it was all off. Con Thien fuggin' off. Now fuggin' on. Now, instead of emotionally locked and loaded, he felt about as loaded as a busted rubber.

Thirty minutes later he stepped into the gloom of that chill monsoon drizzle called the *crachin* and climbed into the back of a deuce-and-a-half. Then gunny Redd, Jim, and three other correspondents trucked out the battered metal gate past quacking geese and went bumping along a rutted road in the slow dark rain toward the airfield. With a light pack slung over his shoulder, Jim wore a Marine helmet, poncho, and flak jacket, carried two canteens of water, two candy bars, a can of tuna fish, two notebooks, and two ballpoint pens in the big pockets of his fatigues, but no iron jock. His stomach still churned with beery belly-wash, and he felt less like a noble news knight on his way to epic battle than a sick yella dog.

Later in the morning, after a fast flight in a C-130 to Dong Ha, a Marine base a few miles from the DMZ, he crouched near a helipad with rain plinking on his helmet, staring at dark clouds closing over them too much like a coffin lid, as they waited for the chopper that would carry them into the action at the small mountain of heavenly beings. Staring blearily at the sky, and the rain coming harder, with visibility less than a mile, he asked their ebullient escort, who had closed down the press camp bar a few hours before, if Con Thien was still taking fire?

"Don't worry about it," snorted Bad Boy gunny, tromping around in the slop, laughing, arms swinging, chewing on a wet cigar. "Don't mean nothing. I'll tell you like the Lord told old man Moses, if the Pharaoh drops one on you, consider it lucky, he's not that good a shot. Now, what's the matter, JJJ, afraid to get your hair wet?"

Now to Jim's left, from under the hood of a correspondent's poncho, came a dry laugh. "From what I hear, gunny, there's been quite a few lucky shots lately."

"Naw," scoffed the gunny, "It's those helicopters you got to watch out for. You know those whang-dangers can't really fly. Rather walk in myself. You want to die healthy, don't you?"

Soon Jim saw the whang-danger whirling through a crack in the coffin lid, mud-spattered, slinging out rain, beginning to settle in front of them.

"The big mystery show is about to begin," noted the hooded correspondent, "and all us little news kids are invited."

Gunny yelled for the news kids to get ready. Jim, the hooded one, and behind him a deadline-fidgety wire-service man ("What time do we get in? What time do we get out?") and a frowning fellow carrying a big movie camera along with a gaggle of other cameras, who grimly told Jim he was doing a documentary on these perverted bastards, though not specifying which perverted bastards.

They heard hollering from behind. A big beefy Marine with a funny face (young Oliver Hardy) framed around a black spot of a mustache splashed toward them through the puddles, rifle and duffel bag swinging. *Bam Bam* was written on his helmet. He grinned and said he was returning to duty after being dusted in the butt by shrapnel the week before.

"So what's it like?" Jim asked over the clattering of the chopper.

"Okay," Bam Bam patted his butt. "I'll walk it off."

"Con Thien!" Jim shouted. "What's it like?"

"What's it like?" Bam laughed and spat brown blobs through missing front teeth. "Hee, what's it like?" He worked tobacco around in his jaw. "Hee, what's it like?"

Before he could answer or spit again, gunny waved them toward the CH-46 with the rain-streaked words *Marines* on the side. Bent over, the big-camera fellow stumbled blindly under the chopper's rotors through whirling rain and slop. Jim grabbed his arm to keep him in a straight line. After clambering up and in himself he pulled in the fellow and his cameras. Up front, he saw a gunner in body armor jerk back on the cocking lever of his .50 caliber machine gun, as if something serious was going on.

The chopper lifted, rocking upward, then clattering forward over a muddy road paralleling the ridgeline to the north. Going to war, Jim thought, peering out, eyes filling with rain and desolation. Everywhere rain and mud and red-brown craters. It looked like World War I out there. Would they fix bayonets upon arrival, blow the whistle, go over the top and meet the Huns head-on? The chopper jerked forward and he told his dream factory to be quiet.

The flight was brief, loud, and then they were there, bumping down. Gunny pumped his fist.

"Out! Out!" The chopper wasn't sticking around for more incoming. "Out! Out!!"

This is real, Jim thought. *Real.*

"Out! Go! Go!"

Jim went, leaping down with the others. Eager for the roaring of guns, he didn't have long to wait. In mid-leap, he heard two sounds, close, busting near his right ear. He saw a big crater just ahead, and went for it, arms spreading — *splat!* Down on his hands and knees, helmet tumbling off, gathering slop in a hole of slimy green water. Glancing up through the slop, he saw the chopper lifting, getting out fast.

Oommph, something crunched down on him, and he looked up into the slimy face of the documentarian of perverted bastards, who was feeling around frantically for his big camera stuck upside down in the muck. Jim heard someone laughing from above, that shy, schoolgirl belly laugh.

"As you were down there, Jesse James," Gunny Redd cackled. "First rule of combat is to get your ass *down.* But not that far down. Now climb on out of there, news *men.* Next time *bend your knees* and you won't hit so hard. You think that was *incoming.* Naw, that was your friendly old outgoing. Must learn the difference before you start doing that expert analysis. Now just scramble out of there before the serious dung starts to fall."

They pulled themselves dripping up and out of the crater, the new correspondent of war shaking his head to get the gunk off, and the documentarian of perverted bastards wiping at his slimy camera lens with a slimy handkerchief. Chomping on the end of his cigar, the gunny jabbed his finger toward several howitzers, 105s, in a firing pit nearby, muzzles still smoking over a wall of sandbags. "*Our* stuff."

"Deflection 3173!" came a shout from the firing pit. "Number three stand by! Number three fire!"

Another kick in the ear. More smoke drifting.

"At ease. Outgoing," laughed gunny flapping out his poncho like a big wet bird. "Okay, *men,* the fun's over. Listen up. Time to start earning that big money. Remember, our boom-boom goes *out* theirs comes *in.* You got that? *Out. In.* Now we want to accommodate the media. Now you can move around and talk to whomever you want. Lots of brave Marines up there, but I'm sure you'll find one to share some hugs and boo hoos with."

He pointed up toward the mountain of heavenly beings, which was not a mountain but several big muddy risings full of Marine bunkers and trenches.

"Whoever wants, come with me and I'll set up a briefing with the colonel. For those who don't like colonels, you can wander around until 1600 hours. Repeat, 1600 hours. Just stay close to some cover in case the big dung starts to fling. And then boogie-woogie to cover. Once peace is restored, double time back to this very spot and look for me and our bird going out. Roger? Or we might fly away and leave you. All right, you fearless typists, go justify your existence."

"Please, gunny, don't leave us," said the hooded correspondent.

"Just hear me. I'll be smoking my cigar in the command bunker up there on the left, under that big pile of sandbags there. Those sticking with me, let's move out. Those not, watch out. There's no cure for bullet holes in the heart, and your blood don't make the mud grow much."

Then the gunny, the wire reporter, and the grim fellow wrestling with his be-fouled cameras trudged off through the drizzle toward the command bunker. The hooded one, whose name was Sean Donlan, pulled back his poncho hood and winked.

"This powder-puff doesn't need another brief by another colonel from Great Balls, Texas. Got to get down and earthy. Down with the grunts. You?"

"Earthy," Jim said, like Ernie would have said.

Donlan, a correspondent for a major news mag, was on the stocky side with piercing green eyes and dark curly hair that ran riot across his head. Jim noticed that he wore a look of skeptical, mildly-pained amusement, which was his bloody little smile. He was from Boston and had spent two years of his life in Ireland.

Now the two set off toward the southern slopes of the bleak muddy little hills past a motley array of bunkers, some sturdy looking and others seeming just built enough to slow the rain. Instead of jungle war, this looked more like the old Western Front, churned by bombs and shells, not a tree standing and craters everywhere full of dirty water big enough to drown in. They mushed on past things bullet-riven, shrapnel-gashed, smoky-smelling, black with gunpowder, past watery trenches, rolls of rusty concertina wire, clumps of slimy sandbags, and empty ammo boxes scattered all over. Past a very grim-looking Marine looking them over like who the hell are you? No place for powder puffs.

Here and there in the mud-bleared sprawl, little groups of Marines turned the color of the red earth were humped over filling sandbags, working on their bunkers in the rain coming down harder again. Mud and rain, everything wet, sticky, falling-apart wet, go to sleep in a drizzle, wake up in a waterfall.

The mustache called Bam had plowed far ahead. Sore butt and all. Jim saw him thumping backs With another Marine on the middle rise. Donlan veered toward a grunt poking his head warily out of a bunker as if sniffing the wind, looking about to howl. Jim slogged on upward, boots globbing over, sinking *jug jug slop slop* into the ooze with every step.

"What's this hog wallow called?" he hollered up to Bam.

"Little valley of death," Bam hollered down. "Better dance on out of there."

Into the valley of death rode the six hundred… the words rode through Jim's head… *Half a league, half a league, half a league onward.* But not swiftly, the mire kept sucking at his boots. He began imagining he might not make it. The correspondent who never got a real story. Couldn't even find the remains of his notebook, not that there was all that much in it. He was a bar correspondent. What would Ernie say?

Plowing on, he reached high ground. Straight ahead was the DMZ. Through the gloom, he saw the mountains of North Vietnam. Bam stood with rain on his face by the top of his bunker, a couple of layers of battered sandbags with canvas, shell casings, and dirt piled on top. Resting on one sandbag was a skull with a bayonet sticking out its crown.

"What's the name of this little hill in the middle?" Jim asked. "I don't see any heavenly beings?"

"Just the little hill in the middle," Bam said. "Only heavenly bean we got here is ol' Tag there. Step on over here Tag."

The Marine Bam had been slapping backs with stepped over. "I'm gettin' pretty wet out here."

"Well, your poncho's got holes in it," Bam said. "Could that be it? You didn't say hi to my friend here."

"Say hi in a minute. Even gonna shake his hand."

Now for the second time, Jim asked Bam for a fast boots-on-the-ground analysis of the battle for Con Thien.

The question seemed to punch a fast red button, because here it came, the first incoming of Jim's war. It came *whoooing* through the rain like a train on sky tracks looking for a place to park.

Bam and Tag dove together, hit the ground, and scrambled through the canvas flap covering the bunker entrance. Jim stood there, tall, fascinated, the objective observer, steeling himself not to go spastic this time, or blink, or twitch, trying to visually track the rush of the streaking shell, to objectively try to *see* that sucker and soak in the sensation of what objectively happened when that sound met the objective ground.

Soaking it in, the observer saw a flash and big smoky splat and the earth rising and raining out a red-brown cloud and felt himself being carried backward through the canvas flap and sent bumping down narrow slimy sandbag steps. At the bottom, the observer lay on his back blinking furiously through a dark cloudburst turning to brilliant sunshine that went ring dinging out his ears.

"You okay?" the sound washed over him. "Close. They swang one down on us that time." Bam leaned over him, mustache twitching. "Roughhouse Rosie rides again."

Jim sat up in a dim, low-ceilinged, dirt-walled room with a candle burning. He felt his nose burning and spat mud. I'm in the war, he thought. He felt something slimy on his fingers and thought it was blood. It was slime. Sitting up, moving his hands, he felt for his notebook.

Roughhouse Rosie? He needed to write that down.

Outside, there came commands followed by hard shouts "Doc! Doc! Need some help, doc!"

Inside, the objective observer heard the Marine called Tag shouting into a field telephone something unpleasant about the chain of chickenshit command he was enduring as Bam and another Marine guided the objective observer over to a canvas cot.

"Dinks nearly nailed you, you know," Bam said, working a chaw around in his mouth. "Now you know what we know."

"I really don't," Jim said, spitting. "Somebody's trying to tell me."

It had been a 130-millimeter shell, a product of the Soviet Union. Jim wiped mud out of his eyes and a clod of dirt out of his ear and slapped at his poncho and pack that looked as if they had spent a hard year in combat. The third Marine, a slim, baby-face from Georgia named Rusty, handed him back his notebook and helmet that had rolled down the sandbag steps without his head.

Holding a can of C-rations, Rusty sat on the cot across from Jim and said, with a kind of lispy drawl, that he had been trying to eat this old chopped turkey three times between shellings. He leaned forward carefully, one ear cocked as if listening for some distant all clear, while he spooned up his *Meal, Combat, Individual, turkey loaf, chopped.*

"Like a taste? We get all the old leftover army eats. Good old grenades and rocks and ham and mothers. Taste like they're leftovers from old World War Two. Some of 'em taste like your old grungy underwear after a long day's march. Some of um taste like your old."

Jim wiped at his mouth, tasting explosive dust. "Looks good. Maybe later."

He watched Rusty dip in for a bite with his white plastic spoon, chewing for a moment, hesitating, listening before deciding to swallow, listening again in mid-swallow.

"If you hear a train comin', it ain't a train," Rusty said. "Sure you don't want a bite? Grab it when you can. Like your last supper, sorta."

"Maybe later."

"Can't never tell," Rusty shook his head. "I had a buddy who'd never duck and ended up gettin' toe shot. Lost his toe. If he ducked he'd lost his head. Me, I don't have no gripe with them Viet Cogs (sic). But it was my duty and here I be. Well, I don't want to say no more about it right now."

"Well, don't," hollered Tag.

Bam, sitting on a box of smoke grenades, rubbed his belly. "Only time we get a hot meal is cold soup. Doc back home told me I had a spot on my kidney. Said just don't eat anymore fried chicken and I'd be fine."

Tag shouted into the field phone again, at someone in the battalion. "Oh, yeah. Well 'ats your stinkin' story and it's stuck on you. You hear me! Oh, yeah. Well, you'd better shed the fug up, peanut balls. You hear me!" He slammed down the phone. "Oughta lock those broke-dick headquarters' weenies up and let us go win the war."

His name was Tague, like tag-you. He was from the Louisiana bottomlands and said in civilian life he had been the second assistant to a pipe-fitter's helper, a gotta-go-fast toilet specialist, a proud outlaw trucker, and a master burger flipper whose rhythmic distribution of burgers on buns, his symphonic flow of onions, pickles and hash browns with flashing fingers, had drawn praise far and wide. He was also a scintillating pool player before volunteering to save his country from broke-dick Communism.

Tag looked as rough as his language with big shoulders, big hands, and a big bumpy nose with a rising boil on the tip. The earth had salted over his fatigues, caused him to spit red, and turned his hair into a gritty reddish mass that snapped off the teeth in his comb. He sort of flopped his head back and forth when he smiled, a big red-mouthed smile, like a big tough rooster with its throat cut.

Smiling, he formally welcomed Jim into their *living* room with its shrapnel-ripped ceiling reinforced with a few wooden beams through which fashionable rainwater dripped. On one side a wiggly flame danced through the empty eye sockets of another grinning skull, found as they dug the bunker deeper. There were three cots, three M-16s, two sniper rifles, boxes of grenades and bullets, some fat yellow candles, a case of spoiled C-rats with the cans all swollen, and a tiny make-shift stove upon which Tag, using the flame from a small slice of C-4 explosive, boiled up a mix he grandly called coffee.

"Want some? Combat coffee. Gotta be a man of arms to drink it. Break a nail in two. All I ate today is three cups of this and a piece of pound cake and a boiled lizard I found in the coffee, kinda rare, and I never felt better. Sometimes I scrape the mud off my neck and throw it in there too.

Want some?"

"Maybe later. What's that fine smell?"

"Must be Bam. Got that fine smell of the rear. All smell like that in the damn rear. Hell, when we come out here, we had clean faces, pressed out camis, and all ready to go catch some bullets."

"With one hand," said Bam. "And look good while we're doing it."

"So why are you out here exactly?" Tag asked Jim. "You crazy too?"

"To write on you guys being out here. Whatever you do, whatever crazy things you say."

"We got some good yarns out here," Rusty said.

"That's what I'm looking for," Jim said, "yarns."

"Well, all we need is the monsoon, a bar of soap, and five minutes of peace. Every time I try to air out these boots, the NVAs get wind of it, and here comes the incomin'. A cruel way to croak," said Tag.

"War's a cruel sport," said Rusty. "Only it ain't even a sport, you lose you're dead, sort of. One day, one's comin' right down our chimney. We mightn't make it out alive or somethin'."

"Well, it ain't today," said Tag. "We got a visitor."

They were all young trigger-puller lance corporals, who said they were born to be United States Marines.

"My feet was burnin'," Bam said, "and I joined up and that's what I am, you're lookin' at one. And they said, dummy, we're sending you to Nam and I said what's a Nam? But here I am and I don't regret nothin', I don't."

Jim sat with pen poised, delving deeper into Marine thought, asking how was the battle going, really? How was morale, truly? He knew the view from on high where the bullets never flew would tend to be rosy. Now he wanted to hear it down and earthy, grunt style. No glossy flimflam. Hold nothing back. Let it all spill out. Could they win? Were they winning? How rough was it out here? No linguistic BS, please, just straight shit.

"Oh," Tag moaned, "I'm all torn up. I think they split my weenie."

The bad news," said Bam, "is Marines wasn't born to sit around getting peed on. We're not stationary men, we're movin' men. But here we sit."

"Don't matter," Tag snorted. "We're called the dogs of war. Bad dogs. With big teeth. Afraid of nothin'. We just roll with it. Let the rough side drag."

"So you're afraid of nothing?"

"Well, yesterday I was out there and all this gray stuff started bracketing me, bing, bing, bing… and I was draggin' a little But this minute, talkin' to you? Hail, no."

Tag laughed. They all laughed.

But could the NVA overrun Con Thien? Jim asked the bad dogs.

Rusty frowned. "Well, like the colonel says, if they won't pay the price."

Tag looked astounded. "Write this down. No way, no how." He burst into song. "*Ol' Charlie's dead they say, he bought the farm today, he's gone underground, he's sort of spread around…*" Warming up, he shyly noted how short the war would be if this *forwardmost* element of the United States Marine Corps was let off the leash to go carve up the Cong.

"Marchin' north, bitin' butts all the way. Less a harpoon blows us away first."

"Typhoon," corrected Rusty. "Like what hit Bam in the mouth there."

"Just a good-natured riot," Bam said, trying to whistle through missing front teeth.

"Sweet gal in a club sold me ten bottles of what she said was champagne. So, I drank 'em. Then I ran into a boot, a good-natured boot. Then I woke up. What country am I in?"

"Listen," Jim asked seriously, "can you win this war, Marines?"

"Well, I didn't come over to get a haircut," Bam said. "Man, I watched all those John Wayne movies. By the time I was sixteen I knew I was joinin' up. Combat arms. Guaranteed grunt. I didn't wanna be locked up in no cotton-pickin' supply room. 'Nam, Nam…' the sergeant kept sayin' in boot camp. 'You are the poor designated fudge nut we're sending over there next.' 'Promises, promises,' I said. Hey, the big boys tell us to come over, so, hey, we come over. The big boys wouldn't steer us wrong, would they?"

"What he's sayin' is…" said Tag, "is he's got a roof over his head and the chow's great. Why we might go chow down at the yacht club tonight, the ol' NVA yacht club. Just look at him," Tag pointed to Rusty. "Tearin' up his skivvies to clean his piece. Done cleaned it three times today already. I mean, like, you know. There is a worried Marine. He even thinks he looks like Elvis. Why maybe he does. Doesn't he look like Elvis?"

"No, I don't."

Rusty had pulled off a boot and was sprinkling powder over a wrinkled foot. He told Jim he had a bad case of trench foot and a worse case of homesickness and that with all the shelling he wasn't sleeping much at all. "So tired I'm seein' double. Can't keep my eyes closed. Though I did yawn once."

"Sleep…" yodeled Tag. " 'at boy's snorin' got heard clean back in Two Egg, Georgia last night. Why the dinks phoned down and said they couldn't stand it and if he don't stop they'd have to surrender. And that's the truth."

"All I know is…" Rusty said wearily, "when I was in my prime I never got tired. This is no life for an old guy."

"He's our old man…" Tag hollered, "and he ain't even a man yet. This *is* your prime, boy. Live it up."

"I'm almost 20 and I've lived my life." Rusty shook his head. "Once I've done my duty and amassed my fortune and get back to Two Egg I'm not doin' nothin' no more. I'll just sit in my rockin' chair and take some red clay dirt and put it in a bottle and just watch it grow."

"Watch it grow *what?*"

"It might not grow much. Can't afford nothin' more than dirt. Guess I'll wind up in the Marine po house."

"You're in the po house now. Hell, ain't so bad."

A sweet-faced tattoo named *Jewel Ellen,* which he said the more he looked at her, the more beautiful she got, adorned Rusty's left arm, his dog tags were wrapped around an ankle, and a St. Christopher gleamed from the chain around his thick neck. When Bam and Tag went up to take a look outside, Rusty told Jim softly that while just sitting here waiting to die, he had been praying a lot of late, because God must be everywhere.

"I just bow my head a little, you know. They saw me on my knees they'd shit. I never say, 'Lord, just protect me,' I say, 'Bless us all, dear Savor, and throw myself in there a little at the end like the olden people did."

"Which olden people?"

"Like in the good olden days when things were good. I mean you're sittin' here with a cup of coffee and cake in your belly one second just waitin' for it to happen and all of a sudden here comes another one. And no one but God knows whether you're still here alive or not. After a little you say, 'Okay, God, I'm back, thanks again, sir.' What else I say is… well, it's all I got to say. Except sometimes I see a little light come in and it's almost like a light from heaven and gives me hope we make it outen here alive."

Rusty scratched his foot. "Don't mention it 'bout the prayin', okay? They might shit and stuff."

"Sure," Jim said. "Not too good at it myself."

"Hey, Mister Reporter," called Tag in the tone of a friendly jackhammer as they came back down, "how ya like it out here? Is this the good life or what? Nobody yellin' at you to get your area policed up. Or make your rack right. Nobody yellin' how come your boots ain't spit-shined?"

"Maybe I'll just stay out here."

Tag seized a can of sliced peaches, held it up, and slurped it all down. "Hell, y'all think this is rough?" he wiped at his mouth. "Not close to real rough."

Jim listened, getting in the heads and rhythms of young rednecks at war. The trouble was, except for getting shelled, they had not yet experienced war very deeply. Rusty was a mortarman temporarily out of work because his crew had been wounded. Tag and Bam were a sniper team not yet called upon to do serious sniping. Both said they were born by the woods, and learned to shoot before they could read the funnies.

"You can see the expression, the eyes, the hairs on the face of the guy who wants to kill you," Bam said. "Next thing you know you do him in. Just squeeze 'at trigger, two pounds of pressure. Just ding him without no feelin'. Squeeze 'at trig real slow and it goes all through your body down to your dong. It ain't so hard to ding a man.'

"Like how many have you dinged?"

"Not 'at many. Like zero up to now."

"What he's sayin' is," said Tag, "they keep the best dang shooters in the Corps back here fillin' sandbags and diggin' holes... 'at's what cracks my nuts."

Feeling more at home in the war now, Jim is jotting impressions in his note-book... *country boy smart... apple pie, and Chevrolet... raise the flag, and open up a can of kick-ass, NVA, chopped... Eric should get his lordly pants up here* ... when Rusty cocks his head and shouts, "Train a comin'!"

"Be-bop-a-lula!" hollered Tag.

A moment later something thunderous slams down near their roof like God's big dirty boot. An overhead beam cracks. Things shake, dirt falls all over, dust fills the bunker. More shells come bursting in. The beam cracks all the way, the roof sags. Another round crunches in even closer and it's animal time.

They're down on all fours in choking dust, grunting, lunging, scrambling through an opening in the side of the bunker... down into another hole, this one very small, very dark. Jim goes with the rush, elbows thrusting, knees scraping, head bumping, squeezing his way in, journalistic inquiry temporarily suspended. Cafe-of-last-resort café, Bam had called it. They wedge into the café. Butts soaking up chill water. Knees jamming against chins. Heads crunching against the muddy top. No light, no sound except gaspy breathing and somebody's belly talking out loud.

Tag breaks out cussing. "What's this I'm fickin' sittin' in? It's a plump of fickin' rat poop. Why didn't we dig the fickin" hole bigger?"

Jim's heart does little wind sprints. Really clammy down here, dank, tight down here, can't hardly move. Stinks down here. Feels like he's choking. Can't see. Dark as dead down here.

"Hope you don't have hole fever," grunts Bam on his left.

"What he's saying' is..." whispers Tag to the right, "we hearda people goin' crazy down here. Gotta get the hell out. Gotta deal with it or go to hell down here."

"Onliest deal you make down here," whispers Rusty "is with Jesus and stayin' alive."

Jim doesn't say anything, staring through his knees, concentrating on breathing, straining to see *something* in this hole the war books didn't quite cover. Now God's other boot descends. Clumps of damp dirt rain down. The hole seems to be pressing in smaller, smaller. Then more shells. Everything's shaking.

"Big one, mutters Bam.

"Roll on, big mama," whispers Tag.

"This what you call the good life?" whispers Jim, wiping dirt out of his ears.

"Gettin' there, son," whispers Tag.

"These are parlous times," whispers Rusty. "Only good thing from down here is you go straight to God, no curves."

"What we whisperin' for?" grunts Bam when the shelling eases off. "Can't nobody hear us but us?"

How often do they do this?" whispers Jim.

"Comes in pretty inregular," says Tag. "Don't letcha sleep."

"Where's Rusty?" Jim whispers.

"Over here, sir. Front ways. Lord, lord..."

It's quiet outside now. But they stay huddled in the dark café talking to the dark. Bam snaps at his Zippo. Dirty, dancing faces light up. "What an ugly bunch," he says. "Why can't I be down here with three short-legged young ladies?"

"I'd admire that," whispers Rusty. "If they were alive or somethin'."

"Long legs, short legs," says Bam. "After five beers, who cares. Boots and saddles, man."

"I know one," says Tag, bully-boy voice going almost soft as he tells of his warm, warm woman back in the bottoms. Her name's Mindy, Mindy Mae Hemphill. He practically sings it, Mindy, oh Mindy.

"Built like a shit brickhouse. Prettier'n a baboon's butt. Don't know why she's not writ. Two months. Don't know. I don't. I'm pissed. What do you think?" He nudges Jim, café authority on women..

"Guess the mail's not too swift out here," Jim says.

"Yeah, better be."

"Married?"

"Was for five minutes once. Now Mindy got my ring. Gone have a Marine wedding. Dress blues. Crossed swords. Hail, after a man like me, can't be nothin' back there for her. Like I taught her pool over at Bullfrog Corners Pool and Foodery. That little lady can clean a table in 60 seconds. Shoot, shoot. Bing, bang. Clean, son. But couldn't drink her beer too good. Like skunk drunk. Got all swoll up and her lip poke out. Fuzz got to screwin' with her and I told her on jail visitation day that next fuzz puts his pistol to her I will personally eight-ball into the corner pocket. 'at goes for the ol' judge too, next time he wraps her in his robe with his paws on her. Hail, everything's all right, long as she don't get slack."

They sit there in the dark café where time doesn't fly, hearing tales of Tag's warm, warm woman between sounds of incoming, not long in coming, showering more dirt down on their heads.

"I say sheet!" swears Tag. "Don't like this. I like it man-to-man. I'll fight what I can see."

"Well, I did my duty and my buddy got killed," Rusty whispers mournfully. "We prayed up together, Posie Shoulders and me, we come over together. Nothin' could be done about it, I don't guess. Posie, he died a fungus or somethin'. I naren't say no more about it right now."

"Well, don't," mutters Tag.

"Just glad Posie didn't get smushed up like us out here. It's hard to put words
to it. I'm tryin' to feel no sadness or angriness. Like out there they got a job to do
killin' us. Jesus just called Posie home, I guess. I don't have the heart to say no
more about it right now."

"Well, don't," mutters Tag.

"My brother in Lost Gap wrote some peckerwoods are throwin' their medals
away in the states," says Bam." "I don't got that kinda blood in my body."

"Lost Gap," whispers Jim, "where's that?"

"Alabam. Ain't much there when you get there though."

Jim scoots around, feeling for his notebook. Must get some of this down.
Where's his damn notebook? Would Ernie lose his notebook? He's trying to sort
out the talk from the storm of emotions he felt in the scramble for the hole. How
does a correspondent remain the cool fly on the shithouse wall, seeing clearly, re-
cording objectively, down here? The cool fly doesn't want to be buried in the dark
café. He briefly ponders the efficacy of the strategy plotted by the wise war planners
back in that strange and distant freaking another world, Washington of D.C.

Suddenly, he jams his hand down to where something leechlike is slithering up
the inside of his right thigh. Scratching furiously down in his britches, he forgets
about the efficacy of the strategy.

An hour, a few leeches, and no explosions later, they belly out of the darkness
into their battered mansion. The living room has largely caved in. Rain pours
through big shrapnel holes in the ceiling. Lumps of warm steel are embedded in
the dirt wall. Jim's cot, precisely where he had been sitting, lay burnt, squashed.
Digging around, he finds his helmet, his blown empty pack, one tattered but a
useable notebook, and one can of tuna, smoked. Outside, there's shouting. A few
fires flicker in the rain.

As they try to put the bunker back together, a soggy, bespectacled lieutenant
leans in and calls them out. He tells Bam and Tag to buckle chin straps, there's a
lot of NVA movement beyond the wire. The famed sniper team will be going out
soon with a patrol to set up an ambush, an all-nighter. Standing in the mud with
rain peppering his face, with dark clouds scudding low overhead, the lieutenant

briefs them intensely. He doesn't want any screw-up city out there. He doesn't want any hot-dogging or shooting your own people or short-term memory loss or getting lost on Mount Stupid out there, he just doesn't. Making his eyes big behind water-speckled glasses, he queries Bam.

"Are your hindquarters now fully recovered, lance corporal? Is it ready to go?"

"Like I said eleventy-two times, butt good to go, sir. I'll walk it off, sir."

"Now this is the real deal, Marine. Now, what's the direction of the ambush? You got that?"

"At's for sure. It's set in my head. Three hundred thirteen degrees, sir. Or somethin' like 'at. Like go out there and mosey around in the mud and turn right. Stuff like 'at."

"Magnetic or grid?"

"Magnetic."

"What's the running password?"

"Step forward and state your business, codger, or I'll blow you away. Cause this is the real fuggin' deal."

"Negative, corporal, the word is *cudgel*. Got it?"

"Got it, sir. Like the old cudgel."

"That's codger, corporal. This is a damn cudgel. C-u-d-g-e-l."

"Roger, sir, I got it. You got it, Tag?"

"Who goes there, ol' cudgel?" says Tag. "Spill your guts or I'll blow yo ass away. That usually works."

"Jesus…" snaps the soggy lieutenant. "Just damn straight remember it. Be squared away out there. It's damn desolate out there, desolate, desolate. Assume nothing and expect everything. Don't stand up to pee with your eyes closed. Don't become incontinent of feces. That a problem?"

"No problem on the continent, sir," says Bam, "How long we be out, sir?"

"Can you make it seven hours and keep your eyes open and not go limber-neck and keep your mouths shut? I beg you, boys."

"With a toothpick, sir," drawls Tag. "You seen us in action. Men of solid arn, or sumpin' like 'at.'"

"Well, arn men, can't offer you a toothpick. Maybe your neighbors from the north can."

Just then Jim spots Donlan mucking toward him, shouting that the chopper's coming. Behind Donlan Jim sees big gun flashes, then forked lightning stabbing into the hills of North Vietnam. A rising wind flaps at their ponchos and the rain whips harder and the sky rolls into a strange yellow-dark glow as Jim tells the Marines he'll see them again down the road.

"Down the long ol' road," Bam says.

"Give us a holler," Tag says.

"Yeow!" See that pop over yonder?" Bam spits a blob of tobacco northward. "We got us a toad strangler."

"Blowin' our way," Tag says. "This could be our lucky night."

"You really writin' us up in the newspaper?' Rusty asks softly, muddy fingers fiddling with his St. Christopher. "If we make it out alive or somethin'?"

"If the harpoon leaves us alone," Jim says, moving off.

"Tell 'em back home everthang's all right," Tag hollers as the correspondents slog downward, We're the Bad Dogs. We'll crunk it up and get after 'em. We don't give a hell. It's war. Tell 'em I'm *pisssed*. I don't care. I don't. Watch out NVA. I'm pissed."

Jim had heard accounts from Eric, who had heard accounts from others, of how terrified the Marines were up here. Must be some other Marines, he thought, glancing back at three silhouettes on a hill under the weird sky fuming over them dark and smoky yellow.

At the LZ their bird is ready to fly, and they clamber in. Lifting fast, it banks low and away in a clattering curve over the road leading out, and they are hardly in the air when there comes the first *crack*. Then *crack, crack*. The bird flutters, then recovers as clouds of explosive light and heat chase them down the road. The neighbors to the north saying goodbye. Jim glances over at the documentarian of perverted bastards sitting shoeless with one muddy green sock on and one-off, clutching his big camera. Having declined to wear the perverted boots, he had lost his footwear running through a sucking shell hole. He looks miserable as they leave the small mountain of heavenly beings behind, chop-chopping up and away through the rain.

Noting Jim's pigsty appearance, Bad Boy Redd leans over. "How's your day going? As my daddy used to say, 'Don't go fishin' in strange holes and come back complainin' about what you caught.'"

"Caught what I went for," Jim hollers back.

"Anything interesting?"

"Went to the Café of Last Resort. Dark down there."

"Hell, I been to places darker than the dirt it took to throw over you. Hell, life's just a breath out here. Suck in a deep one, J.J. while you can."

J.J. takes a deep one. A cherry boy no more. There's a small cut on his arm, a big wet rip in the seat of his pants. Bombarded with impressions, and plenty of yarns, he pulls out his last notebook and jots notes over mud spots. Beside him, Sean Donlan sips from his cognac canteen through his bloody little smile and offers the canteen to Jim who doesn't need any. He's cranked-up on the real stuff. He had justified his existence. Could the first time be the best? What would Ernie say?

As he scribbles in the notebook, his adrenaline-cooked brain is suddenly skewered by a vision of a heavenly being. It's the Sun Goddess, sitting atop a pile of sandbags. Her legs are nicely arranged as she smiles down sweetly and aligns her curves for the muddy lads to get the best view. Her lips move, "Can I help you fellows out, like in any little way?"

Jim shakes his head in the affirmative and holds onto his seat, feeling about to float right out of this helicopter.

The Germans Are Coming

He and his airborne buddies were living in a hole in a forest of blowing, dumping snow-freezing fog. Hands and feet split open and bled. Boots became icy, clumping bricks.

Rifles wouldn't fire. Trench foot, pneumonia, and frostbite were everywhere. Wounded men lay out there freezing to death, faces turned red as wine.

They had no gloves, no overshoes. Some never changed clothes, and never took off their boots in six weeks. Others changed clothes with corpses to keep warm. They got shot and it was too cold to feel pain. They ran out of food and water and ate snow off the pine trees of the Ardennes. They got dysentery. They got dysentery bad.

The old soldier got an open-air helmet when a slice of steel from a German 88 came cracking in, rattled around, and wedged in his cap under the helmet. The cap belonged to a dead German. They hacked down in the snow four feet deep with mattocks and waited for the Germans to come again, and come they did. He remembers them swarming forward firing as they high-booted through deep snow in that weird, wading charge out of the fog woods just thirty yards away, and his gloveless, frozen, bleeding hand jerking numbly at the trigger, as they fought off being overrun.

Did he ever feel they weren't going to make it? The old soldier doesn't even pause to think. Uh, uh. Nope. We weren't brought up that way. We *knew* we would make it. Even though he nearly didn't. He woke up in a Bastogne hospital and spent months suffering from malnutrition, extreme exposure, and frostbite over much of his body. For a long time, he lay naked on a bed without even a sheet touching him. And it took him out of the war.

Years later his hands would crack open and bleed strangely like that again. It wasn't that cold in California. And no one was shooting at him. Just for a moment though, he'd look at the blood on his hands, and he is back in his hole staring at those snowy woods, and the Germans are coming.

Battle of the Bulge (1944)

7
DEEP ANALYSIS

"Oh, rats, stupid me," giggled Susanna Robinson on the bar stool wiping at the drink partially spilled in her lap and trickling down one leg.

"Hey, let me," said Commander Tommy Sullivan, kneeling down and dabbling at her leg with his handkerchief, soaking up the gin coursing down her ankle toward her lemon-yellow shoe.

"Oooh! You are a sight, lady, " he said, looking up at those ballerina legs like a worshiper of the dance

A sight, but she still had to get dry. Fifteen minutes later they were up in her apartment on Nguyen Hue near the International Club. All she had wanted to do really was to change her dress and maybe have one more drink and talk to the commander who was an interesting case and about to go home. The commander had always been playful and never really pushed himself on her any more than the big hairy-chested teddy bear he seemed to be outside of his war troubles.

The next thing she knew, here he came ambling into the bedroom with her still half-dressed. He was rumbling something about having this aching sweet tooth for her for so long and so bad and now he was leaving and so, please, counseling aside, show a little compassion for a poor desperate fellow just this once, you know, just this once, honey, just this... And then he had her down on the bed still apologizing in husky tones, "I hope it's okay, honey, you beautiful, sweet, kind... don't say no..." while pulling off her clothes except for the lemon yellow shoes he seemed to admire

She opened her mouth to say that she really wished he wouldn't, while still letting him. It was the last thing she had wanted and her usual classic dilemma, but the commander was going home. When they are like this, she told herself, you can't stop them, you really can't... and then she felt him getting at her, gripping her in his bearish paws. He was hurting her a little but she kept letting him, as she traced the heroic scars along his neck with her fingertips. "Oh wow, wow, wow!" she heard the commander going on.

It was only because the good commander was going home, she felt fairly certain. He was such a nice, needing teddy bear, and even though he was hurting her a bit, it was all right because she would never see him again.

"Wow!" the commander gasped, "damn, damn, you beautiful… oh, wow, wow, wow!"

Finally, she unstiffed and went with the flow a little more, But not all the way, because she still managed to think of it as just blind connections of flesh on flesh what he was doing, meaningful for him and justifiable in a behavioral way on her part, analytical and relatively well-controlled, because she was simply his stress-reliever, the healing woman aloof from mere raging physicality, and that the act itself had little to do with the heart of what she felt in her true self.

Indeed, a part of her was already redesigning it, lifting it beyond random bed games, instilling purpose, even soul into this mussy bed. It was also registering how good she had gotten at it, *at least that, Robby,* she thought, as she listened to the rumbles of ecstasy or something from that bear throat. She had never heard such noises before. That she could make one carry on out of his mind like that triggered a rush of feelings she had never felt with Robby or anyone. She did not entirely dislike the feeling that she was the commander here and wondered how many women could make a bear moan.

Now the stress reliever found it difficult to analyze whether she was relieving the bear or the bear was relieving her and wished in the worst way for another drink to make analysis easier. Then, inevitably, here it came, cranky gloom-sodden old noise scolding her through some crack in the dark of her head, advising her that she had now almost qualified for her crown of crowns… Queen of Saigon's Sluts. She told it to go away. She told it that it wasn't about being that — which was a highly relative and misunderstood term in the age of the great sexual awakening — and then heard herself trying not to cry under his scarred awakened bulk. I'm doing the best I can. *No, you're not.*

After the bear had finished with his honey and was forever gone, she lay in the mussy bed, unable to sleep, thinking that she had just had a little too much to drink once more was all. This had been absolutely unplanned and unwanted and promised herself not to let it happen again like that, willy-nilly. She also wondered why she was making such a big deal over what many others these days celebrated, and even glorified doing willy-nilly in the great sexual awakening. It was just doing what moved you. *Freedom, natural freedom.* She would have to think more about freedom and what moved her when she got back to thinking.

But if flesh rules, she wondered, why did she feel like some untouchable, bel- lying around on a filthy floor searching for a scrap of the rationale for doing what she had done? Why had she wanted it and not wanted it and then hated herself? I'll study it, she thought. I'll truly analyze it. I will. I won't be just another nitwit. I'll stop it. I must stop it except with love.

Alone in the dark in the mussy bed in a country at war, the analyst rubbed her raw places and gazed at her navel. It seemed off-center. It seemed to be shifting. Was that possible? She tried to analyze it, and what she would feel afterward if she ever felt *love*. They called it true love, but what made it true? Books, movies, ro- mance magazines, various authorities, and some real people said it actually existed. I'll find the truth of it, she thought, one day or night. Surely. And I won't be half- drunk.

Going to Kansas City

LOC NINH, South Vietnam. He rode on a deuce-and-a-half from Saigon un- der a high blue Vietnam sky past rice paddies and banana trees, past coconut and nippa palms, past sweet smelling wild flowers and tail-switching water buffalo tak- ing enormous craps near where two Viet Cong corpses lay decomposing in a ditch. He was on a convoy bound for Loc Ninh near the Cambodian border along a road called "Thunder" infamous for ambushes.

They rode through villages that hit Jim's ears like Bap Dap and Flung Dung, past peasant women working in the fields under wide palm-leafed hats, wearing pajamas rolled up over earth-speckled thighs, making it hard to tell how nice peas- ant legs were in the mud, on past South Vietnamese soldiers with rifles leaning over and taking potshots at fish from the rail of a bridge. One dropped in a grenade that blew up a big spray of water making rainbows in the sun. Mud and dead fish bubbled up in the stream. Bouncing along in the back of the truck, Jim, between watching for ambushes and legs, tried to write the best parts down.

"Bull-ridin', hoss lovin', homesick, Texas cowboy, that's me, hoss," the tall sergeant with the wide grin said. He lay barefooted in black pajamas under a big white beaver hat in an old sagging, French brass bed. He had big hands and big feet.

"Hey," hissed a voice from the shadow of the doorway.

It was another sergeant, short, chesty, in just-shined boots. *Dude of Death* seemed printed on the helmet. Jim couldn't quite make it out. Maybe it was *Dud of Death*. An unlit cigarette drooped from his mouth. "Why don't you do your country a favor and go hunt a gook for a change?" he half-growled at Cowboy. His helmet was pulled down low over his eyes. Stepping from the shadows, he addressed Jim. "If you want action, you're wasting your time on cow shit."

The long sergeant did not lift the big white hat from his eyes or move except for a one-fingered salute that made an upthrusting shadow on the candle-flickering wall.

Pushing words out the side of his mouth, the chesty sergeant sort of snarled, "See you later, porter, unless you're still stuck in cow shit."

"Shut that dang door," yelled Cowboy, and the door slammed shut.

The dude or dud of death, marching off into the dark to take command of the command bunker, seemed to emit a glow in the dark, Jim thought, weird, from a flare perhaps, weird.

Lifting his hat, stretching his legs so that his size 12s poked beyond the bed's end, Cowboy looked over at Jim and laughed. "Poor doggies wore out, took all they damn can. *Oh, the hardest job, the dirtiest job, since ever war began, is pickin' 'em up and layin' 'em down, the job of an infantryman,*" he chanted, then turned up his little transistor radio that was capturing some blast from the country-western past by way of Saigon, 70 dark and crooked miles away.

"A decent little band," sighed Cowboy, "it sure is."

Overhead, lizards lapped up mosquitos and zipped like green darts along the shrapnel-chipped ceiling. Cowboy, whose name was Kitwell, yawned on his saggy bed, smoked some grass, said don't worry, he wasn't gonna float off or anything, just gonna keep a cool little Texas flame cooking in his head. He hummed along with the radio for a minute or so, then turned it down low.

The once-fine but now bunged-up French villa lay inside a small scraggly camp surrounded by miles of rubber trees and populated by a hundred irregulars, known as Ruff-puffs (called the saddest specimens in the South's military), some of their families, and the two U.S. sergeant-advisers. Nearby was an airstrip cut out of the rubber, with a U.S. artillery unit dug in at one end, a Special Forces A-Team camp not far away, and down the road the little town of Loc Ninh.

Jim was getting the story of Americans stuck out in the rubber with the wretched Ruffs. The dude or dud of death, whose bonafide in war had heretofore been as a chronically pissed-off supply sergeant, was the ranking sergeant. But Cowboy, an ex-paratrooper, had seen combat, was more experienced in-country, and the more quotable to be around.

Stretched out there long and loose, sounding homesick under his hat, he talked about life back in Six-mile, Texas, his love of horses, and how he had traded his ex-wife, a female dude, for a true beauty. "As beautiful a hunk of hoss flesh as ever was rode. Can't wait to climb back on her."

Smoking, and signing, Cowboy got to pining about the great times he and his old ranch buddies, Vonsell and Quintas Buffalo and his cousin Wee Wee used to have, and how when he got back there was gonna be a whole lot of dancing, riding, hollering, and all the good things in the world going on.

"So, what's the roughest part out here?" asked Jim.

"Well, my hoss ain't bein' under me is the roughest part. And the easiest part ain't this dude goin' round dumpin' on these poor Ruffs, tellin' 'em they got to kill like Godzilla, dress for success, stand like a man, die with their spurs on, and suchlike bull-funky. See, I'm out here to advise them how to shoot, scoot, and *communicoot*, not win him no medals. Well, no mind. Get the ranch house here fixed up 'fore long, have the neighbors in, and sit around barbecuin' snakes and talkin' world peace and stuff and the good laf (sic) we have out here."

No electricity yet, but Cowboy had patched up the long-abandoned villa, fixed the roof where a mortar shell, a dud, had popped through two nights before, no sweat, and scrounged up furniture and slapped on paint. A few large pictures of wild horses and even wilder-looking jean's-filling fillies helped cover the cracks in the walls.

Jim sat on a cot by a glassless window swarming with mosquitos beyond the canvas flap. The convoy had dropped him and a load of ammunition off a few hours earlier, then turned around to make it back to Saigon before dark. The chesty sergeant had offered Jim a midnight boogie into the bush, said it was no problem at all to lay on an ambush. ("You wanta rumble in the rubber? I can make your dream come true.")

"Dude!" groaned Cowboy. "Few mortar rounds now and then, that's it. Might's well stay on the good side of the VC. Just search a little and skedaddle. Then comes this dude Biggs, who thinks he's the baddest rubber in the forest. Here ten days. Goes chargin' into the woods to piss on the natives. Even shot one of our ruffs in the butt the other night, who's just out there by the wire with his pants down takin' his usual midnight crap. Dude said he saw movement, suspicious movement. Rode a bull like that once. Mean little one-track brain. After it threw you it'd pound your butt and drag you around, stomp on you and try to sit on you. Bad personality. So, they had to shoot it. No shit, Sherlock, I wouldn't mosey out there with him I was you."

Snuffing out his joint, emitting a long, musical yawn, Cowboy lifted his hat. "In the mood for a little sack time there?" And Jim said he could use a little of that, and Cowboy blew out the last candle.

The radio played on softly. *Those were the days, my friend. We thought they'd never end...We'd fight and never lose... Oh, yes, those were the days...."*

"Some crazy days," sighed Cowboy.

Jim, still in his boots, lay there thinking of Susanna and told Cowboy of the mesmerizing filly he was chasing, whom he couldn't tell gave a rusty dusty about him or not.

"What sorta filly? Never trust a filly over three."

Jim pulled out a picture of Susannah. "Except for this one. Enough of her is never enough."

"Man, she fills those jeans. The trouble with a filly like that is they're always itchy to go rompin' off with another dude. One like that... just too much."

"What's that make me?"

"Hooked on jeans, I'd say, hoss. The great-lookin' ones is funny stuff. No comprendo. Bumfuckle you all up. Gore ya worse'n a bull. Grab you by the you-knows and won't let go and then drop you harder than jumpin' out of an airplane. You ever had one grab you like that? I'm through with all that forever."

"The little fillies? I'm gettin' there, hoss."

"Naw, jumpin'. I don't care if there' no wind outside and I'm jumpin' into a sea of sweet Texas puntang, I'm through with it, hoss. By no means will I ever be doin' that again. It's not natural. The only thing fallin' out of airplanes is bird shit and dang fools. You know that."

"It's one thing I have no desire to do over here."

"Course, chickenshit never gets off the ground."

"Maybe I'll desire it," Jim laughed. "Once."

"Well, it's not a jumpin' war," Cowboy said. "It's a huntin' war."

"I'm a natural-born hunter who doesn't want to kill anything,' Jim said. "What's that make me?"

"In the wrong place, hoss."

Strands of pearly moonlight gleamed briefly through holes in the canvas but were soon covered by clouds. Raising up, squinting out, Jim stared hard into the shadows at rows and rows of rubber trees that had once been part of great French plantations but were now part of the war. He thought he saw bad things moving out there. He knew you couldn't just look straight ahead, the demons always looked back. He shifted his eyes to one side, and rolled them around.

"Dark out there," he said. "Damn dark."

"Dark," Cowboy said. "Our sergeant in charge of scarin' the VC to death went chargin' out the other night. 'stead of workin' the area real quite like, just went bangin' through the trees brayin' like a donkey with its ears on fire. Got him on the radio and all he says is he ain't afraid of no dark, the dark's afraid of him. Says,

'I'm doin' this and I'm doin' that and I ain't scared by no little Bing Bang Bungs runnin' around in black underwear."

"Unless they're pretty," Jim said.

"Some people just wanta go out and make noise. A guy what knew the dude back in the world said he'd turn up his stereo until the walls rocked, then go climb on his motorcycle and roar back and forth across yards and sidewalks until people came out and looked at him like they wanted to shoot him, and then he was happy."

It was snowing mosquitos around Jim's head, and he rubbed on bug juice until he dripped. He was weighing a possible boogie into the bush with the dead dude, or was he too crazy? The night belonged to Charlie, everyone said. *The VC is a silent, secretive, nocturnal predator who approaches from the dark side like the mosquito and strikes between midnight and dawn,"* an expert on the night had written.

Night or day, Jim thought, he needed the action. Otherwise, another silent night, no-story night.

Lately, he had been out with infantry beating the bush for some contact in III Corps around Saigon, but Charlie, like Susanna, wasn't in the mood.

He had even tripped out to Long Binh, the huge headquarters and support base near Saigon, and discussed the war with a unit of engineers who said they spent their time in the rear with the beer while building recreational facilities and engaging in vital missions like squeegeeing up their colonel's tennis court. Long Binh must have eight swimming pools, said the merry engineers. The closest they had come to war was hearing far bumps in the night. They laughed and said they saw more war on the boob tube back in the states. What a swell vacation in terrible Vietnam they were having. They called themselves the six-pack-for-lunch bunch.

Jim's editors had been most pleased by his stories on the stirring defense of Con Thien. That was yesterday's pleasing. Now he searched for more battles. Maybe the death freak had it right, just go crashing out there and piss off Charlie.

His Con Thien pieces had shared the front page with a big antiwar march on the Pentagon, the marchers burning draft cards and citing their "hour of conscience" and "high principle" while refusing to be sent to "that place of hell." So, here he was, conscience unbruised, looking to find a little hell. He recalled a friend back home declaring he did not know one sane person not afraid to go to Vietnam, and that he would gladly drink pints of his own puke, knee the doctor in the gonads, and throw up in his face at his army physical before he would go over there. "I'll tattoo 'I'm a proud crazy psychopathic liar and drug fiend with kidney disease and liver failure,' on my forehead," his friend swore. "I'll bribe priests to swear to my peace-loving Christ-likeness."

How, Jim thought, had the great spirit of World War II evolved to this sorry state? Cowards were celebrated as heroes. Heroes were spat on and called criminals.

"So, you're telling me," He said to his friend, "that you're too good to go?"

"That's the kind of guy I am. Too good to get buried because a bunch of rightwing hysterics are afraid of bad old Commies."

At 20 minutes past midnight, the first mortar round fell. Then *whaaaaaa*. Funny sounds. *Whaaaaaa*. Like baby rockets. And the camp began to rock.

"Sheet fire and save the matches!" Cowboy's hat tumbled to the floor as he went corkscrewing off his cot and under it. Then, reaching, clawing out for his boots, jamming them on without tying, he felt blindly around for his steel pot but couldn't find it. Jim sat up, glanced out the window, and ducked. The battered villa was falling down around them.

Cowboy yelled they needed to skedaddle to the command bunker 40 yards away, a mostly underground, stone-and-steel Japanese creation from World War II that spiderwebbed out through six entrances. Jim under his cot kept glancing over at Cowboy bumping and thrashing big-footed under his. Each time Cowboy started to crawl out an explosion sent him rolling back under.

The roof fell in. Plaster and bricks crashed on Cowboy's bed and around Jim under his cot. Shrapnel blew shrieking and rattling through the walls, ripping shutters off the window above him. An hour later the barrage suddenly ceased.

"They're comin'!" whooped Cowboy, getting up. "Make tracks!"

Pell-mell out the door they went, Cowboy galloping furiously in his pajama bottoms, head down, boots flapping, rifle in one hand, waving his big hat in the other, hollering at the Ruffs in the bunker ahead not to shoot them.

Jim saw many shadows moving along the wire at the edge of the camp. Through the smoky light of trip flares, the shadows seemed to dissolve and float disembodied through the rolls of concertina wire and then reform into arms, legs, heads, guns, and bayonets shining in the firelight. He heard whistles blowing, and saw dead Ruffs crumpled all around. Most of the camp's inner perimeter — a few small bunkers, some thatched living quarters, the villa, the supply room, the ammo bunker, the jerry-rigged shower that was a fuel drum with a thatched screen around it — smoked and burned.

The only true defense left was the old Jap bunker, and those inside were shooting out through firing slits in the steel-doored entrances. A rocket round smacked down near one as Jim and Cowboy went for it. There was a thud and flash and the clangs of shrapnel hitting and bouncing off steel even as they crawled on their knees through the door thrust open by scary-eyed Ruffs, then went stumbling down stone steps into the yellowish smoky twilight of a chaotic room 25 feet below ground crammed with shouting Ruffs, bawling, huddled women and babies, even a chicken or two flapping around down there. In the middle of it, the death-tripper was in full voice, calling for volunteers to get off their duffs and follow him upstairs and go out there and smoke some gook ass.

"You *dinky dao*, crazy American!" the Viet leader named Tran shrieked in Death's face. Death laughed.

Jim sat against a stone wall, knees up, eyes watering, scribbling in his notebook, trying to catch the mad dialogue between Death and Cowboy and Tran as they debated the efficacy of the strategy and nobody agreeing.

Cowboy with his punctured white hat pulled down half over his ears got on the radio yelling where was the dang artillery? Where was the dang air support? It came back to him that the whole area was under attack, including the arty unit that was even then skipping shells point blank, fuses timed for air bursts, off the hump of the runway into human wave Viet Cong assaults out of the rubber trees to the east.

Outside now a shrill nasal voice came squeaky-squawking over a bullhorn. "Send out da 'mericans! Trow down your weapons! We only want da 'mericans!"

"How about da chickens?" sneered Death. "Got a mess of them."

The voice squawked again, "Black man soldiers! Throw down your rifles! We will not shut you! Send out da black man soldiers! We have nodding against da black man soldiers. We given good foot and water, let go home to dear

"I'm going up there and put a round down Ho Chi Bung Hole's rice-snapping throat!" snorted death-tripper. "And then I'm gonna rip his nuts off and stuff 'em down his bullhorn." Death's teeth bared as he talked, his eyes fairly glittered. His attack plan was simple. "I' m gonna dust his bongos! Any you girlies care to assist?"

None sprang forth. Jim pondered his role. He had looked for Hell and had found a piece of it but wondered what kind of work it was that allowed people to shoot at you but it wasn't proper to shoot back? When did an impartial observer become a bloody-balls participant? When he was a cornered rat? He watched the dude-of-death robotically brush each boot against the back of his trousers, tip his helmet down low, pick up his bloop gun, an M-79 grenade launcher, stuff his pockets with rounds like fat golden bullets, and go stomping up the steps.

"Back shortly," he called down. "Don't *go* anywhere. Don't *do* anything."

Shortly, just outside the entrance, there sounded intense bursts of shooting. As promised, the death-tripper came back. Several Ruffs carried, half-dragged him boots bumping back down the steps. Jim saw bullet holes in him and about a mile of his sneer wiped off. After dragging him into a corner and making sure he had totally finished his trip, they flapped a dirty poncho over him. Jim stared at the boots sticking out. They had taken his life but left a little of Death's shine. The boots themselves looked curiously alive, almost wanting to say something.. Hard to grasp, Jim thought, kick-ass boots on those dead legs. He didn't even know Death's first name.

Outside, the bullhorn voice came squeaky-squawking again. "Throw down your weapons! Send out da 'mericans! Send out da black soldiers! Send out da puppet traitors!"

Inside, Cowboy shouted for artillery again over his radio. "Bring in the big beef *now* or we're cooked!"

Jim found himself slowly climbing the steps where the dude of death had gone. He kneeled beside the last Ruff-puff up there and peered through the firing slit at what seemed hundreds of the enemy moving inside and outside the wire. Some wore uniforms, others black pajamas, others just loincloth. A few seemed to have gone berserk, leaping from bunker to bunker, shooting in the air, running around like drunken Indians fire-dancing through the smoke. The last Ruff shook his head in the negative, thrust his rifle to Jim as though it was scalding his hands, and scurried down the steps.

Jim kneeled peering out. In the jungle in the dark one rarely knew what one was shooting, but he knew now. He saw three of them moving his way, and it was something to write about but not now.

Barefooted, wearing a loincloth, bulging with satchel charges, the charges slung over their shoulders and hanging over bare chests, they advanced low to the ground through the smoke, moving slowly sideways, crablike, directly toward him. He knew they were sappers and were going to try to blow down the door. And now they were right *there* to his front, jungle phantoms, looking boot-tough with thick black hair, body language loaded with menace, eyes narrowed into wolfish slits. Less than 15 yards away now, crabbing forward weirdly sideways, coming to blow him up.

Jim aimed the M-16 through a firing slit. He had always loved guns, he just didn't want to kill anybody. And he knew shooting... get a good bead, aim a little low, breathe, relax, squeeze. Shoot the deer, not the antlers, hunters said. Or just stick it out there and spray and pray. As he considered these sayings, suddenly BARROOOM... BARROOOM... blinding flashes, crunching in close out front. It was a salvo of 155s, real big beef. When Jim opened his burning eyes the sappers, the deer, the antlers, had all disappeared.

Cowboy could really call it in. One salvo followed another. Soon afterward air strikes bracketed the area with bomb clusters, bomblets scattering like exploding peaches among the Viet Cong now in full retreat. A spooky gunship circled round and round above, miniguns stitching down destruction like a frightful sewing machine of firepower. In Spooky's wake, American troops came cleaving through on the ground, and the VC were running back into the rubber.

When the bunker people finally felt their way out of the smoke into the sunlight, the attack was gone and so was most of the camp. In the crumpled villa, Jim saw a twisted brass bed, cooked bricks, charred wood, and dead Ruff-puffs and their families lying all around. VC, dead sprawled face down, face up, faceless. Whole bodies and odd chunks of bodies and bloody heaps of bodies lay scattered through the camp, across the airstrip, and out into the bombed trees. Hasty burying by the Americans was in progress. Jim had never witnessed the not-so-fine art of hasty burying. He saw a VC body slung into a makeshift grave by the legs as a foot tore off in the slinger's hands. Mass graves humped just outside the dangling remains of the camp's wire. He saw a load of blood-caked corpses tossed off a truck into a shell crater. Nearby, a minefield strewn with enemy dead was torched, burned, and exploded, with body parts flying all over.

Clouds of yellow fumes floated up. As Jim jotted down words describing fumes and flying body parts, someone said something from behind. It was from a mouth of the rear, just off a helicopter.

"Quite frankly," said this colonel frowning over Jim's shoulder, "this is a field of honor and a huge success story. Quite frankly, you could contribute a little by helping us keep the old image up."

The colonel's own image ran a bit puffy, with pockets of fat beneath his eyes, and a too-big bottom beneath his frankly over-expanded beltline. His uniform, however, was razor-creased, headquarters-spiffy as he moved about putting a positive face on body parts.

"Please keep it positive or, quite frankly, it decentivizes the war effort. Just keep it cool."

Jim didn't want to disincentivize the war effort and he didn't want anybody disincentivizing his reporting effort.

As the PR colonel offered advice on incentivizing storylines, Jim's eyes fell on one of the camp's women. There was a bloody rag around her head. Her left arm was blown off at the elbow. Flies crawled on the stump. As for cool, she didn't seem to have much to lose. She sat on an empty ammo box and cradled her dead baby in her right arm and begged a medic to please kill her.

Jim turned to ask for guidance as to how he might work the woman and dead baby positively into the story, but the colonel had departed in a rush to meet the landing of another important helicopter, from which stepped a general.

"Yes," said the general, "I'll say a word to the media."

The general, a blond-gray, two-star striding along trailed by a television team and several print types just up from Saigon, looked pleased. The general halted. He glanced around. Birds suddenly seemed to sing. Two birds high in a skeletal tree did in fact exchange peals and twitter The general folded his arm. and assumed his words to the media stance...

"By damn, gentlemen," he said, gazing all around at the smoking rubber trees, "do you know how much we love it when the bastards do this? We've KIA'd over a thousand main force VC and wounded many times that many and we're still chasing them out in the trees. When they mass and try to fight toe-to-toe, we just kick butt. Yes, you can say it has gone absolutely perfect for our side, and the absolute shits for their side. Just use a nicer word. You can say we wish to hell they had the gumption to try this every day. Listen, gentlemen, we're shit hot. We're on a roll."

Jim wrote it down. The war was getting more complicated but easily writeable was the general. It was a butt-kicking, all right, with friendly casualties not overly heavy. One of the heaviest, a Ruff-puff blown naked and headless, was being pulled down from a tree near where the birds sang. Jim wondered how birds could sing so sweetly looking down on this. How could PR colonels? Well, he had read plenty of windy hoorahs for and blubberings against war and understood that he must keep his own blubbering to a minimum. Death had had total risk tolerance toward death. *Had had.* Jim wondered again how far his own risk tolerance would carry him.

After a while, he went over and found Cowboy down on his knees in his ten-gallon hat with a half-gallon hole in it. Picking through the rubble of the villa, Cowboy found his little radio that was still working but there was not much left of the dude of death's personal effects.

"Only thing is this piece of letter from his momma. Says, 'Nice day to wash. I washed most all. The ironing went well. So did the meals two-legged and four-legged. Every day the same. Wash. Iron. Get meals. Well, I won't read no more. Here's one where he's tellin' some filly by the name of Big-ass Red how dull it was here and how he's workin' with a fellow sergeant so lazy he'd pee in his hat afore he'd drag his worthless carcass outside. Wonder who that dude was? Well, I won't read no more. That's life out here, I guess."

What's Biggs full name?" Jim asked. "Hard guy to write."

"Rodney Biggs," Cowboy said, clicking at his radio. Rodney Harold Biggs was it. Or Herbert? Why don't you say Rodney Harold or Herbert Biggs had balls as big as a bull that couldn't be rode, a smile as wide as all West Texas, and got smoked kickin' butt for his country. They's not much else to say, I guess."

Cowboy's radio all at once burst on with joyful noises about another dude: "Going to Kansas City, Kansas City… there's crazy little women there and I'm going to get me one, get me one…."

Nearby, the woman with the baby not in Kansas City screamed.

8
POSSESSED: THE PERFUME WARS

The Dude or Dud of Death was well received in Washington. Jim had made Death sing. The question to himself was, had he made Rodney Harold or Herbert Biggs sing on key, or even the right tune? Writing a certain kind of brave damn fool hero required writing around foibles like Big-ass Red and thrill-killing rats. He felt good about the other sergeant, a near-solid gold cowboy with perhaps a karat missing here or there.

E. Drudgington Blow was not impressed. "I am not impressed, friend student," he said, lecturing that this was not fine old WWII where any clerk or jerk could to nostalgic applause claim he had routed Rommel or punched out Tojo. This was Vietnam... The entire Vietnam endeavor was just not worthy of any commendable word. He referred to the Communist side as not the Communist side, the enemy side, or as the Red Threat, but as the *other* side, representatives of gallant liberating forces headed by Ho Chi Minh, which meant Bringer of Light. He called this war *that* war, a horror movie of misguided Americans turned demon marauders in a misunderstood peasant land, what?

Whether it was this war or that war, friend student felt he himself had filled in too many blank spaces on Sgt. Death, and wished he knew much more about this war or that war. But it was still his war, and though he tried making politically logical leaps to see things as presciently as Lord Eric claimed to see them, it was a leap far too bleak. He thought of trying one of those pills the lord swallowed each day for his suspected ulcer, as he uttered collectivist hallelujahs to friend student.

In Saigon, Jim moved into an apartment over a bar just off Tu Do Street whose name had been changed from the Wild Wild Kitty to New Moon Over Miami, after the place was vacated by a gone-native, gotta-get-out fellow who advised the new occupant that one way to get the feel of the land was through warm contact with its more liberated women and their wrenching stories on what calamities had brought them to this state of business and that the selection in the ex-Wild Wild

Kitty could prove physically exhausting and financially draining, and, yes, tearful, wicked, and funny, and watch out for the Euro-Asian booby trap called Mia, the most draining of them all. No sweat, no drain, Jim replied. He just wanted a place to lie down close to JUSPAO.

Close contact with Susanna, meanwhile, between Jim's dates with the war and hers with the warriors, had chugged onward like a train waiting for logs to be cleared off the track. But then came that night he took her to dine in a restaurant left over from French days. As always she had to maneuver through the hungry eyes. Even Saigon Fats, an enormous news presence of some reputation and no small appetite, who had been eating like a sour-bellied Buddha, briefly ceased his disappointed chomping and wine-sniffing to observe Susanna's festive charms, a gorgeous piece that looked good enough to sprinkle rare spices before rendering his critic's choice, a chewy umbs-up. *Watch that fork, Fats*, Jim thought.

In the field, he had more than once shaken her off as a super hormonal escape for an observer concentrating on life and death in battle. Now, as she sat at a corner table aglow in candlelight, instead of chicken he seemed to be ordering French whores for dinner. He retained, however, sufficient wit to get the Sun Goddess, or Sunny, as he called her in brighter moments, drinking. It seemed the natural thing for a natural man to do for a natural goddess who liked to drink.

Having observed the way drink spun her mind from relatively clear to mostly cloudy, he found himself instinctively plotting to move this earthly angel, crocked if necessary, to the heavenly sack. This, even as he heard her going on about where she was in her life, how she aspired to do more. *More what?* he wondered. Something more of true worth, she said, and talked about her vacillations over whether to stay in Vietnam or go back and finish her degree in psychiatric social work, what did he think? He was surprised at how the responses he emitted seemed to please her. She was talking now meaningfully, most meaningfully, about something. Squeezing her hand, he gazed into the long-lashed caves of her eyes that seemed at first as sweet blue as a baby's dream, then seemed to dance with a smoky, moody, devilish green, candlelight perhaps, or his imagination. Were devils green?

Just for tonight, he decided he would play Mister Say Whatever Pleased Her to get elected to her sack, like any good seedy politician. Tomorrow he would not vote for himself. That would be tomorrow.

As they killed off the wine, lips poised above glasses, he leaned across and just touched his lips to hers that were like the old song... *lips like cherry bombs,* or was that an ammunition slogan? By any definition it was lucky the VC hadn't exploded anything or Fats burped and cracked the sound barrier, he wouldn't have heard a thing. In this exalted state, he seized her wrist, a little too urgently, and urged that they continue this magical voyage of discovery in her pad or his.

She reclaimed her wrist, and he patiently listened to her talk-talk. It seemed to be about the trials and tribs of womankind making it in a man's world without resorting to if he could imagine it, crass you know what. As she leaned forward with her pleasing anatomical arrangements looking about to set the tablecloth on fire, he didn't have to imagine it, and she said again how she enjoyed discussing the deeper things with him.

She went on about how her Red Cross work was wonderful but limited, and how she wanted to do more. Sometimes she wished she was a battlefield nurse, closer to the ultimate action. Maybe she could get out there someday, somehow. What did he think? He thought of the tablecloth on fire.

"Stay in the country," he urged aloud, "this beats any theorizing in a class-room."

From behind now, he heard a familiar voice. It was Sean Donlan walking over with a Frenchman named Francois Marre, a photographer of rising fashion fame newly arrived from Paris. They sat and talked of the art of photography, and the Frenchman asked Susanna if she had ever been photographed, with serious artistic intent.

"Not that seriously."

"Zat will not do. I must capture you in somezing serious, no?" The camera was already working the possibilities in his head, clickety, click, oh, *merci!* And she hadn't even stood up.

They ordered coffee, and the three men sat camera-eyeing the figure before them, considering her photographic potential. The gentlemen of art agreed she had somezing of great seriousness to offer mankind, *merci!* Just wait till she stood up. What a magical mystery tour that would be.

"I never realized it till now," Jim said.

Indeed, noted Francois, zee camera must have a passion for pure art and imagination beyond zee cheap eye-candy, but what a pleasure to imagine *eet* anyway whatever zee price, no?"

"Yes, can't imagine how I missed it," Jim said.

Donlan broke the spell, saying he and Francois were heading up the next day to catch some guaranteed hot images in the Central Highlands, building into maybe the damndest, biggest infantry clash of the war. He said Francois was eager to capture the latest fashions of battle in a tropical setting.

"Like to go up?" Donlan asked Jim, "for zee hot images."

"Sure. Almost there," Jim said. "What about Eric?"

"He sends regrets." Donlan cracked his bloody little smile. "Said it did not sufficiently pique his interest on Saturday. And never on Sunday."

"I'd like to go up, I really would, I need to see things." Susanna leaned photographically forward. "Could you smuggle me in somehow?"

They looked at her again, concluding that if she went nobody would pay much attention to the chitty chitty bang bang, and they would have little to report. On the way out, Jim noticed Saigon Fats, leaning back and observing over his ample belly, arched an eyebrow at the curvy turkey passing in review and somehow restrained himself from forking her.

Outside, they bid farewell to Donlan and Francois, and Jim escorted Susanna to her place by the river. She just rippled along, the American dream-walker, and Jim, maintaining eyeball discipline, fixed his attention on the potential sighting of the elusive VC in the moon — this could be the night. In this charged state he heard Susanna telling him she had something else to show him.

Six floors up in her place they sat on a couch near the balcony, with the moon over the river shining in, and the sound of an ARVN troop convoy grinding along the road beside the river. Jim looked around at wood, crystalline, and metallic dragons with scary talons and fiery maws, at grinning, balloon-bellied Buddhas, bountifully-bosomed earth mothers, and an assortment of other objects conveying the Romance of the East.

Susanna had disappeared into her bedroom. Minutes later, reappearing in a kimono and holding a pair of blue satiny house slippers, she bent over, slipping off the reds and sliding on the blues, with the kimono flashing open to reveal exotic new heights. She was showing him all right, tease without strip, and held the infernal position, he calculated, about six months longer than necessary. In a cloud of pleasant perfume, she blew softly over and came down sighing next to him.

This was about tea, which was what she wanted to show him, she explained, and happily launched into a paean on tea power, on the joys of the ancient and honorable ceremony of tea, remarking how the great tea adventurers could search for greater wonders beyond war. Positioning the iron kettle off the tea set on her big round coffee table, along with the ceremonial tools that would carry them along the hallowed path of tea, she placed her hands ever so lightly on his, instructing him how to keep the kettle just so, and the dipper just so, and the whisk just so, and then how to perform the turning of the tea bowl gracefully just so, which would make the tea gods smile.

He smiled himself as the sunny one spoke earnestly of how much more there was to draw from the Experience of the East, and how they might enjoy exploring these mysteries stretching out before them together away from war, and how would he like that? Yes, he replied, he would. He imagined making explorations with the mistress of tea into the experience of the East or any other direction she and the gods might take them.

Pointing to a vase by the balcony holding a single, lush, long-stemmed yellow flower, Susanna called it her magical jungle flower, which made good things happen and good people come to her. On the wall behind the flower hung a Japanese scroll with one downline of black characters.

"It tells of one moment..." she said, "one meeting. It tells of the unique design of each moment in life. We may have tea here tomorrow," she went on so softly he could just make out the words, "but it will be different. We have this now, and we will have it only once."

She sat philosophically close to him, too damn close. Forget tea, he thought. Flowers were for later. Talk about unique design, her legs were running riot from her kimono. He felt that if he touched her actual flesh at that moment he would burst into flames. So, he reached out and touched her. He seized her shoulders and kissed her. Gently at first, and then not so gently. He was a natural man. She did not resist.

He kissed her again, harder. Her dimples winked at him, he thought. Her eyes turned devil's green, he thought. *Audacity,* he thought, If he failed it would be gloriously, and he closed even harder against her lips, and then against her breasts as if they were the enemy to be subdued.

"You *don't* need to do that." She pulled at his hand.

"Yes, I do."

She pushed against his shoulders. "*No*, you don't. Not now, *please.*"

"Why not?"

"I don't want back on that piece of road. It doesn't feel right."

He wanted her feeling or no feeling, on road or off. He was a natural man. This seemed the natural moment. His hand shot out as if on its own, brushing away the kimono and landing hard above her unique knee. At that moment he looked possessed. He was possessed, desires for her bumping together like boxcars.

"Please! I don't do *that* anymore!"

What was *that?* he wondered. Is this it? he thought. Tea and chit-chat? He was thinking again, his wires cooling. She wasn't a goddess. Just a female filling up space. The moment passed, his charge quickly done, not very glorious.

"A little faith in me would help," he heard her whisper.

"Listen," he said, "I don't blame you, fighting off the barbarians. Like me. Go ahead… give me some hell."

Susanna didn't know what to give him.

He felt moved to say something sublimely romantic. It came out like a man slowly hanging himself. "Is it possible… including the having of tea and all, if we could be like… you know, like alone, in the future, exclusively…together?"

Susanna sat straightening herself before the word master, and he realized he had never before uttered such sentiments, not even to his idiot model, and was sorry he had blubbered forth now.

"So…" he got up to go, "guess you've heard enough of that twaddle."

At the door, she reached for him. "Not enough," she half-whispered, and then with words too soft to catch, kissed him, full-mouthed and then some. His knees dipped. As she pulled away, she squeezed something into his hand. She said it was a Saint Jude medal, the saint of really impossible things.

"Take it," she whispered. "You need it in those terrible Highlands. Bring it back to me, this one thing. Will you, please? please?" She kissed him again in the way she had,

"Hell yes, yes. Sure, sure, if possible."

And then she vanished behind the door in a puff of perfume or was it a cloud of estrogen, that left him as steady as a love-blinded bull gratefully receiving the sword and bellowing for more

He put Jude in his pocket and made it down and outside, feeling the sword twist. She was impossible, all right. Still, he thought they had reached a mutual understanding of sorts with that kiss.

He hadn't caught the words but the kiss seemed pretty mutual. Go home and perchance to dream, he thought. Bellow your silly brains out. Bleed. Roll in the dust. Didn't she know it was dangerous to tease a natural man into a state of sexual riot and turn him loose in the streets? *(Terence, you get ever stupider.)* She was taking him over. He did not like being taken over. She had gobsmacked him again and he liked it when it was happening, He did not like it thinking about it later.

Breathing deeply of the heavy Saigon night, he walked along. Where had she learned to kiss like that? He didn't want to know. He kept going, hearing shells *poom-pooming* across the river, harassing and interdicting old Victor Charlie out there somewhere. At least out there, he understood what Charlie was trying to do.

The beat went on, the nightly artillery lullaby to lay him down to sleep. He walked past a trash fire sputtering in the gutter, past rats so fat and sassy they paraded in and out of the gutter like rodent royalty. One royal rat faced off with him on the sidewalk, before looking bored and waddling back to the gutter.

He saw shadows of the *Quan-Canh,* Vietnamese military police, patrolling an alley in a machine-gun mounted jeep. Looking down, he saw strips of cardboard jutting from a doorway with a sleeping woman and a small girl close together on top of the cardboard near a pile of trash.

Pulling piasters from his pocket, he placed them carefully just in front of the woman's eyes and stepped around. What a good guy he was. Eric would laugh. *Boobus Americanus.* So *ski-ruuw* Eric.

Back over the Moon Over Miami, assembling his gear for the adventure of the coming day, listening to the radio… *"Now a word to the wise, check your radio for booby traps…"* He snapped off the radio. Susanna was the boob trap. He told himself he was getting pretty tired of playing this ring-around-the-beddy-by. She had carried him spellbound to new heights of spinning his wheels, leaving him stumbling through a maze of bewildering femme signals — yes, no, stop, go, do, don't, slow down. speed up, look at me, worship me, but don't get carried away, kiss, don't kiss, touch here, not there, say this, not that, physically want me but not too much. On further reflection, he thought Susanna was too much bling, not enough blang. What he wanted right then was simple. Love it and leave it. Ding it and dump it. Bang it and bag it. Don't sweat it and forget it. On the subject of women, he was back in the mode of a natural man, roaming free, whatever happened, happened. Nothing wrong with that.

The natural man felt his legs moving, blanging down the stairs toward the Moon vamps. On the hunt, natural man beating the bush, nothing wrong with that. His hunter's eyes raked them over, little yellow honeys full of midnight slink, all so elegant, so intelligent on subjects like sappy Americans and their money bags. He would be grandly selective. There was only one. Across the room, he saw marvelous Mia advertising herself, part sultry Vietnamese, part sultry French, queen of Saigon bar life. She would be the antidote to Susanna. He had never really approached her, just given her a certain instinctive smile, and she had given it back with a certain sultry interest. Could he intoxicate himself on Mia? Break the spell of Susanna? Natural hunter-man walked over to the spell-breaker woman.

"Mia? Would you…" he pointed up, "like come visit… for a little while?"

Mia gave him the smile as if to say, yes, and batted her eyelashes, shook her head, and said *no*. She, after all, was Mia, queen of all she surveyed. Mia surveyed him. Mia was grandly selective. It was Mia. "No visit, thank you."

"Well, you've got good taste," he said.

"Maybe, someday," she said, tossing her head in a queenly but friendly manner. "I say to you maybe someday. Do not feel bad. Maybe someday you get lucky with Mia. Maybe."

He thanked her for her concern about his future luck and then found another Moon-over-Miamian so exuberantly agreeable that she grabbed him in a near arm-lock.

"Hokay. Numba wan. Anyting you say. We go up your house, handsome boy. Hokay?"

Jim was in the mood for a fast silent tryst, eyes closed, but went upstairs with this babbly-bubbly ex-peasant girl with the designation #28, known famously as Gidget Wunderbar, who was a bit flat of nose and walked big hippy and giggled spastically at anything he said and jumped as though goosed at every nudge. Under the ceiling fan, she flapped around advertising her charms in what she called her super micro mini-skirt especially designed to excite the eyes of foreign devils.

"Me *sooo* hot girl."

Moving to the dragon-fire red bar she bounced and jived around like a New Orleans band on Fat Tuesday while cooing out a mix of perfume and fish sauce in his face and telling him of her magnificent irresistible hotness for him

Babbling, sweaty, uncoordinated action ensued around the bar stool, followed by a kind of hand-rasslin' on the floor. After a bit more rasslin', lying on his back on a grass mat, straining to unlock from the lusty grip of Wunderbar, who liked to maul him while cozying up to him, yet another Experience of the East.

"Where you from, Gidge?" he asked, nudging her ribs gently away with an elbow.

"Oh, wow, me *sooo* bary, bary hot girl." she revealed, suffocating him in perfume while blowing demon's breath in his face and grabbing at his crotch. "Me nice on you, you nice on me. You sheat on me, me kill you. Me old woman, twenty-five. Now gimme ten thou. Me stay you all night, hokay?"

"As one highly articulate featherbrain said to another, babble on, baby."

"Oh, wow. Me from Paree. Now gimme ten thou, you bad boy."

"Sorry, Gidge, sounds exciting, but no can do tonight."

"Oh, wow. You no loven me no more?"

"I've got this pain in the brain. It's pretty bad."

"Oh, wow. What main thing you liken 'bout me?"

"Mainly? Nothing."

"Oh, wow. Oh, wow, you bad boy."

"Don't say 'oh, wow' anymore, Miss Wunderbar. It makes it worse."

"Oh, wow."

Jim lay there playing the proud bad boy to gorilla girl's aggressive amour as the ceiling fan creaked slowly going nowhere. Though briefly appealing in a gorilla-from-*Paree* sort of way, it wasn't long before he paid her off, something less than she desired for something he did not receive and no longer desired. Afterward, he lay camped on the top of Mt. Restless looking for the Valley of Sleep while summoning up exotic visions of Sunny's photographic potential that made the tea gods smile. At least his nightmares would be shapely. The only females he would have to worry about for a while might come rushing four-legged and growling out of the bush with big sharp teeth.

9
BADLY INFECTED HILLS

Jim fell asleep and dreamed dreams that made the tea gods smile. Early the next morning he went looking for smoke and thunder. With Sean Donlan and Francois Marre, he waited at Tan Son Nhut to hitch a plane ride north to the Dak To camp in the Central Highlands.

All regular flights had been diverted to rush troops and supplies to Dak To. The correspondents sat stewing in the low-slung terminal building along with many soldiers flopped around on the gritty floor, some sleeping between gum wrappers, coke cans, and weapons and equipment piled all over. Jim gazed at a sign on the wall.

> *In case of mortar attack*
> *Don't panic and run*
> *Lie flat on the floor*
> *And put your hands over your head*

Pacing in and out of the building, peering up the flight line, Francois, eagle beaked, wiry as a fox, nervous, animated, who waved his hands a lot when he talked, waved his hands, slapped at his cameras, and said they got to get going.

"We got to get going," repeated the photographer of Paris fashion fame. From time to time he practiced his moves for a firefight, popping around a corner with his Nikon, snapping off fast shots, then ducking back, esthetically satisfied. These moves had been demonstrated to him by another French photographer, an unlucky late one, but still pretty good moves.

Francois was readying for the Big Snap, the Ultimate Image that would capture and cage the Beast of War. Though this was his first combat assignment, he spoke of it eagerly as his coming defining work, and any further delay toward reaching this pictorial pinnacle was not only intolerable but immoral, because the world was waiting to see the beast as it really was.

"Take me to where zee action was, is all I want. I am ready for eet. I don't care. I must have eet." He went outside but soon came hurrying back all in a conspiratorial whisper so that other prying correspondents with the big ears could not hear.

"Look, Sean, Jeem, listen. I am just seeing some Vietnamese paratroops up zee flight line. Going to Dak To straight like a line. I asked to get on zee plane but zere American adviser look at me like a spy or somzing. He say kiss my ass but I zank we can get on zat plane if you carry zee ball."

The Frenchman had a good eye. Grabbing their packs, they started running. Far up the flight line they saw troops loading into the rear of a C-130.

"Look, zoze MPs in zat jeep," Francois waved at the MPs. "Maybe zey take us zere if you carry zee ball. They carried, the MPs obliged, and the jeep scooted toward the up-swooping tail of the big cargo plane. The props were already roaring. Heavily-armed Viet paratroopers packing weapons and huge stuffed rucksacks jammed hotly against each other nearly flush to the ramp that was starting to close. Clambered on, the correspondents squeezed against the puzzled Viets.

Up front, a towering, red-faced American sergeant adviser to the Viets, pumped a fist and bellowed, "Get offa this plane! Ya can't go! Ya here me you people? Get offa this plane!"

"Can't hear ya, sergeant," Donlan replied softly "Bellow louder."

The sergeant mouthed louder as the hatch closed. The plane darkened, vibrating and whistling curiously, Jim thought, like a whale with digestive disturbances.

"It's a hot mother back there," the sergeant bellowed. "Hope ya fry."

"Hot mother is first class," Donlan nodded in the affirmative. "Many thanks."

Hot mama indeed, everybody jammed in sweating and elbowing as the plane lifted. The correspondents found themselves wedged in on metal rollers high in the undulating tail as the plane flew rising, falling, bouncing through a sudden storm. Several of the Viets bowed their head, folded their hands prayerfully to Buddha, and began puking. Losing some of his effervescence, Francois, gray-faced, gasped an apology, leaned over Jim, and barfed a small amount of effervescence on the plane's side, and then a larger amount.

Donlan patted the Frenchman's shoulder. "Getting to the story is the hardest part," he said soothingly, "the rest is ridiculously easy." Donlan himself looked comfortable with his head nestled on his pack and cognac canteen balanced on his chest as the plane rocked and seemed to float like an elevator going sideways.

An hour of prayerful puking later, they landed at the Dak To airstrip, which was not the story but the jump-off point to the most fearsome terrain Jim had ever seen, where the story was. "You know what's out there?" Eric had warned, smiling at them crocodile-like before they departed.

"Have you been there?" Jim asked.

"I have flown over it, which was too close. Don't worry, I'll write the nicest lies about you. How old were you again?"

Out there were said to be tigers, leeches, scorpions, bountiful killer snakes, and thirsty lethal mosquitos. That was the more pleasant news. The bad news was that regiments of NVA were raising hell under triple canopy jungle in fuming valleys that rolled up into great misty hills full of battle smog, explosive flashes, and all kinds of ugly firepower lighting the sky like leering, smoky-red jack-o'-lanterns.

On the ground around the correspondents came walking wounded in from the hills, dripping sweat and stained with blood, burning up with war fever. One soldier, assisted by medics, stumbled by trembling, eyes rolling around, who seemed to turn shades of white before their eyes.

"Malaria, worst sonbitchin' kind," a medic muttered.

Now the seekers of news trudged past rows and rows of tents thrown up in the last days as reinforcements funneled in. Dak To had been a small special forces camp, with the Berets and their irregulars, before the big stuff started. Now the camp was a swelling sore, with all the pus and fever of war puffing up in the distance like ready-to-lance boils, with troops coming and going in punched-up choppers through those badly-infected hills, and looking a whole lot better going than coming. Outside the tactical operations tent, they saw one of the head lancers about to enter.

"General..." Donlan called to a small man with piercing eyes behind steel-rimmed spectacles, who appeared, and at first, sounded more like a bank supervisor in a too-big helmet than a rompin' stompin' field general, "could you tell us who's winning out there?"

It was the hook that rarely failed, and the general, fastening his eyes appraisingly on the newsmen, said, "I can, and I will because that is a timely question. And the answer is we are. Because this affords us profitable opportunities to smash them on a large scale. Ha. We are,

I should say, extracting the most we can from our battle investments so that we can best utilize our capabilities, hopefully, as we recapitalize our force structures. Ha. Do you follow me? I'm just kidding, boys. That's general speak for saying we are kicking big butt and I think Charlie has been told to get off his backside and finally win a serious battle."

The general said this huge many NVA had already bit the dust and that small many Americans. "We got 'em boxed in and are maximizing our butt kickin', so to speak. Charlie's mistake is he's moving around in daylight in almost set-piece warfare, which means we're stompin' the daylights out of him. Charlie's trying to cut the country in half, you see, and obviously, we're not going to let him."

The general slapped at his pistol holster. "I don't know what you're up here for, but there are ferocious battles for the high ground going on along those sonofabitchin' slopes and ridges as we speak. But we've got the sonofabitch hurting and, hopefully, it won't last much longer. Bet on it."

"How much, general?" asked Donlan.

"How much have you got?"

"About twenty MPC."

"Bet it all. We're on a winning streak, hopefully."

"Sir," inquired Jim. "what's the best way to get out where it's really happening?"

"Well, son, any way you can," replied the little general. "I'd take you out to see the bastards myself, but I'm pretty well strapped down back here recapitalizing our force structure, getting our best shit together. And be that as it may, things are getting better, hopefully. Quite frankly, it seems we are effectuating progress. And by the same token, it won't be too painful, hopefully."

The general pawed at the dirt with a boot. "Wouldn't wander out there alone though. Unless you phone up Charlie and let him know you're a friend of mine. Just kidding, boys." The general chuckled. They all chuckled. "Find some chopper, a resupply, a slick, going out. Best way. About the only way," said the general, slapping at his holster again as he turned toward the tent of operations. "Good luck, boys. Hope they pay you well."

"Thank you, general," Donlan said, "it's been most instructive."

The correspondents walked away, looking much wiser. "Generals can be most instructive," Donlan said. "Or not."

"What zat general mean?" asked Francois.

"The general has hope," Donlan said, "that quite frankly we are effectuating progress, or not. Be that as it may, the bad guys are boxed in, hopefully. And by the same token, quite frankly, maybe not. It's a big ugly box."

A few minutes later, outside the big emergency tent (inside a dying soldier screamed, a sound that went from a wail to a gurgle to sounds not familiar as human) they talked to the other side of hope, a still practically smoking wretch of a Green beret (it was his buddy in there making those noises) and asked him if he knew a quick way to get to the fighting. Sixty-eight minutes earlier the Beret had been trapped out in the deep bush and thought of himself as a dead man. And then he and his buddy had been hoisted out of the jungle, plucked up together in harnesses at the end of a cable from a dust-off, and then, dangling, carried off swinging over the trees dodging bullets and not dodging them.

This Beret, the lucky one, so blood-spotted with bandages and so filthy, beat-up, and used-up looking as he leaned against sandbags that Francois, trying to get his picture, couldn't keep his camera from shaking. Jim asked the Beret again his recommendation on the quickest way to get to the fighting.

The Beret looked at him as if he was an escaped loon. Slowly, he pointed to some resupply and other choppers across the strip. He said only about seventeen had been shot down this day.

"Might make it."

"We really *need* to get on out there," Jim said with deadline urgency

"You don't really fucking *need* to," replied the Beret. "Nobody on earth should order you, people, out there. You aren't even armed. You never imagined in your whole life how totally fucked you can get out there."

"We don't have to take hills or anything," Jim tried a very small joke. "We just have to get you guys doing it, on paper."

"Fucking morons," grunted the Beret, scratching at his rags, peeling off a piece of his lip. There came another scream from the tent, and the Beret shook his head, grunted something profane, and ducked back inside to see that nobody was fucking his buddy.

The job of the story *uber alles* driven was simple enough. Go out there, grab the story by the throat, and be sure to duck when the story grabbed at theirs. In any case, if the country was being cut in half, they must witness it. This was an area of journalism reserved for the extremely new-hungry. Even getting to such a delectable story required a stoic's amount of patience, a goodly portion of physical endurance, and an extra helping of tunnel vision tenacity. A little creative denial and bone-marrow optimism about what all would not happen to them in those smoking hills was also helpful, whether they grabbed the throat of the story or the story grabbed theirs.

After they had waited at helicopter pads for two days in wet heavy heat and sudden thumping rainstorms followed by torrid sunbursts that made the steam rise and boiled off big puddles in an hour and much of the fizz out of Francois' war juices in less than that, as they watched through little dust cyclones the troop-carrying slicks wobbling in smoking and clanking, and then after hearing one bad story after another about birds that couldn't make it into this or that hill because of bracketing ground fire and murderous infantry clashes, and how the dead were stacking up and the wounded had no way out, Francois, with eroding élan, began to reassess the purpose of his mission.

When a wounded paratrooper stumbling off a chopper yowled at them, "If we're not surrounded, they're doing a damn good job of faking it!" Who exactly was boxing in whom became ever murkier, and he began to seriously reorder his photographic priorities. Then, after learning that a chopper they had almost made it onto had been blown from the sky ten minutes later, he began to wonder out loud and louder whether his famous journal had not sent him to capture the broader, more insightful view of the conflict, "Zee beeger picture, not zis leetle nowhere stuff."

Indeed, how could he justify wasting their expensive time sitting out here in nowhere land in blowing dust and bastard heat while drinking 90-degree water to wash down the constipating ham and limas, the evil *beans*, over and over from the gauche leetle cans with their *specialties en grand pain.*

He had imagined he would be magically transported to a more agreeable setting, a challenging yet fascinating scenario with a touch of glamour and a tipple of wine now and then.

Not this grubby endurance contest, this discombobulation of body functions, this clutching of the gut, and constant self-groping and scratching at the heat rash in private places while listening to the leaping hellfire from the hills. How could one concentrate one's faculties, much less produce sensitive, award-winning imagery? How could one? No, yes?

Paris was in a bad mood but Francois had so much rather be back with his bony beauties and outrageous fashions and wanton sex and insane students to photograph. There were still sunrises and sunsets over the bridges to capture as never before. Oh, how he loved the bridges as never before. There was a kissing accordion player and singing and artists along the bridges and love and kisses under the bridges. There were the living art forms who at the first twinkle of sunlight broke out *au naturel* in spontaneous sunbathing along the Seine to warmly embrace on film as never before.

There was the Louvre, and Mona, still smiling, and the Luxembourg Gardens and how he missed Notre Dame and the Left Bank and all the shops and cafes with the five dinners and five desserts to choose from and just walking and shooting the quaint cobbled streets and street people as strange as any object in the museums as never before and the Arc at night glowing like the Gate to God and the whole amazing City of Light and driving the champagne fields and the country of France and the entire continent of Europe on which to do acclaimed work, crying — he could hear it — *hurry back!*

For the glory of art, he had rather be doing the lowest pissing rats in the sewers of Paris or the rattiest whores or anything else anywhere else on earth, even Germany. What aberration of ambition had beguiled him into this descent into masochism? He slapped away another ravenous insect, one of the thousands surely searching him out.

As they sat against ammo boxes in tiny patches of sweltering shade watching American jets dive-bombing out of the fireball sun, with sounds rolling, knocking, echoing back through the hills like some monstrous bowling alley of the giants, Donlan watched Francois' eyes go from a little goofy at every ten-strike to ill-disguised fright in a face burned red and dripping like a strawberry popsicle. To lighten his French pal's load, Donlan began a tale about a touring USO belly dancer with whom he had held warm tummies recently.

"She's a Slovene from Slovenia and fiercely proud of her Slovenicity. She goes by the name of Sweet Katrine the Earthmoving Machine, and we had some true and beautiful moments together until this swine colonel offered her a thousand bucks to bring her bejeweled navel over to his hootch for a little polishing. Well, goodbye truth, so long navels. After we wrap this up, how'd you like to get the belly's-eye view of the war? I'll talk to her. I'll go with you. There's also Bette the Bombshell Brat from Bratislava, also the ever-lovely Tina from Tonga, who's only about fifty."

Francois, his mind too clouded with dreadful imaginings as he listened to the earth moving in the hills, just looked grim and grimmer. Why hadn't he listened to wise Eric? Chewing on his bottom lip, licking it until it bled, he affirmed that it was obvious no chopper was going to take them out there. No one cared for them. And was it not stupid to get lost in some meaningless place out there and cut himself off from the important *beeg* picture, was it not?

"We must stop zis running around like we are *crazee*."

"Maybe a little *crazee*," said Donlan.

"We could head back to Saigon and dig in at the Follies," Jim said. "They give great *beeg* pictures."

"But zere's no way out to zoze hills," Francois said. "We waste time. There is no reportage. You have seen."

Other than life and death there's not much to report," Jim said. "We could knock a paper clip off a desk and put in for a Pulitzer."

"Fock zose hills!"

Francois shook his head sadly and placed his hands on his cramping belly. He looked as if you touched a finger to him he would pop into pieces. He jammed another cigarette in his mouth but felt as if he had already smoked 75 packs and his tongue hurt and he threw the cig down in the dust and burst into French profanities, went quiet for a moment, and then again burst into French profanities. "One hour more I wait. Zat's all. *Finis!* Fock!"

Donlan, speaking gently, told Francois that indeed it might be wise to just fock, and that.

"Look, the fact that we're even out here means we need help from the white-coat boys. I mean, if you swallow this kind of feces once and keep coming back for seconds and thirds and still can't get your belly full, you aren't merely hungry for news, you are a deserving specimen for an NVA rocket lobotomy in what is left of your cerebral shithouse. Hell, Jim knows this. Right, Jim."

"Right."

Jim had once visited Normandy, some of the old French battlefields, and the cemeteries next to the battlefields. Maybe the French had seen too many cemeteries, he thought or eaten too much pastry.

Now Donlan got on a roll about how he was pretty damn tiffed that they were messing with his stories again and that after this, by Christ, the news commandos of the rear had better keep their bloody brain attacks off his copy, screwing it around until it grooved with their notions of the way the war should read as viewed from the jungles of New York, or else he was going to take up an honest line of work. That even when some military genius said the boys would be home for Christmas through the light of Westy's tunnel while swinging over LBJ's rainbow, that's indeed what he had said, not the way it read after the mag's rewriting von Clausewitzes had finished restrategizing hard quotes into the acceptable mush of the day.

So cool earlier he seemed to be dreaming with his eyes open, Donlan was waxing forth in this Irish manner when a well-worn airborne captain they'd seen earlier limped over and told them a bunch of slicks would be landing in minutes to pick up reinforcements and drop them on some hill out there, wasn't sure which, but they were welcome to tag along if they found one to squeeze into.

"No promises on getting back though."

"Thanks," Jim said. "Let's just get out there."

Donlan looked at Francois, who had hoped for a reprieve. "I should reject to go, yes? Zere be not room to squeeze in, no? Does nobody know where zey go in zis damn place?"

A half-hour later, flying under billowing clouds into a glaring red sun, dodging over hills blowing smoke like wild volcanos, nobody seemed to. They were getting down close to it… could almost reach out and touch that thousand-year-old forest, trees ten feet in diameter, two hundred feet high, cloaking the earth like great green dark umbrellas full of burning holes, the country once described as scenic by big-game hunters but now turned twisted and war-ugly as high explosives and thousands of troops bobbing around in there trying to kill each other could make it.

The correspondents rode with a lone, red-headed paratrooper in the twelfth and tail-end slick of a thudding line that went serpent-weaving through the slopes and peaks. One minute flying low, they would start taking fire, then roll sharply, popping up and away before swinging back down again, circling to the other side of a hill just feet above the treetops, the formation sometimes stretching out, other times drifting in so tightly rotor-on-rotor the blades seemed about to clang together.

Francois had his camera out getting it when another chopper whirled up beside his door so close, he froze, shut his eyes, and made a fast little sign of the cross. Below, every landing spot looked hot, battles all over, the next LZ looking scarier than the last, and impossible to land and unload.

Just then a hundred feet in front of them a slick full of troops blew up, puffing out in a red dazzle of light and smoke and plummeting in fiery chunks into the trees. Francois shivered, and shut his eyes, but kept working his camera like a blind man. Now suddenly they were flying over the teeth of an NVA battalion jumping out of trenches and firing up through the broken trees with AK's and machine guns.

The slicks all went in a scatter, pilots hollering into their radios and their machines splitting off this way and that like ducks through shotgun blasts. Jim saw green tracers ripping up and another bird in front go ricocheting off a hillside, bouncing up, down, flapping and spinning and clanking *whang-whang-whang* round in smoky fire before exploding.

Now their chip began taking hits... like wrenches knocking the fuselage, *knock, bang, knock, bang*, metal tearing, and engine trying to die and the ship wobbling and yawing terrifically to the right nearly dumping its load.

"Holy shit!" Flung partly out the open door, Jim heard the paratrooper's voice, felt wind smacking his face, saw trees rushing below and smoke blowing out the ship's belly. For just a moment he swung out pop-eyed over the trees with the paratrooper holding onto his legs and then the craft banked hard left. The paratrooper had him now by the collar shouting, "Holy shit! Holy shit!" as Jim tumbled back inside.

The pilot had corkscrewed the ship in a groaning 180 away from the others, trying to head back to Dak To. Shaking from rotor hits, slinging out fuel, it went. Francois alternated from stark terror to trying to photograph their destruction. Donlan, eyes riveted downward, looked all sweat and jaw-set going to meet the great newsmaker. Jim on the floor had unentangled from the paratrooper as the pilot, unable to pick the ship up, steered toward the base of the nearest hill. The co-pilot turned around shouting.

"What? What?" Jim shouted back.

"*Jump*, goddamit, *jump!*"

"Jump where! Where?"

Everyone shouting and nobody getting it and the slick seemed about to pop its rivets.

With chipped rotor blades whacking air, the ship sputtered over a low stretch of hillside pocked brown with shell craters, deserted trenches, empty bunkers, a few still standing trees, and many jagged tree stumps and nothing moving except blowing dust and whirling garbage. Now the co-pilot, teeth bared, shouted again and jabbed a finger fiercely downward. "Jump! Jump the fuck OUT! OUT!"

One at a time, as the chopper hovered, they jumped the fuck out, rolling down in dirt and garbage. Francois, the last, perched on the rocking edge, looking not at the six feet down but up at the sky, his *beeg* picture. After more swearing and gesturing from the co-pilot, he jumped, hitting awkwardly but hugging his cameras like precious babies.

The chopper careened off, nose sagging, blades beating the air, pitch changing moment to moment, having big trouble getting up, then lifting *pop pop pop* trailing smoke and making it just over the next ridge, trying to make it if it could hang together, back to Dak To.

On steady ground now, the four stood looking up at that heavily-forested monster hill and down at a trench full of garbage. It seemed friendly garbage, a lot of empty C-rat cans, shell casings, and odd trash, scattered all over. There were no Americans visible anywhere through the drifting smoke and mist and shafts of sunlight. Jim turned and saw a single actual bird chirping away in a mangled tree. What did the bird know?

"So where are we?" Jim asked the paratrooper corporal whose name was Clapper, who had *Busted Flush* written on the front of his helmet, who smiled through his freckles while trying to see through his busted spectacles.

"Lost, I'd say."

"*Voila!*" exclaimed Francois, brushing off dirt, and wiping his cameras. "Zis is nowhere!"

"This is somewhere," said Donlan. "Hill something on somebody's map. Hope that chopper makes it back to Dak To."

Jim looked at the smoke rising, and listened to gunfire echoing through the hills. "So what now?"

"Maybe we should attack?" said Donlan. "Or defend? Maybe they'll send a chopper back."

"We are lost," protested Francois. "And zat's eet."

Jim tipped his canteen, drinking, and wetting his handkerchief. He dabbed at the blood trickling from a small cut on his forehead. He stared at his red sticky fingers and felt again the sickening rush of nearly deep-sixing from the chopper. Whether this was *eet* or wasn't *eet*, all at once he resented the *rear*. All the commandos of the *rear*. All the experts and pontificators of the *rear* back in Washington who had never spent ten minutes in battle. Lord Blow writing his Saigon pap. All the *safe* bastards. Well, Ernie knew about all those *safe* bastards. And now I know, he thought, because this is the front and I am at *eet*. Or is this the crazy middle?

Corporal Clapper, aka *Busted Flush*, "just call me Clap," was squinting through his glasses, trying to focus. "It's not good being blind in combat," he said, smiling. Clap smiled, flicker on, flicker off. When he looked down at his feet, or up at the moving clouds, or at inanimate objects like trees and rocks, he flashed a little smile, and then around at those badass hills he smiled like a corporal with a rising toothache who wouldn't admit it hurt a little. He also whistled a lot, little nervous tweets with no particular melody. He also smoked pot a lot.

Their only defense was Clap's M-16, and Jim thought he'd better start carrying something more potent than ballpoint pens. It was damn spooky out there in the middle of those jungled hills full of malevolent burps and thuds, and the unseen enemy as the shadows closed in. An NVA battalion could have us in their crosshairs at this moment, Jim thought, and we wouldn't see a thing.

What he did see was a foot-long very ugly centipede squiggling across the toe of his right boot, before he shook his leg and booted ugly away into the garbage trench.

Then they all got down in the garbage, except Clap, who smoking his blissful pot pipe, sort of floating around outside. As he floated he decided he needed to pee, He pulled a banana out of a pocket and seemed agitated when he couldn't make the banana pee. "Well, If you're going to hang it up, might as well feel good about it."

"If you're hanging dead, it doesn't matter," Jim called up.

So there they were in their defensive perimeter down in the garbage trench, and Clap floating around trying to pee outside of it.

Back home as a boy, Jim had swum in a snaky river called the Wolf, and rowed up the river in a little boat past trees and vines curving out like it was a true jungle, about which he made up great scary adventures. Now he was a big boy, and it was a true jungle looming all around, and he didn't have to make scary up.

After feeling spooked for a while, however, he grunted and climbed out of the garbage and walked out, and stood before what might be the entire NVA nation. Defiantly, he too began to pee. Out here you could think doom was approaching one moment, and think pee on it the next. You could think anything or think nothing and just do things. Now the others climbed out of the garbage to plot their next non-pee maneuver. As they plotted, a brief rain swept over. The raindrops seemed to change color, shining like thousands of tinted diamonds on the big green leaves dripping water off the trees and tangles and twisting vines of the great hill above, which moved Francois back to working his camera.

Busted Flush had stopped whistling. He stared through the cracks in his glasses, freckles on fire.

"Holy shit!" He aimed a finger. "*That there!*" They all looked there and saw something dark, "somzing seenister," whispered Francois, which was moving through the thickets, moving their way.

10
WHEN THE SUN GOES DOWN

Going on 25. She's bright. And she's built. Hips, swinging. Legs, amazing. She's a woman. Not exactly roaring, moaning, or bitching, but searching. Been all over the philosophical map lately. Just being physically arousing and blowing their doors off was not always enough. She-power had to mean more. At the moment she's holding forth brilliantly, not merely as a magical shape enthroned on a bar stool, before an erudite group of the rear echelon — REMFies — at the Brinks Officers Club.

At least, semi-brilliantly, she hopes. Instead of bright and chirrupy or her voice that normally floats out as soft as words on a lily pad, she lowers it, making it more authoritative, talking ideas, an authority figure, but the authority figures they seem interested in are cleaved by her bra. They keep looking but not listening. She's in the arena of manpower stuff. It seemed everything was always men *and* women. Her depth and clarity of thought must connect with them, she thinks, even as they nod, wink, as their eyes keep stealing to the terrain of the cleavage and curves where ideas don't reside, their eyes trying to undress her. She mustn't let it happen this time. She's stating serious views on the war and what it all means and trying not to drink too much. If they would top looking at her like damn *that.*

In fact, to one REMFI, an engineer, it's her legs, those structural beauties that he sees as the key to exciting building plans. To the other two, officers of intelligence, a little carnal knowledge is a dangerous thing, so which will most keenly analyze her data and score first is the big challenge. The gang even laughingly moves away briefly to discuss who will escort this well-known authority figure to the sack of deeper intellectual inquiry. All three? That's a possibility. They might even have to call for major reinforcements if she's half the she-devil as the stories they've heard.

Nearby, E. Drudgington Blow observes. Though discussing with several correspondents, the bad doings up at Dak To, his eyes keep roving to every movement of those flaming legs. Gawd, he thinks, how she rules this mob. Frightful. Unchaste. Makes my flugelhorn honk.

As the gang casts lots, Eric slides to the bar, shows the splendid though yellowing teeth, and makes pleasant mouth music. At first, they talk of his great dear friend, Jim, the mad risk-taker, and chat on. She's connecting, she feels. "Oh, well said," he says. Woman, cease thine inane drivel, he thinks.

So fabulously physically showy, he thinks, but obviously missing furniture in her upstairs apartment. He could not abide these small-talk horrors and their dearth of cognitive depth. "Oh, quite," he responds.

"Isn't that interesting." *So what's the bloody point?* Woman, turn off the jabber machine, your tongue must be exhausted. "Oh, so true. I say you are so beautifully, dangerously, aaah, that is to say, excitingly insightful, so um, very, very, rather." He stares at curves curving into all the cognitive depth he requires.

Eric seems different, she thinks. His smile, his jaunty air, so gentlemanly, so courtly, and he truly listens. Even Mama might not want to blow his doors off. Eric is listening and pressing ever closer when the gang of three, whom he regards as leering louts, virtually charge back in looking daggers at the interloper, who taps her knee and politely excuses himself, murmuring, "I'll be in touch, dear," before sliding back to table. Oh, blast, but it went swimmingly, he concludes. Clearly, she *wants* me to discuss the musings of Nietzsche, no doubt, or the string quartets of Beethoven. If she just wouldn't use the words *I think*.

When Susanna leaves, she's alone, fairly sober, feeling strong. She had not wanted to be blunt about it and had put the REMFies off, nicely. She still showed off a little but is better at putting them off nicely. Everything's changing, she thinks, except she doesn't know quite what to do with herself when the sun goes down. She's been trying to control the drinking and the showing off and things that happen when the sun goes. She wishes Jim was here. She gets these rushes of wanting him close. She wishes she had a true woman friend who knew more about more. She wishes the sun wouldn't go down so fast.

Eric, self-acclaimed master of interpretative body language and seeker of truth in comparative female anatomy, his eye for detail in fine focus, follows. Well, he thinks, the woman has symmetry. I dub thee Susanna of Symmetry. It was amazing

how her caboose flared above those awesome underpinnings at just the right....
No, wait! So royally rambunctious and yet a seeming irregularity in the not entirely
syncopating rhythm of her left quadrant by a half-beat. Any variance in her vital
signs must be truly noted if she's to qualify for his ultimate trophy case. He would
have to speak to her about it.

Gads, he scolds himself. How unfeeling. Am I not the consummate feeling fellow of my time? So slip on me sandals. Where's me wire-rims? Puff a joint. Worship a tree limb. Hand her a flower. Cry and sing to this great piece with a minor
caboose problem a sad song and make it jolly. *Haw.* Just once had the consummately feeling fellow lowered himself, given it a noble try to actually work in what
he deemed a harridan hole of unfeeling femmes, with the head harridan stomping
menacingly up and down the corridors with her whip and combat boots, opening
her mouth to let her brains hiss out, and he had resolved never again to submit his
sensibilities to such tyranny. Finally, he had dressed down the she-fiend on just
who the royal blazes he was and ordered her to be more heedful of her place in the
working peasantry. He preferred feasting on fainting femininity, man-needy lasses
with fine swinging cabooses.

Susanna's alone now. Eric walks faster, ready to bare his teeth and make his
move, just as she bumps into her friend George, the ex-Marine pilot now flying
for Air America. They stand there laughing.

He's a teller of funny stories and he's telling her a good one. He whispers in
her ear, almost seems to nibble it, pats her shoulder, and the good buddies stroll
off together in high humor.

"Drat!" Eric exclaims to the night. "Outlaw that shameless figger. That walk is
unconstitutional!"

Well, cheerio, till next time, sweet pudding, he sings to the disappearing figger.
One cannot help but wonder if she sells it to these desperate lads, what? By the
bloody sweet pound, I'll wager. You cannot look like that and not be worth a
bloody fortune. By my troth, such assets need superior management. I'll put you
in camouflage clingies and charge these leering lotharios cutthroat admission. Why
if I was your promoter O wonder wench of the night we'd shame the competition,
corner the caboose market, restore my castle, and retire in a year. *Hear ! Hear!*

No Fear

On the road to Mount Pasubio
Bomborombom... bomborombom
Slowly a column of soldiers is going up
The march of those who will never come back
Bomborombom... bomborombom...
But the Alpini have no fear

On the top of Mount Pasubio
Bomborombom... bomborombom...
Under the winds the enemy has laid a great mine
There are Alpini digging and hoping
To soon go home and find their love
Bomborombom... bomborombom
But the Alpini have no fear

On the road to Mount Pasubio
A cross is all that remains
Bomborombom... bomborombom...
You cannot hear a single voice
Only the wind that kisses the flowers
But the Alpini have no fear
Bomborombom... bomborombom

Lucky Me

Everything was grounded and we stood in this heavy monsoon rain at the tail of the chopper. The sky was very dark and blowing down all over us. The pilot was hollering quite angrily over the bopping of the rotor blades for one of us to climb the fuck on. Only room for one. It was the weather chopper, going up to see if anything else could fly into the newest hellhole. This spitting-adrenaline TV correspondent had already jammed his camera inside the chopper and this fellow and I were debating most forcefully to determine just who would have the high

honor of flying the fuck into the hellhole. But too much noise. After a lot of shouting and the rotors whanging and the rain whipping us nearly blind, we flipped a
coin that fell down into the mud there. Tails. So I was the lucky fellow to try and
get to that news-yeasty hell. I clambered on and picked up and dropped the camera
back into the hands of the TV fellow down there all wet-nosed and pissed and his
mouth moving as we lifted like a rocking chair about to come apart into the storm.
News competition at its fearless finest. Lucky, lucky me.

11
ONE MINUTE PAST MIDNIGHT:
THE TRUE HUNTING EXPERIENCE

"I hate noose cookies"

— Old Iron Nuts

The advance up the hill was to jump off at first light. It was 1275 meters to the top. The commander of Fox Company made you wonder which side you were on. Known as *Terrible* Twist by some, and Old Iron Nuts by others, with a nose looking massaged by a mallet, a chin scar perhaps planted by a flying meat cleaver, a voice crafted to scare off a rhino, he was no politically sensitive prince of the Pentagon, no neat straight West Pointer, no carefully coiffed ceremonial square-head soldier or shiny-faced fife-and-drum lad, was he? When observing one's unmilitary ways with that wrath-of-god look (*you got the feeling seeing you alive was unmilitary to him*) his black bushy eyebrows arched (*something bad moving in there*), and his eyes riveted on the sinner like a pop-eyed, unblinking bird of prey ready to swoop and tear you up.

The good news was that Captain something Twist seemed quite kick-butt about the impending ascent. "They've got the high ground but, God willing, we're going to have a little fun in the sun and be drinking beer on top of that pile of goddamn toothpicks tomorrow night, or my name isn't...." He paused and gave them the Twist eye. "Well, none your business." From the moment the patrol fetched the newsmen to Fox's position near the base of 1275, Twist had stared at them in amazed disdain. "Christ, I need fighters. and they send me writers, goddamn noose guys."

Donlan smiled. "Well, you nailed us, captain. We're here to gather the noose."

"Noose cookies. Back-shooters. Surrender hawks. And you know who you are."

"Well, we're here now," Jim said. "At your front."

"Hear me well. Don't stray too far from my line of sight, or there could develop some thorny consequences."

"We'll stray out of the thorns," said Jim as unthornily as he could.

"We'll see…" said the captain of consequences, "how funny you feel about it tomorrow."

"Maybe you have us mixed up with some other noose cookies," Donlan said pleasantly.

"Noose cookies I know piss all over themselves in battle," Twist said through his bloody-balls stare, "then get themselves big awards for pee burns. So what're you smiling about, Corporal Clipper?"

"Sir," replied Clapper, "we'd like to glom onto you for a while, if it's okay."

"Exactly why are you with these big guns, Clipper?"

"Clapper, sir. We sorta dropped in together. I'm like out here to do stories on this ops, good stories, sir. We won't get in your way."

"I'm sure," said Twist, and called for a soldier to bring over some weapons and ammo for the non-combatants. "Just think of this as a hunting expedition, and no press turkeys are going with us unarmed because we're going up there and got no time to protect you because we're moving fast and smoking anything that moves — snakes, wild pigs, bad guys or any other creatures in God's great outdoors that takes badass pictures or writes bullshit about us. Where we're going you either *rise* up or *crack* up, see. Now, these belonged to some wily NVA, wily *late* NVA, probably close friends of yours. Know how to use them and not shoot yourselves in the balls, assuming you got one?"

Twist thrust, one at a time, AK-47s and some rusty banana magazines at them. Francois received his weapon as if it was a snake dripping poison and protested that he was a *journaliste* come to shoot *les incidents* of *zee* combat with *zee* fine camera not *zee* shooting of guns.

"You're not of these maggots who sets fires to things, takes pictures of them, and then screams how the terrible Americans did it, are you?"

"*Merci. Zat* not me."

"Where are you from exactly, Roscoe?" The captain arched those ferocious eyebrows as Francois explained in a nervous gabble of French-English the overarching artistic aims of his photographic essay, whereupon the captain, working his mouth around like a man about to spit, spat between the Frenchman's legs. Glancing down, Francois saw a spittle-covered scorpion high-tailing it beneath him and off into the undergrowth. Dropping his AK, the Frenchman performed a spastic little dance backward.

"France?" frowned Twist. "Haven't been there but know what I heard. Damn surrender monkeys. Last to join ya, first to fuck ya. Is he a real nooseman?"

"He is a fully-accredited nooseman," Donlan replied, then asked if the captain had a moment to brief them on how he planned to conquer the hill.

"The captain doesn't give information to the fully-accredited enemy."

"May I quote the captain?"

"Negative. You can say the captain doesn't want a bunch of numbnuts in the same jungle with him screwing up his tactics."

"Might I inquire what are the captain's tactics?"

"The concept of *Balls*. Tell your dancing partner there to drop his drawers. We want to know what we're going up there with. Aw right, don't drop 'em. Maybe we don't want to know."

"Might we learn the captain's first name?" pressed Donlan.

"Negative. Negative means *negative.*" Twist turned to one of his lieutenants. "Keep these powder puffs out of my way. Don't trust 'em... man, woman, or French fries. And get the AK away from Frenchie. She might ding us all."

The captain strode off, fists-doubled, muttering, "I see clean through these phonies like a hundred-thousand-candle-power Xenon searchlight through pieces of dirty Kleenex."

The lieutenant, named Harper, graciously surrendered his first name, which was Al, as he led them off through patches of mist to his platoon busily digging in between giant stands of bamboo.

"Tarzan country," Donlan murmured, looking up at great spreading teak and mahogany trees towering over the bamboo. When Jim wondered aloud what life forms might be moving in that mighty growth, Donlan said, "You don't want to know. You noose guys are such a delicate lot."

Francois had slumped down against a tree, camera bag in his lap, checking film. Back in Paris, he had assumed he could somehow remain aloof from the discomfort, the lack of amenities, perhaps off in some warm press bubble observing from his Eiffel Tower observation post, picking and choosing interesting images.

He had expected picturesque encounters with pajama-clad natives. He had even heard that American wars were mostly hi-tech, push-button affairs these days, little girls could push them. Where were the girls? It was evident that one could just vanish, blown to glop eternity, eaten, licked, and sucked up by any creature in the hunting and killing business out here, because it was all hunting and killing, killing and hunting. The Frenchman's skin itched with real and imagined stings, bites, blood-suckings. The terror in his imagination exceeded even his fear of Twist

Now he was growing cold. When the sun was high in the Highlands he felt like he was in a deep fat fryer, when it dropped so did the temps, fast, at times 40 or 50 degrees. Francois saw this, too, as fate's plot to render him *mort*. That and the infections, everywhere the infections. Especially the vile mosquitoes he heard could cook his brain into malarial soup in hours. He saw them hanging around in the gloom, surely waiting to swarm him, mad to suck French blood, even French hair. "Zis jungle sucks you dry. And zen you die."

He slapped at them. And slapped. He felt them all over him even when they weren't. Though his belly cramped, he could not defecate. Even photographers of great fashion must defecate. And now they handed him something called an entrenching tool and told him to "Dig!" To dig and sleep in a hole in the cold creeping earth was not his idea of *la grande armée*. Where was glamour? A photographer without glamour was like a hammer without a sickle, was that not so? Jim and Donlan agreed that was probably so, as did Corporal Clapper.

Francois' last training exercise, to prepare him for the rigors of jungle combat, had been a piquant fashion spread in Paris featuring bony, long-legged beauties cavorting beside the Seine in lacy underwear abandon. There was no image he had ever captured, not one, that he would not toss into the Seine just to be back at this moment with his ladies of the long legs.

As Francois dreamed of Paris and bony cavorting beauties, Jim saw Clapper stealing behind a tree, hunching his shoulders, tamping grass into a bamboo pipe. "Grows all over the place," said Clap, with a slow drag followed by a slow satisfying release. "Maybe it'll turn me into a groovy reporter."

"How'd you get this job?"

Clap giggled. A few months before, his last outfit had been pretty roughed up. "Charlies crawling all over us. I still smell 'em. Mortar hit so close I woke up with no high tones in the right ear, no lows in the left. Then another hit. If it detonates, I'm out of here. It don't. It's a dud. And then a crazy Charlie pops up and runs at me with his pig-sticker. And I think I'm dead again. Only he gets drilled before he can stick me, so not dead again, and the Army pins a Bronze Star on my chest. Am I a hero? Man, you oughta read that fucked-up citation."

Blowing smoke, he shook his head. "And the highers said, 'Pfc. Clapper, you don't hear so good, but you can spell your name right, can't you?' 'No, sir, I can't sometimes.' 'Well, you know the world is round, don't you?' 'That's hard to believe, sir.' 'We agree. So you have been promoted to be a news ace for the division paper. You are now a writing corporal, with a cushy slot in the rear. That's how we operate. That's our operating system.' So I thanked them kindly. And the operating system sent me out to this cushy slot to learn to write real fast."

The writing corporal was embarking on another philosophical inhalation when… "Holy shit!"

Here came Captain Twist tromping their way like a bulldozer about to crash into an overflowing commode. The corporal wheezed out and faded into the bamboo.

"At your ease," the captain addressed a resting soldier who sat by his hole scratching his backside.

"You hear me? You hear me, Roscoe?" Staring at the scratcher's M-16, he commented. "All you pretty frat boys flopped around better clean the fungi off those weapons. You hear me? You hear me? You take care of your weapon and it'll take care of you. Now *clean* that weapon clean. Better you stayed useless lumps in your mamas' bellies than have your weapons jam out here. Is all you Roscoes ever learned in the army is a half-ass salute and what time do we eat? Don't you know

Victor Charlie loves tasty boy fat-burgers like you? That he'll cut your throat for supper and eat your balls for dessert. Why are you in the fetal position there, Roscoe? Are you sipping that jo-jo juice again?"

Twist paused now to sniff. He sniffed around He looked around. "Now whichever member of this sorry outfit is smoking that sorry zombie stinkweed better dig his hole deeper right now and pull the dirt in after him before I find his sorry ass."

After pounding them into the ground for a while, their captain began raising them from the dead, saying things like, "In Fox Company every day's a victory celebration and every meal's a feast to behold. Is that not right, shit-kickers? Because you're the best. You're the best."

"Right…" groaned a shit-kicker, "Let's eat."

With inspiration class over, the correspondents again pressed the captain on his plan to take the hill. And how, asked Donlan, did he feel in his gut about what was to come?

"*Feel* about it. *Feel* about it? Why if you would issue tissues, the captain would of course fall down in his cry hole and *feel* about it. After you media meatheads wrote about it, the captain would *feel* like he had a hobnail boot up his ass is how he would *feel* about it."

"Would the captain comment on reports the NVA are trying to cut the country in half?" persisted Donlan. "Basic stuff, captain, like when, where, and what for?"

"Negative, negative."

Shrugging, Donlan said that, shoot, had they'd sensed this operation was such a dud, they wouldn't have bothered to fall out of the chopper. And could the captain recommend how they could lam on out of here and hook up with an outfit with a real mission someone could explain?

"I am increasingly sensing that you are full of it, Dooley."

"Donlan, captain."

"Overflowing with it, Dooley. Trying to hurt my *feelings.*"

"All we want is the story, captain."

"Can't hear you, Dooley. My advice to you is to enjoy the social life and stay out of my way."

"So who's winning the war, captain?"

The captain arched his eyebrows until they seemed about to fly off a face infused with not-so-secret anger at why he was having to bother with these journalistic twits. "What kind of patriot asks a question like that?"

"The kind who wants to know."

Finally, Donlan had tapped into some unseen tunnel in Twist's mind. Grudgingly, making noises as if a wad of bark had wedged in his throat, he spread a map out on the ground and made fast slashes with a forefinger. NVA strength on top was a dug-in company, maybe two. So said intelligence. The better part of an airborne battalion would march up there and fire them up. Fox would proceed up the north slope, moving abreast of Echo Company a few hundred meters to the right, while Delta Company stayed in reserve below. Plenty of air and arty support was on hand to soften things up, grunted the captain, which Dooley and friends might begin to comprehend when things started to really shake.

"When my boys get up there, Chuckie boy gets his tail kicked off the mountain, guaranteed. This will happen because my boys are full of *joyful* aggression. Now…" he went on unjoyfully, "perhaps you expected a warmer welcome. Perhaps I did not make myself unentirely clear. Let me make myself even more unentirely clear. Unlike some others, we do not kiss media ass in this outfit. We kick media ass. Because you barking moonbats always looking for one more way to screw us. Do you, as you meatheads say, *dig* me?"

"We do dig, captain. Thanks."

As Twist walked away he further noted that if he ever caught some home-coming queen of the media demoralizing his troops by word or deed, he would personally find the weeping weenie a shithole to drown his tears in. The captain, his voice seeming more attuned to drowning out artillery barrages than conveying secrets in the jungle, said this loud enough for the correspondents and NVA on any nearby hilltop to hear.

Jim liked the part about *joyful* aggression. So much better in war than passive aggression, or blind stupid aggression, or playing dead with your heart still beating. The story was really starting to cook. As it darkened, he moved around interviewing soldiers in .different degrees of aggression. What were they thinking? What did they *feel?* What kind of combat leader was Captain Daffy? What kind of enemy contacts were they expecting for real up there?"

Al Harper, a tall, cheery, loose ("Hey, don't ask me, I'm just passing through") lieutenant from New Jersey, shrugged it off as a likely big-walk, little-shoot operation like many before, and went over and strung up his hammock in the bamboo. "Only thing is…" he said while seizing a stick and practicing his golf swing, driving a rock cracking into the trees, "I've never been right yet."

***

It was all the way dark when Jim bumped into Fox's point man.

"Can't see me right off, can you?" laughed the point man.

He said his name was Leaks, Sergeant Selantheal Leaks. He spoke very softly. "They call me Cat."

As they sat by Cat's foxhole, the gleaming teeth that looked ready to bite the night, were about all that Jim could really see as he tried to get the feel of a black cat's war. Did Cat have confidence in his captain?

"Why? Did he blow smoke on me?"

"No

"Then I blow no smoke on him."

"What about tomorrow? This hill. Good? Bad?"

"This area be fucked up, I'm here to tell you." Cat laughed, cleared his throat, and sang.

"The first time I met the blues, mama
They come walkin' through the wood
They stopped at my house first, mama
And did me all the bad they could."

He sang it softly down low. Then he went on a sort of whispery. "Bad. Yeah. *Bad*. I'm natural born to it. My peoples was grave diggers down Nawleans way. I was just standin' around and this here war come along and grabt holt me. Man like me say, hey, I come over, get some good dope, make a little bread, cut a few throats. Cause I ain't a scared a nothin' or anything but shithouse snakes and crazy people, but, yeah, this hill be gettin' my fur up a little."

"The lieutenant says you won the Silver Star. Pulled in some guys under heavy fire. Some white guys," Jim added carefully because he wanted to know. "What were you thinking? I assume you-"

"Wadn't no thinkin'. Wadn't no 'sumin. 'Sumin won't make it out here. I went out and got 'em and that's it. That's all. Average black cat, me, like to jump around. Can't stay no one place poppin' my pistol. Average white dude, he say. 'Hey, man, I'm gonna stay here where it's cool.' Me, I dig this jungle jive. See pretty flowers, lots of fruit, shoot the snakes, then climb the sumbitchin' hill."

"Who gives you the most trouble, VC or NVA?"

"VC ain't that much. Piss on you a little and run. NVA, yeah, them guys, whoa. We send out fire teams and move around, they send out fire teams and move around. We maneuver it, they maneuver it. Can't touch Cat though. Might see me a second, that's it. Next thing, I'm cuttin' yo throat. This war, I seen men just fall down and quit when the bullets and shells come whamin' in. Fun thing is to do it with your eyes open. When the incomin's comin', just spit in its eye. *Deal* with it. Like jumpin' out an airplane. Just throw you ass out there. And don't be afraid of nothin' or anything. And it scares you no mo. Excuse me, please, I got to go pee a little once."

This was Jim's way. Pick a few good men with earthy tongues and track them through the battle, hoping they were still above the earth when it was over. When Cat returned from his call to nature, Jim asked what was it like walking point on a deal like this, this dark hill looming over them loaded with who knows what?

"Well, it'll kill some folks, or make them lose their minds. Out here, I'm the man. I be fucked, whole company be fucked. Gotta see everything. Don't forget nothin'. Look at the ground, look at the sky, to the front, to the side. See the wires crossin' the trail. Well, scuse me once't mo, must go relive myself again."

Cat eased up, and slid into the mist. Three minutes later, he slides back.

"You takin' this stuff down?'

"Don't worry, sticks like a spider web my head. Anything good."

"'At's least of my worrin's. The worrin' part is knowin' this jungle. The jungle's green. Someone whack at it, it turns colors, different from the rest. I see that, I hand-signal and everybody get down. I got two grenades comin' out and they goin' right over there, and that's it, just step on around. Also must watch the muthas comin' up the trail. Is it round-eye, Marvin the Arvin, or Luke the young gook. Got half-sec to decide. Then shoot, chest or head, or he'll do yours. Well, scuse, seems I must go pee once mo."

Gone again, and quickly back. "Cool thing is, I gotta lotta 'lectric flowin' through me. Somethin' ain't right, my hair do the stand-up. Beats 'pendin' on some old peckerwood with stars on his shoulders and half the U.S. Army standin' round him." Jim asked what his folks thought about his being over here?

"All dead 'ceptin' my old granmama. She can't write no how. Can't walk much neither since her last spell. Man, she started throwin' furniture out the house. Hoppin' around on her cane hollerin', 'What kinna house is this? It ain't got no furniture.' She just sits there now rockin' and holdin' her Bible, cryin' and prayin'. She got nearin' else to do. Somebody even stole her crutch. She can laugh too. Sometime she be laughin' even when she cryin'.

> *Oh, she cries to heal the sick*
> *She laughs to raise the dead*
> *You might think I'm jokin'*
> *Better believe what I said..."*

he sort of hummed and then sang it down low. "Well, must go tend to things now." And Cat, when Jim turned to ask him one more thing, had vanished sound-lessly into the bush, maybe looking for wood to cut his momma a new crutch, or a VC throat to cut. Groping back toward his hole, Jim found Francois all balled up, shivering, afraid to touch anything at all. That foot-long stick there might be a bamboo krait. They were everywhere like firewood with fangs. The Frenchman, holding his belly like a French poodle trying to take a defecation bigger than he was, said he had heard something *seenister* moving in the dark. *"C'est dangereaux."*

"That's me," Jim said, "no big danger."

Jim lay down and briefly covered his head with his poncho away from mosquitos and waited for the night to move. From time to time heavy firing would break out in the hills, then quiet down to be replaced by growls, whistles, whoops, and hisses. During the next hours, patrols went out and came in through blanketing mist and trees seeming to shift all around, and Jim half expected some red-eyed, slobbery-jawed thing to come scuffling out of the bush looking for something to bite. There were Bengal tigers in there.

Now he heard wind rustling those great trees with sap running the color of blood, heard Francoise moaning again like some poor tortured little critter, and thought, damn, be a man, my Frenchman. Poor Francois, better suited to covering the palpitating drama of up-and-down hemlines while armed with a box of bonbons. Jim wasn't the sleepiest soul on the hill either. He listened to others sleep and try to sleep. A few yards away across the slick damp leaves came the breathing of Donlan. Sean had what he and Francois needed a little more of, he thought. The more dangerous the place, the better the snooze. Just lie down, close his eyes, roll over, and in seconds look as if he had occupied that space since Genesis. Turn it on, turn it off. Cool in bad places. Maybe a touch of cognac. That was Sean.

At one minute past midnight, U.S. big guns on firebases thousands of trees away opened up on 1275's top third, turning midnight into volcanic daylight, prepping the hill for their hunting adventure. The hill rumbled and turned flaming flip-flops for hours above them. Even Donlan opened his eyes.

At 0430 hours the soldiers of Fox Company rise from the little graves of the night into the dewy tomb of the dawn. There's no feeling like it in the world, Jim thinks, waking early in the morning before going into combat, the sense of dread squeezing cold into your vitals as you prepare to climb the hill of somebody's death, perhaps your own. This could be the day.

Robotically, they're gearing up, moving from memory, the ritual camouflaging with foliage and grease paint, the ritual swallowing of fuel for the day, the checking of weapons, and not much talking. Some steal away for fast visits to the bush, glancing over their shoulders, listening to every crackle of wood while doing their elemental business, wondering if this is the way the world ends. Even Francois, as if crawling out of his deathbed to attend his funeral, answers the urgent call where fashion, having to go toileting without *toilette,* does not rule. A fat, multi-colored spider dangling before his nose sends him gasping, scooting back through the brush with his britches down. Such is the artless crisis of the morning, what will the glory of the day bring?

Jim watches Terrible Twist sifting through the ranks now with the quiet certitude of a wild pig, cranking up the engines of war with frightful snorts. Planting himself in front of a kneeling soldier, a timid new guy, he arches those ferocious eyebrows, flares his nostrils as if about to blow smoke.

"Stand *up,* young troop," he woofs. "Do you hear me? Let me see your shining face. Do I detect something shaking there? Listen, I am here to tell you it is no shame to feel scared when that first drop of fear runs down the crack of your ass. You hear me? No *shame.* Just grab your nuts and drive on.

Airborne! I can't *hear* you. Stand up straight there. You're not going queer on me, are you, Roscoe? Eleven bravo, *Airborne!"*

"No sir! *Airborne,* sir!"

"I can't *hear* you."

"Airborne, SIR! All the way, SIR!"

"Queer enough, Roscoe. Nuts and guts. Now wipe the dew off your nose and saddle up."

The soldier wipes and Twist moves to fire up another engine. Back in training, he had them butting heads and trying to bend horseshoes with their hands, breaking beer bottles with their teeth and spitting out the glass, flipping chairs and pounding on each other, eating lightning and farting airborne thunder they were so tough.

"All right,' he counsels them now. "Let us move with alacrity, gentlemen, alacrity. And silently motivate our asses up this hill. I mean silently!" he practically shouts.

As if shooting up on primordial chemistry, they commence the mighty climb. Black Cat hurries up to the point while buttoning his fly. Jim gives him a wave. Cat flashes the teeth.

Heading steeply upward now, the gutless news wonders are in the middle of a long, twisting column of hunchbacks bobbing along, chopping with machetes through the misty, clawing thickets that had looked so pretty in the rain. They dodge insect-swarming jungle flowers, swat at webs of spiders looking the size of meatballs, duck through clouds of stinging gnat things, are flailed by branches and get entwined in the saw-toothed brush, and then plunge on leaving little blood trails in their wake. Jim looks at his hands, strange, dirty things getting all nicked and gashed.

"Step along first squad. Tighten the fuck up!"

Going up the hill he hears a lot F-bombs unleashed, and marvels again at how fast language disintegrates under pressure of war in the head. It is not close to a silent, stalking the enemy march. It is a heavy-breathing struggle upward through the ancient forest toward the clouds, boots crunching and sliding, weapons, canteens, and bulging rucksacks clinking, scratching and bumping along, helmets appearing and disappearing through morning's gray-white fingers. It is chilly in there, dank in there, full of floating gloom, cigar-sized leeches.

Then it is sunrise and rifle butts, at first the sun is like an egg dripping through the trees, then it starts to fry. They climb on into noon and beyond, slowly, treacherous-footed over big slippery rocks, over ridges, and down a steep slope gurgling with streams and wet greasy leaves covering a hill oozing slime. Even during the day the strange dark browns and shadowy blues and greens add to the mystery of the next step. They're still just getting to the story.

They slip backward, plunge upward again, sometimes falling, grabbing hold of vines and bamboo, other times jerking themselves up tree-by-tree, big-stepping over logs and around holes, staying off any trace of a trail, making their own trails with their bodies, watching for bushwhacks and tripwires and booby traps, and trying always to step in the steps of the man just ahead, *follow me*....

The brute labor drains off the cold-belly tension, the sludge-like movement of the morning. Jim changes skins, back and forth, trying to remember he's the dispassionate reporter, not the passionate hunter. For a while he feels less like a gentleman of the press and closer to his fighting forebears, but then his mental screen goes gray, he's hypnotically planting one boot after another, part of the flesh-and-blood locomotive chugging hard to make it uphill.

Francois also changes skins, scrambling for position to shoot the march, catching first drops of sunlight and then spectral slants of brightness through the trees that turn sweating soldiers into glowing art ghosts, transfiguring men looped by gleaming bandoliers of bullets into shining phantasms of steel, creative shots rivaling even his lovely ladies of fashion. Francois grabs at Jim's pack now and again to keep from falling, but instead of weaker the wiry Frenchman seems stronger.

As the afternoon and Twist's pell-mell drive toward the presumed enemy at the top wears on, men under the biggest loads begin to buckle. "*Momentum…*" Jim hears the captain's voice ahead, "keep up the *momentum.*" No wisecracking now, breath is for breathing through humidity so thick it seems you can grab it and put it in your pocket, through ripping thorns, leaves of poison, and bugs that tunnel into flesh. Troops worrying less about the VC than just surviving the march. Blowing hard, ankles twisting, rucksacks cutting shoulders, they weave, sink to their knees, helmets tumbling, guns banging trees. "Suck it up back there! Nuts and guts! Drive on!"

On the left and right now are sheer drop-offs. Their column moves slowly along a very narrow spine of that hill that is really a mountain that considers it an insult to be climbed. When a soldier weighing 145 pounds, packing gear weighing 120, shifts his 23-pound M-60 from right shoulder to left, he wobbles, begins to stagger, about to tumble down the slope, Donlan lunges and grabs him. Clap tries to relieve him of his machine gun, but the soldier won't let go. Nuts and guts.

"When they start fallin' and droppin' their stuff, oh, I hate that," mutters Clap.

Jim feels a trickling down his arm and notices he's bleeding from four small cuts on his arms and hands at once. Then, stepping around what seemed a giant elephant crap, he trips and goes down hard, just missing impaling his gut on a sliver of bamboo upthrusting like a slimy bayonet. Getting up, he steps on a huge horny insect that goes *crackle-crunch* beneath his boot. From up ahead, he hears a hard voice. "Drive on… *Airborne…*" The voice adds a note about good hunting, but not about who's hunting whom.

Now with the sun burning, scraping through like hot sandpaper across faces, backs, crotches, they reach the top quarter of the hill that is blown battered and black. An unexploded bomb sticks up from the earth with craters and shrapnel-hacked trees all around it. The march stops. Suddenly, it is very quiet, with only the sound of flies humming over an unmoving lump up there.

Cat edges forward. So does Francois. In the shadow of a cave that had been a command post sprawls a dead NVA officer. Sandals, mess kits, and other gear are scattered around. Blood-flecked trails lead off in several directions. Camera up, Francois moves as if magnetized toward the corpse. It's the first dead face he will see in war. The face is almost lost under the feasting of the flies. The feast of the flies is interrupted by a rat leaping out of the man's mangled belly.

As the Frenchman freezes, staring at the ghastly romance of war photography, he's jerked back down by Donlan. Jim glances at Donlan who gives him that bloody little smile. *Here we go.* Now there's movement just behind Jim. It's Clap, *Busted Flush,* freckles on fire, squinting through the cracks in his glasses. "Charlie, man! All around! Can't you smell 'em? "

"Thought that was us," Jim says.

"Gonna be big contact, man. Teach me how to write them big words fast."

"Little words best. Take 30 seconds."

Lieutenant Harper sticks his head up nearby, a finger to his lips. They're doing it with hand signals now, moving belly-to-earth, low-crawling from cover to cover, dropping their rucks and setting up in craters, behind rocks, stumps, and toppled trees. Jim, steeped in the stalking instinct but not the killing one, remembers his old man telling him that you only shoot it to eat it, or to keep it from eating you and that in true hunting the shooter should feel no braver than he would being shot at. He doesn't know why he remembers that now. That was his old man. And now just him.

The true hunting experience starts to happen. At first, far below, the pop-pop-pings of small arms like bacon hitting a skillet. Then sounds like satanic whispers *whoosh... whoosh...* shoulder-fired rockets. Then a chain reaction from down the hill rolling up the hill and Satan's whispers turned into bedlam.

Moving to the attack, the paratroopers have stepped into it, joyful aggression from the other side. Delta Company below is being swarmed over. Echo on the right is pinned down, asking for help from Fox. But Fox is catching it in the rear, the front, and flanks, mousetrapped it's called.

B-40 rockets and 82mm mortars crash in. NVA machine guns hidden in and under the forest like wasp nests waiting to be brushed against are brushed against. Every ridge, rise, and fall of terrain seems seized by NVA gunners. From the front comes the sound of a bugle, off-key bleatings, a bugle freak out there, followed by more muzzle flashes. Jim hears Harper losing his looseness on the radio, "Six! Six! Shit! Shit! Oh, shit! Over...."

As the paratroopers try to set their positions a mortar drops in right in the middle of the ammunition, even while they are trying to break it open and get it out there. Much ammo, rifles, machine gun, grenades, everything starts exploding inside their lines while the NVA attack from outside.

Someone's shouting, "Get down! Get your asses down!"

"Get down *where?*"

Now there's Twist bellowing through the racket, "Fox Company, get those machine guns *firing!* Second platoon, where are those fucking machine guns? Straighten those flanks! Do *any* of those sixties work? Fire those sixties! Fire those fucking weapons! I can't HEAR them!"

When NVA press in from the left, the paratroopers peel to the right, and maneuver to the center, finally forming a coherent firing line in the smoking tangle. Yellow smoke pops over them and then reds. Firing like a thousand whips comes cracking at them through the trees. A dazing mortar burst hits near Fox's center. Jim watches four paratroopers stumble past carrying a badly wounded or already dead man in a poncho, his head hanging out, flopping up and down. Just behind them another soldier, big tattooed arms bulging from his flak jacket, stops, kneels, and fires blindly into the trees. The true hunting experience is getting a little serious.

Now the scrambling correspondents duck behind the trunk of a fallen tree as bullets come *whock whocking* into it sending wood chips flying all over. Jim digs his nails into the dirt. Hot flashes run up and down his spine. He grabs his AK like a baseball bat ready to swing at something, just as an RPG round skips off the top of the trunk and tumbles 30 meters past before exploding. At the other end of the trunk, two gunners get their M-60 rattling out front into heavy screening brush toward an enemy they have yet to see.

Francois, head down, who has never seen a man getting shot at, sticks his camera up to photograph anything that might appear out there before a shock wave nearly blows it out of his hand.

Moments later, glancing over the trunk, Donlan spots a pile of forest rubbish rising up eerily and drifting toward them through the flashings and the shadows.

"Here they come!" a machine gunner shouts. "Shoot the bastards!"

"*Grenaaade!*" Harper shouts from the left.

On the right, pith helmets with leaves sprouting above them move soundlessly in sync just above the brush line as if on wheels of smoke. Blink, they're gone. Francois pokes his head up. So many mad images, all he has to do is shoot before he's shot. Donlan jerks him down by the collar as the machine gunner at the far end of the trunk screams. His kneecap's been mostly shot off. The assistant gunner tries to stick it back on. It won't stick. Suddenly, an AK round ricochets into one of the assistant gunner's smoke grenades that spew off in his face. He rolls around, choking, slobbering out green stuff.

Out front a pile of leaves charges. From just behind now an American with a light rocket launcher kneels and fires a smoking rope over their heads. They hear an explosive splat. All they see is a green pith helmet sailing up over a pink cloud and leaves fluttering down. The shooter shakes a fist and grins at them wildly, just before a Willie Peter, a white phosphorous mortar round, plummets down and spears him perfectly through the back, direct hit but no boom. His tail fins stick out his back. The fuse protrudes through his chest hissing out Willie Peter all over. Somehow, even with the foaming hole in his chest, with eyes wide open under a dirty mop of blond hair, he keeps crawling toward them. He doesn't seem to know he's dead. With eyes locked open, and eyeballs looking about to burst, he finally stops crawling. He is presumed to be dead. Still staring at them but dead.

Presumed because no one moves to confirm it, except for Francois, the now fiercely focused French Poodle who, camera ready, stalks on hands and knees toward the soldier, whose demise in the art world of true hunting and killing, he already has a name for, an eventually award-winning shot: *Eyes of War*. As art would have it, the lighting at that moment was eerily cooperative.

There are many dangerous places to step. Clouds come down and cover the hilltop. The fighting goes on all evening and keeps going. The hunting experience gets down to Stone Age up there. NVA creep through the mist in the dark, muzzles suddenly flashing, breaching Fox's perimeter. Young men from Hanoi and Haiphong clashing with guys from Sioux City and Sweetwater, shooting left, right, point blank.... bayonets clanging, rifle butts smashing, knives flashing in the dark, off and on all night long.

Two foes death-embrace along the edge of a slope like crazed rock apes and go crashing down through the brush, rolling into a crater full of corpses. The larger soldier bludgeons the smaller soldier's skull in with his pistol butt. America rules in this full hunting experience until the large fellow reaches up to find that his throat's been cut.

By morning Fox has driven most of the NVA into the jungle, but some hug close to the perimeter to avoid the storm of artillery shells Twist calls in. When the shelling eases, you can hear the other side's wounded screaming, hear their dead being dragged back through the bush in the fog. Some NVA shinny up and try to potshot the Americans from tall bamboo blown over like giant curving bows. They climb other trees that lean this way and that like forest drunks before they too are shot out of the trees.

In surrounding Fox, the NVA had wormed through the hills in ways military intelligence had not precisely computed, with hundreds of spider holes from which they could see and not be seen, with whole sections of terrain interconnected with trenches and bunkers nearly flush to the ground and built with logs and overhead cover solid enough to withstand all but the biggest hits from bombs and shells. As the days pass chunks of friendly and unfriendly shrapnel come glowing and banging through the trees like thousands of little killing comets. Jim becomes an expert on the sound of bullets. In reading about war, he had no sense of the hissing, whip-snapping sound of bullets through the brush, the hard pop like a branch cracking just outside an ear, their rockety… ockety ricocheting off a rock or tree, their splats into flesh or dead solid thunks into a skull.

"If the people back in the world could only see this," a soldier, trying to eat, whispers to Jim in the more pleasant early stage of the battle for the hill. This is just after Jim lies down to sleep among a bunch of sticks. Only they aren't sticks, they are bamboo kraits, a foot of poison each. For some reason, they refuse to bite him. Divine krait guidance? So he's not meant to die today.

In the later stages, they sit in the middle of the aroma of the rotting dead and eat anything they can grub up. At one point, Jim picks up his AK and joins the troops in the spraying of the jungle at advancing phantoms. The AK jams. The non-combatant scoops up a late American's rifle and rips off rounds. He hopes, in the interest of journalistic integrity, he shoots without prejudice.

The sun steams the living and bloats the dead. You can see the heat rising from the M-60s before the barrels burn out. Ammo is running out. Rounds thud into corpses. The living crawl under the dead to stay living. The lightly wounded give what's left of food to the severely wounded. Choppers maneuvering through broken trees to pick up the wounded and drop supplies are caught in killing crossfires.

Everybody bleeds from something. By day the lips of the red-faced living swell and crack.

By night, with the moonlight playing over their backs, they wrap up in blankets against the chill highland air. A soldier near Jim, with dirt-caked, bug-bitten hands clutching his rifle, stares zombie-eyed down the slope, until he moans like a little boy and falls over, dead or asleep. At times it's hard to tell the difference. You could fall asleep anywhere or in any position, standing up or taking a crap. Just grab it anywhere, hold it close, and hope you would wake up.

By the sixth day, U.S. steel has blown the top of 1275 nearly bald, burying a fair number of NVA up there. Not far below, Fox, which started up the hill with 140 able bodies, is down to 50 but still able to fight in a shrunken perimeter. Echo has been battered almost as hard, and Delta is under heavy assault in the forest below. To this stage, things have gone with wonderful military imprecision, and the captain cannot look them in the eye. He's certain they will write twisted things about him if there's anybody left to write.

In the last stage Twist hunches in the little cave grumbling over worn maps. A hot flash has painted the right side of his face red, but he's jacking up again, in command, because relief battalions are battling up the hill toward us, he says, kicking butt all the way.

"All we have to do is hang on and, God willing, we can still win this misfuck."

The good captain, who now calls the newsmen his bad boys, appears embarrassed, even apologetic. The one who never blinks. He now thinks of them as not the enemy, just wayward boobs in a screwed-up line of work. As his officers are killed, he invites the boobs to share his office space.

"It's been said that my personality is not too lovable, that I never won a butt-kissing contest with the press," he says in a gesture of camaraderie. "Don't guess you knew that."

"Hard to believe," says Donlan. "I just don't believe it."

"I'll swear, Dooley..." Twist cannot understand how intelligence was so lacking in it. "Well, there's always one more thing to screw up. Be that as it may, Big Mo is on the way."

Philosophy time over, the captain rubs his face and steps out to view the latest airstrike he's called in, trying to keep the NVA off our backs just a little longer.

There's a silvery pair way up there glittering in the sun. He sees the first diving, here it comes, tearing down the sky, blurring over, the roaring of the bombs nearly lost in the banshee shriek of the engines. Nicely aimed, the bombs thud into the last serious concentration of NVA massing less than a hundred meters away for a last defiant charge.

There was another sound in the sky, like a giant wheel with ball bearing problems turning, and the second plane, the usually reliable F-4 Phantom, comes streaking down, banging down its load almost on target, close except for that last one, a big dumb iron one released a fraction too late, hitting a bit too far, like a 500-pound exploding battle-ax where the wounded, the medics, and the last of Fox's sergeants have huddled a bit too close to the command cave.

Twist is knocked down and rolled hard backward. When the smoke clears Jim and Donlan stumble out and drag him inside the cave. He's been nailed with burning shrapnel that's turned his right arm and side into gushing red faucets.

The correspondents shout for a medic but there isn't any. They search for morphine but can't find any. Jim kneels down, puts the captain's head on a rucksack, and then works in his fingers to pull a hunk of shrapnel from his side. Francois offers his undershirt and Jim jams it against the wound. Donlan ties bootlaces high around Twist's arm to try to slow the bloodstream.

"Spread out, men!" the captain bawls out. "Thomas," he bawls again. "Thomas Twist."

It seems he is Thomas E for Edison Twist. He is from Pittsburgh, Pennsylvania and he's suddenly got the babbles. "Well, looks like I'm tweaked again. Where the hell is the XO?" (*The XO is dead.*) "Why are those men bunched up that way? See what happens when you bunch up! Tell Lieutenant Harper to get his butt up here!" (*The lieutenant won't be coming.*) Where's Roscoe? I can't hear you old Roscoe." (*Roscoe won't be able to make it.*)

Twist looks straight at Jim and whispers, "Don't worry, young troop, it is no shame to die with your boots on. So let that put your mind at ease. Is your mind at ease, young troop?"

Jim doesn't know where his mind is but it is not at ease.

Now the captain sees NVA specks floating before his eyes. "You think I'm finished, but you are wrong, Roscoe."

Donlan and Francois get outside searching for a living medic through the howls and the maze of burning bamboo. They see an NVA sniper hanging oddly from a smoking tree looking about to shoot. He doesn't shoot. He's wasted. but hasn't let go of his rifle. They hear a trooper moaning that he can't find his sergeant's missing members, like his head and shoulder, and arm.

Empty helmets are scattered around — *Burn out* written on one. *Sleepy time* scrawled on another. *Mud flap* on another. *19 days to go!* rejoices another. Some of those belonging to the helmets are unidentifiable. One of the still identifiable is Harper, the loosey-goosey lieutenant. Half his face has just stuck, melted into the machine gun he's leaning over. The freckled corporal leaning against him still holds something in his lap, a piece of notebook with writing on it. The ending Clap couldn't find for his good ops story has found him with a bad case of shrapnel in his left temple.

They find Black Cat off in the bush on his back. There's a red rose blooming over the opening where his heart is. They see his heart, still beating. It wasn't the work of the bomb. Three suicidal NVA had come slithering through the woods, and in the confusion following the explosion, ambushed unambushable Selantheal Leeks, doing to him all the bad they could, tying his hands behind him with barbed wire, shooting him, and working on his face with a piece of notched bamboo, then trying to finish him with bayonets. Black Cat doesn't finish easily. What's left of his mouth still moves, asking Donlan to do it with the knife. "Do it, man… *do it*…. Don't mean nothin'."

Donlan stands there looking down. "It's a helluva thing to happen. It's a helluva thing…" He won't do it. A few seconds more, it doesn't matter, the rose trembles, fades. A beat-up soldier walks over. "Cut my poncho off." Donlan cuts it, and the soldier spreads it over point-man. End of ceremony.

"Had to mean something," another soldier mutters. A few minutes later several men gather up

Cat in the poncho and carry him over and stretch him out to lie with the others among the dead. Francois snaps another award-winner of the line of the dead and then of the soldier still muttering that it had to mean something.

Inside the cave, Jim kicks at big ants trying to take command of the captain's blood. Trying to get the last words right, he listens carefully for last words, but Tom Twist refuses to say them. Flat on his airborne ass, he starts again issuing commands. Dirty tears run down his cheeks. It's been whispered that he may appear to be a sonofabitch on the outside, but that what he is on the inside you can't print. He closes his eyes finally, but then his head jerks up. "What's all this woe-is-me crap? Suck it up, boys! We can't lose momentum! Drive on! Soldier on!"

By the time the first relief column breaks through, what's left of the NVA have withdrawn to safer places in the greater jungle. The captain is lifted from the hill in a dust-off and the correspondents, crowding in, hitch their ride out of there. Until now Twist had brushed off steel like the softer species, most everybody else, brushed off lint. He had brushed it off in the Ia Drang Valley and places nearly as bad and this had given him a certain invincibility of attitude. Even now he commands the dying-of-the-light to cease so that he can attend to more urgent duties. "Color guard, keep the flag flying! As you were, mess sergeant, I can't HEAR you!"

All the way back to Dak To a medic hammers his chest and works on him mouth-to-mouth, and Francois maneuvers in the rocking Huey to catch the last eerie blaze of blue-orange sunlight slanting through the smoking hills. He leans left, leans right, working the hellish glow onto the dramatic faces until the medic turns around hollering, "This man's trying to stay alive! And you'd better stop poking that fucken camera in his face or I'll throw you back in the fucken jungle!"

Good quote, Jim thinks, mechanically reaching for a notebook. Only too tired, too drenched in good death quotes to write another dying word.

Soon, clattering out of the hills in the near dark, the dust-off's load of wretches lands back at the Dak To base camp. Medics rush over and hurry the unconscious Twist away on a stretcher.

Only he's suddenly conscious again, eyes locked in that pop-eyed stare. He's shouting bellicosities.

"It's only son of a bitchin' blood, you bastards. I'll walk it off."

Trotting beside him goes Francois, sun-fried and sunken-cheeked, working his remaining film. The once-frightened Parisian has become Francois the possessed, who has used the flashings of shellfire to capture stunning silhouettes of men in action, indeed all the latest ghastly fashions of battle, who seems ready to snap his own bones rattling in the grave if he could get a little more friendly inside lighting.

Inside the big swamped emergency tent, Twist is laid out on a stretcher between two sawhorses. He's encircled by medics whacking off his clothes with scissors and punching bore needles into his veins, getting in the plasma and fluids. The last Jim sees of Terrible Tom Twist are those wild bird eyes and his good arm throwing out a what seems a feeble thumbs-up as they carry him back until he's lost among the maze of tubes and shadows and bloody white coats.

Francois gets it all. Just inside the tent, he gets the tattered uniforms of the wounded piled up in one corner and their weapons and web gear stacked in another. He even gets the iron boots. He focuses in on the white-coat standing like a bloody traffic director sorting out the likely treatable wounds from those who seem too far gone, who are moved to the rear and placed behind a curtain of army blankets.

After guzzling water and gobbling C's and almost the cans, the correspondents hang around outside in the dark, listening to the sounds from the hills and those from the tent. An hour passes before the medic they flew in with comes slumping outside. He advises them there is no way the captain is going to make it, just too much blood loss, they've taken him behind the curtain.

"Wanta take his picture?"

A few days later, Jim hears that the remains of Fox Company, about 40 still standing, have held a memorial service for their fallen commander, with empty boots and helmet, and words of sympathy they would never have spoken to his living face. The emotion was considerable. There was a moment, a long one, of silence. Some tough faces wept. Three weeks later Jim hears that old Iron Boots is rather alive and kicking butt. He's recovering in a hospital in Tokyo, kicking butt without his boots, just his remaining arm and enthusiastic vocabulary, and is plotting how to return to combat arms. One arm, he swears, is more than enough to handle the Jap or Chink bastards, or whoever those other bozo were he can't quite remember at the moment. But he is still a warrior, passionately advises the now Major Thomas E. for Edison Twist, and all else is none your business.

Jim churns out pages but goes too fast that's what they resemble, a churn. Another mixed-up victory for the defense. The savage hills have been retaken, or have they? The country has not been cut in half but is pretty chopped up. Soon, however, MACV announces that 1275 and other hills will be given back to the jungle, voluntarily. It is part of their mobile, war-of-attrition strategy to grind down the enemy until he gets tired of war and quits, or will he? Kill for the hill, get killed for the hill, win the hill, then give it up, and maybe come back and kill and get killed and retake it later. Jim tumbles it around in his head, but still can't grasp the efficacy of the strategy. Surely there was some giant strategic mind pulling mystic wires back in Washington, as surely as other geniuses must have mulled over the efficacy of endless blood-and-shell-drenched trench warfare on the old Western Front.

United Newspapers applauds the stories, but the noose guy knows how much he's left out. It's all there, he thinks, life, death, courage, and stupidity to the max, and I'm just paddling along the surface. That first night back in Saigon, he and Black Cat go strolling through the hills, just walking in the wood, looking for the blues along the corpse-strewn slopes, while discussing what rewarding work grave-diggers and journalists find in places like this.

Waking, he practically jumps out of bed, looking all around in the dark, being careful not to step into anybody's grave. He imagines he hears somebody singing, way down low. He remembers that he himself is alive. Things like making words into neat paragraphs matter again. From the muddy smears in his notebooks, he cranks them out non-stop, until he sees dizzy spots. He knows he's going way too fast, missing too much about a place and people nobody could make up. One day when the fog's lifted and the hurry and get it down fades, he promises himself to dig deeper and talk to Clap and Cat again in his memory and this time get it dead right before he went brain dead or just dead himself. He promises that to himself, to Ernie, and to all the old guys who probably did it better. And through the promising and the dizzy spots he falls back to sleep.

***

Jim's disappointed when he can't find the fair Sunny. Took a few days off, he's told. She's not at her place but she's out there, he's advised, *somewhere*. Jim frowns and shrugs it off. He, Donlan, and Francois, all looking like burnt toast and ten pounds lighter, meet at the Continental. At first, they talk about the small stuff, about how dull life around them looks. After a couple of drinks, everything seems small except for the number, 1275, *oh my lord*. Soon, they're blowing on the smoke, kicking up the fire, talking back the details of memories it would take them years to understand.

In that euphoric exhaustion, they sit there, swapping stories about noose guys making it up the dreaded mountain and surviving the NVA and old Tom Twist. At times they talk as cheerfully and mundanely as if they were in Auntie's kitchen discussing the deliciousness of her gravy on hot biscuits. At times they hear them-selves laughing about terrifying experiences.

"It was only near death," says Donlan. "Some people write better the closer they get to it. Is that a pickle there? Pass me a pickle."

"One man's near is another man's so-what," says Jim. "Look at old Twist."

"Well," says Donlan, "the flow of adrenaline was extreme."

"*Beaucoup,*" whispers Francois.

It's what they're living on. They feel strangely good. Almost too good. It was only near death.

Like charmed immortals, they came out of it with all their moving parts and good stories and great tans, and the more they drink the more charmed they feel.

"What," asks Jim with a shrug instead of a shiver, "can there possibly be after that?'

"Stick around," says Donlan, "Didn't Napoleon say war's so exciting the danger is you might learn to love the sorry bitch too much? Didn't Einstein say there are two things which are infinite... the universe and human stupidity, and he wasn't sure about the universe?"

They sit around, deciding what Einstein said. But for Jim, everything but locating Sunny seems to be clicking at this moment. At least as much as a noncombatant whose sense of adventure and testing himself sometimes overrode his sense of staying alive. And as one all caught up in a conflict declared by many to be illegal, immoral, insane. and other bad stuff. And as one having no idea what the future will bring can know clicking. It was just life and death stuff. Nothing to worry about. He reached into his pocket and gave Saint Jude a little squeeze.

"So how'd it go," a correspondent leans over and asks.

"Well, had duller days," Jim says, aiming his forefinger at his temple. It was not clear whether he was being protected by mysterious guidance or blind freaking dumb luck the guys in Vegas would say was impossible. He would take it either way and not knowing the future seemed not such a bad thing, he might start to worry.

BOOK II
WARS OF FLESH AND LIBERATION

12
DRAGON'S CHILD

Before settling in Florida, Susanna Diane Robinson, a military brat born in Louisiana had grown up in the patriotic spirit. Early on, there was her father, an army chaplain. Then appeared stepdaddy one, followed by stepdad two, followed by an unfortunate assortment of mixed male salads with ingredients she couldn't put names to. Later there was her captain husband, brave, rough, with little patience for and understanding of the subtleties of the female psyche, and too soon dead.

After her husband, she saw the Red Cross in Vietnam as a chance for a real-world mission for a woman who wanted to bear a bit of the burden, without killing anybody. What exactly could she offer? Because there were still mysteries about herself, after escaping from her therapist on the couch, that remained unsolved.

As a plumpish little girl, Susanna was Tubby this and Tubby that, and "fatty, fatty two by four, can't get through the kitchen door." She wasn't all that fat, but she thought she was. She would stand in front of a mirror, dimples and braces gleaming, flapping her dress and twirling around while chanting, *"Aren't I pretty? Aren't I pretty?"* even as she learned that tubbiness was not the most admired configuration in the female design.

Until he was killed in Korea, Tubby had been her daddy's "little dancing flower" as she thumped around to his laughing, clapping applause. First, stepdaddy also clapped, but with rhythmic movements, he saw budding through the baby fat that cracked him into sweats unrelated to fatherly instincts. "Do that again," he would urge, "yeah, girl, oooh *that.*" He was preoccupied with *that.* Which was the first intimation little dancing flower had of things to come with certain earthy men who liked to pluck little dancing flowers, unspoiled yet, at their roots..

Growing up among this species (mama was a man-killing collector), could have turned her into a bitter weed while still very young, but bitterness was not then in her nature. On levels she had yet to find words for, she craved being noticed by even sweating stepdads, while Mama drank and slept a lot, getting kind of fat, kind of bombed, kind of oblivious.

Susanna's true father had given her the Bible. She heard about Holy Scripture long before she began transfiguring into a flower inspiring thoughts more to the fiery side of scripture than the holy. That sudden summer when the braces came off, and she was bursting out of her fatso phase, she walked in that way she had into a hardware store wearing too-snug shorts, and looking about to burst out of her blouse, and evoked reactions ranging from the furtive fumbling smile of the older clerk to the spastic bumbling disturbance of the younger one, who stumbled over cans of paint and dropped his box of screws. Susanna wondered as she paid for the screws if she had done something wrong. That was on one level, on another, she scolded herself for secretly enjoying it. All she had to do was move a little, this way or that, to make them drop their screws. For a while, she wore an expression of beautiful bewilderment, which caused them to drop more screws.

Later, at a class swimming party, an energetic football lad jokingly jerked down her bathing top and, *oh Susanna,* there he came snorting like a water buffalo and nailing her virginity to the side of that midnight pool. For a long time, she dreamed of drowning while sleeping with fourteen teddy bears.

Susanna was always a giving person. In high school, she was voted "sweetest" and "most helpful girl at giving a guy a hard time," and was honored with artwork and verbal tributes on restroom walls while still sleeping with teddy bears. As she grew older, it seemed that relating to the other half of humanity on a level beyond the starkly physical, was as easy as threading a hypodermic needle through the eye of a galloping camel, no matter how giving she was.

Later, still in college, away from mama, and dreaming of a hero, she found herself married at 20. She discovered that her Green Beret, so vigorously physical, felt vague verbiage like *I love you,* messed up basic communication. In two years of wedlock, their exchanges of feelings and ideas were largely limited to his brief charges from Vietnam to torrid, bed-jarring (him torrid, her jarred) reunions in Hawaii, and that once in Saigon. It was on her brief visit to Saigon, feeling the danger and the drama, the heat, and the hunger, that she first felt the breath of the dragon.

Between collisions with her hero, Susanna began graduate school in psychiatric social work. Her most intense work was standing off an army of scholarly gallants who opposed the obscene war while seeking to carry her to the heights of antiwar ecstasy in her choice of parked cars as they smoked a little Mary Jane, or they could motel it. Though she was becoming her own most interesting case study, Susanna Diane did not once during those days and nights of higher education dishonor her Green Beret, as she learned a lot of interesting theoretical stuff about what it meant to be a woman who wanted to know more about being a woman in such fast-changing times.

The day came when the military gathered his remains and shipped him home. And Susanna went around feeling that she had contributed to his demise, messed up his head because of those spats in their last beddings, with her crying out was that all she was good for? And after a few drinks, him looking her over like she was something in a body bag, "Not even that. Listen, I didn't intend to marry. All I wanted was a great lay before I went back to war. You sure looked great but you don't lay worth a damn."

It was his sad duty to report that she just didn't measure up In fact, he had slept with sleeping bags giving off more sparks than her. She was, it was his regret-ful duty to report, simply not enough woman where it counted and, he had to admit, did not compare to *real* women he had had close encounters with in his travels, just didn't have the knack no matter how she looked.

In his defense, Susanna thought back on Robby's sweet side, when he wasn't going off like a bazooka. He had slapped her that first time, he advised, to see if there was some actual red stuff running beneath that hot smear of lipstick. Robby further advised her that a roll in the hay should suffice to cure whatever ailed a woman. In a military way, he informed her that if she was ever going to get up to snuff and max her efficiency report, she had better get with the program like *hup, twoop, threep,* quick time, baby, because where he was going time was not going to be his girlfriend. He had been very brave in a masculine, physical way, but was out of his element in a conventional, married way. They awarded him a great medal posthumously, fired the last salute over his flag-draped coffin, folded the flag from the coffin, and presented it to the young widow who received it and bowed her head and appropriately commiserated.

Enshrining Robby in her memory, she felt she had never been a wife worthy of him, never learned to understand or patriotically please him. In her grief, she was seen by her mother's therapist. That soothing, insightful fellow, becalming her into semi-consciousness with hugs and drugs, explaining how he was freeing her across her neurochemical brain barrier from dark repressed forces in her libidinous deeps, as he buckled up his belt and offered his handkerchief for her lovely sniffles, and prescribed another healing visit. Indeed, he assured her, she was making substantial progress, and how was the lovely Mama coping?

Susanna soon found herself boozing though not doping, which she felt was bad for her. She even bayed at the moon with Mama. One day she decided after reading about it and being urged by a friend that Red Cross in Vietnam, far from mama and higher education, was the way she might be able to do some practical good for herself and others, and that even Robby might have approved.

In Saigon, Susanna was instantly popular, but wasn't sure if Robby would have approved. As she showed his picture around, a remarkable number of stalwarts of the rear seemed to have been his blood brothers. In truth, the few who had known him were less moved by reminiscences of the bravely departed than by the sight of the gin-tippling, knock-out curvy, eager-to-help widow, especially those able to discuss their sadness with the empathizing counselor in the sack of carnal knowledge.

In her work, Susanna sometimes counseled men storming directly from combat, full of those raw, violent, stressed-out primal feelings she had felt in Robby, for which her studies hadn't come close to equipping her to handle. Her sweet voice and non-verbal assets, however, elicited secrets from the psychologically battered that might have blindsided Dr. Freud. She was all feeling. Their stories, even the ones exaggerated for her benefit, made her shudder, as well as the stories that could not be exaggerated. She found herself attracted to them on different levels of light and dark as she sought to emotionally touch their battle scars and understand them. Even during those sudden, unscheduled outbreaks of war on the sheets, she had the power. Or maybe the power, twisting around inside, had her.

Susanna kept trying to rise above all that. She dabbled in eastern philosophies and hip western thought. So much was changing. She tried grasping the sexual revolution thing, the radical reconsidering of all the old moral horse feathers. She thought about how to be a truly ripely, liberated, empowered, in-control female, grooving with nature while working out troubling contradictions having to do with the old ways.

She had dates with Jim, well-controlled — he respected her newly installed old-ways no-trespass signs — even when he was just back from the bush and running hot — and funny encounters with her friend George. She went daily to the *Circle Sportif,* a once-French, now Vietnamese club where one could almost forget, except for shaking thuds in the distance, that there was a killing war going on. The club was open to some foreign devils. One look-over of Susanna in a bikini seemed devilish enough to flame up the pool in which she swam and swam and worked on her tan and her head — *how many laps to clean me out?* — and was looking and feeling really fine and in control again, just super fit it, you know, just so golden shiny liquid beautiful that some observers of the male persuasion would almost as soon lick her sunshine as embrace her.

***

Dressing for a party, Susanna stood before her long mirror by the bedroom balcony overlooking the river. She was studying her reflection in the late afternoon light, and recalling that thing she had read — *the old ways are over, old-fashioned gal out, wow-now female free soul of the sixties in, a sexual revolutionist, redefining the power of womanhood* — as the last of the sun slanted in shimmering, painting her super-fitness with pretty pink fire. Looking like this, feeling like this, maybe that *was* the Sun Goddess looking back.

In celebration, she was permitting herself a sip of a drink, just a wee sip. After tonight she would completely rise above all the silliness, she felt fairly certain. Tonight was a Christmas Eve, rather paganish bash tossed by George and some of his flying friends for all sorts of Saigon types. There was still a war out there, and about 90 degrees, but Saigon went on being Saigon, and Susanna had some serious dancing to do, and her friend Georgie was a serious dancer of sorts and a very fun fellow of sorts.

As she sipped a gin and tonic, her first in weeks, she felt lonesome but also worked herself up into a certain mood. She had counted on Jim going with her, but Jesse James was still out in the field somewhere, robbing trains no doubt, blazing his trail to adventure. I'll go alone, she thought. Georgie will take care of me. No, I will take care of myself. Maybe Jim will gallop in at the last minute to rescue me. Why do I pick the wild ones? Why do they pick me? At times she felt just part of the body count. She wagged a finger at the mirror. Nothing crazy tonight, fine gentlemen. Redefining womanhood could wait until tomorrow.

Sipping her drink a little faster, wriggling her miniskirt up over her hips, watching her legs glow in the pretty pink fire, the former Miss Beach Bombshell felt that old stirring. She had not felt that in a while, but the biology was cool, under control, she was in command, and she felt fairly certain.

Susanna remembered her beach friend Annie once saying, "I refuse to walk a beach and not create a disturbance. That's no life for a woman." Such was Annie's way. Poor sweet Annie. Whatever became of Annie? To think that the two of them had once stormed the beach together like curvy twin tornados blowing sand in the bad boys' faces. It was all very innocent. They just got ogled and sighed, slurped, and drooled over from a distance. Poor Annie, such a slave (*"Dear god, how do I look? How do I look?"*) to what any of them might mutter in the negative about her physical appearance. Susanna thought how, after Robby, she herself had begun to free herself from such female slavery.

On this night, however, which she considered pure fun, excusable, no army prepared for combat assault with more attention to detail than did Susanna preparing to knock *them* cross-eyed It was not entirely that she wanted to show off a little. It was that she had stayed in self-imposed restraint, stayed quiet, and been very good, and though it wouldn't change the course of human events, her mirror told her that she was looking just stunningly gloriously bad, again. She giggled at being bad, and poured a bit more into her glass while affirming to the figure in the mirror that you command the eyes of the night more than even Annie ever could.

She promised herself to seriously think more about all that when she got back to thinking. Tonight was not think-night. Tonight was just a feeling-great night. It was statement night. She looked at herself. What body language would she convey to the high priests of body language?

Zipping up her skirt of white silk, smoothing it down over her hips. Susannah smiled, remembering her girlish trauma at being called "Little Miss Meatloaf" and other words of corpulent indelicacy. She looked back at that once tubby fanny and remembered the first time she heard a guy gasp *"Wow!"*

Now she wondered if the skirt was *too* tight. But nothing seemed *too*, these days. And what if it was?

Tonight wasn't *forever*. She felt loose, laughing. On how she might shock-treat the boys at the old gentlemen's club. Gentlemen scholars of course would focus more on her grasp of quantum physics, at least until she flashed a daring curve here, a little flare to the rear there, perhaps unfairly too exciting for mere scholarly words to grasp. It was just too easy, she thought, unless you were blessed with ugly.

She poured herself another taste. Smiling, empowering her lips with lipstick, touching tongue to lips to make them glisten, plumping them up to irresistibly kissy, making a warm little sugar kiss to the mirror, turning her face in the light to this angle, coyly back to that one, widening her eyes in mock surprise, narrowing them to burning invitations to eros. Another remembered lesson from Mama the manslayer. Mama bragged that she was the torch who flamed them into submission, that stripped the bark off their hotshot egos, and made them do any stupid thing she desired, because they deserved it. The power of Mama. Let instinct do the thinking, Mama said. Mama should have been in the movies, Mama said. Mama had said enough to drive her chaplain to sin because he deserved it, Mama said.

Letting instinct do the thinking, Mama's girl unleashed a pretty pirouette in her powder blue shoes that made her calves slowly ripple. Mama's darling breathed in deeply to make the physics of her breasts strain as if to burst their earthly bonds, past the perhaps too low cut, too translucent blue blouse clinging to her shoulders like windswept leaves certain to fall before the hot winds of oohs, and ahhs sure to come as she danced, she imagined with a giggle.

Perhaps they would name the dance after her. And wasn't it amazing how such fleshly maneuvers could send guys into rushes of irrational over-drive, just crack them up? And how she herself felt these overpowering rushes at times, which caused her to shiver, over-reach for her drink, and lose her balance for a moment.

She told herself in more analytical moments that it was primal bordering on infantile when she made *them* carry on like fools. She didn't really want to blow their doors off. Or hurt anybody, although she knew women like that, full of calculated female cunning, who got what they wanted or made some poor heavy-breathing garter-gazer awfully sorry like the notches on Mama's garter. Mama's not *you,* she advised the figure in the mirror. And promised to deeply rethink all that when she got back to thinking.

But just this night she would concentrate, in all good fun, on the project of achieving that certain *look.* She saw it in her head. There was an art to it, beauty, even science, she mused, achieving that fearless can't-take-your-eyes-off-me female drama. But still not quite *there* yet.

Glancing up, Susanna thought she glimpsed the Old Scold in there, glowering at Beauty's art and science. Beauty shook her head, reached for just one more taste, and assured herself that she was doing just fine, thanks, truly in command. But still, she worried if the skirt was a touch too short, too fearlessly fashionable, too revealing, too naughty at the rear, and just a killer if it didn't split.

She had thought of going to the Saigon Cathedral after the party. Because it was going to be Christmas. Dare she drop to her knees? Was it too fearless for church? For anywhere? Well, the worst she would do was to throw a little fire at the bad guys, making them not much crazier than they already were.

On that triumphant note, she strode into the living room, and put on a record. Returning to the mirror, she looped on a string of pearls. Better? Worse? She took them off. Not quite *there* yet. Where was she trying to take it? In the next room, the voice on the record shrieked about having a fit for freedom and nothing left to lose.

Susanna snapped her fingers and poured herself a smidge more... She had the knack now, all right. Robby would snap to and salute, she thought, throwing a half-salute and a full giggle at the mirror. So I drink sometimes, but at least I'm over here trying to contribute something. *And doing such a dreamy job of it.* There it was again, closed-minded mean-mouthed old scold of things past with no current enlightened perspective and no sympathy or forgiveness. *And exactly what were you contributing in that sex swamp you call a bed last night?*

Listen, it wasn't last night, and I'm doing the best I can. Why don't you learn to laugh once? she admonished the mirror. Learn to dance. But on another level, she knew that this running loose in the animal kingdom must soon cease, and mostly had ceased, and she pledged to study how to make it cease absolutely forever, once she got back to studying, absolutely.

A few years earlier she had the magic bod numbers but not the knack, had the moves but not the mischief. Robo beauty. Now she had it all and drank and began to reflexively sway her hips, *aren't I pretty?* Indeed, just so damn pretty she felt about to set the looking glass on fire. She hadn't felt this incredibly thrillingly free and pretty for a long time and she played with her hair which was also incredibly free and thrilling. But not quite *there* yet.

Standing there, preening left, preening right, repositioning it, teasing, spraying, as concentrated as a commander priming his awesome weaponry to use on the outgunned foe, they didn't have a prayer. Mama, that once-beauty *uber alles* who thought she should have been in the movies, had issued instructions on how satisfying it was to bring the enemy begging to his knees because there was nothing wrong with making *them* suffer a little, and looking great while you were enjoying it, because they deserved it. Mama was from winding them around her little finger and making them beg school because they deserved it.

Susanna remembered Robby's explosive response to such sagacity. All guts and gunpowder, grab it and growl, who pitied poor knuckleheads who got off on the silly poetry of romance and making any babe more than she functionally was, a handy, eight-puffing-minutes, heat-generating mechanism efficiently executing what a babe was trained and equipped to do. As for Jim, Susanna thought he had his own way of suffering, and for that moment really missed him and wanted him.

But still not *there.* yet. Wearing her hair long tonight, she sighed and reached back and curled one hand smoothly under, tipped her head forward, and tossed the golden shining mass of it over her left shoulder and breast. Now she redeployed a strategic curl, the critical nuance that could make all the diff.

In the beach town where she grew up, a growing girl was most rigorously educated in the school of thought that one revealed who one truly was in the shining glory of one's hair. Such wisdom elicited another giggle.

Now, sipping the giggle-juice straight, fastening golden hoops to her ears, she gazed into the mirror. Suddenly, there, she had *arrived,* absolutely *there.* The sun had gone down. And in the looking glass looking back was the masterpiece of herself. Should she show her masterpiece off to public view? Well. You know. A little. Just tonight. The scholarly gentlemen would surely applaud Mama's girl

It was all just fearless female fun and from the next room, she heard that voice jerking the chain for freedom. She listened to the music in her loins that made her hips move, redefining hips if the skirt didn't split. How she missed dancing. She could have been a professional, she thought. The barking boys at the beach swore to that. She and Annie had made them roll over and actually howl one wild night. How many Magna-cum-laudes could take their brains off and do that? She felt that other rush again, warm, warm. Snapping her fingers, moving her hips sort of sweet and slow, little dancing flower could feel the dragon breathing.

Soon after the proclaimed victory at Dak To, Jim spent a week down in the Delta along the MeKong River with an attack helicopter squadron called the Sea-wolves, blowing VC sampans out of the water. Running on no-knock adrenaline, he switched over to the Riverine force, the brown water navy outfit that dispatched heavily armed boats up and down snaky little streams off the big river, looking for Charlie's place.

And found it early one morning when the boat ahead got ambushed by rockets streaking from a brushy bank twenty feet away and then his own boat took hits from rifle fire. All Jim got hit with were splatters on his helmet and flak jacket of other people's bad luck. Five minutes before he hadn't even had his helmet on, just basking in the morning sunrise and grinning at somebody's joke about hoping Charlie had breakfast ready.

Out with Navy SEALS on a river patrol boat two nights later, he hit the deck in time to see the SEAL just behind him lose most of his hand to .50 caliber machine-gun fire flowing like little red rockets that seem to come out of the moon, then from much closer, from just around the bend ahead, *smack smack smack*. It wasn't from the Viet Cong, it was from a U.S. Army patrol boat, friendly fire coming around the bend. Midnight Madness on the Mekong, two boats finally bumping together full of hair-trigger Americans trying to blow each other out of the water and cursing and growling at each other's mistakes under a big yellow moon over deep dark water. It was turning into an odd week of off-beat war reporting.

Jim had developed a bloody nose for it all right. It seemed every combat sleepo-ver he went on during this time, death and destruction dropped around him like loose change even when the other side wasn't spending any. "Boys," the wise old sergeant said as they were about to dig in for the night, "keep your eyes open, the friendlies will do it to you for nothing." This, minutes before a big friendly mortar round, a four-deucer, slightly errantly dispatched, one of those technical glitches by an American crew miles away trying to zero in to protect them from a possible night attack, fell short. It exploded among them scattering body parts and nearly destroying the weapons platoon Jim had been interviewing, getting their feel of things, including the wise old sergeant he was joking with about the no-action action, who literally had his head blown off that nobody could find. Americans killing Americans, friendly fire visiting in an unfriendly way.

It only blew him down flat, white-knuckled holding onto elephant grass. Four seconds before he had walked away, four seconds, or he would have been among the body parts. Three more times that night as he lay in a shallow trench in the foggy jungle did this greenest of outfits nearly whack him and each other out? The first time somebody mistakenly fired a round that if he hadn't turned his head at that moment would have hit him in the temple; the second time a spooked ma-chine gunner jumped up and started ripping off rounds just over his own troops' heads; the third time an M-60 machine gun was jammed down onto his gut by another spooked-out friendly who thought he looked like a VC humping along in the night mist there. After hearing Jim shout "American, American, Stupid! and receiving a kick from Jim's boot in his own gut, the gunner expressed regret at being a split-second from blowing the man of the media's belly out. Bad things went on all night and the battalion commander later ordered, then beseeched Jim not to write the story of war's fickle fury, think what it would do to morale.

"Sorry, sir," Jim said, thinking about what it had already done to morale. How could he not write it? There were more wild stories out there than a sane man could ever write. He had to do the next one on the heroic gunship pilot so hypno-tized by his own firing, so dedicated to saving Americans trapped in a tree line, that he followed his tracers *Boom! Flash!* straight into eternity. One day Jim got a note from his editor: "Are you trying to make us cry? You succeeded." The story, the story.

In the hairiest places, like the hill beyond theoretical journalism, the good guys might shove a weapon into his hands and urge him to use it if the story got too personal. By now he could carry the M-16 as just part of the story, the part he didn't write about in the interest of journalistic purity. But he was there to feel what the troops felt, and he waded the paddies and rode diving gunships like Jesse James or his old man or Ernie would have. He was feeling it, all right, and had yet to lose his life or something occasionally useful like his mind.

One day he got a letter advising him that Ernie had checked into Walter Reed Hospital battling the Big C, but was biting the bullet all the way to the cutting table and swearing he would be back pretty damn fast. Jim wrote Ernie to say how much he admired him and the grit of the World War II generation, even as he struggled to define what strange stuff his own was made of.

Ernie wrote back: "Yeah, kid, we had rare spirit back then, and maybe we'll rev it up again someday. Anyway, thanks for thinking of me in this ridiculous battle I'm in. Just tell my Marines, I might see them again one fine day, maybe just pop over and see if they've still got it, and they know what I mean." Ernie was hard to keep down, but that was the last sentence he ever wrote.

By now Jim had talked to enough dead faces to begin to grasp what Ernie had tried to tell once, that something nearly inexpressible at the heart got lost in the telling of most real war stories. He remembered how Ernie had shifted in his chair that night in the Washington bar, the sudden concentration of darkness in the old guy's eyes… *you really don't want to know this and I don't want to tell it.* For that moment only, and then back talking as if it was just another story, like covering city hall on the battlefield, routine write, rip, and forget. And if you believed that, Jim thought, see you at the war movies, where some folks get exploded and other folks full of popcorn courage just keep on munching.

Jim returned on Christmas Eve, too late to catch the fair Sunny, or the sassy Susanna, whomever was in charge that day, at her place. He expected to find her at George's big holiday do, to which the cooler crust of the other Saigon, the night-life Saigon, and a number of VIPs, were invited. After cleaning up, he would meet Donlan and Francois, the fierce French poodle being celebrated by his magazine as "…*peerless photographer of beauty, fearless canvasser of the beast of war…*" Also, back on the scene was the peerless E. Drudgington Blow, all chirrupy and full of glad tidings about his latest doings, who had buzzed in from another tiring rest-and-relaxation adventure in Hong Kong for another spot of war coverage.

Jim burned to see Sunny. He had followed orders, keeping hands, glands and cave-man urges under heavy guard. This was to allow their relationship to flower. Because it would mean so much more later. That was the working hypothesis. It was easy work except when he looked at her moving or thought of her in cave-man ways. Or out in the boonies where he had decided more than once that he would speak the unspeakable words to her. That he cared for her even more than being shot at, that he wanted her for keeps. He might even really say it this time.

When she had suggested, sweetly, that it was probably best that they keep their relationship a little open for now, Jim did not press her to define the interesting word, *open*. He understood her to mean that while he was out having field fun, she might see others, compatriots in counseling, platonic conversational buddies, tellers of funny stories, the friendly sort, but nothing feverishly physical going on, heavens no. Still, there was that four-letter word... *open*. As in I pledge to you my undying openness. As in I can't give you anything but openness, baby.

He had learned in the field to assume nothing and expect everything. But this was about women. And not just women. This one was a fuse blower who made his hair smoke. He still could not write her Story on what the hell she was really thinking and wondered if she knew half the time. Such was the tactical state of their relationship in his mind during that time, not signed in blood because times, people kept reminding each other, they were a-changing, and were about to change a lot more. Even in Saigon, just look around. Listen to the music. Smell the strange air. It was almost 1968, not being open wouldn't have been cool.

Sez Old Hollywood

They were going into a village. You know what that means. Roll out the clichés. They may have been just ordinary American boys back home, but in a Vietnamese village, scratch below the surface a little, and out jumps the devil, the crazies, the druggies, the sadists. That these hoary sayings shall ring with moving-picture truth, you just know they're going to burn down the village. What normal American sadist ever went into a Vietnamese village full of innocent peasants without wanting to burn it down? *"I may have been born in Alabam, but I grew into a mad firebug in Vietnam..."*

Out pops the Zippo. Torch it. Burn, baby. To the ground. Shoot anything left. And let these poor, undernourished Viet Cong huddling in their damp huts and caves be advised who the big boss man is around here. It's the American way, said soothsayers in old Hollywood. And a good testing ground for the Zippo. If you went into a village and didn't let the Zippo do its sparky thing, obviously you were not with the program and needed to see one of those award-winning moving pictures about the way it really was.

Flashback

It didn't matter anymore that he was back home taking orders from people who had carefully avoided the war and was being severely judged.

It didn't matter anymore that people like him were being called wanton baby killers happy in their work. It didn't matter that he felt anger, and betrayal, and that he had been deserted by much of the American people.

It didn't matter that the psychiatrist said that if they had tried to clinically create a psychological experiment for a soldier, they couldn't have created a more perfectly devastating one.

It didn't matter that the ex-soldier, during a picnic in a heavily-wooded area, suddenly took on the look of the thousand-yard stare. "He was not with us," his wife said. "He had left us. He was seeing things nobody else was seeing. He was all the way back *there.*" What matters is that out in the woods it is not so bad now. A damn tree is a damn tree. A movement in shadows is not an ambush about to happen. The best news is that he does not have to be tied to his bed at night anymore, like that time he mistook his wife for the creeping enemy and started to take her out.

13

IN POT THERE IS HOPE

We are winning
This we know
The old general told us so
In the Delta things are bad
In the Highlands we've been had
But the Viet Cong they will go
Stonewall Johnson told us so
And if you doubt us who are you?
Boom-boom Macnacrackers said so too.

They sang it around a big piano, laughing, drinks in hand, in the crush of Susanna's friend George's Christmas Eve blowout that rolled and thundered over the top floor and roof garden of one of Saigon's newer, taller apartment buildings, built since the American presence had burgeoned into seeming irreversibility. Hundreds were there, diverse and colorful elements of the American as well as other presences.

Jim, reconnoitering through the hubbub from room to room, searched for Susanna but couldn't find her. Over in a corner of the room with a piano, one of George's embassy friends was holding forth, instructing a skeptic on why the United States was bound to achieve success in Vietnam if it held to its present wise course. This official, a sophisticated mind-handler of the prickly press who normally spoke on condition of anonymity, was in an elevated mood, unloading with vigor in leaps of platitudes to bully certitudes about how absolutely splendidly the limited war of containment was proceeding. Sean Donlan, the skeptic, was more skeptical than usual about the limited war of containment. "

The man of the embassy, having been elevated this very day to a more weighty position in the American Mission, explained with chesty cheerfulness how neutralizing, that is, relentlessly dispatching to eternity as many Viet Communist digits as feasible within the confines of South Vietnam, in concert with nation-building, in concert with the USA's unflagging will to win, was steadily making the foe so weak and weary that, finally, they would just have to call it a lost revolution.

Donlan's bloody little smile stretched into a wide bloody grin. "Well, they live here, and it's been reported they breed like rabbits who can't say no."

"Oh, I rather think the United States of America is capable of ferreting out these fierce rabbits from their holes," chuckled the other. "I trust you have not become one of those kneejerk retreatists who think our success in war is not in the national interest." He continued with an expansion of his chest under a bright red vest. "I rather have faith our boys in Washington know what they're doing, don't you?"

"Then why don't they do it? What's the solution?"

"The solution is that we are moving the process steadily forward is the solution, while making all necessary adjustments as we go is the solution."

"Like patching a flat tire with the wheels still rolling?"

The official, a tall man leaning forward, responded with no trace of exasperation. "The central truth is that we are *here*, man. It is inconceivable that we depart before the job is done. There's nothing flat about it. Because the US of A gets it done. Always. Crunch the *numbers*, man, the *numbers*."

Now the tall man leaned rather more sternly forward, as if he were Uncle Sam in one of those *I want you* posters, and aimed a stiff finger at Donlan. "Our powers of projections are unparalleled since WW Two, half-a-mill strong and building." The finger softened. "Having said that, we must apply our power gracefully. On the one hand, we must continue attriting the enemy. On the other, there's a world opinion to consider. There's China and the Soviet Union to consider. And of course, there's public opinion, the home folks, swaying in the balance." Thus, he noted, the necessity and efficacy of the limited war of containment which was working so splendidly.

Donlan agreed, a whole lot of swaying going on.

The tall man looked benignly down at this correspondent whom he liked more than most of the pestiferous breed, and asked him to let it sink in that they were talking about the resolve of *the most powerful nation the world has ever known.* To suggest that the Vietnamese Communist spirit was stronger than good old American steel was ludicrous. With rising ebullience, he stressed how the awesome firepower, superior soldiery, and fighting techniques, backed by the inevitable meeting of its victory quotas — so many zapped, so many pacified, so many tons of rice and ammo and weapons captured, so many air strikes laid on, so many bombs dropped, so many, so much — well, the bottom line being that the US of A could not lose even limited war, it wasn't in the math.

"As Napoleon said, 'God invariably favors the side with the most artillery.' The *numbers,* man."

"Sources close to the story and God report that Napoleon may have lost," Donlan had to say.

"I'm sure you're aware," said the other, pulling at a loose button on his vest, "that the soft belly of the journalistic experience is its anecdotal nature, drawing helter-skelter conclusions from encounters here, there, out of the mind-boggling milieu of the great geo-puzzle."

Fortunately, he went on, pushing the button back in place, the sophisticated war planners in Washington considered every option and every contingency everywhere, maintaining a veritable Matterhorn of data that dictated strategy not merely in Vietnam, but around the entire whorling globe. Given such expertise and wisdom, it behooved less informed observers to genuflect before the wise and steely strategy and determination of those directing this inevitably successful limited war of containment.

The button had come loose from his vest now, and the embassy man of the big numbers put it in his pocket, gave Donlan a reassuring finger poke, lifted his empty glass of Christmas cheer, and confided, off the record, of course, that he doubted the beat-down foe hiding out in the jungle had one more serious battle left in him as the light at the end of the tunnel grew ever brighter.

"He's hurting, hurting bad. In the real world, we cannot be defeated. It's simply not an option. So trust us, young doubting Lancelot of the media. Trust us."

Young Lancelot mustered up his most trustful face as the big-hitter stiffed him with a last friendly finger poke before marching off to refill his glass of Christmas cheer, looking right bloody merry.

> *Oh, Saigon, Saigon's a wonderful place!*
> *But the organization's a terrible disgrace!*
> *There's captains and colonels and civilians too!*
> *With their hands in their pockets and nothing to do!*

caroled the gang around the piano.

While Donlan was learning to appreciate the success of the splendid limited war of containment, Jim drifted through the crowd, looking to locate and contain the splendid beauty of Sunny.

"Corruption?" he heard a sweating red ham of a face, munching a martini olive, laughing amongst a serious cluster of faces. "Who says there's corruption here? Those charges are a blatant fabrication.

Why anybody who says there's corruption here has lost his sense of humor."

"You should get out of Saigon," insisted a most earnest face. "You city slickers should get out and see some real Vietnamese for a change. There are some very, very real Vietnamese in the countryside. All we need to make this thing work is a massive new program that would...."

> *"Oh, dear, what can the matter be?"*
> *Ninety-nine generals and no future policy*
> *All I can say is, oh, what a tragedy!*
> *Nobody's running the war!"*

sang the gang around the piano.

As Jim searched, he saw a bevy of attractive faces purring around Susanna's interesting friend, George, who seemed wired into the most exotic elements of Saigon's society from its spooks to its swinging femmes. George was demonstrating close air support to a lovely young Viet just returned from Paris, spaced out on hashish, who kept exclaiming in her latest English what "oodles and gobs" of fun she was having as George swooped close to her with his arms and made machine gun noises with his mouth while maneuvering her expertly into a corner.

Nearby was the emotional face of a man once close to the Cambodian royal family. Sporting a big smile, a bald, gleaming head, and a Clark Gable mustache, he rolled his eyes around furtively and dramatically while announcing, "Clandestine! Clandestine! I am always on a clandestine mission! No one must know I am in the town until I am out of the town!"

Squeezing past the clandestine man, Jim came upon E. Drudgington Blow in animated discussion with a group that included Pamela Graves Dicemore, just back from America, whom he introduced to Jim as an important and serious writer for a great American journal, whom he regarded as the reigning doyenne of the Press Corps, whom Jim should perk up and listen to closely. They were conversing with a wee, bespectacled Vietnamese in a baggy white suit who kept reciting, "As soon as 'mericans gets out, great piss and happiness come back Vietnam. We do anything for piss. All we want is piss." And also one Mr. Pathomkolma Samboonlokahorn from Thailand, called Pat.

As the discussion continued the serious lady journalist maneuvered Jim away from Eric, Pat, and the piss-loving Viet, and got him alone in the crowd. Pamela Graves Dicemore, whose writings some called a throbbing pulse of peoples, wore big glasses and a green ribbon in her strawberry hair and spoke with an air of supreme mission. In her writings, she had rhapsodized over Mao-inspired people's work in China (*"Even beyond sunset the peasants remained in the fields en masse, strewing seed with eager sweeps of arms..."*) and even dampened with a few tears what she considered her usual logic of revolutionary steel, when gifted with a Mao jacket and Little Red Book.

In enchanted Cuba, she had written hymns to young Fidel. (*"Tell us more, el commandante, of the glorious liberacion..."*) In Cambodia, she saw revolutionary promise in a porky fellow with an engaging smile named Pot (*"The purity of the man moves one. Villagers break into spontaneous song, strewing flowers upon his approach. In Pol Pot one senses transforming vitality and hope...."*)

Indeed, her important reports had been written, some said, not only for the intellectually soaring promises of such world visionaries, but also for people everywhere who were throwing off colonial chains and living victoriously in a new egalitarian dawn, a fresh breeze to history sans the greed and gluttony, the racist, fascist oppression and lip-smacking sexist and sexual dung so typical of that supermarket of flamboyant decadence, post-World War II *Amerika* and its sickening arrogance of power.

Now, from the moral high ground not available in the mob, with hand on hip, she assumed the lecturer's position. Yes, she noted, the U.S.S.R. had its glitches, the so-called purges, gulags, carpets of counter-revolutionary corpses, and the mostly mythical iron curtain, but, she submitted, in this heroic pivot toward world social justice, the negatives were so grossly, even viciously exaggerated, as were Mao's, and were without question superior to the *Amerikan* bully-boy alternative, absolutely. She in fact is doing a book on all that, she said, linking all the movements of oppressed peoples to the awakening spirit of Che Guevara, a friend of man. What did Jim think of the friend of man?

Jim's impression was that he was also a son-of-a-whore killer of men. Aloud, he said that although he did not yet grasp that style of friendliness, he would think more about the awakening spirit of Che, as well as the purity of Pot, and the magnificence of Mao.

"I am a gentle soul, Jordan, but liberation theology requires more than weasel-worded, garden-party dispatches, don't you think? Vietnam is the defining crucible of our conscience, you must agree."

He would think more on it, he said, looking around for the shapely crucible of Susanna. Pamela Graves Dicemore, however, was not easy to look around. She talked passionately of struggle in the streets, of grand revolutionary knowledge beyond the mob's crude grasp. And, yes, she knew Jim's so-called work. She laughed and waved at balloons adorning the room. And such a pity, he had a flair, she said, and in the world of jackass journalism he would get by, but he must seriously work on his attitudes. She would assist him. There would be a meeting of minds, she thought, perhaps like freight trains colliding in the night. But she believed that the transcendent truth of her positions must inevitably prevail, and that guilty *Amerika* must, to put it in archaic terms... repent and sin no more.

"I do not want to lecture you, but this is a heroic age," she lectured, "but not your heroes, *dadadada,* that I don't care to hear about in a war in which the re-fuseniks, in their quest for peace and justice are our true heroes, the most brilliant flowers of our generation, who with great and noble inquietude of spirit refuse to fight in this tragic war, you are forced to agree

"And they won't have to pick hot steel out of their butts."

Pamela Graves Dicemore visibly shuddered. Why should she bother to out-reach to this refugee from the journalistic turnip truck? Yet she felt it her duty to try. "For shame, Jordan. What you airily mock and dismiss *dadadada,* I call a badge of honor. Obviously, some political sensibilities are dangerously une-quipped to grasp what is going on here, and should be sent home to slop the super-patriot pigs."

Jim felt moved to respond as any super-patriot pig would… *"Oink."*

The lady was not, simply *not* amused. She spoke passionately and waved her index finger at him.. She spoke passionately about political things from molehills to mountains. "Someone in some backwater might think that's cute. I grope to locate your mindset. I passionately refuse to do *oink."*

Behind the glasses were round brown wonderfully earnest eyes, an up-tilt of nose that some considered a sniff of arrogance, over a body curvesomely slender bordering on frail, though very long on intensity. She kept taking off her glasses to make a point and quick-brushing her hand through her hair, crooking the rib-bon before, thoughtfully, returning the glasses to place as she warned Jim to beware of the increasingly decadent, beastly, out-of-control nature of the *Amerikan* sol-dier.

Jim replied that he had seen quite a few undecadent soldiers out there just do-ing their duty, quite a few in fact, and the lady ran her fingers anew through her hair.

"Do not wave that oppressive flag at me, Jordan, that holy symbol of the *Ameri-kan* Empire and its bombs-bursting-in-air billionaire war criminals who have earned the moral opprobrium of the community of nations. What's clear is that war is the ultimate expression of masculinity gone mad, Jordan. I feel strongly about that. The power-crazed, testosterone-gorged *Amerikan* male charging

around with his reactionary erection on, when not out robbing the planet with his
fat wallet, tries to blow it up. Can you deny it? You *can*. But, I suspect, is beyond
your revolutionary cojones. It's not that I call for the entire bull male species to be
lobotomized and reprogrammed. Though, perhaps, at some point, I will consider
it. Or not. Perhaps. Indeed. You know, I mean. I think I...yes... I do feel *strongly*
about that."

Turning, she aimed a beringed finger at the merry man of the embassy. "I come
looking for reportable, historical truth and get lost in this cloud of deceit and delusion. I see *him*. I see the face of Germany, in 1939. Those cobra eyes. When
some snake of the right hisses words like *victory*, putting a heroic façade on this
horror as we ooze down into the pit, would you have me just blink my big dewdrop
eyes in cooing acquiescence? One can almost hear *When the SS Comes marching In*
and that goose-stepper and his attack dogs rising in howling salute, can't one? To
be fair, Jordan, can't you sometimes, question whether you're out there on the
wrong side? Can you not?"

"Yes, I can't. But rest assured, we are only out there killing innocent peasants."

Pamela Graves Dicemore slowly removed her glasses, and stared at him — *how*
to penetrate such density, such a cold hard rightist lump of brain rot? — "I am so
war-weary..." her voice rose. "Unreconstructed naifs like you make me so war
weary, repeating that fevered twisting of history by cold-war zealots. I feel *strongly*
you should be outraged at the smell of fascist rot in this room, that needs plowing
through with the jawbone of an ass."

How metaphysical, Jim thought. How sappy. "In lieu of a jawbone, would you
care for a drink?"

"So, you fancy yourself a humorist," she said, resituating her ribbon. "If it helps
to summon sanity to this room, yes, a drink. A gimlet. Do they do gimlets? Yes.
Indeed. Thank you. To me. Do. Make it strong. In the spirit of Che."

Escaping to the bar, Jim scanned the mob for the physical radiance of Sunny,
not yet visible. Reluctantly returning to the teachings of his latest mentor, gimlet
in hand, he found her sitting on a couch, hair a bit frazzled, face set in revolutionary grimness as she scratched at a fresh mosquito bite on her ankle. She crossed her

legs with a certain up-swooping grace and esprit, perhaps in the spirit of Che. She touched her hand to her head and confided that her feet hurt her terribly.

"So what do you intend to do about it?"

"Rub them, I suppose. Massage? Have you tried…"

"The line, Jordan. The *official line*. Promise not to write it. I feel *strongly* that if you do you are nothing more than a willing instrument of the tools, fools, and grotesque partisans of the killing machine, and should find a dark place, fall to your knees and slit your throat for being in contempt of serious journalism. Now that…" she engineered a smile, "is funny bleeding, I'm sure you agree."

As one who saw Uncle Ho's teachings and Mao's Little Red Book as guideposts for the masses searching for light at the end of the liberation tunnel, who bled for Vietnam while abhorring the sight of blood, Pamela Graves Dicemore sat one moment with chin up and out, imperious, her great reporter's voice bespeaking superior intellect at work, and the next looking nervous, vulnerable, warm, feminine, her voice trailing off. After another swipe at her hair, and the readjustment of her ribbon, however, she returned to the imperious mode, her stare gone blank hard as the eyeballs of a Greek statue.

"Why are people like you here, Jordan?"

"Just trying to elevate my agenda and shape my biases to the highest art form."

"*Agenda?* I have no agenda. *Bias?* I do not see that at all. As journalists, we must not be fabulists.

Nor let our sympathies influence our reporting. I call it passionate dispassion, Jordan. Someone, after all, must render the first draft of history. I write it only as absolute truth, absolutely. Because someone must convey the reality of our chest-puffing bully boys pushing around brave little southern patriots who only want freedom and justice in their own land. I am so sick of whooping *Amerikan* bellicosity and macho gee-whiz crowing about victory that strikes the ear like a bad case of whooping cough in a cause doomed to lose the way the French were doomed to lose. Did you know there were legionnaires so tough they could crack the cement bars of Saigon with their heads and still they lost?"

"Weak cement, ma'am, shocking."

"Do not call me ma'am. I am not your *ma'am.*"

"Okay, lady. Such cement should be rounded up, stood against the bar and shot."

"Don't call me lady. You are *trying* to offend me," she said, eyes slightly bulging as she gulped at her gimlet. "I am at least semi-offended. As a humorist your attitude is as *Amerikan* as corporate looting, capitalist piggery, patriarchal hegemony, and your war coverage rank Stone Age as our bully boys are out there basically storm-trooping around, deliberately slaughtering day after day... raping, beheading, poisoning the water, burning, marauding across the land, shooting even dogs and chickens for *fun.* And did I tell you I am war-weary of all this, so war-weary?"

"To be so weary how much of this have you seen for yourself?"

"Enough. I have heard as much of it as I can bear. Others have seen it as much of it as they can bear. Now comes this nerve gas business, murdering randomly with nerve gas. Surely, you know of it. It must be true, and I feel so *strongly* that one must write of it unflinchingly until one drops."

This was spoken with such feeling that Pamela Graves Dicemore touched her hand to her temple as if struck by a bolt of such searing pain of thought that it stood her straight up. She seemed about to stagger off, but then turned. "Yes, I am outraged, Jordan. I am in a state of constant outrage as lackeys like you write *Amerika* is the hope of the future which is like saying the Chicago stockyards is the hope for lost animals. *I feel...*"

"I know, *strongly.* So how much of this nerve gas business have you observed or sniffed yourself?"

"Yes. Mock me. But we know it is out there and must write of it till we drop. I do so pity you.

Once they wake up from their slumber I'm sure The American People will agree, don't you agree?"

"I'm not sure The American People agree what is American anymore."

Pitying him, Pamela Graves Dicemore sat back down, lips on the verge of a tremble, the revolutionary voice almost warm again.

"Would you care…" she said, "that is, even *dare,* to venture roofward with me to source out that racket. It can't be an air strike. Is it dancing music? I sense a bit of dancing would elevate our moods."

Despite her conviction that most degrees of masculinity should be animal-controlled, she somehow liked this feisty (most of the species buckled at first bite) throwback, his simple starry blue-devil eyes, the gunslinger's walk, the drawling (the turnip factor?) though profoundly irrational bravado in his voice, quaint relief from some of the precious-mouthed word-slingers and rat-a-tat tonsil artists of her world. But the liking, indeed, was on a lower evolutionary scale, hormonal nitwittery, biological trickery (she must speak to ill-conceived nature about that) for which she as a crusader for her great journal and for the greater revolutionary mission had no time to play some fool sex object.

Still, the raw fellow needed her mentoring, and on the way up she urged him to stand strong and write fearlessly of *Amerika's* crimes and perfidies, because she was morally and historically correct in her conclusions, she insisted, before excusing herself to go do restroom. While waiting for Pamela to use the restroom, Jim looked over the dancers moving hotly, cheerfully in dance on the roof garden, but still no sighting of his sweet Susanna.

When the great reporter returned, they tried to do dancing. The band only came close to drowning her out, and he saw her face infused with intensity and eyes burning large through her glasses, and her mouth ever moving. She was lamenting the thousand-year-old forests being shattered by the barbaric *Amerikan* bombing, ecocide on top of genocide. She pulled back. She gave him the gimlet eye. Was he listening? She was marshaling her arguments to buttress her conclusions over the *boomp* of the band. She passionately waved her finger at him over the *boomp* of the band. Once the U.S. was out, Vietnam would shine as a revolutionary beacon to the world as did progressive Cuba. Did he not feel solidarity with progressive Cuba? Was he not absorbing?

"Yes," he fairly shouted. "I was not."

"To be historically fair, one *must* consider the Communist position."

"Yes," he fairly shouted, "We must always figure the Communist position.""

The roof was aglow with balloons and Christmas lights, the floor spread with sawdust and the action of the dancers, the boppings of the band harmonizing with distant crunches of shells across the Saigon river, the twinkle of the strings of colored lights blending with the sputtering glow of flares descending over the jungle by the river, from which red and green tracer bullets sporadically spewed upward decorating the sky in sparkles of steel, all mixed with the animated offerings of Pamela Graves Dicemore's inspired analysis of the Communist position, truly lent the night before Christmas with sounds and illumination Jim would not soon forget.

Trying to do dancing was difficult. They went to and fro, bumping sideways and back midst the laughing, babbling, and shuffling in the sawdust, and no one seemed much bothered except for the crusading lady journalist bravely remarshalling her arguments to rebuttress her conclusions, ceasing only when they literally butted into one of her great media heroes. Indeed, it was none other than that siege gun of the great pundit rear, the towering Beltway sage himself, indeed the crown jewel of current Washington Big-think. It was Pecunias Odvard Crock himself, also known as P.O. or "Uncle" Crock, whose searing analyses after presidential addresses about what the man ought to have said, sent shivers through officialdom down to the tingling roots of the White House itself. Wherever P.O. led, wise heads predicted, the president and the country would inevitably follow.

Now, tiring of dance, addressing Pamela, P.O. rose on his toes and gazed as if seeing the political beyond, as he recounted a recent epic encounter. "'Who do you think you are?' I put it to this poor fellow, 'the President of the United States?' As I recall, the fellow *was. Ho, ha.*"

Uncle P.O. had flown over for a five-day, first-hand look-see at the war, which had confirmed his direst convictions about Saigon's inferior restaurants and no damn nozzle on his hotel shower, as well as pro forma (there was more *substance* in his drippy shower, he said) meetings with the military and diplomatic brass. He did not indulge in battlefields, but being a quick study he was now ready to return to render his report to the American people. "Accommodate, accommodate!" asserted the great accommodationist. Critics might unkindly call him an egghead with its yoke leaking, but Uncle was the august voice of a club of pundits who believed that a mild dose of Communism would work adequately for peasant Vietnam, without high-flown, impractical notions of democracy and such. As P.O. and Pamela stood suffused in higher analysis, Jim edged away.

Overhead, he saw bats dipping and flapping just above the lights. He listened to the band whomping away and saw five-star clusters popping across the river and then parachute flares drifting in much closer, shimmering, making shadows and trailing vapors over rooftops before snuffing out, some of the little chutes hanging up on wires and in trees and gently flapping in the breeze over the streets below like lost ladies' undies.

Suddenly, the band began really beating it up. Strings of lights flickered low and Jim saw a section of dancers hollering, clapping, and stomping, closing a circle. The grinning bass player took off his dark glasses, the drummer pounded his drums trying to keep up with the rhythm of a dancer's fire-breathing hips.

"*Mein Gott!*" It was Eric, striding over, grabbing Jim's shoulder. "The curves, *mein Gott*, they never bloody cease!" he gasped. *Bumpety... bump.* "Save me!" he downed his drink. "That is primal! That is preternatural! Hark, Jimbo! Why isn't that your squaw with her caboose on fire? The eyes of a mere man were not built to absorb such a sight. Look, look, um, ah, at *that! What is that? Bumpety bump* Is that not *bally* power? And her outstanding intellect. Her writhing fertility. She's redefining the hourglass. There is the female Arc de Triumph, or is it the daughter of the devil, in motion? Look, Jimbo, how can you not *look?*"

Jimbo tried but was unable to not look.

"Out of the way, slavering swine." Eric pushed on through. "Come along, Jimbo. Don't you feel her aura? We must capture the essence of her aura."

The bally action was steered by the airplane-driver George doing the great dancing adventure with Susanna, handing her a drink which she sipped and handed back without missing a writhe, while shaking out her hair, while kicking off her shoes in the sawdust. And George urging her on, and on, and Susanna teasing with her skirt, and then a little more, until she shook her head *uh, uh.* But then George got her going again, and she leaned back flushed and glazy-eyed until her bosom seemed about to bubble right out of her top. *Aren't I pretty, so damn pretty?* and the mob clapped and cheered as pretty one's blouse slid further down her shoulders and daring George, holding out his arms, snapping his fingers, urged her onward downward. "Come on now… a little more… I double dare you. Do it for the boys. Do it for your country."

"Only the master sculptor can make boomers like that," whinnied Eric. "I dig your luv's subtle charms, Jimbo. The woman is an uncaged animal. Those she-devil eyes, that white-fanged smile. Out of the way, rude people. Show some respect. I'm all agog at the cut of her jibs. Move those jibs, I say!"

Jimbo bit his lip gazing at her jibs that seemed to be trying to move the earth.

"Isn't it just bloody wild when they know how to move it," celebrated Eric, waving his glass. "How few do. As a highly evolved male, I'm upright on my bi-pods, I say she should be locked in a cage as an affront to the dignity of the mind of man. She arouses the jungle in me, what? Could you arrange a midnight interview, Jimbo? All quite high-minded. I'll bring tea and lemon-curd tarts and we'll analyze the economics of her aura. Quite."

"Quite," Jim said. He saw Francois down on his knees mumbling *"Merci… merci…"* while lustily working his camera to keep the economics of her aura in focus.

"Quite," Eric said, giving Jim the jolly elbow. "It's said they're just a rack of hank and a pair of bones. What a rack, what a hank, and that running-amok bum. Oh, the glory. Best of Show!

Gendarmes, seize that hank, arrest that rack! What say you, friend student?"

"Watch your elbow."

"Come on," crooned daring George, "keep doing what you're doing. Mess with their minds."

"What's she doing now?" A Saigon warrior hollered.

She kept doing what she was doing with the *boomp* of the band, and most everyone was aroused and cheering except Jim, whose mind she had already messed with. Now Susanna, breathlessly hip-rolling around George in the skirt ready to rip, and George's fingers tickling down her blouse an inch from the points of no return, and the mob jostling forward, going whistling, clapping bananas for the public peeling, but then... another hesitation... her bally losing its sizzle, the banana ceasing its peeling.

"Aww..." came the groans. "Downer! Teaser! Prude! More!" demanded the deeper voices.

"Booo... whooo..." George grabbed another drink to restoke the flame, but uh, uh, no, no, all flamed out, the dancing adventure all done. As Mama would say, leave them cross-eyed lusting for more.

Carrying her shoes, George led Susanna off the floor, flashing a thumbs up with the shoe hand, while fanning sawdust off his dance partner's smoking derriere with the other — her skirt had finally split — and the mob laughed merrily at the dancing good sports.

"That grinning baboon is canoodling your luv!" declared Eric. "And I protest! I thought she was a mere goddess, but have decided any creature put together like that, supposedly by particles of mutation through natural selection, is quite another being, what? In any event, follow that caboose! No telling what natural chaos it will create next. Where are you going, Jimbo, to lodge a formal protest? Buck up now. I shall accompany you."

"Don't accompany me."

Jim pushed through, slowly following the dancing good sports down the stairs, watching George patting her evolving backside, and her laughing and with hair all damp and wild, going along leaning against him, full of hot laughter as they disappeared into his rooms at the end of the hall.

Jim followed, his emotions not well sorted out, that ran around ferociously, the green-eyed bull with the sword sticking out. He wanted to charge and gore, leave them bloody in the sack. He held on, remembering his damsel singing to him her sweet nightingale (*"Oh, don't, please...")* song, now serving herself up as prime snack to the town canoodling house.

So she had been brought into this world by one of those compulsive hip-swishers. Her old dad found out about his sweet poison in the course of his war, and now Jim had caught his own dose of it, and at the moment wouldn't have enough sense to come in out of an artillery barrage. Such was the quality of his comprehension as he climbed slowly back up the stairs as if gut shot.

"Give my regards to Saigon. Remember me to Cholon too,
Tell all the girls on Tu Do, that them and me are through
Oh, I'll miss my nook mam, Bah Me Bah and Biere La Rue
So give my regards to old Saigon and to hell with Madam Nhu…"

sang the gang around the piano.

Back on the roof garden, the dancing gang was still going strong. Jim walked over to the railing. Leaning out, he stared across the river. He could hear a psy-war plane circling over the jungle, just high enough not to get shot down while squawking out Christmas carols over its loudspeakers.

"Inspiring, isn't it?" She was the great reporter. She placed a hand on his shoulder. "How we of the Christian persuasion invite them to Jesus before blowing them to perdition. When we invoke God, we kill more. But enough, Jordan. The Alpha male is the plague of the universe, don t you agree? The answer is that the Phallocracy must fall, don't you think? Selective castration of these power-besotted, barbaric yawping misanthropes might be the antidote to this period of dystopian macho kakistocracy, don't you agree?"

"If that doesn't work," he muttered, "try enhanced radiation."

"I am glad, Jordan, you've retained your twist of humor. I was concerned."

Pamela Graves Dicemore, who despite all her higher instincts was drawn to this refugee from Phalloland, and it was her duty to instruct him on nuancing his hawkish sensibilities, and how the revolution must deal with criminal elements of rapacious, pitiless *Amerika* in its pursuit of world dominance.

She squeezed his shoulder. "The Amerikan dream of *capitalisme sauvage*, aka dog-eat-dog Robber Baron, Inc., aka Wall Street excrement, should be sentenced to life at hard labor cleaning up the outhouses of greed, don't you agree? So tell me Jordan, of what is dog-eat-dog Amerika dreaming?"

"Bitches in heat? World dominance? "

"I sense a small grimness in you, Jordan. Forget the sentimental tripe, that synecdoche for female fecklessness." She swiped at her hair. "Feel passion for things writ large. Shouldn't we march on the White House by torchlight? Shouldn't we weep, howl, gnash our teeth and smite them with the truth? Not over some poor woman using her body like a toilet mop for the male brain. Feel Jordan, feel *large.*"

"What I'm feeling you don't want to know."

"Jim Jordan, Jim Jordan. I sense you are beset by ennui."

"Who's Ennui?"

"Jordan, there's much for you to learn about the struggle before it is too late. And it is late."

"Who the hell's Ennui?"

"Jordan, Jordan, a mood has overtaken you. A little knowledge is a dangerous thing, and you are in the greatest danger I've more to say. *Later.*"

Dismayed, moving away, and readjusting her bow, Pamela Graves Dicemore paused to offer Donlan her concern over Jim's shaky attitude and her sense that he was beset by ennui.

"So," said Donlan, coming over, "what about the fabulous Ennui?"

"She got rhythm. And trouble keeping her clothes on."

There was laughter behind them. Eric and Francois walked over full of bubbly and cheer.

"I say," said Eric, "who's that tortured-looking chap slumped over there? Why it could be old Raskalnikov himself, all a pother over his war crimes. Just joshing, Jimbo. Merry Christmas, lads. More excitingly, to where did the divine Salome twirl off? Did I say what great respect I have for her... *art?*"

"*C'est magnifique!*" grinned Francois. "I have zee images."

"I would try my arm on her, Jimbo," said Eric, "put my super dreadnaught move on her if it wasn't for you and my ulcer. I've a dreadful ulcer, you know. But pip, pip, it's not like she's some squiffy old French tart with a false eyelash hanging off her puffy cheek. Did I say what great respect I have for her remarkable... um, portfolio? Enough to, gawd, can't believe I'm saying this… if not die for, actually *pay* for. No, on the queen's dear hat, I did not *say* that."

"Yeah, you said it, but save it," Jim muttered. "She donates to the extremely needy."

"That's awfully good for an extremely needy lad to know. Material for my forthcoming masterpiece, *Romance at the Front: Bad War, Great Pieces.* But tell us, Jimbo, who's that scurvy yegg your darling was doing the *pas de deux* with? Close friend of yours?"

"As close as you."

"That's so not true. You *know* how I feel about your plight."

"So what?" Jim said

"So this," Donlan said. "It's early, we useful idiots should hit the bricks, and find some real action."

"First, let us raise our glasses to Jim's plight," Eric said.

Eric drank, face aglow. Donlan drank cheap champagne. Francois drank and puffed on a joint. Jim grabbed something purple-looking from a passing waiter.

"What's that purply junk?" Donlan said. "Never seen such purply junk."

"Who cares," Jim said, "it's purply."

Eric raised his glass. "To Jimbo's purply plight."

"I'm caring of nozing," noted Francois.

"Nor I," said Eric. " But *tra, la, la,* this grows dull. Let us tear ourselves away from this gala, knaves. Let us conquer the bloody night. Fight them in the fields, in the cat houses. Surely some poor lonely Viet Cong beauty huddling in her leaky tunnel with a hand grenade clutched to her revolutionary bosom yearns for us. But we shall never surrender. Isn't it almost Christmas or some place?"

"You go ahead, Santa," Jim said. "Take her a revolutionary teabag."

"No, you must go with us," Eric insisted. "I promise to straighten up and fly, how do you highly articulate Yunkie featherbrains put it, purply right?"

On the way out to conquer the night, they bid Pamela Dicemore and P.O. Crock, standing off the barbarians while discussing the perils of Wall Street excrement and the fate of The American people, adieu.

***

The dancing darling did not make it to the Saigon Cathedral. Nor could she remember what she had made with daring George. When she awoke in his great big bed from Bangkok, staring up at the gold-embossed bull elephant with the huge tusks and upraised trunk carved in the headboard, she guessed whatever they had made must have been wild.

She had been just so way up there, expressing herself, floating so free and letting herself happen, and found herself in his talented airplane-driving hands, and him confounding her with all sorts of funny dares and compliments and mad-funny stories and sudden caresses and, yes, they drank a little more and something surely happened. He was great to dance with and made her laugh, especially when she was drinking. Woozily, she rolled out of bed now and went feeling around for her things in the dark like a staggering soldier groping through smoke after a battle, finding her split skirt and sliding it up over her boom-boom hips, and grabbing up her bra that wouldn't fasten and then her blouse like bloody laundry and throwing it on and all she knew was that she had to get out of there.

She felt sick stupid drunk. She couldn't seem to put life together. She heard Georgie sprawled out starting to snore. She had just meant to look great and dance free and have fun was all it was. Lord, she thought, it's almost Christmas. Or is it Christmas? Why do I get like this? I will stop it, I *will*. What comes over me? Was mama this bad? How long can a woman carry on like this?" She saw her panties draped on a bedpost and thought, *all I want is to damn die, I really do, just please let me die.* A few clawing brushes with her hand at her hair that looked trampled on, and wow-now woman got out the door with shoes and torn panties in hand, fleeing her latest conquest. She had blown his doors off. Mama would be proud. No whispered bye-bye or even a glance toward daring George, pleasantly snoring under his bull elephant.

14
CHRISTMAS HEAT

The beat went on. Out in the swarming streets now, Saigon in heat, a juking soldier came cutting toward them, radio blasting: "*From Saigon , ladies and gentlemen, the beat goes on….*" He half-crashed into them. "Oh, man, I'm high, man, I don't feel so bad, man. Dig what I'm sayin', man? Want some, man? Hey, don't know what I'm sayin' man. Sorry, man. Bye, man."

It was almost Christmas. The calendar said so. Eric said so. "Merry bloody Christmas, lads." A wrinkled face man behind a cigarette stand reached out. "Numba one feelthy pictures. You wanty? Nice marijuana? Changee money? You wanty?" But they no wanty.

Other Vietnamese squatted around a three-wheeled rolling lunch stand working their chopsticks, scooping up rice from bowls held chin high. A stumpy barefoot fellow wearing short pants and a white pith helmet hacked stalks of sugar cane into bite-sized chunks with a machete and sold them to passersby. Donlan rubbed his stomach and stuck his tongue out.

"Hey, papa-san, help the foreign hungry."

The machete man smiled and fetched them four chunks on the flat of his blade, no charge. It was almost Christmas. There was black market Scotch for sale, firecrackers, paintings of slant-eyed Santas being towed through the sky by reindeer built like water buffalo. A sign in a restaurant window advertised:

Blessed American
You Com In Here and Christmas Dine
Turkis and Fruiti Cak
Like from Home, by famus cook Nguyen Phu

They rounded a corner and stood, sucking sugar cane, in the rising racket of Lam Son Square.

Numerous street photographers hustled through the throng, vying to record the American presence. With arms looped over shoulders like close war mates, the correspondents smiled into the Saigon night. Jim smiled as he watched a Vietnamese guard across the street, one of the White Mice, zipping up his fly after urinating with a pained look into his guard post.

They walked over to the Continental and sat with the crowd on the terrace. It was not a silent-night crowd; it was a babbling, lighting-up-for-Christmas crowd, making itself heard over firecrackers and the clacking din of scooters in the streets. A Vietnamese fortune teller circulated through the tables telling the fortunes of the American *messieurs*, who listened and laughed. He was good at telling the *messieurs* what they wanted to hear.

Now from a television set on the lizard-dappled wall above them, an Army newscaster read a "Year of Progress" report on the war. What a very profitable year it had been, according to the charts and graphs of progress. More Americans were in the country than ever, Nation Building was proceeding apace, hearts and minds were steadily being won, kill ratios were up over last year, as were all the numbers, all the indices of success.

"Hear, hear," crowed Eric, smoking, sipping Beaujolais, "You are winning 'em and incinerating 'em at the same time, what? Jellied gasoline, some say, is good for the skin, what? Jimbo here insists that brain damage from concussion arouses patriotic fervor. Jimbo writes that war is hell so why not enjoy the warmth? Jimbo, as quick to the mark as Rip Van Winkle with a fly on his nose, is a master storyteller. He writes whoppers that would make Mark Twain cringe. There's a whopper he was born more or less legitimately on a riverboat stuck on a sandbar out in the Mississippi. Just joshing, Jimbo. Actually, it was in the middle of a cotton field at sundown with darkies singing all around, is that not a fact?"

"I won't soon forget it," Jim said. Nor would he soon forget Eric.

Now the American president flashed up on the screen, paying a Christmas visit to an airbase in

Thailand. "Your cause is a just one," he told the airmen. "Let no one misread the American spirit. From our course, we shall not turn.."

Eric groaned. "The he-coon leader vows to the numb and the dumb there ain't no outhouse bombed in this yer Vietnam he don't know about. If the war was fought in outhouses, you can't lose."

And then the commander-in-chief was shown briefly stepping onto the soil of Vietnam itself, assuring troops at Cam Ranh Bay that "the enemy knows he has met his master in the field… We're not going to yield and we're not going to shimmy…."

"What drek," scoffed Eric. "What air he be talkin' 'bout? What fur we be watchin' him shimmy? He air too unequipped to do a real shimmy. We just saw a real shimmy-buster, ay Jimbo." As the commander-in-chief faded from the screen, a minister appeared, blessing the troops.

"Americans at home are with you. Your courage in Vietnam will be long and warmly remembered. And history will say that this was the place where freedom under God was saved by you. In God we trust."

Eric thumped the table. "Kill a gook for Gawd. Hear that, chappies. Well, the war is almost over. All the whores and generals will be very sad."

"Who says it's almost over," Jim said, "hardcore veterans of whores like you? We have been silent too long."

"You silent boys just go round lickin' your chops and burying your axes in Uncle Sam's back, don't you," Jim said,

"Ridiculous. I do not go round lickin' my chops. I am a highly decorated wine-and-cheese veteran of the French front. It is the secret of my intellectual and sexual prowess. That and brushing my teeth with hot chili peppers. Tell him, Francois."

But Francois had meandered to the bar to converse with another wine-and-cheese veteran. As Eric looked around, checking out the crowd, Donlan discussed with Jim reports of an enemy troop build-up around Saigon. "The dry season could get pretty interesting."

"Bah," Eric turned back. "The lads on the other side are hardly as hot to conquer the cathouses of Saigon as are your panting horn toads, although they easily could."

Donlan went on to say that another highly-placed horse's mouth had advised him of a serious buildup of NVA around the Marine base at Khe Sanh up in I Corps.

"How now.." protested Eric, "what's a Khe Sanh? Zounds! We are noodle merchants of information here, not bloody war horses. But drink up, in case you forget to come back."

"Come with us, fellow noodle merchant," Jim said.

"Phaw! I should commission a scientific study of your brain circuitry to fathom what low pleasures you paleo-scribblers find out there. Being one with bloody nature? Screams in the night? The dead-eyed stare of your *enemies?*"

"It's all good," Donlan said.

"Especially the night stuff, " Jim said. "The screaming."

"Your rhapsody in blood? Aren't Americans foreign policy morons, half asleep with the telly on? Some gentleman said, I believe it was Captain Ahab, that if gullibility fed the whale, the Americans would have been long swallowed already. So who're you trying to impress, Jimbo, your missing-in-action Lady of the Dance?"

"Screw you, Blow." "Oh, *screw* me. So *rugged* . So gosh darn tootin' creative American. Fresh from the grits factory. But where is humor here? Are we attending an embalming class here? It's Christmas. We're just having a dialectic with bellicose Bubber here, the dashing war aesthete. Back in the hinterlands known as the beer-belly South, celebrated home of jerks in pick-up trucks, it is rumored, on good authority, that as a child of the southern rebellion, the little nipper here roared around wavin' his wooden saber and hootin' and a hollerin' all the way to the hangin' tree. But since he grew up and winnin' that goober pie poetry contest, old Bubs here is full of blockbuster metaphors and commitin' near witticisms in the languorous monosyllabry of the young-men's-Christian-lynching-division of the Old South Will Rise Again Association. Tain't that so, Marse Bubber? What?"

Marse Bubber sat there, face spotting like red measles through his tan.

Now the army newscaster on the TV began recounting the growing number of Communist violations of the Christmas truce, then warned everyone to stay "wary" over Christmas because "old Charlie never sleeps," and closed with the caution to Saigon's warriors to be "careful" and drive "defensively" so as not to mar the holiday season.

Just then a hot wind came blowing through the archways, and the potted palms thrashed and tablecloths billowed and glasses and bottles went crashing. The correspondents stayed in their seats, holding down the cloth, until the lizard that tumbled into Jim's glass came ricocheting out across his nose, Eric managed a coughing chuckle while balancing a bottle in one hand, glass in the other, and clenching a smoking cigarette between his teeth. "Friend student…" he observed through coughs, "must learn to organize…" *Cough, cough,* "his," *Cough,* "thinking under…" *Cough,* "pressure." *Cough.* "Lord knows…" *Cough.* "I've tried to teach…."

After the strange whirlwind vanished the waiters came mopping and sweeping, and soon the crowd at the Continental was back in full chorus across the little white tables.

"Don't!" Eric suddenly snapped, recoiling. "How dare you touch my person!"

The elderly waiter, the same fellow whom he had bugger-booed him months before over the efficacy of a screwdriver, had tapped the coughing lord's shoulder to gain his attention, then jumped back, drinks sloshing across his tray.

"Go away! Stop pestering me!" Eric brushed hard at his shoulder. "Leave what's left of the drinks! Bugger off! Be gone! Take immediate flight!"

"Gee, Eric, how intellectually neat you are," Jim said, as the waiter fled. "Eric knows all the folks out here intimately as Asian fucked-up masses. But he's in the bag for Chairman Mao and all a twitter about New Communist Man, while detesting little economic digits who assault his senses by touching his living flesh with their rice-pickin' hands."

"Yes," affirmed Eric, "I wish to say very publicly that I will not have this uppity scum laying hands on my person. These stinking, scrofulous whang doodles trying to cozy up to people like me. Do I look like some scurvy specimen in their infernal flea markets to be picked and haggled over?"

"Long March Eric insists on spiritual cleanliness and not being haggled over," Jim said. "All these uppity underlings out here need a good cleansing, a serious defying, a sound spanking until they get with the program. Eric wants to purify the masses, eradicate the irredeemables, and consolidate the constipated. Slaughter of U.S. lackeys is no vice. When he hears the words *People's Democratic Republic* he practically creams his knickers with people's-republic joy, as long as he doesn't have to live in the bastard. So let us drink to the better class scum."

"Conversely," Eric said, lighting another cigarette, "I do not make heroes out of war criminals, nor do I reek of U.S. napalm cologne. It's said on good authority that before he goes to battle Captain Bloody Balls America here calls on Jesus, Socrates, and Elvis for divine guidance, whoever's really rockin' that day."

"Wow," Jim rejoined. "'I reek not of U.S napalm cologne,' a well-showered former filthy rich limousine earl and current spiffy blow-dried pseudo-Maoist news-cruncher said today as he urinated on contrary facts and brushed a goober-pie-munching capitalist-roader off his sleeve."

Eric puffed smoke. "I say again… this dung heap country is not worth one damp cow chip, to perpetuate, much less this evil war. Moreover, I do not always agree with Chairman Mao," Eric crushed his cigarette. "Nor does he always agree with me."

"That's the way it was with my dad and Mister Hitler," Jim said, "when he got his ovens really cooking, there were days they just didn't agree on things."

They carried this on until Jim turned to Donlan and told him about Ernie Johnson, busy dying back at Walter Reed. "Said another day, another 10 BMs, what a hell of a way to go."

"He was such a funny chap,' Eric interrupted. "He wore those glasses that were never level, his eyes all foggy and bloodshot. And that cigarette dripping ashes in his booze, smoke coming out his nose while the booze went down his throat. I wondered how he did that. And the hair poking out his shirt where his button never buttoned. And his pants too short and zipper half-zipped and coughing on you. I almost asked him to please keep the saliva in his mouth instead of showering people. Such a fun fellow, but he did not evoke laughter. The chap just went around sneering at us, like only he really *knew* things. Just a lost relic from an ancient time full of that feigned bravado, all rather tiresome."

"At least he had something to be tired about.," Jim said, "that you will never know."

"Yes, the thrill of the clean kill," Eric laughed. "I lean to eighteenth-century stylings myself, more richly textured, worthy of the *London Gentleman's Quarterly*, appealing to the intellect, beyond crude intestines. Ask me about anything beyond crude intestines."

"Are you now or have you ever been a spittoon, comrade?"

"What rot. For all your maudlin hero worship, your mysterioso Ernie is of the dimmy past, so WW Two. I had two meaningful contacts with him. Once he came half-falling down some stairs as I went up. The other occasion he came swinging out a toilet door nearly hitting me in the face. He threw a roll of paper at me. He did not say hello. What is sadder than a rummy old correspondent hanging on for one more war, especially *this* dreadful war?"

"How about a dreadful young correspondent who couldn't carry rummy's bullet-riddled jock strap?"

"Oh, so witty. But I was just *not* impressed by the fellow, Eric said. "Tell him a plane crashed in the trees and he'd say 'what kind of trees?' And wrote in that brute, telegraphic, polysyllabically challenged dissonance I found rather off-putting. Hardly Proustean. But what a great read when he was drinking, like a blind man slinging grenades. He read better from bottoms up, actually."

"I asked you," Jim asked, "are you now or have you ever been a spittoon, pseudo-comrade?"

"Oh, let's make peace," Eric said, showing the teeth. "Guess I am running on. It's the frightful heat. Just unnatural to swelter like this at Christmas. 'tis the season to be jolly, *tra la la*. Go on, stand by your ancient Ernie. Because for a spittoon I am a quite open, loving, soul-of-tolerance spittoon. *Hoot! Hoot!* But let us cease all the higgledy-piggledy. Let us decamp and march this rum bunch to fields of fun and frolic. Surely, there are wild, insatiable nymphomaniacs waiting to swing

down upon us from the Christmas trees. Cause 'tis the season to be insanely jolly…
tra la la, la la la la."

Soon they were marching past the bars of Tu Do Street. "Where you go?" called
a little man.

"You want girl?" Doors swung open. Clouds of smoke and perfume rolled out.
Inside, American young men far from home mingled with native young women.
A sign in a window advised:

> *Soldier boys – come into us!*
> *Glamour girl hostasses!*
> *Enjoy Leixure hours!*
> *Tunefully Chrimus music!*

"Hey, sheep Sharlie," called a glamour girl leaning out a door. "You buy me
tea, I love you ever."

"Hey, *mon Cherie,*" called another, who looked about 300 pounds, "you takee
off your shirt, I takee off mine."

"Spot on," laughed Eric. "They think we're classy, rich, movie-idol Yunkies
come to save them from the red terror. Did you know that this once was the Rue
Catinet, so quiet and gracious, before mad wooly mammoth America came and
sat upon it?"

"PASHUNN," bleated a voice from a jukebox. "Gimme your sweet
PASHUNN…."

"Not a trollop in the bunch," said Eric. "But these dreadful bars must close. I
am all for that. As soon as I depart I will demand it. Try your luck, Jimbo?" Jimbo
was feeling no luck with women. He felt more sat upon.

In front of the Golden Hands Massage Parlor a scantily-clad hostess ran out
and enveloped Francois like a praying mantis, screeching, "You no good mudda
fucka butterfly! You numba wan pissing ant!"

Clawing at his shirt, shoving her hips and hiney against him, she tried butting,
then dragging him into the Golden Hands.

"Your true love goddess," said Eric. "Worth fighting for, what?"

"*Mon dieu!* She say she having *my babee.*" Francois kept pulling away. "Tell her I am the most gay fellow!"

"The little rosebud says she's eighteen," interpreted Eric, "and never been boinked by anyone but you. Well, people forget. *Liberté! Egalité! Fraternité!* One must strike a blow for French pride, admit *l'affaire,* gallantly accept fatherhood and dwell on the *joie de vivre,* all the happy years ahead."

The girl, 38, whom Francois knew not, kept raging around him.

"Hey, let's beat it to Jim's dump," suggested Donlan. "See what's happening at Jim's dump."

"Bung ho," echoed Eric. "As me, great Uncle Mephistopheles use to say, 'To the dump, stout lads.'"

Soon the stout lads were up in Jim's dump. They had four glamour girls up from The Moon Over Miami "Unbound the hounds!" trumpeted Eric. "The game's afoot! Bring on the pleasures of mad flesh! Allow none to escape!"

Donlan's mad pleasure ran to the balcony and threatened to throw herself to Buddha Eternity. Gidget the Wunderbar draped herself across the dragon red bar and pushed Eric away as he propounded on his need for deep, barn-coupling togetherness.

"Now lean back, Miss Crab-dip. You remind me of a sex symbol of the early 30s. Resist me not. Bacchanalia calls. But touch not my nose. That fills me with consternation. If you wish to curry my favor, be still me warty beauty and we'll read classical Greek together. Have I met my intellectual match here? Now cease your caterwauling. Now let's have an orderly orgy here. Now don't make my feathers fly. Are you sure you're not the lass to whom I read poetry in Oxford days?"

A couple of the half-dressed glamour girls kept shrieking and running around the room. "What I adore about Asian damsels is they're such shy, inscrutable little buttercups," declared Eric. Francois the possible gay fellow galloped on all fours after one buttercup, her red bra dangling from his ear. The really good-looking one, whom Jim knew as Mia, reigning queen of Saigon's bar life, bit him on the shoulder, and then kicked him and he laughed. This must be what he wanted from the fair sex. She ran to the door, turned, and threw her shoe that grazed his head and he laughed harder. This he could understand.

The glamour girl pursued by Francois the possible gay fellow crawled out the door squealing like a pig with a fork in its rump and he went after her on all fours out the door, bra hanging from his ear, until she slipped and bounced twice on her well-buttressed rear.

"Red Knight, you have wounded the little snow blossom," Eric scolded. "You must pay reparations to your fiancé. A cup of tea, dear, a few scones while you describe your tragic moment?"

"No tea! No tragy!" little snow blossom squealed, then leaped onto Red Knight's back and started riding him using the bra as a bridle. Jim, stretched on the floor, was trampled over. They crashed on top of him. He hurt as he laughed. He laughed so hard he thought a blood vessel would blow he was laughing so hard. The semi-orgy was becoming a semi-success.

Later, after the others had left, Queen Mia sat in the shadows, a dark river of hair tumbling over her shoulders, She was trying to look super sultry. She was succeeding. She was Mia, who knew a thing or two about stoking the furnaces of men far from home.

"Blond 'merican bad for you," she whispered. "No?"

"Pretty bad," he said.

"She so terrible for you. How you stand it?" She reached out and touched his chest. "You need Mia stay this night? I think you do."

"Well…" He shook his head, yes, no. "It's a hell of a night."

Drawing herself up super proudly, Mia told Jim of her many love-afflicted American admirers, even mighty generals, who would gladly offer her all the gold in the gate of the golden bridge to be in his position at this moment. "Oh, please, Mia,' they beg and cry. 'I die for you, I give you anything.' She then said dramatically that Buddha himself had ordered her to come to him this night. She said that she would lose her poor face forever and Buddha would be very angry if he did not consent to her simple this-night desires.

"Have fun tonight, Buddha say, because maybe VC come the morrow."

Now she was telling him of her French legionnaire father who had wooed and deserted her Vietnamese mother and left her to die all screwed and broken like the country. Mia began to edge closer, eyes half-closed, baring her little white fangs and pink little tongue while running her fingers down the sun-blond hair of his forearm as if it was really quite extraordinary as was the whole marvelous rest of him. Then she bit him on the shoulder, gently.

"Make me warm," she whispered, raking his face with silvery nails, softly. "Make me too warm all over."

"You're boiling over now."

"Maybe I love you," she flared her nostrils, dug in her nails. "I see you watch me. I remember you ask for me before in bar. Mia say, no, then. Mia say, yes, now. When you look at me you have the crazed eye, you know."

"I am plenty crazed," he said.

"Listen, I watch you, too. My head be so dizzy when I watch you. I say, 'Mia, this is first time you ever love stinkin' 'merican with face of lamb, heart of wolf.'"

"Maybe you're crazy too."

"If I say I love you, I mean it. I never lie."

"I believe you."

"Okay, I do not lie to you *yet*. Mia know many man, but Mia have only one heart. Why when I lie everybody believe? Why when I tell truth nobody believe? So I not say I love you."

"I'll believe anything. That's why they sent me."

"Okay, I be frank to you. I say I cannot sleep alone tonight, because I am dreamin' very bad. Everything go wrong with me. Sometime I pay mamasan five hundred P to sleep with me. Sometime I stay up all night, worry, worry, think, think. Maybe VC come the morrow. So if you will please come by me and make me warm tonight, you will never, never forget me. All man," she whispered, closing her eyes, pressing close, "same, same."

Mia lay back across the pillows now, eyes doing the fire dance. "Look at me. Make me too warm."

Jim looked at Mia. She seemed to want to be adored. Didn't they all?

"Why?" her eyes suddenly widened, amazed, "why you have no heart?"

Jim looked at her. It was not a matter of the heart. He started to say something. Mia interrupted.

She sat up. It was no good. Her astrological charts had warned her of this, she said, shaking her head. Because it was almost the Year of the Monkey. All the heavenly signs pointed toward disaster. Obviously, the Year of the Pig, in which she was born, clashed with that of the Monkey, whereas if she could just make it through the Year of the Chicken, which always got along well with the Pig, in heaven as on earth, then her life and love would flow with much good fortune and sweetest harmony.

"Why?" She stared at him. "Being with me could be your best happiness through life."

She wriggled her shoulders and stuck out her chest. "Is it 'merican who walk like too hot stuff? Is it? Tell me truest. Yes, it is."

"Something like that."

"What is her name? No, I do not want to know it. Do not tell me it. Never mind. Maybe one day you wake up and be very, very sorry. Okay? *Xin Loi*. Excuse me. I go now. I tell you I must go. Do not try to stop me. Many man wait for Mia. Mia must go. Mia say no more."

She stood up, shook out her hair, and gave him a last look-over. He did not try to stop her.

As she left, a possible tear, or bead of perspiration, trickled down her cheek, He hoped she wasn't going to cry. Why did they always cry? Then she asked him, almost incidentally, "What is your name?"

He spoke his name as she left but she did not reply. He watched her from his balcony fading down the street, and then lost her in Saigon Christmas morning. Fiddling with a button on his shirt, he silently wished her much good fortune and the sweetest harmony in the Year of the Monkey.

Susanna's Secrets

One day I went to see the weserde. He gave me some magic seeds in a bag. I ran home. I did not tell anyone where I was going or what was in the bag. I ran up to my room. I dumt the seeds out of the bag. Then I grabt the seeds and ran outside. I planted the seeds and when I was finish it I went back home and went to bed. The neaxd morning I woke up and went out to see my tree. It was a secrit tree with all kinds of good things on it and I will keep it always and always. I loved my tree. I'm still theiking about it now. l wish I still had my tree. O I wish I still had my tree.

Dear Miss K, (Please)

This is the second note about Sus. I am not pleased. I don't want you to go as far as Suspension. She is in fits almost every day and talks back. Her grades are really droping. The other day she hit a boy in the eye just cause he pinched her. She is a problem. She thinks she's pretty.

Out of a class of 29 children, 28 and one-half percent of the time is spent dealing with Sus. She thinks she's so pretty. I would like to schedule a convention with you for Tuesday, February 28 9.00 (second period) to tell you more if this is OK please return this note PLEASE but don't let Sus see it. She is my best friend.

In all of sincerity yours,

Annie.

15
SILK WRINKLES

The Eighth Earl sat in the café across from Susanna's digs observing odd, fecal-like matter floating in his coffee. This, after observing queer crawly things cavorting in his soup. Vietnam grew ever worse, not better, despite what the rationally deficient Yunkies said. Well, blast. Too hot to eat. A spot of spirits was the thing. And *she*, no mistake, that shameless *thing* was *up* there. Another spot got him conjuring up visions of that pulchritudinous phantasm whom he had seen earlier on the Street of Flowers, just high-stepping along in that way she had, that dimple dazzling blond bombshell prissing along popping eyeballs like Lady High and Mighty on parade. Mesmerized by such blatant female effrontery, and having telexed to London his latest epic poem on the evil-doings of the Yunkies, he felt heated up enough to give it the old royal Blow go and drag that heavenly thing down to mortal ruin. And dare she deny him his manly due? She wouldn't dare.

Oh, I see the magic in your eyes, he hummed a ditty while swatting a small bug trying to unstick from the sweat stream of his neck. Yes, he thought, her ladyship was worthy of his steel for a thump or two. He lit a cigarette. He blew lusty smoke rings. As a master of wowing the wems with cunning jaw-jaw, it was comforting to know he could prevaricate equally with aplomb or without aplomb. He could be a little lost lamb bah-bahing for sympathy, with a catch in his throat one minute, or the devil with his teeth on fire the next. That's how he got them. Sometimes he forgot to whom he dallied with the truth, and about what, tut, tut. But why should one of his rank apologize to his inferiors, practically everyone, for having the gift of pulsating power of personality? Indeed, a little spanky-spank on that incredibly ripe pink caboose might show Goldilocks what a real lover was all about. Lucky her.

Why, he mulled on, she should be all a twitter with gratitude that I take the trouble to render my services at all. Why, if truth be told, beautiful loose wenches were like beautiful loose words, briefly entrancing, but not seriously memorable.

Haw. Moreover, crowning the good deed, with Jordan off playing war with his moronic Marines, I'll ambush ol' Bubba where it hurts most… in his imbecilic ballocks, *hoot, hoot!*

As a proud pagan and discerning erotomaniac, he deemed regular wenches no longer worthy. His dynamic libido rightfully demanded more rousing romps with classic young *belle tournures* to rub sparks against him. Now he blew smoke and tried not to think of his hag from hell in London, with fat lip poked out and probably chewing something. Or how one of his proud lines had married so low, even when desperate for filthy coin. Nor did he want to think of the minor chinks in his own psyche. Or of his blasted ulcer. He knew he had one, though never so diagnosed. It was dreadful and he endured it so bravely. And despite his peerless analytical acumen, he brooded over a basic lack at the heart of his war coverage. True, he could charm a nun out of her habit, or spin a mummy out of it sarcophagus, admirable qualities certainly. But if he was to become the unchallenged Grand Mufti of the Journalistic Word in this beastly war, the media grandee than whom there was no grander, he had to get out *there* more. He couldn't do a Dicemore, guilt-tripping her way to the top, weeping, and shaming her readers into submission. He did not weep well. And shame was for sissies, not true Blowdom.

But he would not sink to charging up a hill like some hairy yahoo throwback to a stinking cave with a knife between his teeth, like some slobbering, yawping baboon with club and notebook scuffling through the body bags for information fit to print. Just not his forte; his journalistic code required no such barbaric theatrics. He loathed that, loathed all things military. His values, his sensibilities, more deeply felt, he felt deeply, did not allow it. He did not need to talk loud and wave his hands. He had style. But he could not forever dodge events in the bloody field, even with his blinding word games.

Those well-turned words, those broad-brushed fuzz phrases, strained at times to fill the blood-and-guts gaps of war. Sophisticated jabberwocky, predicting everything (how soon the fools forget!) had limits, though he did it so marvelously. As a spinner of golden fleece, his ace was the political story: finely nuanced rumor, conjecture, savage second-guessings, juicy hypotheticals, transcendent hind-sight insight, and, if necessary, maximization of minimum content, and, if necessary, well-massaged prevarications for the *(his)* greater good. Speaking on condition of anonymity, a well-fudged source familiar with the war whispered whatever galloping mood Eric, master of the pestilential question to elicit the diseased answer, was in that moment. He would out-Orwell Orwell. Why, if properly put, the informed source was likely to forget what was the question until Eric shaped the answer. *Why do you beat your silly wife? I don't have a wife. But if you had one, the odds are you would beat her silly. Do not deny it.* Not every correspondent had the gift.

But the bad doings in the field. The actual shootings, the messy doings his swinish editors kept harrying him over. Surely, they pressed him from the safety of behind their desks, something of consequence was going on *outside* Saigon. Like this damn Khe Sanh flap that Jordan and Donlan were off to. But he would not be pushed into following those maniacs. As if he should grab a battle ax and body armor, don his brass balls, and clank on up there. In truth, he had done a bit of the risky stuff early on and quickly gained a sense of his possible sudden, unattractive demise. Indeed, his awful ulcer had sent him retching to the hospital, even though the fools there refused to locate the ulcer.

He came to believe that what had happened were the worst things that ever happened *in the history of war (could Christ on the cross have endured such horrors?)* because they had happened close to his own living person. It could have been *him*, although not that much had happened. It's what bloody *could* happen. One heard the stories. All the stories. And he swore not to go out on anything again whiffing of the perfume of fleshly danger, and never overnight. Let some other hyperventilating muttonhead meet his midnight deadline with his excuse-for-brains oozing down a banana tree.

Even the low-risk, back-by-nightfall junkets were dodgy enough to convince E. Drudgington Blow to form his view that the Colonials, those hopelessly delusional knuckle-draggers, with the historical depth of fruit flies, had charged up the wrong hill this time. America's WW II roaring triumphalism was steadily turning into confused bleats in blind alleys. He yearned for comeuppance time for the bloody show-offs. Who did they think they were? Best to lobotomize them all, what? Old George III had it right about all along.

America Quits! Dare he dream? But the story and battles grew ever bigger and more ferocious. And his editors, the swine, slavering for their blood meals, kept urging him not to dally in Hong Kong with the China-watching thing, as marvelous as it was. He assured himself it was just this cruel and unjust war that spooked him. Why in a decent war his pluck would rank second to none. Why in old WW II he'd have written them all dead on the floor.

He did not think of himself as a rare breed of an attention hog, as rare as he was, still his psyche bled for a spot of fame, brimming with bags of coin, and a sip or so from the cup of the glorious past to restore the Blow legacy. But no need to get carried away, he thought. I'll allow my friend Jesse Jackass James and that death-flirting fool Irish Donlan to continue to exhibit their moronic macho indiscretions all the way to perdition. Why you would have to drive nails into those reptilian brains to inform them they were attending funerals — *theirs.*

As he blew smoke, dreaming of old Blow glory, and whetted his appetite to consume that irresistible female hot fudge sundae up there, he worried a bit about his looks, this hellhole ravaged one so. Still, the eighth Earl fancied himself a natural for the telly, with his dazzling teeth and commanding nose, the rich confident broadcast voice, the sonorous rising, falling cadences, indeed, his sheer overall gravitas and stunning authoritative presence… *Bulldog Blow of Britain here, reporting from the deepening shadow at the end of mankind's last bloody flicker of a weeping rainbow and suchlike. There were also rumors of patchy fog today.*

Or should he give big politics a go? Wasn't he a natural? Why, he could bully-rag pols all day long. He could whoopdeedoo the masses, arouse the rabble the belching blokes, the blissfully idiot screaming lasses. He would champion the poor little people with perfumed words with blue smoke. He would be their Hammer of Thor. He'd grip and grin, press the flesh, flash the teeth, ooze, schmooze. If challenged, he would obfuscate the obvious, deny, stonewall, shut his lips like a little old lady snaps to her purse. Then out-fork the most fork-tongued lawyers, spit in truth's eye, and make a speech blaming opponents for motives most vile. Blowspeak rules. He'd feed the media what they hungered for, cruising amongst them and issuing fluff press releases, and they would slobber for more and not edit a word. *Good reporting!* The thinking man's hero would stride the corridors of power in jackboots, or do the soft-shoe shuffle in velvet slippers, leaning left while pressing the right's buttons and massaging the mob with magical elocutions until their eyes glazed over. But all rather tiring to think on just now.

Just now the thinking man's hero was finalizing his plan to conquer that un-natural force of beauty, and how she must show her gratitude by begging for more. Was she the sexiest woman alive? The issue might be in doubt but for this night he would not dismiss her with a lordly wave... Am I not a randy dandy? he thought. And how she looks at me, sensing my power. *Save me, O gallant knight, sir.* But even as he visualized his knightly errand, his amorphous mass of a rhino-rumped mate, his frightening cow of the apocalypse, gone cold and fat and frumpy on him, kept butting into the reverie. He also held her nose against her, gone bulbous on him. Tis so unfair, he thought. I'll drown that one in a drink.

Eric carried a bottle of gin with him, saving it for that gravity-defying high stepping perhaps sexiest woman alive. He sat marveling at how this bubble-bath birdbrain could create such a fireball in his own extraordinary dome. 'Tisn't fair, but a*mazing.* All she had to do was whorl those hips, agitate that hourglass and she canceled out Einstein's most relative curve. But now, silly bird, your master is coming to cage you, he thought, blowing masterful smoke rings. Perhaps Salome would dance for him, wrap his head in the sweet cloudy fire with nothing on but a veil or two, no need for seven. *Hoot! Hoot!*

***

Jim hadn't answered silly bird's calls, staying away from her physically, trying to avoid serious thoughts of her, trying to disconnect the hot-speed wiring that had him reacting to her every twitch and tremble. And trying to rid himself of the early morning stuff when she drifted like sexy smoke into his dreams in the arms of daring George. Donlan advised him to stop going around hangdog-shufflin' stupid over her and go make some sort of peace, or treat it as another wound in the old war where everybody bleeds and nobody wins, and then scrape the dead skin off his brain and move on. Maybe there was still space at the Café of Last Resort.

So Jim was about to move on, going up to this Khe Sanh. From what he'd heard, if that didn't blow the dead skin off his brain, nothing would. Before going, he decided to give peace with honor, no matter how pitiful, a try. He would head over to her place and surprise and shock her with his open and forgiving nature. Maybe that would divert him from the feeling he had about Khe Sanh, something death gray, caressing his spine with long cold fingers while whispering he might want to go somewhere else. Jim whispered back that he had to go, it might be *the* story, epic Dienbienphu all over again, and he did not want Sunny fogging up his survival instincts as he committed his possible last days to the Marines.

On the way, almost there, feeling less hangdog, he spied this truly sinister figure and fixed it with the laser concentration usually reserved for fresh blood on a trail or the swing of Sunny's hips. There went his old mentor loping across the street of flowers, bottle tucked under his arm, pausing now at the far curb to light up, taking one lordly drag before tossing the smoke away. Then, boldly straightening, head high, he went clip-clopping like Lord Wellington's horse into Susanna's palace of pleasure.

Jim started after him, too late. Hurrying to the lobby, he watched the elevator tick-tock up to floor six. Screw peace, nuts to tranquility. Whirling, he steamed back across the street to the café and slumped into Eric's still-warm chair. Staring up at Susanna's balcony, he felt the sword twisting.

Perhaps she and his lordship would appear and do a balcony scene together. And then would fall off the balcony shrieking eternal verities at each other. He could only hope. But they did not appear, and he sipped hemlock beer while in his head he painted pretty bedroom pictures in wild and wicked detail.

A couple of hemlocks later, he got up and wandered down crooked little streets that ran around like the past bumping into the present, past new crooked buildings thrown up slab-sided, gray, windowless, all leaning over and whispering to each other about another crazy American on the loose. He heard a helicopter thudding along somewhere, maybe in his head. He wondered if Ernie before he died heard that. Head swimming, he passed a potted palm. "Don't I know you?"

Turning down a quaint refugee street, he nearly knocked into a crouched old woman with a face like leprosy with hairs growing out of it, her scabby toes curled over the edge of her chair like monkey feet. She sat by an army cot jammed against a building. She seemed to be nursing something down in the rags of her bosom with one hand, a grenade perhaps, while holding out the other. He gave to the grenade. "Don't I know you?"

So he had a bit of the wobbles. He sat down at a sidewalk table at a no-star café. Ordering a glass of beer with a chunk of ice in it, he studied a brownish thing wriggling up from under the ice. Fishing it out, he was not familiar with the species. Ice lice? It did not look particularly menacing, so he pursed his lips and blew it away, thinking, so now she's all wrapped up in delirious delight with that tea-sipper who would stab himself in the back if he could reach around that far.

Out front now, a tiny boy, drooling papaya juice, cheerfully sailed his card-board boat with a paper sail in the gutter floating with crap. Nearby, a Viet man with a big knife stood behind the fly-buzzing, dirt-smudged glass of his rolling lunch-stand slicing cucumbers, tomatoes, and cheese, before waving the knife at a soot-faced rat investigating scraps under the stand. Ants crawled on the soft shiny cheese and loaves of twisting bread stacked on the counter. Diners squatting around on the sidewalk, gobbled ants on bread with blind gusto.

"Ain't good for you," a smiling and-eater advised Jim.

As good as wild women, Jim thought. Booze was a bore. Pot was for petunias. Women were... He had once thought that in their heart of hearts women were better than men. Soft versus hard. Nest and nurture versus fornicate and kill. This one, Sunny, the sweetheart of Blowdom, was already a legend, he thought. She should be awarded battle ribbons, with naked asterisks, though not from him. He still had his sweet war to sleep with.

Now the tiny boy stood up from the gutter, walked over with no britches on, and gazed at the sad-eyed round-eye. Big-knife whacked open a fish, cleaned it, and slapped its pop-eyed head down on brown paper on a slanted box, pink fluid trickling down the paper. Big-knife smiled at round-eye and offered him some of the ant-bread and trickling fish. Round-eye smiled back and patted his full tummy.

It was beginning to rain. Jim got up and, bid his pals at the inedible eatery goodbye. He saw a sign on a window that said "Welcome happy 'mericans. He looked through the window. There were no 'mericans. No furniture. Only empti-ness. The door was shut tight. Now his eyes fell on a cat, three-legged, black, limp-ing in the steam rising in the street. Jim walked along with his faithful new friend,

Three-legs until the rain began to pour, and his friend rose up, black cat hissing at the rain, before doing a fast, three-legged goodbye. Jim marched on, catless in the rain, trailing clouds of trouble on a dark wet afternoon. In this frame of mind, he would proceed to what doomers said was the most dangerous place on the planet, Khe Sanh.

***

"*Ooomm....*"

Susanna sits in front of her mirror, legs in the lotus position, with a glass and gin bottle to her left. The bedroom is growing dark except for the little flame of a candle smoking to her right. Her shadow starts to quiver along the walls and ceiling. A blue silk robe is draped over her bare shoulders. Her voice rises and falls in slow, rhythmic tones, just as she had heard her teacher do it. It's her latest revealing dress to try on, spiritually speaking. She is meditating to invoke the cleansing spirit. Thinking about how she might go to India and get guru-fixed, or Japan and get Zen-fixed. Or back to her roots and get Jesus-fixed. She must go somewhere, get fixed, and liberate herself from even primitive notions of liberation, from the mongrel pack of jerks, rakes, and snakes, the deceivers, ravagers and rotters, the pawers, maulers and howlers, and mostly herself from herself. Her revolution's having a bad time. Will sex ever make up its mind? She tries not to look at the razorblade glinting, seeming to whisper *why not?* just to her front.

"*Ooomm...*" Taking it in and breathing it out, and feeling *something terrible going to happen.* Desperately into it now, head bowed, swaying slightly, the way she had seen it done, trying to quiet the mind chatter, cool down the dragon, breathing slowly, deeply into the shadows, seeking union with the universal soul, the great unconscious or something.

"*Ooomm...*" Back perfectly straight now. She's trying to float in the deeps of herself, whispering, inner harmony, purity of spirit, quietness of heart. But something was amiss. Something always amiss. Like going through life with her bra-snapping, or being snapped. Yes, she's done things she's not too proud of. Slowly, she gets to her feet, and lets the robe slide away, looking at the cursed figure in the mirror.

"Ooomm…" Something shimmering in there now. Pretty little girl telling her tooth dream… *I was walking through the big house and my tooth came out. And Mama said, "Wash it and that'll make it shiny and bring you good luck." But I lost my tooth in the big house and never could find it. I looked and looked but never could find my good luck.…*

"Ooomm…" Let me see you walk like that again, honey. How old are you, really? Hot, hot. I don't care. That's right, sugar, hips forward. Um… a real show-girly, aren't you, with certain, um, photogenic qualities. How'd you like to be a cat-walk queen? I can make that happen. Glam hair.

Gorgeous gams. I saw you prissing along the beach with a mouth full of cookie. Oh, *bad.* You turn guys on like a wall socket. Say you love dancing? Do you know poles? Good things are happening in poles.

Okay, hold it just like that, yeah *that.* Hot, hot. hot. Will you strip for me? Good things are happening in stripping. Then pose in these little see-throughs. I'll make you Miss Picture Perfect. Don't you want to connect with the camera? Be the feminine ideal. That men look up to and go bananas over. Don't you want to be gone bananas over? Hold still now. Slip those classy legs through. Be careful, silk wrinkles.

Here, let me help you. All right now. Just lie back. Don't talk. Got a surprise for you. Be still! Be quiet! You came here, didn't you? You were showing it off, weren't you? Shut that pretty face or I won't take your picture anymore. We're just having fun here. Don't you want to be famous? Lie back, girl! Back!

Back! Scream for joy if you want to. Quietly."

Ooomm… See, mama. A rainbow. See, it's getting bigger and bigger. Look, mama, now it's going away. Please, mama, my pretty rainbow is going away. The mean clouds are spoiling my rainbow. Why does it have to go away, mama?

Ooomm… Going deep into ourselves, everything is revealed.… So he took me to this strange old place and I sit waiting in a small room staring at the wallpaper. The wallpaper is purple. A woman in a heavy coat with a face like cracked granite and long black dyed hair under a flowery hat, sits silently rocking in a corner. A man steps out of a larger room and motions me to follow him. No how are you? He is a tall, thin, buzzard-looking man wearing thick glasses and a yellowed white coat. The room has one window with a curtain of faded paper roses, a big sink, an instrument table, and a metal examination table under a 15-watt electric light hanging from a long cord. A brick supports one leg of the table. Cigarette burns spot the table. The table slants.

He tells me to remove my clothes and climb on the table. I undress and sit on the cold table. He keeps squinting at me through his glasses. I can't look at him. I'm trying to cover myself with my hands. He tells me to lie back and close my mind shut. He bends over me and I close my eyes. When he touches me I open them and focus on a crack in the pink plaster of the ceiling. He's in me like a plumber with some instrument and it is painful and it would slip and he would have to get me right again and readjust it. The pain is so bad I don't know when he's in or out of me. I claw the table until my nails break.

On the drive back it was raining and cold and the windshield wiper broke and her great love of that time who seemed too wonderful for mere words and, as he often observed, was simply marvelous at everything especially the making of love, kept slapping her knee and saying, "Listen. it's done, so just cool it and please shut it the fuck up so I can drive." So she shut it up. And he explained how busy and all he had been in his work, so swamped and backed up and in a hurry and having to take the time and trouble to set this up and bring her down here and all, she must understand how hard it was on him. She understood, all right, mister. Now. But it pretty well messed her up inside and the good part, she guessed, was that she could just let things happen and not worry about going through this again while doing whatever fun she wanted, isn't freedom liberating?

Ooomm… Spring rain can be lots of fun. You can splash in puddles and get wet. The tires of cars sounds like whoosh. When spring rain hits the windshield it makes the dirt go away. The rain drops off the trees and when you step in the grass the water squooshes up. Spring rain helps baby flowers to grow. I love to get my face wet in spring rain. Spring rain is very fun. I don't like winter rain. Spring rain is the very best kind of rain. I will always love spring rain.

Ooomm… At times like this she feels so unsubstantial it's as if she's hardly there. *Do I exist?* She retreats into sleep, waking up on a slow boat to nowhere. Her eyes dim out as if she's fading away as if she can pass her hand through herself. She feels so down low that if someone on the phone says "hello" in a negative tone she hangs up. Even Jim, who she really had feelings for, despises me, she thinks, looking at the cursed figure in the mirror. Maybe they could meet again someday on a less emotional level, and converse like cool clinicians, or a reunion of mellowed old warriors who no longer desired to cut each other's hearts out.

Why are you staring a hole in this looking glass, you poor thing? Susanna can't see her but she's there. The Old Scold letting her have it one more time. *Don't you know that humans are one of only six species to recognize their image in the mirror, including chimpanzees, bonobos and orangutans? Which are you? The most ravishing bonobo on the block? Or the half-naked she-ape on television selling the latest junk? Aren't you sick of being female junk you silly creature. You always say you are and then you do it again. Great boobs do not a deep-thinker make.*

Her reflection, the glorious swoops, and curves that made the flesh-hounds howl, scares her. *Sic transit...* Glory is passing and *something terrible going to happen.* She sits down again and feels for her empty glass, then the bottle. Nothing there. Nothing but the gleam of the blade. She sits there like a little girl waiting to be spanked, who really deserves it, and anything else they want to do. How messy will it be? How will she look? *Aren't I pretty? So who cares anymore?* Pressing down with her hand, feeling the blade's cool sharp sting, she wants to scream something at the shadow in the mirror. *Are you maxing your efficiency report?*

But then comes a noise piercing her trance, an insistent buzzing in her head and she isn't even drunk yet. No, it's the door, perhaps the great unconscious or a zealous bill collector come to collect.

16
BATTLE OF THE BOUDOIR
LORD LUCIFER WOOS THE DAUGHTER OF THE DEVIL

As to the fair sex, he was their absolute master. he felt. Great fake emotion was his game. He saw the ladies breathlessly craving him in the loving mirror of his mind. Now Eric the Bold stood at her door, girding his heated loins for conquest. His irresistible brio, that smile, his likeability quotient was top hole, his mellifluous eloquence preternatural, he felt. He didn't need to say anything, but it sounded so good if they didn't know anything. He had the knack. His was not just another pretty voice, he could descend from the high road of a true knight from Old England to a gotcha-baby low in the blink of a sentence, spin any argument round and round until a poor ladyship seized with sexual vertigo must swoon. He could flow from lordly aloofness to a bedroomy lip-curl over a brisk cup of tea or stiff drinkie-do and not miss a silky beat, which drew oohs, aahs, and tee-hees and ushered him under any number of forbidden sheets where, he felt, he surely outperformed any-man-jack twice and on good nights, thrice over. Of such were his thoughts.

Revving into character now, he stood punching the doorbell, brushing away still boyish locks spilling over his brow, then spreading and patting down thinning hair over the first traces of baldness (which he *refused* to accept) creeping across his beloved. Was he not still Jack the lad?

Jack's first maneuver with this dish would be to flash his bowl-of-cherries, man-of-passionate-sincerity smile in all dental splendor, at which point the sheer pulsating power of his charm should wriggle him past the first obstacle, the door, whereupon he would engage her in simple chin-wag, innocent yet subtly stimulating, and then proceed to scramble egg her brain with spinning conundrums about the great galactic wheel of life and this and that. After which he would generously gin-soak her and carry her, bodice-ripped, bosom likely heaving, aboard his stallion as they galloped toward the promised land. Of such were his thoughts. He hoped she was in a mellow mood.

When Susanna slowly opened the door, all wrapped up in her robe, she focused on the gin before she did the knight. He entered cheerily with awesome toothsome display. "I say, hope I'm not disturbing you. Just passing, wanted to chat a bit, you know. It's not easy finding someone to share feelings with, who truly gets it, in this balmy cock-up. Hope it's not a bad time, my dear.

Hope I'm not intruding. If so... why, what's the matter, dear?"

"Nothing's the matter."

"In this place? Why not? We all suffer tired-conscience syndrome." He patted her arm.

"I don't know." Susanna shrugged. She pulled the robe tighter. "I don't know anything."

Eric seemed nice in an old worldly sort of way, some kind of old ex-lord of something. She looked at the bottle. The living room was in shadow except for a small orange-shaded Japanese lamp by the couch, and when Susanna moved to turn on something brighter, Eric said, please, dear, no, this so fit his mood. He was just shockingly dry, he said, holding up the bottle like a lad with a secret goodie. Could he fix them something cold? Yes. Minutes later they were on the couch, gins and something in hand, with orange glowing droplets beading the glass beneath his lordly hot breath.

They talked. She talked about her late heroic captain husband, poor Robby. "He was such a tough man," she said, "so aggressive. And that's what got him, I guess. "

"I, too, am a man," responded Eric. "I have seen, been through quite a lot, though I don't speak much of it, the existential angst of being here and all. You see, I, too, am just surviving."

Perhaps, he suggested, sighing deeply, they could survive together, and explore their angst together. But was she properly listening? he wondered. Her mouth was still moving. What the devil was she gabbling about now? Did I ask you to speak? Words are not required from the drunken dumb. Just show your wares, woman. I'll sort it all out. Gawd? Was that a gawd reference? Have I stumbled upon one of *those*? Hardly gawdly in the way she moves that wicked caboose. Carry a fiery joystick, I say, only gawd a man needs with her kind. "Are we, who feel so deeply about things, doomed?" he asked softly.

"I don't know about doom. I don't know anything."

He liked that she did not know anything. He rarely went wankers over a logician. She was not going wankers but she liked his great smile, his fine beautiful though stained teeth, his engaging humor, and the sensitive, deferential way about this ex-lord of something. Could he do this for her? Fetch her another drinkie? Well, one. Well, cheers, dear. How else could he please her? Could this use-to-be lord, so responsive, possibly be a friend, platonically, she wondered, without the old smothering other?

At first, she held the robe tightly around herself, curling her legs and slippered feet cocoon-close beneath her. But as they talked and drank and the robe loosened up enough to reveal, he thought, a sudden swell of savage breast. Her body was simply dynamite and the fuse was lit, he thought, , which triggered in his lordship the clenching and unclenching of his left hand, as if he were a starving peasant about to seize the goldenest ripest melon in the market. Of course, he maintained lordly aplomb with his right, his drinking hand.

When Susanna unfurled her legs toward the big round glass and bamboo coffee table, Eric thought of golden panthers, sleek muscled, stretching in the sun. His left hand, draped along the back of the couch, twitched, but his eyes remained suave. Now she casually crossed them, leaving a slipper dangling, What a lovely dangle. What was more exciting than the well-shod female footsie? When the slipper fell, Eric thought she had more sensuality in that royal arch of ankle than his galumphing wife possessed in the entire length and breadth of her lumpty-dumpty, ever-expanding frame. He could not abide the ugly-ankled.

I'm doing it to him, Susanna thought. *Aren't I pretty, aren't I pretty?* It was a little amazing, even to her, how easily she pressed their buttons. She did it so reflexively that it dawned on her she must be related to Pavlov's mindless bitch, Darwin's dumbest whore, doing it for free.

Pavlovian or who or whatever, the sight of such a constellation of gorgeousness bathed in the lamp's glow triggered in Eric a change of tactics. *Fait accompli!* Almost. Was that not an expression of near orgiastic surrender? Clearly. And went forward with all deliberate speed, tending to get high on his own fumes. From the untidy state of the human condition, he waxed ever more warmly on how wow-now he was by the *why of her,* why a person of such delicious wit and beauty, who could write her own first-row ticket anywhere in the eyes of males from great apes to gentlemen like himself, was here sacrificing all that for this, wasting herself in this malignant swamp of tears.

"I sense melancholy in you, what? A tantalizing mystery. Who *are* you, actually? Helen of T? Marilyn? Sophia? An original from Gondwanaland? Do you know Gondwanaland? Are you responsible for the Cambrian explosion? Never mind. You seem so deeply caring, as am I. But the wheel of wayward circumstance rides us both hard, hot, unrelenting. Another little drinkie?"

He fetched it and continued dissecting her with his eyes. He remembered her wild-wheeling Christmas dance. She would be his Lady Bountiful, his Venus Van Voom. "What a visual poem you are," he rhapsodized, "and yet a flesh-and-blood woman." Not quite the nose of choice, he calculated, and those dimples, a bit bourgeoisie, but I generously forgive, for now.

She crossed her legs (*those wanton attention-grabbers, he thought*) again, as her other slipper fell. She had been feeling so wretched and here he came, crooning of his infinite respect and admiration for her very personhood, and how she deserved so much more. Then going on about the wheel of circumstance and his angst over this bloody awful war. It was not, he made clear, that he was in the least afraid of going into harm's way himself, and made a manly fist.

"By nature, I am a high-risk person. I've had fencing lessons, you know. I'm confident in my physicality. I've tennised at the Lawn and Croquet club. My sang-froid under fire is… well, enough pollywaddle about me. Listen, dearest, how would you like to toodle off to old England with me some fancy day? We'll stomp at the Savoy. And then nip over to Paris. Do you know Paris? We'll feast at Maxim's. Have you done Maxim's? We'll cruise the Seine. Do the Tuleries. Do you know the Tuleries? I'll scent you in perfume of gardenias and roses. We'll sing and dance. I'll sing to you

La Vie en Rose. Would you like another little nip?"

She wanted it. He rose and fixed them both little nips. Hurrying back, humming *La Vie en Rose,* he sat so chummy close that drops from his glass fell *drip-drop* into the dimple of her right knee.

"Oh!" he made a face, most caring, then leaned over, and with his little finger elegantly brushed the dampness off that electric pulsating knee. His finger rested there briefly, enjoying the velvety shock of the terrain, and… tallyho! Receiving the non-signal he sought. No frown, no uh-uh, no-no-no, not a negative twitch, not the weest murmur of protest. So there she is, he thought, the perfect prey. *Heel.*

Fetch. Sit. Disrobe. The perfect prey. So classically stacked, those golden goblets crying for his touch, and the master ready for the moment at which she would abandon all hesitancy and beg him to cease further tongue-wag, as thrilling as it is, and just do it.

Now, in the style of great power lovers, as he fancied himself, he favored her with a bit more of his famous talk-talk. "I am a purist, and yours is a passionate presence to one whose *raison d'être* is pursuing and beholding beauty sublime." So he moved closer, beholding it. "Do I strike you as a bit stiff, cursed with understatement? Help me express myself, dear, as a stifled-in-silence member of your secret admiration society, since I first gazed at the magic swing of your… ah. movements. Because in this drear land you are just so very, very… and, I confess, I too am so very, very captivated at… yes, your incomparable, well, movements. Do you grasp my meaning? Because we are so alike. I'll sing to you my poor poetry someday. I've perfect pitch, you know."

Susanna did not answer, her eyes seemed glazed. Had he carried it too far? No, he thought, marveling at his locution, the transition flawlessly made, disarmingly delivered. Now he watched her stretch those pantherish legs again. *Tallyho!* Then at her robe slipping away — *Mein Gott!* — high on the surely rising heat of those savage thighs. Her beast bloody *let* it, he surmised, as she pulled the robe slowly back. He had seen nothing, *nothing* at all underneath except beckoning bikini lines. By Jove, got you now, O daughter of the devil.

"Ah, woman," he crooned, "so deliciously good, so delightfully evil. All that woman was meant to be. You inspire in me that *ur* feeling. Do you know *ur?* Why do you clutch your robe so? Aren't you warm? Gawd, I am. I say, enjoy expressing your beguiling humanity, your free-woman sexuality.

Unbind thy curves, woman. Let the sun shine in! Let freedom howl!"

As he caressed her robe, Susanna closed her eyes, which he interpreted as another signal of surrender to the master. "Yes, yes, tuck in. Let the stars in your hair down. I'll sort you out, dear."

Indeed, he had never felt so lathered up over a commoner. He felt her bubbling up to a boil, so now he would steep her. His left hand, looped carelessly around her shoulders, actually (so unlike him) trembled as he edged the robe on downward and looked ready to bury his face to sip from those goblets of desire. Don't stop, he seemed to hear the goblets gurgling. I dare say, dears, the queen herself on her morning gallop couldn't stop me.

Tuning up his music box a passionate decibel, he flexed his lordly voice and raced onward, words a tumble *(when in fine form awkward silences and tiresome commas were banished, periods made rare, and never, never perverse semi-colons)* as he dizzied one worth the chase them with his sine qua non of seduction, a twinkle-tongued trove of hot-breathed similes and moonstruck metaphorical delights. After all, 'twas sage Sophocles who said, "tis the tongue that wins and not the deed." *Hoot!*

"Oh, I know you wish me to quit breathing so hard and just seize you. No, speak not. I will complete your sentences for you. Just be there. Because you are indeed so very, very *there*. What may I call you? Venus undraped? Pagan moon goddess descending? Sun goddess burning her bodice? But looking at you renders me speechless, virtually."

Speechless, virtually, he sang out, "Oh, I see the magic in *your eyyeees.* Devilish blue? Wanton green? Lusting for me? How came you by those, actually?" He was appraising her goblets. "Sprung full-formed from Mother Nature's fiery bosom? Michelangelo's caressing hands of flame? Exercise?

Running the beaches? Ah, a stray freckle there. *Formidable.* Nay, speak not. Kindred spirits need not empty words. You are just so very, very... Now just lie back. Breath. Breathe to me."

Eric felt transported up, up, and away on his metaphorical balloon. Flapping his rhetorical feathers, he waited for her to swoon. Hand a tremble, he inched the robe all the way… down. "O sweet liberation!"

Susanna suddenly shivered and made a face. "Don't touch me *there. Don't!*"

"Why not *there?* Here, there, everywhere? Dance of the butterflies."

"No, damn you! Don't touch me *there!*"

"Into my hand, thy bosom flows…" Eric hummed a ditty while pressing forward. "Sic itur ad astra. It's written in the stars. Don't you *feel* it? Let no man put asunder our right to *feel. Tell* me you *feel* it. Swear you *feel* it, woman. You are so very, very… now unfurl your legs, woman! Be grateful, woman. I've fooled with you long enough. Yes, you may temporarily speak. And guide me to the spot of mindless rapture. Playtime is over."

Here he was sharing with her his most inspired poesy, and the hussy refused to swoon into a helpless mush of idiot ecstasy. Her response was to stare at curls of drool leaking from the edges of his killer smile, at his face in popping sweat descending, at the yellowed fangs in that long wolf jaw, at black hairs sprouting from his lips, at the elongating tongue like a thing snaking from a dark closet, then hearing from the closet ss*sing* sounds. She thought it was old Lucifer himself, a leer plastered across his face like a salacious dripping pancake as he rubbed himself against her, all con, fire, pus, and calamity.

It was when he tipped the glass toward her, sending gin trickling onto Mother Nature's fiery bosom, it was when she felt his breath crawling across her face and breasts, saw the balding spot on his pate with a bead of sweat oozing up, and that large nose growing monstrous as he sniffed at her, *sniffed,* and his head bobbing over her like a yellow-toothed goat in a can of trash, that she pushed, pulled, and jerked hard sideways back and away.

Undeterred, Eric crooned, "I noticed you beholding my hair. Should I let my locks flow? Isn't it exciting where bliss carries us? Dance of the butterflies, here… there."

"You are disgusting, butterfly.."

"Disgusting. Me? *Phaw*. One can be disgustingly desirable. Woman, you must not irritate your legendary lord." Every inch of this wench below her alleged thinking cap fired his furnace.

"Don't touch me *there*, old Englishman!"

"Obey your lord!"

"Get *out*, lord!"

"Don't be cheeky, silly fox. Tally-ho!"

Here she's panting to make whoopee with me, he thought, must have me, yet making these little obligatory no-no noises. Gone potty on me, she has. What an odd wad. Who's the cock of the walk here?

"Cease the gib-gab, tart. Gab-fest time is over. You're in the master's hands."

"Get them off me, you *evil thing...*" She slapped his hands.

"A bit shy? Shall I out the light?" Eric thrummed in his most prosecutorial tone. "Jog your hippocampus, fancy lady. I've seen your tainted toodlings about, your dalliances with the knuckle-draggers. That debauched, come-take-me smile. That damsel-in-distress routine on street corners, discussing Plato and Socrates in your rags of righteousness, tail feathers up, waving your pom-poms for the military rabble. To which I say *poo*, I say *faw*. Because I *know* you and your kind."

"You don't *know* me and I'm not your kind."

"If it pleases the court, I submit the weeping-wench defense won't work. The sob-sister scenario won't play. Your emotings move me not."

"Stop it, Robby, damn you, *stop!*"

"Who? Do I look like a Robby? Now behave and your legendary lord will reward you with the romp of your dreams."

"Are you crazy?"

"I am old English. Now assume the position and experience the most empowered moment of your earthly existence. I command you, assume the position! But first, kiss me! A rousing good smack!"

"Get out of here, old Englishman! *Out!*"

"*Au contraire.*" Tactics in the joust of love gone slightly awry, Eric turned on his fount of jocularity. "How delightful. You're having me on, Little Puss. I so admire that quality in you. Now, that we're socially comfortable, we can gallop forth in our royal romp."

"You gallop out of here, old Englishman… *out!*"

Oh, tut, he thought. He would delve into her well-known well of empathy, and find her sweet spot. "You daren't refuse me. My mental health depends on it. And my dreadful ulcer. Don't you sense our deep interconnectedness? Our unique synchronicity? So, Little Puss, another drinkie?"

Little Puss declined. Eric called on evolutionary purpose, the mating of superior bloodlines. Little Puss declined to evolve. Eric tried pushing her down while summoning forth biblical principles.

"Don't you love baby Jesus? Doesn't the Lord thy Gawd, knowing how teleologically in tune we are, insist we have a good time? By all that's holy, submit, woman. *Submit! Capitulate! Stop wriggling!*"

Never given to violence, Susanna wriggled out from under and gave generously, a cracking smack to the lord's probing nose, bringing tears to the lord's eyes.

"Let's not get frothy!" blurted the lord. "You have been defrocked! Don't you sell it… as you spread democracy and gonorrhea to the troops? How much? Three farthings? Four? More?"

Susanna pushed up, gripping her glass ready to throw. The robe fell open and Eric's eyes corkscrewed as he backed off. He saw her warts and all — no warts, just those devil woman's curves.

"So…" He retreated, half-staggering out the door, then rattling, into the elevator. "I'll pop along now.

No curtsy? Well, ta-ta to you, too. You may apologize later, minx. On your bleeding knees."

"*Get ouuut!*"

Suppressed passion? Rejection? he pondered going down. Never, he assured himself. Did I stutter? Was it the heat? A tad more dilly-dally? *Phaw.* These runny-mouthed females grumping over the least little nothing. Necessary for brat-making, some say. I say the issue of the stork is not settled. Beauty is the beast here. Stay out of my sensibilities. Fear the wrath of Blow, vamp. Go sleep with wild wolves in purgatory. May the blood-red moon bleed down upon you. Gets you breathing hard, and reacts in horror when you reach for what she's doing her dance of the fruit bats at sunset to show you. May those curves turn to squares of corpulence and crash, shrew. And was that not an unkempt hair hiding in that vulgar dimple? *That* I cannot abide. But enough of this female crinkum-crankum. *L'affaire finito.*

On the ground floor, the cage door of the elevator stuck. Eric gave it a stern rattle, but it would not budge. Well, no hurry, he thought. Should I return, give the vixen another go? *Hoot!* Her figger's bangers-and-mash riffraff really, an ordinary voluptuary, gross flesh with no redeeming spiritual component. Hardly an example of classic Anglo-Saxon womanhood. As the Puddinghams would put it, *To the kitchen, cookie!* You will age terribly. Your show-off chest will lean poverty-stricken upon your bloated belly. Bad show. Your face will wrinkle into a sat-upon map of the dead sea. Moreover, we will never listen to Wolfgang Amadeus Mozart together. Just *not* one of us.

Lord Eric rattled the cage door again. He thrust out his jaw, thinking, full marks for superior bloodlines in this sort of endeavor. Master Euripides knew women are of every evil the cleverest of contrivers. As the good Friar Cherubino of Siena rightly observed, when a hellion throws a hissy, goes stiff-necked on you, put the stick to her, apply the old rammajamma, by Jove. That she-devil called *me* evil, fancy word. Such women are possessed by demons. Vain! Shallow! Selfish! Provocateur! Fascist fishwife! Well, the woman lacks gravitas. Hie thee to the fainting couch, poor player. *Hoot!*

He shook it now, and beat at the elevator door. It remained unbudged. He jammed at buttons. Well, he thought, she likely waited above, properly contrite, crying out to him. Perhaps he'd give her another go, to better herself. But the door stayed stuck, would not, *not* bloody move. "Help!" Eric, loins gone cold, hollered. "Have you no feelings for a fellow being? What's *wrong* with you miserable people?"

17
1968: NEWS TO DIE FOR

"You go in there, that circle of hell, and bring out the good stuff as straight and true as you can. That's merely terrific reporting. You go in dripping the feverish BS of the day all over the story like malarial sweats, that could win you some wonderful bullshit they want-to-hear award."

— Ernie

KHE SANH, South Vietnam. Frames of mind in war change quickly. They had stayed high, then banked steeply, dropping through thick layers of mist over the cratered, smoke-blowing hills, then leveled off going in fast. Jim glanced at his watch as the wheels bumped down rattling over loose shrapnel. It was nearly four in the afternoon. He and Donlan crouched beside the loadmaster near the rear hatch whining open. Just behind them, strapped on metal pallets, were the 50,000 pounds of ammo, explosives, and fuel they were flying with into the kill box called Khe Sanh combat base.

They were alone in the belly of the bird with just the explosive stuffing and the loadmaster named Coffee, he of the pale, twitching, electric-chair stare. Now they felt the creaking C-130 with the machine-gun hits in the wings slowing down. What they must do, shouted Coffee hoarsely, is be sure it's slowed enough or they might get split open departing the plane and blown into confetti by the prop blast. "So wait for my signal and then jump the fuck out, man, and run like hell to the first hole you see, man, because we truly ain't stoppin', man."

Sean Donlan, looking into the haunted beans that were Coffee's eyes, managed his bloody little smile. "I truly believe you, man."

To one side humped the brute hills bashed with bomb and shell holes. To the other side sprawled a junkyard of war — bunkers powdered over with gritty dust like rust-red snow, tangles of barb wire, sagging huts and tents, leaning antennae, torn metal, weaving trench lines under waves of sandbags, everything all ripped and red and lice-and-rat infested and shell-battered and hung over with monsoon mist and three colors of smoke.

Bad, here, Jim thought, bad. A great story is not worth your health, it's said, except when it is.

Now Coffee, who had begun spilling over after machine-gun thunks to the wings of this flying bomb in two earlier aborted landings, shouted, "Go fucking go right now! *Go! Go!*"

They went, jumping, ducking, holding onto their helmets through the prop blast. Behind them the pallets came bumping down the rollers, skidding out the rear of the plane still moving slowly out from under its load. The seekers of fresh news, expecting incoming to blow down again any moment, trotted off the strip's shell-gashed matting, looking for a hole to hop into.

Strung out a mile long and a half-mile wide, stuck off in a foggy corner of the country near the DMZ and Laotian border, Khe Sanh's demise could be near, or so it had been much predicted and gloomed and doomed over. There were 6,000 Marines entrenched on that plateau of volcanic red earth, mostly surrounded and hugely outnumbered by NVA relentlessly firing down their throats much as they had before overwhelming the French years earlier at doomed Dienbienphu. Uncle Sam's likely demise in this mist-shrouded and deadly inconvenient place was a story beyond the gloom still to be finished. *Dienbienphu. Dienbienbhu.* You needed only one look and smell of the place to come down with Dienbienphu fever.

NVA infantry had zigzagged trenches ever closer to the Marines' perimeter, and their big guns deep dug into the high hills and great ridges looming through the mist, dispatched shells day and night into the unmoving target with the big hit-me on its chest, the airstrip at Khe Sanh. When a plane ventured in, it was on an earthquake about to happen, and the correspondents galloped across it now, expecting the earth to move.

The first and only Marines they see are crouching beside big crates at the edge of the strip.

"Leaving this place!" howls one wild-looking, red-stained mask under a cocked helmet. *Born to Bitch* was scrawled on his helmet, which perhaps explained his lack of positivism.

"Better move it!" Jim shouts over the engines' racket. "Not stopping."

"Goodbye, fucking Khe Sanh!" shouts the bitcher. Then he and three others get up dashing toward the moving plane, reaching the ramp about to lift, clambering and clawing up it like spirits escaping the underworld.

The correspondents move like spirits descending. At first searchingly, *is this the way the world ends?* big-eyed, senses strumming, weaving through a jumble of crates and fuel drums as the plane, gunning down the strip, lifts ahead of the first artillery round bursting behind it. As if waiting to let them know what they are in for, more blasts follow, exploding off left, then right, then more stuff blowing in like a blizzard — rockets, big nasty mortars, 130 mm artillery rounds. Welcome to Dienbienphu II, idiots.

Perhaps they're hearing voices of bad things to come, or shouts and cries of French ghosts, these seekers of breaking news who drop down on hands and knees, then up, down, back up, dodging through a crazy-house of explosions, helmets bouncing, packs and flak jackets flapping, eyes expanding as if in that terrible brilliant last focus to suck in all there's left to see. Dodging past rolls of rusty concertina wire, running across a narrow red dirt road now, Jim stumbles over a Marine corpse, eyes, and mouth wide open, one hand raised as if strongly debating his demise. They duck on past a 105 mm howitzer with its tube peeled back like a rotten banana. Another round pounds in. This one is close enough to shake them all over and take their breaths away.

Now, just ahead, rising up through a smoke cloud like some battlefield savior, there's this big, red-dusty, black Marine bellowing, "Rat here!" Standing there in the flashes, legs spread, waving them on. "Rat this way, Marines! Rat this way, boys!"

Just as they make it there, so does this rocking explosion chasing them from the rear. The red-black Marine smacks down on their backs with the flats of his huge hands, jamming them down into a slit trench, just as another shell, a Russian

130, cracks in very, very close and waves of burning earth sends them sprawling in a wild tangle of legs, torsos, guns, grunts, and curses between blasts.

"Say again?" their savior bellows at the side of Donlan's head. "You ain't Marines? You don't gotta be here?"

"Don't gotta nothing," mutters Donlan. "Just messed up again"

There are eight of them down there now, heavy breathing in that smoky quiet.

"Always like this?" Jim asks the body squeezed in next to him, who's holding a rifle with one bleeding hand and a fresh-lit joint with the other.

"Other than being blown away in a few seconds, not too bad. Need some?"

"No thanks. Your sergeant don't care?"

"I am the sergeant and he don't care."

"He don't care," says the black Marine, spitting dust. "It's home sweet home."

Forty minutes later they crawl out of the trench stiffly, like old grandfathers out of rocking chairs, wondering what's broke this time and looking for the next smoke signal from the north, and the next hole to jump into.

Decapitation by incoming explosion was mainly random rotten luck, Jim had always believed, and in some places almost sang to himself that the odds were with him. But after diving around Khe Sanh for a while, his singing commercial between blasts took on darker tones. He begins to think of them as alive, evil-souled things, malevolent presences seeking him out very personally, banging on doors down in dank little rooms he never knew he had. Hearing them hit close, but not too close, crazily lowers and lifts confidence from moment to moment. And then a barrage descends that could make grown men moan for Mommy and the Holy Ghost, that could tilt a man's center and move him around inside like haunted furniture, one-moment thinking coherent thoughts, the next feeling for all his parts.

Here it comes again, like a loaded TNT freight train out of howl *shu whooo...* *CRAASSHH!* Jim sees lightning blur through the fog outside the bunker they're in, and a reddish smear that is a Marine torso disintegrating. Ten minutes earlier he was asking that smear how did he feel things were going?

Quiet again, sweet murderous quiet, then amber flares popping and blooming like sky flowers, before hissing and dying over scattered fires burning below. Inside their chill bunker nothing to fight back with but singing commercials and the cognac swishing around inside Donlan's canteen. Jim begins appraising the Marine PIO, the public information officer named Hackenberry, whose hoot-owl eyes blink in the bunker's dim interior almost as eerily as Big Rat's glittering over in the far corner. The PIO major is more articulate, but Jim knows where Rat stands.

This PIO had earlier stood by the smoldering remnants of a bunker advising them how well things were going. Explaining how the sun was shining as the fog crept in curling over them like funeral wreaths. How he wished the media would stop doom-fucking Khe Sanh and

Now from somewhere, a tinny voice sings out. "I'm comin' over... Just say it's okay and I'll be on my way... Baby, let me come oooverr... Cause here I go down that old wrong road again...."

"Dammit, shut that damn thing off!" snaps a gruff voice out of the dark. The voice commands them to look straight ahead. Don't go to sleep. Don't smoke. Don't talk. "And by all means silence any frigging radios and did I see a flashlight? Douse the glim, dimwits. And who might that be with you, corporal? Who *is* he? What's he doing here? Jim shows himself. He explains what he's trying to do if he can stay alive. "Well, keep it down, okay? We got a war to do out here, okay?"

"Well, that's it," snorts Tag, as the voice goes away. "See what I mean. We run into them newby officers. They do dumb things. They don't know nothin'. They say this here's the way we do it in combat by the book, I say no matter how many times you do it by the book you never know how you gonna do it in real combat. He's jumpier 'n a squirrel with its nuts on fire."

At 0400 hours Jim and Donlan, following a not-so-nuts company commander showing them along a winding, pitch-black section of trench, all freeze. There are sounds just ahead, heavy gnawing sounds. At night rats by the thousands prowl Khe Sanh, and the trench travelers, through the pop and sputtering light of a flare, spot this huge, humped-over shadow, gnawing away at something.

"Good lord," says the CO, edging closer as the flare sputters downward, "I know that shape."

He moves forward. "Damn, gunny, what *are* you doing?"

In the flickering light, they see the company's big gunnery sergeant, called Ox, crouching, the good news. When the big noise dies down, the major gratefully accepts Donlan's offering from the cognac canteen, which cheers him enough to declare that being surrounded by twenty or forty thousand fanatical NVA is not such a bad deal. "When they bunch up, we ding their rice bowls." And in retrieving a positive from a negative, he requests Donlan to pass the joy juice one more time *bao chi.*

Jim doesn't want any, but Big Rat could use a shot. When a shell explodes close-in, Rat scurries around the bunker, trips, drags his foot-long tail over Jim's boots, reverses field, scoots back, and jams its head in the corner, quivering all over except for its tail. Only the three of them in there, plus the resident Rat. Why did Rat choose this place? Jim feels bad, almost, for Rat, and also for himself in this joke of a bunker covered only by a layer of steel-punched sandbags.

"Why can't Marine gentlemen learn to make a decent bunker?" asks Donlan.

"Same reason news pukes rarely get their facts straight," replies the PIO, "not in our job description."

Donlan takes a slug from his canteen and claws grit from his wild-curly locks.

"Mustn't boff off the old generals," says the PIO, smacking his lips, "under lots of pressure, lots of pressure."

"First time I ever heard a PIO puke tell the truth," says Donlan, passing back the canteen.

The PIO advises them that before he took shrapnel in a soft place and was reduced to this sorry flack state, he was a line officer. "They called me Hacksaw. Now I blow pretty bubbles for Bullshit Central for people like you. Just call me Hack. I'm lower down than you guys."

"I doubt that," says Donlan. "I was accused of reporting once that we could actually win the war. You can't get any lower where I work. I should quit, and go play piano in an Irish whorehouse with no editors."

Donlan seemed always ready to quit, not the war but the magazine for which he was covering the war. After being close to so much elemental combat, surrounded by desperate life and desperate death, he wondered if he could ever fit in back with the spoiled children of the western world. He wasn't a war lover but he wasn't a bullshit peace freak either. The thought of going back and becoming a creature of Washington, covering the overflowing political sewers, the huffing-puffing wind tunnels, caused him to reach for the cognac. Did people really get the government they deserved? What collection of saps was that undeserving? He knew he'd have to go somewhere and do something. He couldn't live in the past, even if the past was the most interesting part of his life. Perhaps someday he would belly up to a bar with Pamela, arm-in-arm with the eighth earl, and after hours of illuminating drinks and blah-blah, be converted into believing that red star rising was the light of the future. Probably not. Maybe a place like Khe Sanh was his true home. All he knew, for now, was that he would keep on listening while the war tune played, and write his own song later, if later made it.

Another warm gurgle, and quiet outside, gets Hack cranked up and expounding about where he stands, where they stand, where it all stands.

"Half-ass in war, half-ass out, is where it stands. We've got amateurs, political operators, calling in air strikes from the White House. They should let us cut the Ho Chi Minh Trail with infantry. Stop that toilet from leaking on us now and for good. Chase their little red wagons into the North. *Force majeure,* gentlemen. Let us go clean their clocks on *their* sacred soil. Because we're playing underwhelming force, win a battle and back off, splitting the weenie, enough to hang in the war but not win it.

Winning of course would highly piss off you geraniums of the media. What's that old saying? If you got no shit to report, don't report?"

"You've got us mixed up with some other geraniums," says Donlan, "although I like that saying."

"Listen, all I'm saying to the gang-bangers is that I'm not a serial killer, the Marines I know don't cut babies' throats, and even more radical, I cherish my battlefield experiences and don't need any weeping Willies of the press to come in here crying all over us Marines whether we know what we're doing or not. Whatever happens, we'll salute smartly and march on, gnashing our teeth. Well, that's my story. Might I taste the joy juice one more time? No telling what I'll say next. Just don't print it. I'll say you made it all up."

"All I say," says Donlan, passing the canteen, "is that I *really* need to take a urination."

"Anyway, that's my story," Hack smacks his lips. "Don't dare print it a word of it. Let the unnamed source stays unnamed. Under lots of pressure, lots of pressure."

"My story," says Donlan, "is I need to take a big, I mean a really *giant* urination. Under lots of pressure. Should I step outside and risk it?"

"Risk it," says Hack, swishing the cognac. "Stand up and pee like a man... a man of the media. A giant urinator of the media."

Donlan starts to stand up.

Hold it," warns Jim. Earlier the major had loosed a burst from his can of mosquito spray and Jim had ducked, had thought it was a rocket. Now he feels a tingle in his scalp, and then an electric chill running all over him...

"Do it in your helmet," urges Hack, "your media helmet."

In the next seconds where he does it is of no concern. The bunker trembles and sags under another hard hot shrapnel wind outside that blows away levity but doesn't quite collapse the bunker. Jim stares through the burning chill at a broken toothpick on which sweat dribbles from his forehead. If it's the last thing he'll ever see... what does it mean? They all press heavily earthward, away from smashing echoing sounds rolling over their senses now like trains thundering through a tunnel.

When the trains thunder off, Hack mumbles something not nice. Mumbling something else even less nice, he fumbles around and switches on his radio. A prim nasally voice crackles forth. "*Have you checked your uniform lately for missing buttons, brass, and discrepancies? Don't embarrass us by embarrassing you. And remember, a good soldier is a neat soldier,*" scolds the voice. "*And don't forget, no matter where you are, if you lose your toothbrush you're in trouble. So take a piece of bamboo, shred it, and use the bristle to...*"

"Shove it up your discrepancy hole," advises Hack.

Jim lies there in the explosive stinking dust, a temporarily spent shell asking himself what wild illusory concept of journalistic élan, what foggy pursuit of Fourth Estate glory, had driven him this far into this place for... *news?*

And how different it was than hunkering down in the armchair trenches of the home front reciting over stirring books and thrilling music and a beer or two heroic incantations about being...

> *...it's on the way again shuttling down the sky, landing in a sizzling*
> *CRUUNNCH so close outside the killer wind blows earth through*
> *the canvas flap and Jim lies there all stiffed out for seconds in the*
> *flash and the dust before he stops hearing the explosion...*

where the action is.

Curled up there trying to shrink into the ground, the intrepid worm correspondent wonders how he can write this stuff straight. Can anybody write it straight? What's that saying, he's a journalist, a creative liar by training. Is this worse than Dak To, or Con Thien? Or is he getting worse? Straight or bent, the ghost of Dienbienphu rides again. Luke the gallant Gook trying to outshoot Johnny the merciless Wayne. And the great white news shark gobbling it all up like hot buttered nightmares, bones, blubber, and all the overripe tripe ever written or imagined about where the action is, and yawning for more ever more.

The fog creeps, the wind mutters, the rat quivers, old *Schweinehund* prowls around trying to get inside even as Jim juggles what he's felt, what he's seen, trying to drum up deathless phrases to capture death and destruction at Khe Sanh. The good news is he hasn't had a vision of the high-skirt dancer for fifteen or twenty minutes.

He's reaching for his notebook to jot something down *(shit bottom of the world... will they print that?)* when he hears an earthy laugh and glances over at Donlan in his corner addressing his rodent compatriot, Rat, still quivering in its corner.

"Excuse me, old guy, for not introducing myself, but I think I've pissed my pants. Hope you don't mind. I've been in tense places, but this is getting tenser."

Sean Donlan, he may be very angry about some things, but he has this quality about him, of one able to interview and relate to situational rats of all kinds with relative calmness and with a fair amount of objectivity though he has wet his pants and may or not be blown to the back of oblivion at any moment, a quality that takes him anywhere in this war, that and a little cognac.

They've been ducking around Khe Sanh for a few days, and now they are outside in the dark, moving slowly along a deep curving trench between bunkers that form part of the outer defense line. A heavy night mist, shapes of fog, roll like slow white dragons over a section of concertina wire through which the NVA had cut the night before. During the day Marines had patched and adorned the wire with dangling skulls to scare the spooks away.

Spooks are all around, and every night is Halloween. A Marine with a stethoscope carefully examines the lungs of the earth, listening down here, up there, for sounds of digging. There's scary talk that the NVA are burrowing beneath them and will rise up one night like shrieking, killing ghosts. What they know for sure is that enemy trenches are steadily zigzagging toward them like snakes full of poison as they did at Dienbienphu. There are more bites into the wire every night, and the Marines keep waiting for the really big one when all the poison out there comes hissing and snapping at once, and it will be another crushing Dienbienphu or it won't.

At two in the morning, they stare through the wire at objects that seem to float forward and backward in the same motion, at grid coordinates uncoordinated, at stumps of trees, ravines, and hills dissolving and reforming again among the slow white dragons. Then noises, like metal hitting rock. Up and down the Marine trench line there's the clinking of rifles being raised, the cocking of machine guns.

"I seen one! I definitely seen a gook! He had a shovel!"

"They're diggin' in. They're closing in."

"Movement! Over there! Fifty meters! Get ready!"

Marines along the line unleash three mad volleys of fire toward the movement. Then silence.

"Shhh…" a sniper whispers to Jim. Jim stares at him. The sniper is Bam Bam, his old Café of Last Resort down-in-the-hole buddy from Con Thien. "Hear it, Mister Reporter ?"

"What?"

"There, right there in the wire, *there!*"

"Get the sumbitch," urges another sniper. This one is Tag. "Shoot it."

Bam lifts his bolt action rifle with the starlight scope and flash suppressor, aims it toward the wire with the hanging skulls, steadies it on a sandbag, then squeezes off a round, a swift solid rush.

"Hear it?" whispers Bam, easing back his rifle, slitted eyes still on target.

"Hear what?"

"Blood squishin' out his air holes. No lie. One shot. Clean kill. Caught him in his shorts. Blew his jewels off."

"We kill the fucker every night," says Tag. "He never hardly complains."

"So whatcha doin' in this fun place?" asks Bam. "Not lookin' for us?"

"Why not? The famous sniper team. Heard they never miss. That's Donlan over there."

"Jim asks the men of arn how they're making out in the fun house?"

"Just tellin' lies and killin' rats," says Tag. "Lots more them than us."

"Where's old Rusty?"

"Caught a little shit here and here. We got him out aw right. He'll be aw right."

"So what's it like out here night after night? What's it take?"

"Mental illness, I guess," says Bam. "Give us a wet paper bag and we'll break it in a week anyway. Just don't try sleepin' at Khe Sanh in the dark. Nobody sleeps at Khe Sanh in the dark."

"Still want to be Marines?" Jim asks, peering out at the dark.

"Oh, hell yeah," says Tag. "If it wadn't for the dang rats."

"He's our big rat killer," says Bam."

"I killed about a hundred last night.. It's your turn," says Tag. "I hate 'em."

"Well, they don't love you neither. And it's your turn."

"I still hate 'em. Naw, it's your turn."

Just then, reverberating through the hills, come these big rumblings, then a great shaking and flashing and splitting of earth. It's rolling toward them.

"Like God marching through the mountains," whispers Donlan between blasts...

"Close," says Jim. Out front then, way too close and moving closer here it comes cracking earth *pound pound pound thud thud thud.* Midnight turns into yellow-orange daylight.

Smacked by shock waves, the correspondents and men of arn go flopping like rag dolls to the bottom of the trench. God is surely louder but this is B-52's bombing closing in enemy trenches, part of a sound and light show called Niagara, said to be the heaviest bombing in the history of bombing, and what the NVA will have to fight through to take Khe Sanh. Even the dragons seem blown away.

Dig deep, Jim thinks, when he's able to get the sound out of his ears, the rolling light out of his eyes, about the shadows out there and hopes he will never have to feel what they're feeling.

"Hail," mutters Tag. "they still can't touch us,"

Now from somewhere in the dark, a tinny voice sings out. *"I'm comin' over... Just say it's okay and I'll be on my way... Baby, let me come oooverr... Cause here I go down that old wrong road again...."*

"Dammit, shut that damn thing off!" snaps another voice. The voice commands them to look straight ahead. Don't go to sleep. Don't smoke. Don't talk. And by all means, get those frigging radios and other junk out of his sight. "And who might that be with you, corporal... the mail clerk? Who are you? What're you doing?" Jim shows himself and explains who he might be and what he might be doing. "Well, keep it down, okay? We got a war to do here, okay?"

"Well, that's it," snorts Tag, as the voice goes away. "See what I mean. We run into them politics. Dumb shit officers. They do dumb things. They don't follow through. They don't know. They say here's the way we do it in combat. I say no matter how many times you do it you never know how you gonna do it in combat.

Just loses his mind. Twitchy as a squirrel with his nuts on fire. But, hail, ev-erthang's all right. Dumb shits."

At 0400 hours Jim and Donlan, following a not-so-nutsy company com-mander showing them along a winding, pitch-black section of trench, freeze. There are sounds just ahead, heavy gnawing sounds. At night rats by the thousands prowl Khe Sanh, and the trench travelers, through the far pop and sputtering light of a flare, spot this huge, humped-over shadow gnawing away at something.

"Good lord," says the CO, edging closer as the flare sputters downward, "I know that shape."

He moves forward. "Damn, gunny, what *are* you doing?"

In the flickering light, they see the company's big gunnery sergeant, called Ox, crouching, jaws bulging, face screwed up over an open box. He's eating something. It looks like old bread, he's going at it like he's starving.

"I'm sorry, sir," the gunny replies miserably. "I'm sorry."

"Hell, it's okay, gunny. Go ahead and eat."

"I'm really sorry, sir. I don't ever want my boys to see me eat and think I'm weak."

Jim reminds himself that back in the world he would never see such a sight. He could be back at Walter Reed dying under a ghastly white sheet, and wonders what Ernie would give to be out here covering elemental Marines like Ox one more time. Outside the wire, the B-52s are raising hell again. As long as you weren't under them, the thunder never sounded so sweet.

"Goodbye, word jockeys," says Hack. It's time to say goodbye if goodbye makes it. They are huddled behind a line of sandbags near the edge of the airstrip. "Don't ride away all weepy. Don't get sloppy with little details, like who's winning and losing. Keep it simple… Marines happy with a chicken in every pot. One Marine and a mule. And don't believe a word I said. Under lots of pressure, lots of pres-sure."

They keep glancing at the sky, listening for incoming and for the C-130 that will carry them out of there. It's been quiet for a while, but with the exception of waiting on top of the ammo dump, this feels like an earthquake central about to happen. Finally, it appears, cutting through the grayness, swinging down fast under a 400-foot ceiling.

One part of Jim wants to stay and grind it down and bleed it out with the Marines, and the rational part says that if he stays he might not be around to write the first part. He watches their bird leveling off now, touching down, and so far no boom-boom. He picks up his pack and an AK-47, a gift from Ox ("Just write something good about my boys") wrapped in a blanket and tied with tent rope.

"Time to egress, gentlemen..." advises Hack. "Go..." he gives them the thumbs up "and sin no more. Move with alacrity.'

The plane taxis along. Two dirty newsmen and six dusty Marines step forward briskly, eyes fixed on the 130 that keeps rolling. They begin to trot. Jim turns for a look back, another moment of defiance. *And then with good conscience and honor one can fall back from the battle,* he remembers from something somewhere. At least he's got the falling-back part down. Or does he? Interrupting the reverie, *bum bum bum,* a burst of machine-gun fire whacks up dust in front of the plane still slowing to dump its load. He sees several Marines and correspondents jumping out the back. Then across the strip, the shells start blowing in again. One, two, three. Each closer. The guests arriving and departing dash past each other, exchanging unhealthy vibes. Bad here, *bad.* The 130 keeps rolling. The ramp starts to lift but the loadmaster leans out, waving them on. More shells whistling in, closer. They are wild dogs chasing their ticket out. They are moving with alacrity. Catching up finally, the pack goes plunging, kneeing, finger nailing it up the spinning, lifting rollers. Trailing the pack, Jim lunges to grab onto something and smacks his cheek against the rifle butt of the Marine scrambling ahead.

Inside now, hearing explosions outside, Jim buckles up in the parachute seat next to Donlan. He glances over at the haggard, dusty faces across the aisle, all listening for fate, with nowhere to duck and nowhere for cover. A couple of them look about to pop, tensing for the next big burst. The plane guns forward. They hear thumps outside and sounds like sledgehammers banging metal. They feel their bird bumping and shuddering all over. But then it's off the ground. It's climbing and groaning, scudding as straight up as it can go in a big-bellied tremble toward the sky.

After the furious rising, they begin to level off, riding free on top of the world, slipping off the death masks. The Marines look like Marines again. Jim remembers to rub his cheek. Donlan raises his canteen and cracks his bloody little smile. The chosen ones have ascended.

Back at the DaNang press camp, it is difficult for some of the latest, rushing up from Saigon correspondents, marinating in doom vibes, visualizing ghastly red carpets of Marine corpses, to accept Donlan's less-than-apocalyptic analysis. "Well, we went in under fire and we came out under fire. Otherwise, it was not always unpleasant except for a few thousand incoming shells and stressed-out rats."

Don't try to understate it, they urge. Give it to them straight, they urge. Okay, he gives it to them straight, Khe Sanh seems very defendable. It doesn't look like American Dienbienphu after all. The Marines just have too much big-time air and artillery support, like the French did not.

A couple of the more dedicated doomers exchange exasperated looks. Perhaps Donlan is seeing the battle through his rose-colored cognac, or Khe Sanh has sat his and Jordan's dirt-gummed heads too long. For his part, Donlan believes that once a doomer decides on what the story should be, and this one clearly reeks of the intoxicating perfume Dienbienphu II, that's got to be the story.

"I think they'll make it through," Donlan says finally, scratching something small and dark and possibly animate out of his hair. "Of course, anything could happen."

After flying back to Saigon, the shellshock suspects plan to write Khe Sanh as straight as they can when their ears stop ringing. And then, in perky contrast, so that Mac and Muffie back home do not have to swallow too many loose guts and broken brains with their morning cakes and coffee, record how Saigon observes the beginning of the new year, that festive time known as Tet.

With the Year of the Sheep nearly shorn, now swinging into view comes the time of the exciting and often mischievous Monkey, known to get along with the Rat although not compatible with the Snake.

They Went With Songs to the Battle

Forward, gentlemen, to the war! He went joyfully singing toward his ultimate adventure.

Here was the just cause, the shining quest at last. He was ready, so eager to meet Fate in a most stirring joust. How wondrously challenging it all seemed. How absolutely the right thing to do, this half joy of living half readiness to die. The very sound of it was so loaded with mystery that his creative juices went volcanic. Going to Gallipoli. The very sound of it.

"Do you think," wrote the warrior poet, "perhaps the fort on the Asiatic corner will want quelling… and they'll make a sortie and meet us on the plains of Troy… Will Hero's Tower crumble under fifteen-inch guns? Will the sea be polyphloisbic and wine-dark and unvintageable?

Shall I loot mosaics from St. Sophia and Turkish delight and carpets?"

So clang the gongs of glory, of honor. At last, he would reach the burning center, and lay his pen to the meaning of it all.

Foreign Affairs

E. Drudgington Blow stood on the balcony with one hand on hip gesturing dramatically and shouting something to the peasants below in mixed obscene languages. The Vietnamese colonel's wife below looked humiliated. Other Vietnamese gathered under the balcony looking confused and angry. The colonel's wife's face had deepened into greater grief as if about to lose that face.

"All I asked her was to come to my party," the one above shouted to those below waving fists and fingers and a broomstick. "There's nothing wrong with that even with you silly buggers, now is there? All right, I apologize, on the queen's dear hat," the grand Earl roared with laughter. "So don't come to my party. You bloody well wouldn't fit in. Consider yourself uninvited, unqualified, unworthy. So any of you other lovelies desire to come to my party?"

18
CALUMNY

Late in the afternoon at the end of January 1968, the first month of a year surely smoking up from the bowels of Hell's news factory, Jim Jordan and Sean Donlan flew back into Tan Son Nhut, squeezed into one of the ratty-tatty taxis and rattled into town. On the flight down they had heard that DaNang and other cities had been hit by the foe in violation of the truce for Tet, but how hard the hitting was unclear, they were almost too tired to care, and the reaction in Saigon to whatever was happening elsewhere reflected little alarm. Saigon reflected noisy, manic, perhaps going-insane manifestations of gaiety in streets festooned with colorful symbols of Tet, and swarming with Vietnamese banging away with fireworks as if trying to out-blast the war.

Straight out of battle, and returning suddenly to the Pearl of the Orient, could throw Jim into a bit of a contemptuous funk, and with Khe Sanh still clanging in his head, never more than now.

"Can't believe it," Donlan said, "they've started without us."

Arriving at the old yellow-walled villa he shared with others at the end of Pasteur Street, Donlan said goodbye and good sleeping, and Jim went on downtown to file his first Khe Sanh piece. He left the cab in the fire-cracking bedlam of Lam Son Square, dodged his way through Viets laughing, dancing, waving balloons, putting on dragon faces, and grinning, whooping Viet cowboys weaving and gunning dizzily through the merry mob on motorbikes. There was a war not far away but in these wild streets, no one seemed to hear it except Jim in his head.

As he made his way through the crowd in his fatigues, stained reddish with the battle crud of Khe Sanh, spotted with other people's blood, with his scowling face bruised and hairy, carrying his shrapnel-gashed pack and AK rolled up in the dirty blanket, he looked like a most wretched reminder of life beyond the pearl. The sight of the celebrants made Jim feel just really out of sorts with the ways of the East, and the sight of him might have made small children think of wandering demons, said to be released from Hades for seven days to roam the earth during Tet, come to fetch them away.

Reaching the Vietnamese Press Center, he trudged up the stairs and poked his head around a corner. There sat a Viet operator, alone, picking at his feet by a telex machine.

"Can send this, please?" Jim asked. "Now?"

"No, now," the operator shook his head, yes.

"Yes, now?"

"No, now, " the operator shook his head, yes, no.

"Too busy?"

"No busy. All machine brokee."

"All brokee at once?"

"Come back 'morrow. Can Do?"

"Really need to send it *now*. Number one important."

"All brokee. No can do."

"All brokee for Tet. How about you fixee?"

"Come back 'morrow. Eight…" he held up four fingers "o'crock."

Jim started down the stairs, looking even more wretched. Halfway down he encountered his old pal, the Eighth Earl, bounding upward to file his commentary on all the merry doings.

"Ah, Jim…" Eric recoiled, nose wrinkling at the fellow who smelled like burnt toast, or was it old cabbage? "is that you there, *still?*"

Jim said he thought it might be. He advised Eric that he no can file. "Come back 'morrow. Eight o'crock." They began bumping back down the stairs, Jim's pack doing the bumping..

"Longish time no see, old duck," said Eric. "Been off sightseeing again?"

"Khe Sanh. Did you make it?'"

"Ah, yes, the Khe Sanh thing. It did not sufficiently pique my interest."

They heard the revelers waving over the street and sidewalks outside, going crazy with firecrackers, chasing away the scary spirits. Near the bottom of the stairs, looking pretty scary himself, Jim suddenly felt moved to asked Eric about that certain debauched evening with Susanna.

"*Debauched?* Frankly, I'm a bit taken aback by such an interesting fantasy."

Eyes narrowing, Jim detailed which debauched evening.

"*Calumny!*" Eric looked aghast. "*Bizarro!* Nothing of note happened. I say, let's go have a drink."

They were at the bottom of the steps now. "I asked you a simple question. *What* happened?"

"It's simply insane out there," Eric peeped out. "I need a drink, um. Don't you have need of one?"

And a bloody bath, Eric thought, sniffing.

"I don't need one."

"Really, old cockatoo, after you go dunk your doughnut, we'll talk."

Jim stepped forward like a possibly rabid animal in a one-yard space. "I asked you a question."

"Thank you for asking." Eric extended his hands, palms up, a study in injured innocence. He did not look Jim in the eye, knowing better than to look a wild creature in the eye. "Ah, what a delightful colloquy. My lead to this story is a simple declarative sentence. Perhaps, I saw her. It's that female thing inside her. Ergo, to be seen. But may it please the court, of what am I accused? Did I haw when I should have hemmed? Pray, tell me you have not been seduced by gossipy Dame Rumor."

"So *what* happened?"

"Let me be clear, firstly, I cannot be certain of all details," said Eric. "I think… that is, I do not think, yes, um. Secondly, this was in the dimmy past. Dear gawd, that noise. I've been under great strain, you know. Thirdly, I'm a bit fuzzy on that. In other words, having said that, and not to repeat myself, in other words, um, to be completely honest, this much is clear, I will speak to that. Um, yes, quite frankly, what is a journalist? *I* am a journalist. One could say so, um, so there you are."

"*Here* I am. So what *happened?*"

"Let me be more perfectly clear, friend student, quite frankly, what happened was — yes, it comes back to me a shade now — I stopped by on a perfunctory Red Cross matter, some tiresome business, and she invited me, not at my behest, into her digs. Such a fine lass of rare and formidable qualities."

"In a sentence of simpleton English… *what happened?*"

"Simple is not my style, though I will recast my sentence if it exceeds 75 words. Continuing on, don't you feel it, she has a terrifyingly mystical power of seduction. All the lass has to do is wave those famous legs and what's a poor laddie to do? Such endearing modesty, not like some hot-garter Gertie who spends hours pretying herself up to look irresistible but not, heavens forbid! seen as a carnal object. Yet, who can divine what mysterious code she's sending? From the power position, fixing those *eyes* on you, um, as if lusting to be lusted over? It's a female thing. I almost gave up smoking trying to decode her mixed messages. It is clinically proven that the female brain, ah, sweet mystery, is like thinking through a cup of hot chocolate with three marshmallows on top. And that *look.* That *look.* Cleopatra had that *look.* You *know* it. Naughty but imperious. Inviting yet off-putting. That bloody *look.* Incomparably attractive, yet teasingly distant. You know how these super seductresses are shaped and programmed to prey on vulnerable males. How's a laddie supposed to react? And what say?"

"Say what the hell *happened?*"

"Do not unfriend me, friend student. I am entertaining your excellent question. First of all, and by the way, to be perfectly honest, let me be clear, the dear sweet savage imbibed one or two. You know what *that* means. Her head, her heart, her sexual doo-dah murks over. She speaks in strange tongues like, Don't look at my glorious chest like that. *Don't.* All right, *look.* Why aren't you *looking?* And then slides those burning legs around. Am I some blind ruddy priest? You know, I once considered priesthood. But then came misfortune's this and that, and my priestly ambitions were diverted."

"Diverted priest, nothing creates heartburn like listening to you wringing a chicken's neck out of poor clucking truth."

"How now? I don't entirely gather your meaning. But I plunge too far ahead. No. I did not pat the supplicant on the head and bless her. Yes. I may have misremembered an unfact or two. But trust me. I speak absolutely truthfully in that I say what I intend to say. I say I behaved in a most priestly manner and am puzzled by all this Puritan foofaraw. Aren't we good mates sharing the womb of war together?"

"I'd sooner..." Jim thumped his pack down, doubled a fist, "share it with a stinking trench rat I slept with recently." Even a cornered rat will fight, he thought, but not E. Drudgington Blow.

"*Trench* rat? That smells of cruel Dame Rumor. I do not accept such defamatory algorithms. You are assuming facts not in evidence. Is it merely because this is super-blood-moon-end-of-the-world Sunday? If so, I'll confess tomorrow. *Haw!* But in fairness, even Beelzebub is innocent until proven guilty. Only decent thing to do. To be even more perfectly clear, firstly, lastly, tweenly, nothing of note happened. My feelings for the lass may be too complex for primitives to grasp. But let's not get all cobby-wobbly over this. I did not, technically, lay a meaningful hand on her person, *per se,* even if she incites poor lads to sexual riot. On my honor, the awful truth is, we had a taste of wine, white, non-sparkling. Or gin? Or was that another gentle lady? I'm a tad fuzzy on that. And a lemon biscuit. But let me plunge ahead. Let me contextualize. Let me recalibrate. On my honor, after a moment of confusion, we wished each other warm, respectful adieus and proceeded with our normal duties."

"Would you regurgitate that about your honor...slowly? "

"Um. Another excellent question. Let me answer that in eight parts. On my blood oath, on my Englishness, I'm as sure of that as I am practically anything virtually. My conscience gleams. And yours? I gathered you had given the bi... ah, your sainted inamorata up. So why the truculence? Would you turn me into a smoking lump outside the fuehrer-bunker because I exchanged a few words with your exalted lass? So there, um... I have explained it, with multitudinous clarity. A sweeping summary of a minor non-incident with rhetorical proximity to the truth. Now don't be a wag. Remember, henceforth, that your sources be worthy. Treat Dame Rumor with the contempt the sly old hag deserves."

Outside a string of firecrackers, a half-block long went ripping off, making a continuation of the delightful colloquy unhearable. Scooping up his gear, knocking his pack against his womb-mate, Jim strode out into the maze of smoking fireworks and dancing dragons.

"Well, cheerio and piss off, trumpets tooting," Eric addressed Jim's vanishing back. "Go hose your foul self down. Get medicated for lice. *Hoot! Hoot!*"

Well, poor devil's gone off the boil again, he thought. Isn't he aware that the aroused bull moose will attack anything messing with his cow, even a locomotive? Well, I'm done with his cow, what? She was party pastry, a dimwitted surf, a female well-digger. And how dare *he* joust with *me* in semantic swordplay. That is up something with which I will not put, *haw*. Fight on my turf, molasses-sopper, I'll CRU-CI-FY you, and you will be dispatched to the monosyllabic bog from which you failed to evolve, without your cornbread and rubber ducky. And without pity, pip, pip.

"Out of my way, coming through, miserables!" he commanded, pleased with another exhibition of gallantry under fire as he marched, escutcheon unstained, pitilessly into the merriment, pip, pip.

2:36 a.m. Monkey Revolution: Not a Zoological Event

The year of the Monkey will
Effervesce with the unexpected

— Old Vietnamese calendar

"The sons of bitches are everywhere!"

— American soldier

"Hey, bad boy. Why you no come see me?" It was the perfume machine, Gidget of Wunderbar, laying on hands. Wrestling clear, Jim made it up to his place.

"You betta no buttafly me, crazy 'merican," Gidget called up, "or I send you to monkey house."

"This is the monkey house."

"Then I drive you more crazy."

"It's a short drive."

He wrote for a couple of hours, struggling to impose the mood music of Marines under fire at Khe Sanh over the wham-banging Moon Over Miami below. The Moon was noisy but lacked Khe Sanh's big heat. From a head full of no sleep and bitter fog, he had the battlefield blues, throwing out dyspeptic paragraphs about Americans dying in another epic defense in a land trying to drown it all out with dragon faces and firecrackers.

Fingers still twitching, he fell into bed, but couldn't stop listening to the bedlam in his head and outside and below. An hour later, he phoned Donlan and asked if there might be a spare rubber room for a refugee from Din Bin Foo?

"Bring cognac," yawned Donlan.

Again, escaping the clutches of the ever-preying Wunderbar, he managed to find a taxi out to Donlan's, and broke like a brick into sleep on a bed in the villa behind a faded yellow wall with a big iron gate. In the field, a snapping twig could bring him to red alert. In Saigon, he could rock himself to sleep to the soft thunder of distant artillery. Suddenly, it seemed neither soft nor distant. Half awake, he thought he only dreamed he was out of Khe Sanh. The thunder came clap-clapping again. He rolled out of bed. Down on the floor in a tangle of sheet, he looked up to see Donlan standing in the doorway in his shorts, tripping on adrenaline at 3 o'clock in the morning.

"Let's go! Let's rock!"

"I'm rocked out. What the hell?"

"And plenty of it. Let's get to the roof."

Donlan had already made a fast phone call to JUSPAO. But this wasn't supposed to be in the cards. "It's not in the cards," an authoritative MACV source of intelligence had briskly assured the two correspondents in a private briefing in early January. They had queried about captured documents in which Ho Chi Minh called for the "final victory," for massive synchronized assaults throughout the South, and for a glorious general uprising of the people. The briefer of numbers and graphs, aiming his pointer at illustrative fever charts, all favorable if it were a business cycle, had waved off such language as just more propaganda. And chuckled.

"To keep his spirits up. He knows he'd get crunched if he tried anything big. He'll keep nickel-and-diming us until he runs out of small change. Don't sweat it too much, gentlemen."

Smacking his pointer against a chart, here, there, and there, the officer of intelligence stressed how the Americans had largely turned over the defense of Saigon to the ARVN, the South Viets, as a mark of confidence, to show how well things were going. "So," briskly assured the officer of intelligence, with a punctuating smack on a chart, "it sounds sexy, but hardly the hot stuff you're looking for, gentlemen." There were knowing little laughs followed by a thank you or two for the latest cool intel.

Now the correspondents not laughing in their shorts rushed to the roof, the stuff getting hotter with every step as wrecking ball explosions sounded from the heart of the city. Up on the flat roof garden, a shadowy figure dashed about nude except for his flip-flops and transistor radio from which blared the news. Here came the news: *"Ooo ahh! Betty Ann's in town tonight... Ooo ahh! Betty Ann's in town tonight... Ooo ahh! Betty Ann's in town night... Ooo ahh!"*

And then a voice weighed in with commentary. "An important word about your feet. No matter where you are, from the Delta to the DMZ, keep those dudes clean and dry. Rotate those boots and change those socks once a day. Twice a day if you're out in the boons." Foot wisdom was soon lost in the sounds of more thunder not far away in the streets. They saw explosive fireballs over Cholon, the Chinese section of the city, the sky turning into a glowing red smear.

"Wheee, wooww!" whooped the naked man, flapping around, "I hope they blow this whorehouse town off the face of the earth!"

From several directions now came the rattle of small-arms fire. They saw tracers ricocheting hundreds of feet into the air and flares beginning to ring the city. Then so close down that they couldn't hear the whoops of the naked one, a U.S. gunship came fanning over, rotors whapping red lights winking as it went round and round over them like a mad firefly on a string before rushing off across the rooftops.

"Thought we were bad guys," Donlan said. "About to hose us down. Stay here, be back in a sec."

"I swear I still hear firecrackers," Jim groaned. "Damn firecrackers."

After more fast phone calls Donlan returned. "Not firecrackers. Looks like they're hitting the whole damn country!"

"Wheee," sang the naked man running around in the dark.

"Haven't filed Khe Sanh yet," Jim said. "Haven't even…"

More explosions flamed up, these toward the American embassy a couple of miles away.

"Christ! Let's get going," Donlan said.

Hurrying downstairs, throwing on clothes, grabbing notebooks, running outside, they heard shots close by the villa like whips snapping. Just then a bunch of American airborne on foot came bursting through the front gate yelling, boots tromping, waving guns, psyched up, way up. A truck packed with more airborne barged in after them. Some of the troops jumped out and positioned themselves along the yellow wall. Others tossed sandbags off the truck, quickly set up a machine-gun emplacement just outside the gate, and crouched down, pumped up, ready to fire, behind their big 50 big caliber.

"Who's out there?" Jim grabbed the shoulder of a hurrying soldier.

"VCs and NVA. Shooting up the town's all I know. We just got here."

It seemed that his platoon was one of the first American units to come racing back to Saigon.

"Snipers down the street there," the soldier said, jabbing his finger to the left along the narrow street running parallel to the villa wall. "You two better get back inside. Better…"

Now his platoon sergeant hurried over.

"What's going on down Pasteur?" Donlan asked.

"Can't tell," said the platoon sergeant. "Who're you?"

"Press. Looks like they're hitting the embassy, and we need to get down there."

They all knelt behind the sandbags next to the gunner. The gunner pulled back on the cocking lever of the fifty, aiming into the shadows of the little street where the snipers were supposed to be, where nothing visible moved. They peered down big, wide, dimly-lit Pasteur, running from the town center and dead-ending at the villa gate. Nothing moved on the street except reflections from the Saigon sky thumping and flashing.

"Sergeant," urged Donlan, "please tell your guys not to shoot us. We're heading down Pasteur. Gotta get to get to the embassy."

"Better think about it," said the sergeant. "Might get wasted."

"Got wasted last week," Donlan said.

"Wasted," Jim said

"All right. Move fast and low," warned the sergeant. "Don't know what's down there."

"Thanks," said Donlan. "All set, Jim? Let's move."

They got off their knees and ran low across sniper street, then fast into the shadows of the high wall running beside Pasteur and by big spreading tamarind trees along the sidewalk, and at every step time watching for VC or NVA or trigger-happy ARVN or Americans or anyone who felt ready to shoot them.

Jesse James was on his horse again, galloping out of the *schweinehund* of Khe Sanh that had briefly curled him up inside in the coldest corner of his psyche. Whether the passionate pursuit of the story had again crossed the line of carefully calibrated good judgment was again ignored. There seemed no time to carefully calibrate anything; they were smoking and had already crossed the line of good sense so many times that they never spoke of it anymore and never wrote about it, it wouldn't have been cool back in the land of theory and propriety. They made it up as they went along and went forward with what seemed renewed ferocious energy, or perhaps just more sleep deprivation.

They heard plenty of firing ahead, and then the sound of movement behind, coming toward them slowly, ridiculously... putt-putting out of the shadows, an old motorbike driven by a young Vietnamese under a baseball cap, the only mover on the street and looking not very sinister.

After a quick consultation — screw it or do it — they stepped from behind a tree. They waved their hands. The Viet slowed. He didn't shoot them. He smiled under the cap as if it was routine to pick up strangers in the roaring dark. With a slight bow, he granted their request to give them a lift toward the big noise. He might be an enemy strapped with plastique, and late to the attack, but at least heading in the right direction. So they climbed on, and thus locked onto one another puttered down deserted Pasteur toward the racket to their front.

"Thong Nhut," Donlan said. "We go Thong Nhut."

Thong Nhut was a wide boulevard and they soon reached it, slowly turning left toward the embassy. A block to the right, near the presidential palace, they saw a dim figure, a Viet in civilian clothes, moving at a walk from the park across from the palace, then suddenly dashing toward the palace gate swinging what looked like a satchel charge. It was a satchel charge.

Just then an American military police jeep came screeching up and stopped 20 yards from the Viet, who veered and ran straight toward the jeep firing a pistol. Two MP's stood up in the jeep firing M-16's *brrrp brrrp*, muzzles jerking, whole magazines gone in a blink. The Viet sprawled. Then from a bush in the park a rifle-propelled grenade came flashing. It blew the jeep sideways, blew the MP's out, dumping them near where the dead VC lay in the street.

Now their bike driver whipped hard left. Heads low, holding on tight, the three sped up Thong Nhut toward the embassy under attack a few blocks away. Getting light now. They heard gunfire rattling, and saw tracers burning back and forth over and around the embassy.

"*Dung lai!*" Donlan snapped, grabbing the driver's shoulder. Stop! Stop!"

The driver braked, and they hopped off, thanking him profusely. Jim stuffed some piasters in his hand. The Viet nodded under his baseball cap, leaned over his handlebars, and scootered off, away from Thong Nhut.

"Who was that son of a gun?" Jim muttered.

"One of ours, I hope. Hell, who knows? Let's go."

They moved forward in a trot. A block ahead, they saw American soldiers crouched in front of the high white wall surrounding the embassy. Tracers, reds, and greens, ripped in, ripped out. Now, running, shoulders hunched as if in blowing rain, they reached an MP jeep mounted with a machine gun. The jeep blocked the sidewalk about 50 yards from the beginning of the wall. An army ambulance, blood-splotched back doors swung open, sat catty-cornered to the curb beside the jeep.

"How's it going?" they asked, moving in and crouching beside one of the MPs.

"How's it going? Well, besides getting shot at and fucking dead people all over and dumbass questions, it's going just fine. Who're you?" The MP was a big guy with two big bottom teeth protruding out of his gums and a face like a scowling hippopotamus under great stress. The other MP, a small blondish fellow, told them that Viet Cong sappers, commando types, had blown their way through the embassy wall and were fighting inside the compound.

"How many?" asked Jim.

"About twenty maybe. Not sure."

"Did they take the main building, the chancery?" asked Donlan.

"Can't tell. Wild up there. Keep your head down."

"I asked who're you guys anyway?" Hippo wanted to know.

"Press." Donlan said.

"Better beat it out of here. This ain't no jack shit press party."

"Are they inside the chancery?" Donlan persisted.

"What's a chancery?" Hippo scowled. "What difference it make?"

"Makes a difference," said Donlan, trying to determine just how far the VC worm had penetrated the heart of the American apple.

Something was playing inside Jim's head, some stupid little song… *Fifty-nine bullets in yo head… bing, bang, bung and still not dead.* Strange things in his head at strange times. He half stood now, as if to go forward.

Hippo grunted. "Where're you going? There's snipers on the roofs, shooting dumb shits like you.

"Dumb shits have to get closer," Donlan said, peering ahead. "Much closer."

"Get caught in a crossfire too. Be back in a meat wagon just as quick too. Wind up in a body bag too, a used one. This ain't no jack shit! You be crazy? Gonna get wasted."

"Got wasted last week. Khe Sanh," Donlan said. "This be fun."

"Wasted," Jim said.

Donlan gave Jim the look. And for that moment Jim felt almost bulletproof. They said thanks and so long to the MPs, and were up sprinting the half-block along the embassy wall, then on through the busted-open front gate toward the uncertain heart of the American presence.

Bulletproof or not, when the shout came, "Sniper! Sniper!" They ducked. Hit the gravel and crawled up behind one of the big white pillars of the chancery. They lay flat on their bellies peering around the bullet-pocked pillar. Then a burst of gunfire, then another, and they jerked their heads back.

Rising above them was the six-floor white chancery building with the once-ornate, now-battered concrete rocket screen. Just behind them, three VC sappers lay dead in a bed of gravel.

The sapper a few feet from Jim, missing the top of his head, showed bits of his brain like coffee grounds spilling out. The sapper beside that one had his crotch shot up. Blood was spattered up the side of the chancery. The sappers wore civilian clothes with red armbands. More of their dead lay humped on the lawn and sprawled beside the big white concrete-enclosed flower beds. Grenades, rockets, AK's and ammunition were scattered across the bloody grass.

It was nearly over now. Twenty or so sappers had blown their way through the eight-foot-high embassy wall with plastique, killed a couple of MP's guarding the side gate, taken up positions behind the flower beds, and began shooting the shine off the symbolic center of the American presence. The sticking point was that they could not make it through the chancery's three-inch-thick teakwood front door. They had blasted away at it, wounding one of the Marine guards inside, but the big door did not swing open. A rocket had whacked a hole in it, but the door refused to open.

Another Marine guard had crouched, pistol in one hand, shotgun in the other, behind the lobby's reception desk waiting for the worst, but the worst couldn't break in. With daylight coming on, MP's more combative than Hippo had counter-attacked in force, crashing through the locked front gate with a jeep and swarming in behind it shooting.

Not far behind came Jim, Donlan, and other warriors of the media charging the shootout at the embassy corral. It ended when a retired American colonel turned diplomat, waiting with a grenade on the second floor of the villa behind the chancery, faced the last sapper still fighting.

At the bottom of the stairs, wounded, red-eyed from tear gas, the last sapper raised the muzzle of his AK and started up the stairs firing.

Just outside, a red-faced young MP from whom Jim was eliciting fast quotes (*"I killed nine, ten myself! Got one on that wall there, two, three more over there! Excuse me a second"*), turned and ran toward the gas-floating villa. Stopping, he pitched a .45 and a gas mask up to the diplomat-turning soldier again, who caught them leaning out a side window. Inside, the sapper wobbled upward, ripping off AK bursts. Seconds later came another eruption of gunfire. The last comrade had missed. The old colonel, firing point blank, hit the target of his life.

Smoking drama, historic, no hook required, no hype, no word jazz needed. Jim made it back to his place over the Moon Over Miami and rapped out the eyewitnesser. He was in that furious focus again, words leaving his fingers like grasshoppers leaping onto the typewriter keys with the missing "n" so that it came out... "The Viet Cog made their boldest attack of the war today..." And got the story telexed along with the first Khe Sanh piece, the second missing in action somewhere. He noticed that The Moon Over Miami was all shut up, the first time it had ever shut up for anything, the Viet Cogs apparently not good listeners. Even Gidget was gone. Mia was missing.

Donlan picked up a car at his office and he, Jim, Francois, and then, in his guts-and-glory safari outfit, here came Eric cramming in with them, and they all sped forth to cover the fighting. Tet was cooking up the whole country and Saigon was the biggest weenie in the roast. Beyond the embassy, there was fighting around the palace, along the river, at the race track, in alleys, pagodas, the cemetery, the radio station, Tan Son Nhut, and plenty of hot stuff blazing up over in Cholon.

"What's Eric the Blow doing here?" Jim muttered to Donlan as Eric settled in back with Francois. "Said he's going to commit an act of actual journalism," Donlan said, revving the engine. "Thinks this is the Bolshevik Express. Said he needs a spot of revolution to top off the morning."

Jim carried his AK wrapped in a blanket, a map of Saigon, binoculars, and a can of potato chips. He slipped the AK under the front seat.

"What's that you're carrying there? Lunch?" asked Eric.

Jim winked at Donlan. "You're with the VC-for-lunch bunch. Can you handle it?"

"Testing my mettle, are you?" Eric said. "I assure you, friend student, I can handle anything you can handle. I'm feeling right frisky, thank you. Stand and deliver, cads. Your story or your money."

Donlan carried a snub-nosed .38 caliber revolver, but Eric, who had not made it to the action at the embassy, did not know that either. The haphazardness of war, of covering basic shoot and bleed, had finally cornered the eighth earl. Though reporting from the terrace of the Continental was his war of choice, Eric felt in cracking good form, brimming with snappy chatter, cheerily up for the scrum.

Courage, oh, flighty floozy, no more hiding of eyes when old man Boom-boom comes calling. If rogue specimens like Jordan and Donlan were so drawn to it, so could he, by gawd. Though an absolute terror on the typewriter, he was a late, late bloomer to this sort of thing. What did he know? Well, everything. He imagined himself a great pointer, nose majestically uplifted, sniffing the wind for the action. He felt suddenly gluttonous for glory. He saw himself storming the beaches of Normandy.

Astride Napoleon's horse, though not in the snow. He was the crouching cat, pouncing on the Defining Story of the War — the Yunkie *Gotterdammerung* — that his prescience had divined. Delusions of grandeur? *Phaw*. He thought not. Enough of this feckless codswallop. A dash of irony, a bucket of blood is all it took, and he would show these popguns what the corresponding of war was all about. He would show them what the House of Blow under fire was made of, by gawd.

How bracing, he thought. Many are called, few are chosen. I shall write in glowing mixed metaphor. *The will of hot-dog America, pure cur at the core, crumbled like a stale crumpet today and slunk whimpering from the field, tails drooping while wee-weeing their knickers as they fled. Bring our poor rotters home, squealed the mob from Mickey Mouse land. Hoot! Hoot!* So they're the toughest blokes in the pub, as long as it's a tiny pub full of puss 'n boots, *haw. But now the people's cock is a crowing. The VC fox is in the henhouse. Comedown time for the uppity Colonials. Tallyho!* Of such were his thoughts.

"Well, gents, let us poke our schnozzles straightaway into the fray and witness *people's war*. And isn't it fine how easily they liberated the embassy of the American imperium with its big, bald, and, extremely ugly eagle? Accept my condolences. Ba boom, ba boom. Bang on, boys, I'm on fire."

"All your *peoples* liberated was the lawn," Jim said. "Yard work. Damn flower pots. And couldn't keep those. You've been swallowing too much red belly wash."

"*Au contraire*, friend student," chirped Eric. "My sources, dead-bang accurate, say otherwise. Say took it all over. Gobbled it all up. Floor by cheesy floor. And all the denying bats in your belfry can't change reality."

"Bologna, bologna," Jim snapped. "Eric has insider sources, close to the war from a distance, in all the bars. You see them in full combat gear interviewing each other at the old comrades' club."

"Which are superior to your bloody apes swinging from trees. Still, you have to admire little blokes who can wheel off a cartful of scrap iron one day, and next day bring back machine guns to take over the mighty imperialist embassy. Lads who are given two rockets and a bicycle and told to go kill Yunkie tanks. Almost too marvelous for words. And that's a fact."

"That's bologna," Jim said

"I say it's a fact. That is definitely a jolly fact. A fact that jolly is."

Ahead now, they heard rattling gunfire, saw American and ARVN troops moving, saw roadblocks and sandbagged positions being hastily set up. They drove on toward the big fighting in Cholon, blasts of smoke, billowing black and gray-red in the distance.

"So we're off to capture the beauty of scenic Cholon," Eric chirped. "Perhaps, too, we can locate a bite of lunch."

Untethered from fright, the eighth earl was soaring higher than the smoke, feeling the thrill of imposing his personal imprimatur onto the battlefield. Because no one would or could *dare* write it as he would. Because he now saw himself as not just another bloodless, chair-bound, big–think, frozen-mackerel, smoke-without-guns word master. Because he had viscerally evolved. He was now an on-the-scene writing machine. Indeed, the guts of the story, in blazing color, were already written in his head, all he needed were a few more quasi-profound nouns and catchy, juiced-up verbs, adjectives were easy.

"Just keep your dead-bang eyes open," Jim said.

"Right-o. Scold me if my eye-witness discourages you. Even with them closed, can one doubt that friend Bubber here is 100, no, 500, no make that 1776 percent swooning, slobbering Old Glory, by gum, by cracky. Won't say red-blooded because he'd warn us to beware of the *Red* baddies of the interplanetary criminal *Red* conspiracy lurking out here in evil *Red* commie land, by gum, by cracky. Why is he here? To stalk the *Red* devil. He sees *Red spots* staring at him from the stars. *Reds* swimming about buck nekkid in the deep blue sea. He sees phantasmagorical Reds flaying in his bath water. Well, he can get away with that barbaric yawp writing for the beer-swilling bubs and bimbos huddled in their sheep-think back in the bowling alleys and *pissoirs* of his provinces. Whereas, I, more discerning, refuse to tell the rabble what they want to hear."

Jim turned and sliced at Eric's throat with a potato chip. "*Pissoir* on that. You forgot General Giap, the *Red* Napoleon."

"The fact of the matter is," Eric went on, "I know the subject much better than you. I know the noble Cong. I know their true heart."

"His discernments suck, but he knows Cong heart," Jim said. "He sings Cong love songs."

"We'll see whose discernments are suckable, old sweetheart, and whose fierce objectivity has drawn intergalactic praise. The fact is, readers who seek truth beyond bowling alleys trust me."

"Truth, " Jim groaned, "sliced, diced, dismembered, and repackaged as forget-me-not Commie crap."

If truth was the first casualty of war, objectivity seemed the blind, stumbling wounded of war coverage, he thought, and he knew he wasn't the steadiest bloke himself.

They kept hacking at each other, even as the gunfire grew louder. Listening to this, Francois was nonplused. Not a word on Susanna had passed their lips, but Donlan knew how far it went beyond differing passions on the war, as differing as they were. Jim practically snarled, and the words of Eric wrenched from his throat like London phlegm. And he was having a ball.

"*Mein gott!*" He slapped his knee. "Bub here sounds like my old roommate, Kaiser Wilhelm the

Second, assuring the Better Business Bureau that victory is near, strudel production way up, death of schnitzel down. Oh, how the fog of this scurvy war foozles you all. It seems that Uncle Sam, lost in clouds of glory dust past, went to the well once too often and fell in. *Hoot! Hoot!*"

Now they worked their way down side streets in the Volks. Some streets running wild with new refugees. Others empty, too empty, ominous, suddenly erupting with bursts of automatic fire, blowing smoke, then empty again.

"Here it starts," Donlan said softly. They backed up, circled around, not wanting to get caught in a crossfire. It was like chasing fires in a forest, break out here, flame up there. Hard to know which street to go down. For Jesse James it was old Dodge City, looking for the white-hats and black-hats at every corner.

"Enough Tweedledum, Tweedledee! Push on to the fray!" exclaimed Eric, with rising fearless inflections. "We don't want to play catch-up. You news' suspects are wasting valuable time."

"Valuable time may be wasting you in a few minutes," Jim said.

But Eric was feeling at the top of his game, at the prospect of actually physically linking up and exchanging views with the People's Army, the terrible swift justice of the valiant liberators. He needed photo ops. He needed to look the part of his transformed intrepidity. Fight or flight was no longer in question. He now thought of himself in the third person. *Bulldog Blow of Britain. Blow the nonpareil.* Indeed, he seemed to be evolving on the spot. Who could prove he had not led men into battle before, reincarnations ago?

"Do I detect hesitation here?" shouted the reincarnated at the back of Donlan's head. "Push on!"

After pushing on and passing some of the valiant dead, bleeding, and butt-shot, Eric's élan cooled a bit. He decided to stay with the Yunkies until he could determine how things were shaking out. I'll not go wobbly, he vowed. Me knickers refuse to dampen under pressure. So take cover old life of the mind, I am passing into a bold new phase. Which I swear to by all that's edible on the queen's dear hat.

They had reached a dangerous section of Cholon now, catacombed with alleys and packed together shanties and winding narrow passageways full of menace and shadows. The Viet Cong had set up command posts in there. When the newsmen pulled up, an American company commander, gritting his teeth as he glanced skyward, told them he was nearly out of ammo and did not want to commit his men further until he was resupplied and could get his worst wounded out.

His new battalion commander, however, a few days in country, kept aggressively circling above in his command helicopter and urging him to push forward, *pronto.*

"You're good to go! Pursue the enemy! Spray the area! Quit pussying around! Finish the attack!"

"Be advised can't do that, Six," radioed the captain. "Have no problem attacking, but we badly need ammo, and have to get our bad wounded out first. Over…"

"Urnghkh… bzzz… Crank it into gear, captain. Nothing down there. I can see it from here. Don't drag it out. Say again, move in, spray the area *pronto*. Do you copy? Over…"

Looking up, it was possible to track the chain of command at various levels in the air. At about 1500 feet flew the new battalion commander, a light colonel, and circling over him at 2500 flew the brigade commander, a full colonel. Both were monitoring the action, but it was the commander of the battalion who kept ordering the troops on the ground to move with greater *pronto* against the invisible foe.

"Move forward!" came the command from above. "Quit jacking around!"

"I told you, Six, we're out of ammo," replied the captain. "What're we supposed to do, grind them under the wheels of our jeeps? By the way, that air strike you called in, just missed blowing us up! Over…"

"Do not hand me that bow-wow! I want you to move your men in there! Spray the area! Go wrap 'em up! Press the attack!"

"Wrong answer, sir. Just can't do that. You want me to get my men killed? We'll have to pull back. Over…"

"Denied permission to pull back! Listen, I am going to *help* you. I am going to drop a little air-to-ground persuasion. If there's anybody left in there, I'll *gas* their dead asses!"

The command chopper fluttered down and over. Cannisters of tear gas tumbled out.

"Advance! Recon by fire!" commanded the radio." Get going. That's a direct order! You know what *that* means!"

"It means you are gassing my men! You have dropped your goddamned gas on my men!

If you want this attack to go forward you will have to come down here and lead it yourself. Only you won't have anything to fight with. Over…"

"Urenghkh… bzzz… Then I'll come down and relieve you! You are relieved! Consider yourself relieved! Over…"

"So come on down and relieve me. We're waiting."

"Listen, you. I'm coming fast. That is my judgment. Because I am *giving* the orders! You are *taking* them! I am the *superior!* You are the *subordinate!* I am the..."

"Are you coming down or not?"

"Roger. *Mui pronto.* On the way. We're rolling in."

As the chopper descended, one of the captain's gas-choked troops raised his rifle and fired a couple of bursts skyward.

"Am taking fire, heavy enemy fire!" sputtered the radio. "Am in the middle of a damn firestorm up here! No way can make it down right now!"

"Does that mean I am unrelieved?"

"Yes, you are temporarily unrelieved."

"Then get off the radio! You're tying up the net!"

"Urnghkh... bzzz... guu. What's that? Say again?"

"Over. Out. Goodbye. *Ciao.* So long."

"Say again? Not reading you. What say? What say"?

Minutes later. The first little dwelling in the alleyway, packed with explosives, blew up. Then the next, and the next, and then others along the stretch the captain had been ordered to advance exploded *kaboom kaboom* and the helicopter of the colonel superior flew higher and higher *mui pronto.*

They were back in the car now. Near the western edge of Saigon refugees came fleeing all around, swarming panic, running, shouting, pointing back down the road. "VC come! VC come!"

Donlan stopped the car to form what he called his battle plan.

"Watch right, Jim, I'll watch left. They hit you, we go out my side. Hit me, vice-versa. Boots and saddles. May have to go out shooting. Everybody got that? You got that, Eric?"

"*Battle* plan?" The Blow smirk twisted as if he had bitten into a rotten spot on a pretty peach. "Boots and saddles? What are you talking about? We are not here to do *battle.* We are here to! You crazy Kamikazes!"

"Just sit back," Jim said. "Going down in flames might actually feel warm and fuzzy."

"Let me *out* of here!"

"Here… at this juncture?" asked Donlan, driving on slowly, watchfully. "Hold on back there, old Nellie. Stay put, stay low."

"Or you could seize a pedicab," Jim suggested, "and start pedaling. At six miles per hour you might make it to the Follies in time to get briefed on what you're doing out here."

"All right, push on," Eric waved a finger, "You are not dealing with bruised fruit here. I will not be intimidated. But *clearly* we are *non-combatants. Clearly* in violation of the journalistic code. *Clearly* in violation of the Geneva Convention. *Clearly* in violation of the rules of sanity. *Clearly…*"

Clearly seemed to Jim the most misused, murkiest word in the journalistic defensive lexicon.

"*Clearly,* once they get wind of our battle plan, you know they'll *di di,*" he said, snapping a magazine into the AK. "Years from now you'll think all this was funny."

"Everything's funny years from now!" Eric blurted, mouth going dry as he stared at the AK, his voice growing less lordly as the words gagged out. "You are *not* funny. You are irresponsible renegades. You are… Yes, you certainly are… And this road is fraught with danger!"

"What kind of cheese do you want with that fraught?"

"Baffoons [sic]. Some of us don't have to go around proving our manhood over and over." tate-298

"Or not proving it over and over," said Jim. *Into the valley of death rode the 600,* played in his mind.

"How faux heroic," said Eric. "In my experience a hero who doesn't know he's a hero is a hero. One doesn't speak of it. And I need a drink. "

"That's the old drinking spirit, " said Donlan. "In the fullness of time you'll recall this as just a ripping ride, dotty good fun in the countryside."

Stopping the car again, he pulled a flask of cognac from his jacket and handed it back to Eric who, eyes closed, guzzled at it.

"I don't give a toss," Eric said bitterly, eyes watering "I've had *no* lunch. Are you even aware I've a wife to think of? That people count on me?"

"A fam man," Jim offered sympathy. "He's screwing Vietnam but loves his fam. Shall we pause for high tea?"

"And I'm not at all well," Eric said. " I didn't want to mention it, but I need to be in hospital. Even steel rails wear out."

"One lump of steel or two?" Jim asked.

Curs, Eric thought, full of that moronic heathen insensitivity, with no feeling for the raging of his ulcer, the chug of his arteries, of his bladder agitation, of his circadian rhythms gone awry, and how he can feel it coming *right between the eyes.* "Heathen imperialists!" he addressed his fellow newsmen.

"As a proud imperialist, I say award this family man a Purple Flower. He's got a boo-boo on his chin," Jim stared at Eric's chin. "It looks really bad."

"You call it boo-boo," Eric touched the scrape on his chin, "but things wildly infect here. Things rot before your eyes."

"Maybe we can find you a rabbit hole and you can sit in it and shiver"

"That is dangerously dumb-dumb even for you!" shouted Eric. "I renounce our friendship."

He renounced all things having to do with idiots risking their lives covering other idiots risking death and destruction for an idiot flag and idiot country. *How did these idiots get me out here?*

Just then there came big gun racket and lots of smoke up ahead. A helicopter gunship, a Huey Hog, clattered across the road just to their front, rockets and machine guns hammering at enemy shooters on the other side. An old woman, arms full of clothes and household things, bumped against their fender and stumbled on, dropping stuff. A man clutching a pig wrapped in burlap lunged past. Then another gunship, hanging back in the sun, came diving firing ugly rocket smoke streaks 50 feet above them *shuu shuu shuu...* while its sixty gunner, harnessed to a monkey strap, swung out burping down slugs as the chopper rattled above, hot brass raining out like afternoon sun sparkles.

Out front now a VC in bloody khakis lay spread-eagled in the road, big red splatter on his chest. Donlan swerved around him but in the refugee chaos stopped the car. They saw the gunships rolling back. Scrambling out, crouching beside the car, they watched VC rockets streaking up from the smoking shanties to the left beside the road, then the wild back-and-forths of rockets swooshing from shanties on the right as the gunships came diving again.

Francois, eager for air art, stood up with his camera. He caught them buzzing almost directly over the car like a war dance of mechanical hornets, then tracked them over and up through the smoke of the exploding shanties. "*Alez!*" he shouted to the artists of creative destruction.

Eric knelt beside a wheel holding his belly, veins bulging, neck extended, pressing his hands over his mouth now as if to keep his innards from squirting out.

Trying to stand, he gagged and staggered, caved all the way down, puking.

"You all right?" Jim asked.

"Yes. I'm puking joyously."

Up the road, somebody's rocket blew up in the middle of refugees near a truck full of pigs barging along with its horn honking and headlights shot out. The truck jerked to a stop. The driver half-fell out the door, then crawled up under the truck's front as the crazed swine, plunging out the back, went squealing and snorting back and forth in the road across the dead. Jim pulled Eric up by the collar and shoved him into the backseat. "Wipe your mouth."

Donlan ducked in and got the car going. Francois leaned out his window snapping away until a wad of bloody stuff spatted across his lens. Rambling off road, then bumping back on, they made it through a ripping crossfire that put three holes in the hood, chugged on past a stretch of burning buildings, got lost in the smoke, almost hit a smoke-blinded VC reeling along with his AK, stopped, backed up, then gunned on around and kept going until they were out in the countryside.

"Where *now?*" bleated Eric. "Is there no end to this, no end, no end? Where's the American Army? I do not feel comfortable. This is VC country!"

"Comrade does not feel comfortable meeting his comrades," Jim said. "Tell them who you are. Do some collectivist bargaining. They might not execute you right away. "

"Idiots!"

"They're just your simple people's army," Jim shouted, "with cranky Communist tendencies." "Imbeciles!"

Soon they were caught in another refugee mob, this one streaming from a village near the main road. Eric, hand over mouth, face twisted, refused to leave the car. "I reject to go!"

"You're a reporter, aren't you? So get out. Report!"

Eric rejected to get out. "Doesn't it move you at all, what I am enduring?"

Leaving the lord frozen staring out a window, the rest went over to some women on their knees rocking and wailing over fresh graves. Some graves were just big shell holes. Francois snapped men in blood-streaked raincoats wrapping up bodies and pieces of bodies with rope around bed sheets. He shot others furiously digging and then lowering collections of anatomical debris down into the holes.

As they lowered a bundle, a wailing woman at the edge, rocking on her knees, rolled herself down into the grave. The diggers pulled her out and dropped in more bundles, dead on dead, like bags of bloody laundry. A boy leaned over the bags containing the bodies of his parents and pushed down dirt with both hands, crying and pushing down dirt.

Now a woman prostrated herself before the journalists and wrapped her arms around Francois' legs. *"Troi Oi!* My God, my God! Help us!" she screamed, begging the round-eyes to save them from the liberators who kept killing them and from the big friendly shells their own militia had called in that killed everybody. Francois stared at her and whispered how *beaucoup* sorry he was. They all said they were just really *beaucoup* sorry, but that they were just journalists. Francoise got the picture of her tear-streaked face pleading up at him, and another of her dead husband face down beside the village well.

In this village there was to have been great New Year's giving of gifts and honoring of ancestors. The people had adorned their dwellings with branches from the apricot tree *(for good luck against the evil spirits),* and the white-pedaled narcissus *(more good luck),* made new clothes, stocked up with rice cakes, watermelons, and other lucky fare to make the heavens smile and sing. On this day the heavens sang only thunder.

The Viet Cong had invaded, proclaimed liberation, raised the banner of the National Liberation Front, executed the village chief, his family, and selected others. The defenders of the village had fled, hidden in the trees, and called in barrages of friendly artillery fire, driving off the liberators and puffing away the people, the houses, the gifts, the altars to ancestors, the good-luck flowers and evil-spirit repellants in black and red roaring winds.

Now villagers were packing up and trying to leave except for one old woman who vowed that where she had lived, she would die, until her people dragged her away and put her on a cart crammed with the half-alive and already dead. Nobody seemed to be uprising for liberation but everybody was getting out, had enough, Nation Building having a bad day, Liberation having a rough day, it was try-to-stay-alive day.

Francois shot the misery as fast as he could, until it was almost too much. A half-clothed mother, mouth open, eyes rolling, staggered by with her crying baby bouncing between bare breasts. Suddenly, she put the screaming baby down on the side of the road and fainted. Nearby, a girl with big dark eyes sat in the dust with nothing on but a bloody towel wrapped around her head. Her tiny, vacant-eyed sister squatted under an ox cart, dipping her fingers in blood dripping from the cart, making circles in the dust, then wiping it across her forehead. The observers of war watched bawling children, wandering dogs, squawking chickens, bucking oxen pulling carts jamming up as they maneuvered around unexploded shells in the road, on past a raggedy flag of liberation tied to a tree next to the smoking hot lumber and crumpled pink plaster of the new school the Americans had built. On the one bullet-riddled wall still standing hung a picture of the president of the Republic of South Vietnam, one eye shot out and half his nose missing.

Francois, kneeling now, aimed his camera at a woman being carried swinging in a fishnet tied to a bamboo pole. Her eyes were fixed on the man taking her picture. Part of her brain showed through her skull. Her arms and legs still moved. As she was carried past in a trot by her wispy bearded husband on one end of the pole and her son on the other, Francois lowered his camera. "Fock zis!" His concentration had broken. He had done the eyes once too often.

Piling back in the car, the correspondents snaked their way through the mad parade and kept going through clouds of smoke, dodging firefights all the way back to downtown. During Tet, this kind of travel was not unusual. They arrived in time to attend a hurried briefing at the Follies and were told, amid much heavy breathing, various facts and figures, some of them even accurate, about a war going on out there. Jim now knew two things for sure. Don't believe anything in Vietnam if you don't see it. And do not go into combat with a chicken earl.

***

"Between the stutter of machine-gun fire and the thump of rockets," wrote E. Drudgington Blow, "I rode through Viet-Cong liberated sections of Saigon today...." In fact, nothing had been liberated for long, but what a read. The man wrote doom-crackers and his London paper panted for more. Though critics would later say first reporting of the Tet Offensive represented some of the more muddled reporting in the storied history of muddled reporting, few caught in the whirlwind of attacks understood that at the time, but Eric could write the whirlwind, or what he imagined was the whirlwind. Back in his room at the Continental, however, he was not a happy whirlwind. Damn them! he fumed, stumbling bedward again. Correspondents had been brutally killed out there. *"Bao Chi! Bao Chi!* Press!"

And Eric out with the maniacs Jordan and Donlan, had come much too close himself. Hadn't the VC dunderheads understood he was rooting for them? Where was sympathy, understanding? The fools. He must repair to his sick bed.

Now he lay gray under the ceiling fan going around *snick-snick-snick.* He lay a little nauseated and sweating heavily in his underwear. He wore his underwear inside out, so unlike him. He kept remembering a particular American soldier, eyes tumbled back, the death grip on his rifle, and the way other soldiers had flung his body thumping onto a truck. He got up again and wandered around the room, then back again past his typewriter to the balcony. He had so much more to write, but couldn't keep his eyes off the fire and smoke still boiling over Saigon's rooftops. Still, he could write doom-crackers. He could write American chaos. There was such an appetite for it. Ah, where to start? Is there no end to it, no end, no end? Such were his thoughts.

It just wasn't ending quickly enough, he thought. Like berserk bandits, the brave little liberators, the surviving ones, those uncooperative pricks, were still holing up in parts of the city. He saw U.S. gunships circling ceaselessly in the sky hunting, hunting. He heard ambulances coming and going klaxons howling. There was fighting in other parts of the country, and he did not want to go back out there or anywhere. It takes a peculiar kind off son of a bitch to revel in this work, he thought, and he was not of that blood line. But the war was still in Saigon, where he had felt reasonably safe.

So why did I write it so bloody brilliantly? he put it to himself (as he wrote he could be heard . chuckling brilliantly at his brilliance). But they keep yowling for more white-knuckle drama, the shallow swine. For more bright shiny new blood, the unfeeling oafs. As if all I have to do is go out and purchase calamity off a rack to satisfy their animal spirits. One feels so used, so profaned. I'll leave that to those loose cannons with their screws popping loose, Irish Donlan and that son of a bitch of southern decadence Jesse Bonehead James.

Eric wandered around the room. Oh, how lovely to be in Singapore now, he thought, back at the old Raffles. Or Hong Kong, yes, much to do in Hong Kong. There was China to watch. Was he not at heart a great China-watcher? Had he not dashed off rousing analytical pieces on the good works of the Great Helmsman and the splendid Cultural Revolution, on the Miracle of Mao and the Great Leaps forward, indeed, on benign Communism at its people-caring, compassionate, Utopian best?

Oh, rot, he thought. Let the agrarian reforming rotters all go take a great bloody leap into their rice paddies. And leap me out of here. I can write vintage Vietnam nestled among the happiest whores in Hong Kong, leaping perspective pieces from above the battle. Will my editors buy more Hong Kong? Of course not, those Fleet Street garbage collectors. Why in a decent war like WW II I'd show the chappies what pluck was all about, by gawd. Why I could have been a great and very brave. soldier or whatever. Yes. Surely. Too bad that's over and I won't get to show them. Oh, rot.

He wandered about, thinking, imagining, trying to keep his internals from falling to pieces as he waited for the next explosive bump. He kept wiping away personal moisture. I am running rivers, he thought. Why don't these night-crawlers just crawl back to their bloody glens and bogs, hide in their spider holes and rat tunnels and eat their roots and buffalo chips until I phase out of here? I must find a convincing maneuver to ease back to London. A major family crisis? A malady most grave? Requiring my instant full attention? Of course! Even if it means one will have to ring up, actually exchange comprehensible *words* with *The Creature*. 'Tis so unfair.

His wife in London, her feminine qualities congealed into a cold fat bitter pill, as he saw it. He had first seen her at an outdoor shower at the beach, had admired how rich she was and the way the water sprinkled down her legs when she still had legs instead of beer kegs. How patiently he had watched Lady Blow's belly and mammary glands bloat, her galloping cellulite multiply as she galumphed about like a pregnant camel. How sturdily he had endured the feeding of that face in order to briefly enjoy silence noise from that mouth. How she knew his love of beauty and grown brutally, evilly *ugly,* as if to punish him.

Each time he appeared she seemed possessed by the Furies, dismissing the maid, seizing her witch's broom and galumphing about while commencing to clean things maniacally, thrashing around as if in a windstorm, mopping, dusting, crashing dishes, shoving furniture here and back there, crashing more dishes, rearranging things in vicious delight, as if vicariously flogging his very own person.

Now he pictured himself escaping to a villa on an island in the Med, nibbling grapes while floating in the brine next to that consummately shaped booby trap, the vile-tempered Susanna thing, hopefully by now chastened into a less combative mood, eager to seize the rare and wonderful chance to showcase her beauty while soothing his wounded spirit and patty-drying his tears after all he had through.

He scratched at a new mosquito bite on his rear. Hadn't he been such a grand sport about it all? He scratched more. Why did they bite him so? Was it their

unquenchable thirst for superior bloodlines? He gazed into the mirror at his beloved countenance. Were those diseased skin blotches, or gallantly-earned ma-
turity spots, evidence of smashing good character? But soft! What belly through
yonder chest bloats? Were those actual bags beneath his eyes, or minor mudslides?
He so abhorred bags. Graying hairs there? *Not* acceptable. Were those tasteless
intrusions on his classic smile lines? Was that a balding spot on his pate, or a flashlight beam? Was he coming down with saggy neck syndrome? Desperately, he
flashed the smile, those fine, once-pearly teeth. What would the Puddinghams say?
Yes, mirrors do lie. Some are kindly, some are cruel. He was at heart still one of
the beautiful people. He surveyed that princely almost Roman nose. Full marks
for his proud beak! Blow, he had to confess, had a crush on Blow. He was regaining
his dash, but restrained himself from kissing the mirror.

Now a *whummp* somewhere nearby rattled the bedside tray. Stipples of perspiration appeared around his lips. He sank back down on the bed. He was not on
an island in the Med. He was in this damn Saigon cell sweating. Hardly out of the
shower and oozing again, the sweet smell of his revered flesh rising around him
like swamp gas, the bones in his skull screaming, "This is not your venue!"

Now, back up pacing the room. He saw a lizard on the ceiling, tongue flicking
out laughter at him. A lizard laughing at an earl? That could not stand. He threw
a shoe at it. His center wasn't holding. The blood-dimmed tide was loosing upon
him. Now outside came an encroaching thump from the left, followed by crump-
ing thunder too near from the right, causing an acute saliva shortage, bad breath,
or was that a whiff of The Reaper? Was he cracking up in slow motion? He retched,
fought back another gag. His nose was running. 'Tis ever so disturbing, he
thought. I must bugger on out of here.

Now he inwardly moaned, felt frightened. He felt frightened of the birds and
the bees. Of the wind in the trees, of the glowering moon, the beastly sun. Now
he cursed the cursed Yunkies, the cursed VC. There were at least 70,000 ways to
die and having his pulverized guts scraped off a sandbag was not his demise of
choice. Still, on principle, rather than let the rotters see him slouching off into the
sunset, violins weeping, as much as he detested this ugliest of alternatives, he would
soldier on, stand like a Blow, and ring up the Creature Trying to Eat London, no

doubt hunching over her cauldron, sprinkling in spider legs and scorpion tails and calling down curses upon him, which should earn him the Victoria Cross thrice over. Why he could be at death's door, and she'd warn him not to scratch the door.

He sat on the bed and picked at his almost Roman nose. He swatted at a mosquito and got the blood-thief smack on his pillow. But it was his blood, and he felt sick at the sight of it. Indeed, no report could describe what he had been through, he thought, but as a survivor of combat, and dashing knight of the plume, and for the rule of the illuminating word, he must write on. He was Oxford. He was intimate with the Puddinghams. He owed it to world literacy and world literacy certainly owed it to him. He did not want to even imagine himself referred to as the *late great* correspondent smeared on a banana tree. He was, after all, an Eighth Earl of something once grand, and also close to the Puddinghams.

By any standard he was of mind-blowing brilliance, he thought, no cheap fame whore was he, but wasn't he owed something more? As for that Susanna beast of the blinding curves and angles, he now only drooled out of the left side of his mouth. Even if she threw herself at him in her scanties, clawing and slavering with wild unprincipled desire for his manliness, he would stand at the gate of the fortress of his conscience and turn her from the House of Blow with no mercy. *Hoot!* Of such were his thoughts.

Thus he had done his bit, and now it was only fitting for his wallowing walrus of a mate, before she caved in the ice, to do her bit. Surely, there was some creative malady that his miserable mutant who would scare Jack The Ripper back into the shadows suddenly let seize her. But now even thinking about her got him dry-mouthed and stomach churning again. 'twas ever so disturbing.

Biologic Necessity

"War is a biologic necessity of the first importance, a regulative element in the life of mankind which cannot be dispensed with... It is not only a biologic law but a moral obligation and, as such, an indispensable factor in civilization."

— Friedrich von Bernhard *(Germany and the Next War (1912)*

The Well Dead

"Those who remain after the battle are only the inferior ones, the good ones will have been killed."

— Adolf Hitler *(Near the end)*

The Story

The story, supremely challenging, and cursed, kept pulling him back and back like a spellbinding temptress sizing him up for a green plastic body bag, but he still chased her and wanted her as she smiled and sang of better times beside the blast-furnace door. Why are you here? someone asked. Having a nose for news didn't really cover it. To witness fascinating life-death struggle was part of it. To pan for that elusive gold they called the *truth* was part of it. To feel the adrenaline spike of rare adventure, to feel worthy. even noble, to test himself in the shadow of death. To find out how the story was going to end. To feel all that, you needed a war in which to sweat and bleed over and live on the absolute edge with the fighting troops in the brave tradition, Ernie's tradition. And then explain to himself one more time why he's still doing it, with half of him grown to despise it, and half drawing him on and on toward the deadly beauty whispering *"Come to me"* from the flames, and all you have to do is dance out of range as she swings open the blast-furnace door. Maybe old Ernie knew, but he didn't quite live to write it.

— A correspondent *(Near the end)*

19
THE SECOND WAVE?

As explosions rocked and gunfire echoed through the streets, near paralysis gripped Saigon. In a city swollen with fright and fleeing refugees, the civilization of elevators, cars, businesses, newspapers, and mail jerked mostly to a halt. Lights went out, food and water were hard to come by, travel by day was dicey and deadly in the dark. Martial law was declared and people shut themselves in their houses and ate by candlelight.

Unable to get to their quarters, U.S. workers slept by their desks with pistols and rifles. Correspondents running copy to cable offices at times found operators gone and doors locked. Carrying a story to be telexed late one night, Jim got slammed against a wall by shouting, trigger-happy, wild-eyed ARVN jumping out of the shadows who seemed to think he was a Russian spy just because he was carrying an AK-47. With five rifles ramming at his chest and belly he was a finger-twitch away from being dispatched as the latest friendly road kill before shouting his way out of it, waving his story in their faces, "American! You know, *American! Bao Chi!*"

Enemy 122mm rockets, imprecise area weapons, sailed in with the abandon of wild boys slinging rocks over a back fence, killing 99 per cent civilians. One morning a rocket, contrails streaming like a fat smoking cigar, crunched down into a clinic full of pregnant women and screaming babies. Soldiers, firemen, and police dug out 23 large and small bodies. Another rocket fell in front of the Saigon Cathedral behind the Madonna of Peace, knocking the nine out of the cathedral clock.

Yet another dropped on a schoolyard gate driving an iron stake 10 feet into the ground. Another snuffed out the lives of five refugees sleeping on the sidewalk by a doorway. Another made a direct hit on a taxi driven by Mr. Go, the greatest driver in all of Vietnam. That was the 32nd. The 33rd crashed into the sixth floor of the apartment building with the scenic view of the river, caving in Susanna Diane Robinson's bedroom and blowing to pieces her magic mirror. Susanna herself had exited the building 20 minutes earlier, on her way to pull emergency duty at the 3rd Field Hospital.

By the third week of the Tet Offensive, leaflets came fluttering down urging what was left of the eleven battalions of Viet Cong that had slipped into the city, to surrender. As the action in Saigon receded, non-combatants, drinks in hand, expressed rooftop oohs and ahhs from some of the higher structures while observing American air strikes and other booming pyrotechnics lighting up the nights, far enough away to dig the flashes without feeling the heat. Though still great balls of fire on

American television and front pages, the actual heat put out by the combined North Vietnamese and Viet Cong forces over the next weeks steadily diminished.

"Are you saying," pressed Pamela Dicemore, with a frantic run of fingers through her hair "that the main threat is over, that the other side is now truly *hurting?*

"What I am saying," said this stony-faced general to the packed at the Five o'clock Follies," is that the enemy is going underground, running, hiding, and is basically whipped. A fourteen-to-one kill ratio in our favor is what I'm saying. We have been, if you will excuse the expression, kicking some serious butt."

"*Hurting? Kicking butt?* Words that will never die," said Pamela Dicemore, followed by a smattering of Follies' laughter. Like last month's *hurting*, and last year's *butt kicking,* yadda, yadda?"

"Worse," replied the general. "Much worse. We believe the cream of the Viet Cong have been destroyed."

"General," persisted Pamela, " I beseech you. Everyone I know is ill, near exhaustion, and before I go entirely mad myself, can you stand up there sans the military jargon, the we're-kicking-butt hosannahs, and the peerless Aristotelian illogic of your numbers, and explain to us in a language mere English-speaking mortals can fathom, what is now the situation in the field?"

"I thought I just did," said the general. "I haven't discussed it with Aristotle, but even in Hue, where we've essentially mopped up, we've pushed enemy forces out of the cities all across the country. They came to visit but they were sent home early. There's been no uprising of the people, as called for and predicted.. The enemy has been heavily attired across the board. There is still a situation at Khe Sanh, but we feel the enemy there is also basically beaten."

"*Attrited?* you say. *Beaten?*"

"Yes. I said that."

"But is a second wave about to happen?"

"Who says a second wave is about to happen?"

"Some informed media are reporting a second massive assault from the supposedly *beaten* and *attrited* other side is imminent. With all due respect, general, are they massing for another assault?"

"Who? The media?" The general's stone showed the first crack of a smile.

"You are being very cryptic, general."

The crack widened. "Massing? No. It is more accurate to say that they are retreating in circles north, south, east and west, like a few of you folks were seen doing lately. Ha. I'm just kidding,` of course."

"In all seriousness, general, you just don't know when you've lost."

"We lost you, Pamela, but we do not lose wars. Seriously. "

E. Drudgington Blow, seated beside Pamela, leaned over whispering. "Never in the hallowed halls of flackery have I heard such nonsense. Listen to General Eyewash, that nauseous nobbler up there oozing American arrogance. Gawd, these trained assassins of the truth. These steam shovels of mendacity. Well, what can we do? I'm storming up a hot write on this one, what?"

If the confusion, and hysterics, triggered by the Tet Offensive had simmered down a bit, waiting for the Second Wave now became the spooky drama in Saigon. Jim Jordan, Sean Donlan and other correspondents had rushed up to the Battle of Hue and then down to the Mekong Delta and then back to Saigon to get a fix on things. The physical damage wrought by Tet was bad enough, but it seemed even worse devastation had occurred in the psyches of observers far and near. And now, despite the general's optimistic words, it was all about the dreaded potential coming of the Second Wave. Having painted too many rosy pictures before the arrival of the first wave, generals, even telling the truth, were not easily believed, and more likely mocked.

Whatever wave was to come, it would not wash over Pamela and Eric. They were taking leave. They had done all they could in reporting the truth, they told each other with feeling. Of course they would return, Pamela told Eric while quaffing her third gimlet with feeling, to celebrate the full liberation after the little people of the revolution had kicked the corrupting, rat-racing *Amerikan* gigantism back to the land of smothering skyscrapers and Wall Street whore houses. Indeed, agreed Eric with lordly concern, oh, absolutely. Moreover he had a few bullets left to fire at the rotters on his way out. *Hoot!*

20
THE NONPAREIL

Now the acclaimed correspondent, with his almost Roman nose up-thrust, with coat draped over a shoulder, moved there on the hotel balcony with the easy swagger of a conquering bulldog, secure in the knowledge that he was not just another all-knowing egomaniac and insatiable attention whore, while thinking of all his heart of oak had endured with such quiet dignity in his Homeric journey. Of how Fate had fired its brute broad-sides of excruciating malapropisms, driveling doggerel, and crude Americanisms. Of how deftly he had routed the word-mongrels. And how he never had need, like some hairy bozos, of strapping on his giant jockstrap and marching to the story with an actual firing mechanism. Of how, despite his principled revulsion at the whole ghastly scene, brightly he burned again and would no longer grace this nether world with his shining presence. He wished a photographer was about to picture his look of heroic ascendency.

So roll out the red carpet. It was back to Britannia in a cloud of scribbler's glory. He was in such a mood. Was it merely superficial self-adulation? He thought not. Was he ever, ever, deep down, truly daunted? He thought not. Yes, there were minor perturbations. A fever had seized him a time or two was all. But he had come through, by gawd. Who could deny that natural selection had selected a Blow to be leader of the pack! If he wasn't Big Bang man, by Jove, who *was?*

Bellying up to the railing with a fine bold snort, he assumed a triumphal stance and made inspired noises to the cheering crowd that wasn't there He thrust out his jaw. He made a fist. If he smoked cigars he would have smoked one in a show of bulldoggish Churchillian vigor. How alike he and old Churchy were, actually. Filled with ebullient optimism, he offered Saigon an animated finger. No, he was not going wa-wa, he told the crowd that wasn't there. He was re-establishing perspective. His re-established perspective was that as a highly evolved Eighth Earl his center had held together more purposefully than all the heathen lowbrow insulters of the language who had dared impede his talent.

"So fie on you, bloody Saigon! I blow you away like lint in my belly button, as I pass into a great new phase. " So his horse-ass editors had come to their senses and summoned him to London for a major, major award, *"As a nonpareil among correspondents, this daring heart-of-danger traveler, this displayer of incredible stoicism and grace under fire, and superb above-the-fray analysis, whose cool, elegant, yet harrowingly realistic prose from ground zero vaults the reader to the highest level of journalistic discipline and excellence. Indeed, his is not workaday news, his is the art of news art...."* and this and that. The good news beyond ground zero was that he had not vaulted to ringing up Lady Fat Money, and now felt absolutely certain that he would never, never return to Vietnam for a second, third, or thirtieth offensive. If necessary, he could still put his dear bloated beastie to useful purpose with the malady-most-rare maneuver, for which he would, out of duty, *haw*, unstintingly sacrifice himself to remain caringly at her corpulent side every mournful moment until her porky end. *Hoot!*

He strolled back into the room. His bags were packed. Having addressed the crowd that wasn't there, he now rehearsed in front of the mirror the next phase of being back in London town. He would of course, while exulting in the admiration of his peers, show restraint most humble, while wowing them with the dramatics of his war coverage. He furrowed his brow. Occasionally, doubts crept from a corner of his ego. Well, yes, a bit touch and go there for a while, until the pent up British bulldog in him had unleashed, and he now practiced before the mirror the unleashing of the British bulldog position.

"I do not wish to shock you, ladies and gentlemen, but there is such a terrible awareness one comes to in the jaws of battle. And I confess to, yes, feeling a crumpet of shame for the dangerous pleasure I felt under the most intense fire. All I can say is that, at times, under pressure of events almost too grim for words, in order to prevail over The Reaper, one finds oneself calling up, reluctantly, the ancient British warrior instinct buried in one's breast, for which I beg your understanding. Aye. Hear! Hear!"

As a shooting star in things journalisimo, he now had on the telly the film of his reveal-all war documentary in which his personal heroics were touched upon, and also a lucrative book deal, his magnum opus, *Defying All Odds: An Englishman*

Under Fire Reports, was in motion. And, as always, if all else went *kaput,* his silver bullet, the sudden mysterioso morbidity of his beloved over-stuffed love hag could be resurrected to spring him from further dangerous dalliances.

Thinking things over, he wondered if he shouldn't play the reluctant hero, the damaged, though steely-hearted scribbler, sporting a red badge of something, what? A black eye-patch for the book jacket? A pain-wracked limp? Trembling hands? Agonized, incomprehensible poetic mutterings for the worshipful dummies blinking and straining to interpret his every mutter? He'd muss his hair to appear properly, broodingly poetic. He would strike a pose and gaze tragically into lost horizons. Sensitive ladies of intellect would swoon and paw him. He would work up a mighty righteous mad and in his best Stratford-on-Avon baritone rave at the unrighteousness of it all. Right bloody good that.

And as was his natural right, it was time for him to assume his station as a blazing star in the galaxy of notables. Let no one lay the dead hand of the past upon his ambitions, with no blind subservience to yesterday's quaint notions. His Mao phase was done. He was not cut out to be new Mao man, with red ants marching over him. Moreover, Vladimir Ilyich Lenin, red flags flapping, had grown so revolutionarily tiring. Ideas colored peasant drab and worker's gray in drear Utopia were simply not sympathetico with his lordly tastes. He longed again for exquisite richness, the filthier, the better, *haw.* Whispering sweet nothings into the ear of sexless socialism was no longer satisfying, just too taxing to make serious moola at, what?

E. Drudgington did not see himself as a legend quite yet. He saw himself as blood royal in the Sturm and Drang, the yin and yawp of war. As a master of tongue and pen. And a future cascading with unrevolutionary gold. He certainly did not view himself as a case of incipient megalomania. So sound the trumpets! he thought. I'll be high-teaing with Her Majesty ere long, sipping from gold-trimmed crockery. I'll wear my royal ascot. Unfurl the Blow banner! Jog awake the mumbling masses! Make them roar. Nothing inspires like the roar of the mob. Hark! There, on the horizon… appears Sir Eric, galloping into the maelstrom to save us. Oh, we few, we admirable few. He wished a photographer was handy to record his charge into the maelstrom.

Again, observing his countenance in the mirror, the Bulldog of Britain dismissed creeping signs of droopy eyelids as evidence of fire-forged character, and stood there, jaw jutting, and flicked on his smile. His teeth lit up as he luxuriated in the applause of the vapid invisible mobs of screaming mindless buggers celebrating the historic return of Blowdom. If one runs for office, he mused, one must shove those buggers right up front, especially those inspired with inebriation. Must insist they vote twice, thrice. We need their valuable input.

No, I'm not going crackers, he assured the crowd that should have been there. Just now, he thought, I must gird my loins for the Old Blighty social season. Scantily clad beauties of noble blood will surely come a-rioting, breathlessly yearning for my loins reborn. Step on around the love-wrecked corpses of my latest admirers, dear ladies, and let your lack of impulse control carry you to your dream-lover. So, now, the burning question, right honorable gentlemen acquainted with my heroic propensities is, do I sing to them the epic poem of myself and then without further ado boink 'em all? Well then, queue up, your ladyships. Let's get started. Now don't be tardy.

On Daring

"The credit belongs to the man who was actually in the arena, Whose face is marred with dust and sweat and blood, who Strives valiantly; who errs and comes short, and short again… And who at the worst, if he fails, at least fails while daring greatly…."

— Teddy Roosevelt

On Courage

"Courage is… the first of human qualities… because it is the quality that guarantees all the others."

— Winston Churchill

On the Way it gets Way Out There

Listen, man, if they don't trust you, they get rid of you. One screw-up can lose a whole company. Whatever was wrong, the platoon took care of it. We had one guy who says I'm not workin' with no nigger. Instead of a black guy sluggin' this guy, a white guy says, "I'll take care of it." So he walks him off a little ways into the jungle and beats the shit out of him, saying "We are one, we are one." And then he brought him back and things worked out. And then we came out of the jungle back to the rear, and the REMF's those candy asses sitting back there treat us like shit. Said we couldn't use the *regular* showers. Hey, what are we gonna do about it? We innovate. Okay, you take the north side, you move in from the south. So we go in and tear 'em up and that's it. We go back and sit down and wait for the MP's. What's going on? they inquire. Nothin'. We're just sittin' around drinking sodas. Who did all this? Who knows? Because the REMF's never saw our faces. We made sure of that. Us jungle rats.

In the Jungle in the Dark: A Dateline Too Far

Returned to Britannia, E. Drudgington Blow was assuming his rightful station among the galaxy of notables and exchanging sentiments with his loving mate, who threw crockery at him and ordered him about like some female beast of Buchenwald. This, after all he had been through. No doctor could find his dreadful ulcer, though a hemorrhoid was indeed located. Francois was back in Paris doing lovely sane photography with his ladies longlegs, but with something missing at the heart, the intoxicant of viewing life or death with the next camera click, perhaps. P.O. Crock was in Washington issuing Crockisms about how slow history was finally coming to its senses seeing his side of things. Pamela Dicemore was in a New York frenzy writing on the land of burning bras and draft cards and mobs of an enlightened tomorrow marching the streets waving flags for freedom in the spirit of Che and such as Che.

In Vietnam, it appeared to observers there was a lack of aggressiveness in the prosecution of the war. Perhaps it was the foreboding look of the countryside, of the smashed, gloomy cities, of the prospect of a thundering Second Wave, all egged on by the palpable loss of nerve by the man who had boasted he was not going to yield and not going to shimmy. It didn't matter that the other side had been roundly defeated, at least in numbers, on the battlefield, the shock of Tet had bent the minds of too many pols and opinion makers into junkyard wrecks. Speeches about victory seemed but faraway shouts in a hard red rain, if the junkyard listened at all. There was war in the newsrooms; hawks were in disfavor. "The war's as good as lost," came the growing refrain. And who wants to risk more when the war was as good as lost? Jim Jordan for one, who refused to cut loose from his instincts that America had always won and must win. And Sean Donlan. "You want to know what's real, go out there and do the damn work." And that's what they were doing.

The jungle is growing dark. The working correspondents lay flat on their bellies by this misty trail along the Nam-Cambodian border, looking for the rising of the Second Wave. They lay near the Lurp leader, the sergeant called Lightning, once struck nearly dead by a bolt, but even with the scar that swirled across the part of his head where the hair wouldn't grow, considered it just in the top ten of the heavy heat he had come through and, gentlemen of the esteemed press, he always came through.

Lightning is in the center directing this adventure in what he called hide-and-slide. On the left flank is the snarling shotgun from South Carolina *("When I went home I'd as soon whip your candy ass as look at you. People my age so full of love and piss, I didn't have nothin' at all to say to. They sneered at guys with medals and cheered damn draft dodgers. I figured each time I came back to Nam I'd get killed, even when they said go work in the post office. I said screw the post office.")* who packs their radio and swears he's taking no more shit from the army's letter-writing office which keeps advising he is listed as dead. Beside him is Bird Dog who talks in near whispers when he talks *("When I went back a buncha students threw balloons of pee at us, shoutin' we were nothin' but baby killers and get on the hell back to Vietnam. So I did.")* and who once was so shy he nearly fainted when a general pinned the Silver Star on him. "He don't look like much, but turn him loose in that jungle and he'll tear 'em up for you, the Lurp leader had observed, describing his team's "philosophical thrust."

On the right flank is Thin Man, thin as a stiletto and as deadly *("When I went back I knew I was dangerous. I was such a different person that my mother and sister walked right past me at the train station, and I was the only one standing there. I went walking in Central Park in New York City alone at midnight just to do it, hoping some patriotic citizen would try to mug my ass."*) If he's thin, the Lurp next to him is close to invisible, you see him but did you really? He's a light-footed Filipino named Blackie whose best trick is to dress in black pajamas, carry the AK, melt into a column of Victor Charlies, and mess with their minds before doing serious damage to their physical well-being.

Donlan knew Lightning from a previous mad mission. Hoping to gain a sense of what big stuff the other side was capable of throwing after Tet, he had set this one up ("It could be the bleedin' shits," warned Lightning). They were going into the bush with the sergeant's long range reconnaissance team, known as Lurps. Having once daisy-chained a trail with grenades, taking out 80 Viet Cong, the team was noted for its incredible lethality. "We put the shock to them, split them up, got them head-fucked and running around shooting each other in the butt," Lightning had elucidated on the wily ways of his philosophical thrust.

The Lurp leader has had them slithering along as quiet as midnight snails. Quieter than any Americans Jim had been with. Creeping through bamboo thickets, past trees so densely woven they smother sky light, hearing a twig snap like a firecracker, then pausing for four minutes or forty, staring into trees dancing with shadows, listening to birds, insects, animals squawking, skittering, darting, before they move on again. It starts raining and rains for a long time.

Sneak and peak, they call it, hide and slide, stealth or die, and if things go well roll the dice, get bold, do damage, shoot and scoot. In the rain it goes very fast, speed-balling, until a hand signal slows them to ballets of silence, just sneaking along in the tall-treed gloom, gray ghosts through the moving mist and sudden twinkles of sunlight. They move through areas of booby traps where even the booby traps are booby trapped. Now and then they hear *tapa tapa tapa...* more raindrops.

At times they lay as still as lizards waiting for mosquitoes to come tickle their tongues. Jim hears his joints creaking, sees his sweat dripping. They wear dark greasepaint under floppy hats and stay swallowed up in such deep cover and if they do it right are invisible from five feet away at noon.

Eyes rolling, ears straining to hear a bush whisper, Jim is back to basics again, to the pure physicality of the what-happens-next adventure story. (*"Hadn't you rather just ride,"* someone had asked Lightning. *"I can't stand mech,"* he responded *with a wink and a sneer.*)

For four days, the Lurp leader keeps them tracking in and out of rain through the jungle like an instinct-driven pack. He's reading signs, moving closer, seeking *the* spot, not 50 yards off this way or that, but the bulls-eye of the magic target. The evening of the fourth day they are *there,* seeing dropped equipment, web gear, strips of snagged cloth, buttons, worn-out sandals, would-be NVA liberation money. Bird Dog growls at wads of toilet paper. Squatting now in the thick brush near the trail, Lightning's scars seem to light up. He whispers that this is shaping up into an outstanding news event, and the correspondents are beginning to believe.

When unflappable Blackie, out front in the darkening forest, flaps his hands, flashing five fingers, ten, then rolls his hands, pumps a fist, makes the sign of the cross, everyone believes. Down the trail appears the first column, moving through the mist, wearing camouflage brush all over, while the Lurps lay a few meters off the trail watching.

The first column of 30 has hardly passed when through shadows of bamboo appear more, many, many more, filing by both in pith helmets and soft hats, with AKs and mortar and rocket tubes slapping thighs and backs. They wear tans, greens, and blacks, as if they've come from all over. Having been exhorted ever onward by their political cadre, who keep things simple and lie a lot, these latest move almost carelessly, talking to each other, full of liberation fever, heading east toward Tay Ninh City, and then on to Saigon where the last great battle of the war, they've been told, was nearly over. It was to be just routine mopping and dusting up after the smashing success of Tet, and they will be smothered with kisses, hugs and flowers, and all they will have to do beyond the kissing and hugging and flower sniffing is to pull guard duty in the happy liberated zones, goes the script.

To the Lurp leader it's as if he's found the epicenter of the whole Communist Jungle Nation, or at least the rolling crest of the biggest wave he's ever seen. Earlier, boldly, he had advised Jim that whatever situation they came upon they would likely handle themselves.

"What if the situation is too big?"

"So far that situation hasn't fucking existed."

If it exists, this is it, Jim thinks, but at least it's not flying into Khe Sanh. As Lightning pulls the team slowly back in the dark now, he does a 360 with a starlight scope, his fingers fast fiddling over the scope. He suddenly rakes his nails at his face. His eyes, his scars, seem to gleam. There, not far from the trail, all of it down under overhead cover, virtually invisible from the air at treetop level, spreads a vast Communist supply depot and staging area. It is teeming with troops and all the stuff of war being wheeled and carried about.

He can't see it all but the prospector for recon gold sees enough to know he has hit the mother of all lodes. There are storage bunkers above ground and underground stuffed with thousands of rifles, with grenades and machineguns, rockets and launchers, artillery pieces and shells, some of it smelling of cosmoline and wrapped in brown paper and still in crates and cases. There are classrooms, dispensaries, and VIP hootches covered by palm fronds and overlays of foliage. There are tons of ammo, rice, radios, medicine, sewing machines, needles and thread, animal cages, coops full of chickens.

Lightning's recon cup is running over. "We're going to *get* them," he advises in a crackling whisper. "Get them *all*." Now he's on his radio giving out grid coordinates, calling for artillery, tac air, B-52's, BB's, jelly beans, spare spitballs, anything at all lying around in democracy's big ammo box. Just bring it. He rakes at his scars. He's got a look about him you wouldn't want to meet in the dark as if he's unloading that round too many.

"Ready to touch off a round or two?" he whispers to Donlan while stuffing an unlit Lucky in his mouth. "How's the story so far?"

"Fine," whispers Donlan, "fine." It's always fine with Donlan. It was fine at Dak To. Fine at Khe Sanh. Fine at Tet. It's all fine and he's feeling for his cognac canteen.

"Must move closer," whispers Lightning. "Get you some interviews."

"Fine."

Some of the other Lurps sense they are already too close and stepping into something too big, you can tell by the eyes. Lightning, in his fourth tour, already mythical in his tracking and killing skills, passes it on that after they hit the jungle jackpot they'll depart by circling into Cambodia, *neutral* Cambodia, old *secret war* Cambodia. Let the bullshit roll.

Creeping yet closer, they mount a small rise that seems to be, it *is*, a graveyard, a Communist graveyard. Stretching out into the jungle, they see rows and rows of what can only be graves. Some are topped by small stone markers with stars on them. "*Dead soldier...*" read the inscriptions in Vietnamese..."*Sacrifice... May 1967... Sacrifice... August... 1967... Sacrifice... Sacrifice... Sacrifice... Sacrifice... Life the great life, die the glorious death.*"

"Some of these boys might be waking up after this one," whispers the Lurp leader, kneeling now, waiting for the first incoming, checking the view from the high ground, the highest hump of graves.

"We're steppin' in it," mutters the shotgun from South Carolina, "a shitload of it." He doesn't like spooks or graveyards. Blackie believes they're taking a step too far. Thin Man wants to fade. Bird Dog shrugs and moans inside. The correspondents wonder if the thrill of surfing the second wave will ever get reported. Jim thinks of Susanna. He has the tendency to think of her in the very worst places, sweet Susanna. He shakes her out of his mind, another puff of dream smoke.

The first round arrives. It sounds like a train wreck at a comfortable distance, somebody else's wreck, always somebody else's. Now more shells come tearing down the sky from interlocking firebases miles back across the border. They come blowing into the trees, whacking and crunching.

The Lurp leader calls them in yet closer, and closer still, drumfires of shrieking death as Jim and the others flatten themselves out between the graves.

"Fire!" Lightning sings, "fire!"

Salvos from 105's, 155's, and 175's arrive in threes and fours, then sixes and eights, storming through the clouds.

"Get a little fucking serious!" he sings, "fire!"

The sergeant called Lightning has become the guzzler you can't drag out of the bar. The leader of the perdition band. He's in love with the big, big beat. He keeps calling them in, more percussion, more wild strings, more devil drums.

When the shelling pauses, Jim sees North Viet soldiers staggering out of the camp, arms flailing as if paddling out of a waterfall of fire. Secondary explosions leap all around the soldiers of sacrifice lost in the roaring winds dying the glorious death.

Soon arrive the airstrikes. First the Phantoms, tac air. And the graveyard visitors, bracketed by rocking explosions and shrapnel hissing over and around them like graveyard snakes, jam their hands over their ears, their heads against broken gravestones.

Only the Lurp leader, directing the band by firelight, deigns not to stay down. But this is not the worst. The worst in their world arrives shortly before dawn. Cruising along five miles up the monstrous avenging angels, the great planes diverted from another mission, begin servicing the target and all things above ground and below ground in or near the target.

Jim opens his eyes enough to see stampeding NVA picked up and hurled down, picked up again, and pounded back down. Half-buried soldiers are blown skyward only to be swept back down under the heaving earth, locked in place reaching for air, fingers clawing, senses screaming. Silhouetted in a bomb flash, a raggedy soldier falls on his back and waves his pistol at that thing 30,000 feet in the air before the thing buries him.

Bombs, friendly bombs, now come visiting the far end of the graveyard. Some who have been very close to it say you have not seen war's true light until you have seen the aurora borealis of bombing, and Jim has seen the B-52 light from near enough at Khe Sanh but never so close to the heart of the blazing bulb. He feels heat, pressure, eyeballs wanting to pop, eardrums ready to rupture. The sky falls, the earth cracks, pitching up, raining down, flames suck the air.

Nearby the soldiers of the glorious death crawl around in the infernal clouds, howling, gibbering, looking for gravity to stabilize. Dead are heaped on dead, old dead rise to welcome new dead. Jim glimpses gun barrels, hands, feet, skulls, bones, tree limbs tumbling eerily through surging waves of earth before being swallowed up again. Holes are blown in holes, graves dug in graves. Bodies are blown up and then buried and unburied and tossed all around and reburied. Jim keeps telling himself this is not Dak To, it's not Khe Sanh. It's may be worse.

The last bombs begin reshaping the lower end of the graveyard where the Lurps are, and the first to go is Thin Man, dissolved as if he never existed. A moment later Bird Dog's chest is crushed without a whimper. Shotgun covers Dog with his body, plants his hat over his buddy's dead face shouting, "Why'd you have to do that?" Shotgun, who had been heard to swear after five beers,

"I ain't afraid to die," does it now, glass on empty, and won't need to worry about filling out the forms from the letter-writing office anymore. The last Lurp, with nothing left to prove, stands with his lighted Lucky in his mouth proving it anyway. There had been whispers in the ranks that the sergeant was missing something vital at the center of his philosophical thrust. It seemed that he did not know fear as ordinary soldiers knew it. Perhaps the lightning strike had cooked it out of him, and because of the boiling flash that dispatches him now on his great ride with the Valkyries to battlefield eternity, he will never feel that queer human emotion.

Sean Donlan, who knows what it feels like but can't stop writing about it, rolls toward Jim and starts to shout something, but never finishes the thought. Jim is briefly blinded because he's smacked in the face with what seems like a bag of leaky hot water. He wipes at his eyes and face but there's no blood. He's staring dizzily at Donlan, at his buddy's belly wound that he could slide his hand into. Having once read up on such a thing, Jim thinks in this moment that he knows intestines.

Cover wound and protruding intestines with a dry, sterile dressing. Do not try to replace intestines. And do not eat or drink. He had read that after Dak To and must convey this info to Sean and also advise him not to worry much about the likely coming feast of the maggots, they contribute to the cleaning of the wound.

It seems all done now. The action seems over. Well, it was their turn, the immortal bright boys, but they're still here, aren't they, and got the story, don't they, the damndest one yet. Right, Sean? Jim gets to his feet in stages, swaying in the firelight as he talks to his buddy who looks up at him with his eyes open but Sean doesn't hear it and will never hear it.

For some reason — it seems terribly important — Jim kneels down to attend to his right boot. The lace is flopping about in a most peculiar manner and seems to insist, even demand, as one of those small but critical details that it must be properly tied at that instant, or at least tucked politely out of sight because the good correspondent under most circumstances is a neat correspondent. Moreover, the good correspondent must never become too emotionally invested in the story. The good correspondent, no matter how hard or nasty the story is breaking, must retain a steely amount of internal cool banked safely away from the horror of the moment or the story will take away all the credit he has. That is an inviolate first principle laid down by Ernie, and it seems that Sean is dead.

It is exactly 0300 hours when he hears it… a late arrival whistling down the sky and before he can run, dive or blink there's another burst and shaking *whop* and big light flashing all around and in the same moment the sensation like the Big Babe Almighty swinging from the heels and hitting him with a thunder stick. He can feel himself going up in a high breathless float as if defying some law of gravity and looking down through blowing iron and glowing ash and wondering what am I doing up here and then he sees himself slowly going down and mud falling off his boots onto the field of glory.

There's a softer bump and he's all the way down, belly-deep in dirt good Mother Earth, always eager to welcome a son returning from adventure, has rushed to cover his eyes and warmly, smotheringly embrace him.

At times in the past, Jim had scratched out poems, sort of poems, short ones, a few fragments in the jungle on the tops of C-ration boxes. But he never came out with any. They got lost in the rattle of battle or he would toss them away. They were probably not very good. This seemed a curious time to write a poem but he felt he finally had something to say once the dirt was out of his eyes and the writing part of his brain was working on the subject of experience beyond the pale, that he had finally found after much searching and the outcome of which remained in doubt

On Dying Well

Who opening to them your glorious ranks
Gave them that grand occasion to excel
That chance to live life most free from stain
And that rare privilege of dying well...

Wrote Alan Seegar, a true volunteer, who experienced that rare privilege as bravely as a fighting poet could at Bellow-en-Santerre, by the Somme, with six dum-dum bullets in his bullet-stained chest... World War I

Wasted

He sat against a shrapnel-battered tree in half-laced boots, bare-chested, sweating heavily. When Jim walked over he looked up woozily. One hand clenched and unclenched making a fist. His rifle lay beside him. His face seemed to go one way and his hair blown the other. He tried to rise but his legs failed and he fell back. This was just after the battle. He wasn't wounded that Jim could see, although there were a lot of dead and bloody wounded spread out nearby in the clearing and out into the elephant grass. A green bug flew down and walked across his nose, then down into his blond mustache. He didn't seem to know the bug was there for a while, then reached up and mashed it and rolled it around between his fingers. His other hand held the stub of a cigarette. The smoke of battle drifted all around. The sun was a bleeding red eye in the sky.

"Well, it's been a party, he said, speaking low, squinting up, when Jim tried to interview him. "A real party. I'm afraid to take my boots off. Somebody'll take 'em. Ain't got a dime in my pocket, but they'll hit you with a hammer for a quarter. Yeah, I can say life under a tree ain't too bad. It's the ones that get up in the trees that are bad. Nights get pretty wild. I don't sleep till daylight. Folks from the crazy house come out and wander around hootin' and hollerin'. I guess they just turn 'em loose. They come sneakin' through the grass in the dark, then runnin' back and forth nuts. Shootin' and jumpin' up and down. Doin' the war dance."

Not far away the sound of artillery drummed in the jungle.

"Guess you're a mess." the soldier said, as if to himself. He answered himself and told this other self what a strange fellow he is and the strange fellow agreed completely. He kept talking, mumbling, drooling, head bent, head shaking, stub of the cigarette smoking in the hand in his lap.

Off to the left now someone screamed "Morphine!" Medics worked over a man on the ground. They had cut off his pack and uniform and he lay nearly naked, not moving, as ants swarmed around him. The soldier by the tree flicked away the remains of the bug between his fingers.

"That's about it."

Deadline: The Hard Stuff

Susanna had been attending the war but not truly in it. It had been more about her than it. She was working as the Red Cross rep at the field hospital near Tan Son Nhut when the Tet Offensive hit. For many in the old Pearl of the Orient Tet was the ultimate shock treatment. Susanna didn't leave the hospital for weeks. She did everything she could, helping out in emergency sections as wounded were carried in, some tight-lipped and screaming and cursing pain. Susanna had this feeling t she wasn't doing near enough. *What else can I do?*

All of a sudden there would come lots of static and the radio crackling, "We're coming in, inbound! Got a multiple head wound, severe chest wound, probable three KIA…" And then a voice cutting in from a second chopper wobbling behind punched with holes, jammed with wounded, "Be there in five, if this thing holds together."

A soldier choking in his own blood demanded a cigarette. He died demanding it. Another uniform practically smoking, seemed to shake to pieces. Bleary-eyed doctors and nurses who had slumped out of fifteen hours of surgery came rushing back, shaking off sleep, dressing on the way.

Susanna, the empathizer, had this feeling about the dying, gazing into their eyes, seeing life waving goodbye. She would sit beside one in a dim room, holding his hand, thinking, I can at least do this last little thing for you. Men had so often looked at her like the hottest babe they had ever seen, not the last thing they would ever see.

There was this shot-up airborne trooper grinning after surgery. "So what happens now." And she winked. "I'll think of something." She went to get a cup of coffee and came back and put her hand on his pillow and started talking to him, and the hard-hit fellow with the sweaty curls and crimson stumps for legs, lying there a smile tracing his lips, closed his eyes and stopped breathing. She gripped his hand.

"Don't... *please...* " He was there, just resting his eyes because he surely wasn't dead. he was... goodbye, soldier.

Saying words for just one didn't seem right, so she said a little for them all, words from long ago that Mama never said. At one stage, with red alerts going on all night and rockets exploding outside, and even bad-off patients rolling under their beds, she put on a helmet and sat in a corner with a small gold cross pressed to her chest. The war snapped and growled around the hospital, and she was a little girl again whispering to someone who might understand even in crazy Vietnam.

Susanna felt guilty for going to bed exhausted, for closing her eyes when others were closing theirs forever. They're coming in here in bloody pieces, she thought. Should I say, 'I'm tired, come back after I've had my princess nap? She felt guilty. She felt stupid. She started shaking.

She went to see a young psychiatrist there named Summers and he told her, "Well, you've come to the wrong person. I think I'm crazy myself." They shared a couple of brief embraces. He seemed like a nice shrink who had had it with the war. "Dear," he said, "the last drops of counseling have been squeezed out of me."

For Susanna, it began working the other way. The show-and-tail show starring herself was over. She kept thinking of Jim, so determined to be in the first row of the big thundering picture show of war, lost now out in the thunder himself.

They carried in this wounded Marine who reached out and snatched a pistol and waved it wildly around, looking ready to shoot the doctor. Susanna helped pull the pistol away, then talked to him in little ways she had, soft music floating in that soothed the beast. "Young lady," said the doctor, "you should get battle stars."

They carried in this soldier and moved him to what some called the *dumping ground*. Everything bad, his vital signs, the doctor said there was nothing more to do, goodbye soldier. He was young, scared, with a face turned cold-moon white, and Susanna stayed with him, whispering in the darkness. "Don't be scared, we'll take care of you." He seemed in a coma but snapped awake once as she whispered words as uncomplicated as she once had with her father *"Just let this one live, please."*

She kept saying it and the next day it was like one of those old movies when the hero sits up from the sleep of the dead and the sun is shining and you know he's going to make it. The kid indeed made it, and the sun was in fact shining. If that can happen, she thought, anything can. She had come to this surreal place to do some good, and in the worst of times was doing it with what her father had called a serious heart. It was that evening when, feeling very tired, she found herself in this sudden, uninvited embrace trying to put her down. The nice shrink had cornered her and uttered the prescribed words and pushed the prescribed drink at her. "I know," she said, "I know." She *knew* in ways the temporarily wrapped too tight man-of-the-mind never would, he wasn't built right, and she told him she had serious duties to attend to. She said it gracefully as she unglued herself from his arms and moved away. That was the moment she knew that her dragon, trying for one last bite of flesh and what she remembered as her soul, fled to wherever such spirits flee.

***

"Uh, oh, bleedin' down there again," says the first face. "What kinda uniform is that?"

"Damn buzzards got at him," says the second face.

"Who're you? Can you talk a little, sir?" says the first.

"Wants to know where all he's hit." says the second.

The first face leans down, an etching in dirt and sunlight that could be the angel Gabriel if Gabriel was a 19-year-old medic with big ears under a dented helmet. On the ground Jim feels hands ripping at his rags, entwining him with bandages. "Just caught some, sir," Gabriel advises. "Not too terrible. The reason of it is…. Well, just caught some, here, there. We've stopped the bleedin'. You were sorta buried over there a little. Just hang on, sir. Dust-off on the way. Right there now, comin' right there over them trees now. Settin' down there now. Just hang on."

Three minutes later they have him on a stretcher. After the chopper settles, an uncommon battlefield shape emerges through the dust, had to get out here, and she has. She sees what is left of Blackie on his back. Over there the last shreds of Thin Man. And in a heap nearby the shotgun from South Carolina nearly sawed off at the legs, and it comes to her why people go mad in war.

She sees the young medic with the dented helmet working over Jim who doesn't know what he's seeing. He hears a machine gun clearing its throat somewhere. There's a face bobbing over him, like a red cross blurring. He hears a helicopter winding up, boots tromping, words shouted through swirling dust. He half-rolls nearly tumbles off the stretcher into a shell hole. Then for a moment, they're out in the open, very bright. Then more gun rattle as they shove his stretcher into the chopper. "Who're you?" asks a blood-streaked face rising up before him, babbling out blood before falling back.

Swamped now with body bags of the Lurps, the chopper lifts slowly, almost too slowly, nose rocking sharply just over the smashed trees. Jim hears a shout through the clattering, that they're up and the hell out. Then another voice, a softer presence, a certain touching, and he's out himself again.

***

"Bite down! Bite down! *Can do?* Not hurting so much now, is it? The hell it isn't. Just relax."

It was a surgeon doing damage control, up to his wrists in red stuff. *"Can do?"*

Jim Jordan replies he can do, or someone does, from somewhere in his head.

"I said relax, *relax*. We're doing a procedure. What impressive veins you have."

For a day or so he runs fevers from infection. He goes back to surgery and feels like they are laying track for the Red Meat Express. Though it looks sexy, says can-do doc, it's just random bloody shrapnel bites and odd flesh gouges from sharp beaks, nothing in a kill zone. Still, there's an untidy situation in his right lower leg, and Jim hears the docs conferring in low voices as to whether to do a procedure, another damn procedure, as to whether to take some of it off, here, there?

In theory, in chemistry, covering combat seemed his best subject. He had the temperament, all right. That night he hears a soldier two beds over cursing theory through his oxygen mask. From up the ward, a sound starts low and builds like a firehouse siren into a single, sustained, pain-crazed scream down to a gurgle and nothing left to say. Jim's pain makes him laugh like he's leaning over life's last edge but not enough to scream. In the corners of his eyes he sees things moving that may not be there and hears this voice from radio paradise, *"All around the islands we go, taking it sweet and slow, just show me how to hula... and remember, soldier, no matter where you are, if you lose your toothbrush, you're in trouble."*

After the news come the visitations, battalions of ghosts, yesterday's hot copy, shuffling out of the fuming mist in red-blown rags, with eyes blacker than bullet holes some come stooped and limping, and others dragging along badly shot, and others bent over ghastly burnt, but bearing up right sturdily under the circumstances. There's *ain't-a-fraida-nothin'* Tag and behind him trudges Bam, Marines of iron, all busted up. Here comes Black Cat gliding in the dusk, hand over the bleeding rose that was his heart.

"The first time I met the blues, mama... they done me all the bad they could...."

Now a figure drifts from that smoking tree-line. Got that look. Jim hopes it's him. Damn, got to be, Sean. So they patched you pretty good? *Good enough, man. Little sew-up, holding things sort of together for a while, but other than that...* The Cognac Kid, always good enough. Who offers the last drops from the canteen to Jim. Says he's off for the big one, the last one, yeah, that pretty baby. *Want to come along? Sure he does. Those were the days.*

Sean and his bloody little smile, already moving away, going for pretty baby. At the edge of the tree-line, he looks back, shakes his head, takes the last slug from the canteen, and tosses it into the bush. Then, fading, even his dead shadow, lost in the smoke of the trees. That's jungle for you... dark in there.

It is exactly 0300 hours, and Jim feels again almost being dispatched to mad old history in bright rainbow bits in that last whistling thunder of a second with nothing left but close his eyes, grind his teeth, squeeze the medal of the impossible, and whisper to this appearance… surreal, a burst of light and shadow and he opens his eyes and it's still there, beyond the light, beyond the shadow, beyond even seeing, a burst of desperate imagination perhaps, but which many came to prefer over whispering to nothing.

***

Early that morning after the last surgery comes nothing, the Demon of Sorrows, tapping out of the dark, prodding the remains all around with the big stick. Prodding Jim once, twice, then bending over him, breathing down the death rattles of a thousand battles as it puts the question to him, the one never answered, *why are you still here, bright boy, and so many others more worthy are not?* With the sun setting low over his father's last position on the high ground, and the river running in streaks of fire below, bright boy tries asking his father's grave that can't answer.

When he opens his eyes there's another figure. She's floating in and out of light near his bed or is the bed floating around her? *Don't need that here, fancy lady, go pop somebody else's stitches.* Maybe she's really there, and he seems still there in one cracked but moving piece. Ghost or flesh, she's shades paler if it's her. Her hair has lost some of the sheen, her figure some of the boom-boom, or maybe he's perfume, then a touching like no other, moist, warm, moving, rippling with feeling, *alive.*

Perhaps it's supposed to mean something more than sweet lip service. Perhaps that's all there ever was. Like the old song, when a lovely flame dies, smoke gets in your eyes after its burned the loving guts out of you. Maybe it's a story going nowhere but where it's already been. He's still groggy in the fever swamp, searching for the formula that could transform sexual shallows into substance beyond anatomical attractions. That piece of work, scratch her and she bleeds fingernail polish, warn old bitter voices, that she-devil's touch is like being caressed in the gut with an M-60 machine gun.

Don't dare even look at her, or let her close enough to breathe on you, that's how she gets you.

Having in fact been caressed in the gut with an M-60 he knows the thrill, but as he is prone to do he risks it. From outside come cracks of thunder, thumps of blowing rain. Inside, there's no dance of the pitchfork, no hungry howling under the wolf-red moon, just tired blue eyes trying not to cry....

The Burning Center

The warrior-poet, though never reaching the Homeric battle of his dreams, approached his end with perfect serenity. The funeral was splendid. His burial by torchlight amid the olive groves and lemon trees on the lovely Aegean island of Scyros was an event, it was reported, of "gathered radiance." He apparently died of blood poisoning brought on by sunstroke, or perhaps an infected insect bite said accounts. He was in admirable spirits to the end, some said.

On the shores of Gallipoli, meanwhile, there were some half-million other casualties less splendidly demised. Most of them had lost their serenity long before they paid the butcher's bill. "God, pity all us poor soldiers," lamented one of the no-longer radiant, standing with a handkerchief clamped to his nose in a field steaming with thousands of the dead and battalions of roving rats. The hot Turkish sun was baking the romance out of things. As it turned out, the warrior-poet was spared the details. If not, he might have penned rather different songs for the battle.

When It's Over

"In some ways it was a great kick in the ass," says Jack. "How did we ever get through it?"

"In the air, never worried about dying," says Ty. "If it was your turn, it was your turn. If you made it back to the ground, it was better him than me."

"You never said it out loud, " says West. "But what we did was very, very emotionally wearing. I say this in all sincerity. Depending on each other. It goes deeper than being a brother. It goes deeper. Because if it wasn't for you characters right here, I wouldn't be alive. Flying those slicks and dust-offs into hot LZ's all shot to shit, smoking, on fire, then doing it all over again. Can't explain it to anybody who wasn't there. But hell, we *know*."

"I remember everything," Jack says. "Getting shot down. Freaking everything."

"The three of us," says West. "The lucky three. We ought to write it down."

"It all comes back, Tet, everything." Jack says. "How'd we ever get out of there?"

"We should write it down," says West. "I swear, man, I swear, we coulda won the damn thing if they'd ever let us just go do it."

"We should write it all out, but too much to tell," Jack says. "It would take years and years, and who would understand the no-good ending and being treated like garbage coming home?"

"There's a long dark wall with three names missing," says Ty. "We must have done something good."

As The General Said

"We knew we could not defeat the Americans on the battlefield," noted Vo Nguyen Giap, North Vietnam's top general. His analysis was that the war was won on the American street, that the mighty Americans defeated themselves.

"The lively, merry war is no more..."

— The Bloody Red Baron (1918)

"Experience: that most brutal of teachers. But you learn, my God do you learn..."

— C.S. Lewis

What It Was All For

There are places where the bones of the fallen have been mostly removed, that are rather beautiful for death forests. And then you move into a stretch of nearly impenetrable jungle and are gobbled up in green-dark, absolutely silent, absolutely motionless, almost claustrophobic gloom. Through the hush comes a vague, unidentifiable sound, maybe a groaning wind. Only there is no wind. All there is a busted-up American bunker, with old twisted steel sticking up, that was once sat upon by a great force. The noise comes again, not really human. Perhaps, a wounded animal in the bunker. There is no animal in the bunker. Perhaps, some wandering soul of the name less dead whispering for guidance. Or maybe one is just hearing things. That's probably it. Still, one is tempted to drop little things to mark one's way out of such a place. A subject experts, even the fatally misinformed, finally agreed on, was that in Vietnam in the rainy season it rained a lot. Other analysts analyzed that if you were looking for a happy ending you went to the wrong place. An encouraging note was that back home a civic group offered puzzles, card games, dominoes, and free classes in line dancing for recovering veterans. Line-dancing experts stepped forward smartly, noting that good things were happening in line dancing. Precipitation experts predicted skies sunny and delightful, perhaps.

> *"Wisdom is the principal thing: Therefore, get wisdom;*
> *And with all thy getting, get understanding."*

> — Proverbs IV 7

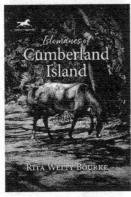 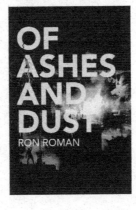